"WE HAVE A BED, MARY."

"Will ye share it with me?" Alex said quietly.

I nodded, unable to speak, and rose to meet him, pulling his mouth down to mine. He tasted of whiskey and tears and I clung to him, then slipped my hands under his shirt and slowly peeled the material away, and then repeated the process with his other clothing until he was naked before me.

"Now kiss me, Mary," he whispered.

"Your lips are bruised," I said softly.

"So they are, lass, but having ye kiss me is the best medicine." He sat on the edge of the bed, pulling me down next to him.

"Then, my love," I said, pushing him down, "let me heal you all over." He laughed softly and ran his hands through my hair, loosening the pins. Suddenly, he pulled me against him and kissed me soundly.

"Your lips," I cautioned, but he laughed.

"Healed, lass. Quite healed. And now, Mary Rose, it's yer turn. Come, lassie, let's get these clothes off ye. I've some healing to do also . . . "

Dell Books by Kathleen Givens

Kilgannon

The Wild Rose of Kilgannon

THE WILD ROSE OF KILGANNON

Kathleen Givens

A Dell Book

Published by
Dell Publishing
a division of
Random House, Inc.
1540 Broadway
New York, New York 10036

ISBN: 0-440-23568-5

Printed in the United States of America

Published simultaneously in Canada

November 1999

10 9 8 7 6 5 4 3 2 1

OPM

For my wonderful husband, Russ,
who makes my life an adventure;

For my daughters, Patty and Kerry,
and son-in-law, John,
who make life full and always entertaining;

And for my parents, Richard and
Violet Wall,
who taught me what's important.

ACKNOWLEDGMENTS

I WOULD LIKE TO THANK MAUREEN WALTERS AND MARIA Angelico of Curtis Brown, Ltd., for their encouragement and constant kindness; Maggie Crawford of Dell, for her trust and latitude; Russ, for still being my hero after all these years; Kerry and Patty, for their suggestions and for reminding me of the joys of young love; my mother, Violet, my brother Rich, and the whole family for their enthusiasm; my sister Nicole for her speed-editing in the "Nik" of time; Peggy Gregerson, whose support kept me going; Mary Meyer Lewis and Patricia Crumley Meyer for reading and rereading; Georgene Fairbanks, Rick Capaldi, Julius Panikowski, Forrest Petersen, Judy Sand, the Lunch Bunch and the Go Ask Alice Writing Group for their partisanship; the staffs of the London Museum, the Tower of London and the National Maritime Museum of Greenwich for their assistance; and the countless historians, librarians, and museum staff members who guided me back to Mary and Alex's world. Any inaccuracies are mine alone.

PROLOGUE

December 1716

KILGANNON. HOME. THERE WERE TIMES I'D THOUGHT I'd never see it again. The air was cold this winter morning, and the sun glinted off the water, turning it from sapphire to silver. Above us the mountains loomed deep blue against the pale sky; white clouds scudded overhead. And the bare branches of the trees reminded me that this was the season of death. So much death.

All those months, when I had dreamed of coming home, I'd assumed we would all be together. If we were wise, we would visit those who were still here, and the grave, and then we'd leave, away in the dark like the criminals we'd become. I glanced at the blond man standing so quietly next to me, then gripped the rail of the *Mary Rose* and watched us turn into the inner loch. And a few moments later, as we sailed around the headland, there it was, the most beautiful home on earth. The dark stones rose into the sky, the roof of the keep pointing at the clouds. The gulls overhead called their welcome to us. Kilgannon. Home.

It was the same and I sighed with relief. There was our room, there the parapet where I'd watched so many sunsets. And there, in the meadow beyond the castle itself, was the knoll where Alex had given the prizes, and where I had welcomed him home. And in front of us now, the dock where we had welcomed the MacDonald to change our lives. Next to me the boys bounced impatiently and I smiled at their eagerness as I took a deep breath. Nowhere else on earth smelled like Kilgannon. The sea met the mountains and their scents mixed with the fragrance of roses. Roses. Impossible, but there it was. Kilgannon smelled like heaven. I turned to look over the boys' heads, to the other side of the loch, where the grave was, and I sighed. It would be, I knew, the first place we'd visit.

"Home," I said.

"It seems so strange without him," said Matthew quietly, following my gaze. "How can it be home if he's no' here?"

"He is here," I said softly, turning to him as he towered over me, his handsome face drawn. "He is here, Matthew," I said again.

Next to me, Ian nodded. "It is home," he said and looked up at me. I smiled and put my hand on his shoulder.

"And I'm glad to be here," said Jamie, his voice bright.

"So am I," said the blond man next to me, his voice full of emotion. When I turned to him, he gave me a weary smile and I patted his arm, knowing he felt the empty space next to us.

I had imagined that Kilgannon would be deserted, that all the people would be gone, but the hills were dotted with tartan-clad figures running toward the loch, and on the dock a small group waved. Despite my best efforts, I felt tears fall as the first lonely strains of "MacGannon's Return" came over the water to us.

Home.

I closed my eyes for just a moment. And remembered.

PART ONE

Let me wander, let me rove,
Still my heart is with my Love;
Nightly dreams and thoughts by day
Are ay with him that's far away.

—ROBERT BURNS, "ON THE SEAS AND FAR AWAY"

ONE

Regret is a cold companion and I lived with it for months after Alex left me. It was with me always, but never more than at the end of the day, when I would climb the stairs of the keep and watch the sun go down behind a blue island. Alone.

It kept me company later that autumn, when we women tried to keep Kilgannon alive with the children and the handful of men left behind. And was with me as we gathered that meager harvest, tried our hand at fishing, rounded up the cattle and moved them to their winter grazing. At night I tried not to think as I bandaged my blistered hands and laughed with the others at our new skills. But regret was never far away. It stood with me as I watched the last of the men leave on the brigs to join the others, their sons gleeful, their wives crying.

Regret came into its own as the autumn nights approached winter and I stood at the windows watching icy rain run in streams down the panes. It was mid-September when Alex left to go to war, four weeks after his birthday and a week before mine. Regret was the guest of honor at my scanty birthday celebration, organized by Ellen to cheer me. I did my best to appear merry as I thanked her. And I was grateful to have her with me, for I could not imagine life without her now. It was difficult to remember that she had once been a housemaid in my aunt's London home. She never complained, though she was suffering the loss of wee Donald, her sweetheart, gone off with Alex. That regret was also Ellen's companion did not ease my burden; it only sharpened it.

The long October and November nights passed so slowly. Sleepless, I roamed the halls of Kilgannon, making speeches in my head, remembering what had happened in each part of the house, staring at the family portraits as though they had something to tell me. I regretted I had let him go. I regretted that he went. I regretted that he had not chosen mine above all other claims, that I could not accept his choice with grace. And that I had let my husband leave knowing my anger and my fear. I should have told him I had every confidence in him and his people, but I had only wept and told him he would lose. And I regretted in those long hours that there had been no child of this union, and perhaps never would be. I stood on that parapet every evening, watching the blue islands and bartering with God for just one more night with my love. How many women, over the centuries, I wondered, had stood staring off into space and wishing their men home? *I don't care who is king*, I told the stones. *I don't care who wins the war. Just bring my love home to me*. But the stones kept their silence and eventually I descended and joined the others.

One thing I did not regret was loving Alex nor marrying him and coming to this impossible place. Meeting Alexander MacGannon that summer night in 1712 had changed my life forever. He was unlike any man I'd ever known, and I'd been fascinated from the start with the blond giant who strode into my aunt's ballroom with his Highland clothing, impeccable manners, and enchanting smile. He was honest and direct, full of humor and disdainful of the conventions London adhered to so slavishly. And the most handsome man I'd ever seen. That had not changed with marriage. I still caught my breath when he moved toward me, still was enthralled by his touch and still moved to passion I'd never known could exist. Even after two years of marriage, all he had to do was flash those blue, blue eyes at me and I was his. And now he was gone to war and with him had gone all my hope for happiness, for it was my own country he fought. And how I had struggled with that. And with him, begging him not to join the Jacobites, not to commit treason. For it was treason. And folly. I knew they could not win, could not hope to taunt the might of the English military and win. No matter how glorious their intentions, no matter how heartfelt their convictions or gallant their warriors, they would lose.

But I would not go home to England. I would stay at Kilgannon, the home for generations of MacGannons, safe for now in this formidable fortress. His home, and mine, perched atop a hill that overlooked a deep sea loch, was amply buttressed. Alex's wife and sons would be well protected. But for how long? I could not shake my fears. Alex might never return, might die on some far-off battlefield, might be captured by the English. My people. The enemy. My heart had made my decision to stay simple. I was The MacGannon's wife, and whether he forfeited his title of tenth Earl of Kilgannon, and I my Countess title with it, did not matter. I wanted him alive and home with me, with his two sons from his first marriage, now my sons.

Politics did not matter to me. Alex did. And in my more honest moments with myself I even admitted a grudging respect for his decision. I knew he loved me, but I also knew he would always put duty and loyalty, as he saw it, first. I did not regret that in him, only that I had ever let the MacKinnons and MacDonalds through the door. When they'd come to ask Alex to raise the clan in James Stewart's defense, I should have been ruthlessly rude and driven them away. But I might as well have tried to stop the tide as prevent Alex from joining.

Regret was with me, of course, on that cold and windy evening when the news came that the battle of Sherrifmuir had been fought on November thirteenth. The runner, a MacDonald, shivered as he stood before us.

"Five Kilgannon men killed," he said. "Andrew, Earvan, and Cian MacGannon, Fergus MacManus, and Sim of Glendevin. Angus hasna a scratch, nor Matthew. Had any other Kilgannon men died, I would have been told." Ellen breathed a sigh of relief. "Yer laird is well, Lady Mary, but he was wounded."

The boys exclaimed and I rose from my chair, Ian with me. "Alex was wounded? How is he?"

"I'm told it was not a bad wound. He's much better the now."

I nodded and sat down, pulling Ian with me, while the weary man told his tale. The women and children gathered around, and when he talked about the battle, I watched my sons' eyes light up.

"It was a big battle," he said. "The Jacobites under Mar were twelve thousand strong. The English had many fewer, and Campbells"—he spat the name out—"among them." *Robert*, I thought, recalling the Campbell family member who had courted me in London, as the runner continued. "Yer men were with us MacDonalds and with the Macleans in the right wing, under General Gordon."

He sipped his whisky while I envisioned the scene. Alex, and the men of Kilgannon I knew so well, fighting alongside the MacDonalds and Macleans. Murdoch Maclean would be delighted, I reflected, remembering Alex's closest friend outside the clan doing his best to persuade Alex to join the rebellion. Murdoch, a huge man, always passionate, was better suited to laughter than slaughter. Despite his best efforts, he'd been unable to convince Alex to join him in the uprising. It had been Sir Donald MacDonald, leader of the MacDonalds of Skye, who had known what would sway Alex, and Donald who had used that knowledge. And I'd never forgive him for it.

Ian spoke into the pause. "Who won?"

The man looked at him without expression. "No one."

"No one?" I could not keep still. "No one?"

"No." The runner looked uncomfortable. "Both sides withdrew. Mar has gone to Perth. Yer laird wanted to press their advantage, so did many of the others, and he was verra loud about being ignored, but then word came of the loss at Preston. . . ."

"Preston?"

"Aye. In England. Have ye no' heard? Part of Mar's force went south and joined the English Jacobites. They fought at Preston and were defeated. Lords Kenmure and Derwentwater were captured. Many left Mar after that."

"What is happening now?"

"I hear now that troops are coming from the

Netherlands to aid the English. Mar is in Perth. Argyll is leading the English troops and he can only hope Mar doesna press his advantage now. But when the Dutch troops arrive . . ." His words drifted into silence. If Argyll led the English, I thought, then Robert, never far from his cousin, was also at the battle. Opposing Alex.

"How can no one win a battle?" Ian asked.

The runner glanced at me, then at Ian. "I dinna ken, lad, but that's what I'm told." Ian nodded, accepting it for now.

Unhappy as the news was, at least we knew they were still alive. But Alex had been wounded, and regret filled the room.

I visited the families of the men who had died and we held a memorial for them, but I had no words to soothe the pain and I don't know that I helped. On my visit to Glendevin I learned that Lorna's husband, Seamus MacDonald, had been killed in the battle, and that Lorna had come from Skye to stay with her mother. I held Lorna's son Gannon while she told me, thinking of their wedding such a short time ago, the same summer that Malcolm, Alex's younger brother, had wed Sibeal MacDonald. And where was Malcolm now? I wondered.

I detested my brother-in-law. I always had, from our first meeting through all the revelations that had come out about his perfidy, about his murderous attempts to hurt Alex. Malcolm had poisoned Alex to prevent him from discovering that Malcolm and a sea captain had plotted to fake a sinking of one of Alex's ships, then kept the proceeds of the "sale" of the *Diana* to the captain. The ship had been recovered, but I had never forgiven him for it, nor for the two attacks in London, which I believed had been orchestrated by Malcolm. I'd almost lost my life in one; Alex his in the other. No, I would never forgive Malcolm. A liar and a thief, he had tried every ruse to sneak back into Alex's good graces. And it had worked. For a while. But when Malcolm had beaten his wife, after she'd discovered he was unfaithful, and then threatened me, it was too much for even Alex, who had banished him from Kilgannon for good. Even then Malcolm had persisted and had written to Alex begging his help when the Earl of Mar threatened to burn him out if Malcolm did not join the rebellion.

Malcolm lived at Clonmor, on the lands Alex had given to him, lands their mother had brought to the MacGannons as her dowry. And Clonmor, as well as the area around it, was under the control of John Erskine, the Earl of Mar, who had it within his power to demand that Malcolm raise troops to back him, whether Malcolm agreed or not. I didn't trust Malcolm nor had I been moved by his plea for help. Where was Malcolm now? I wondered uneasily.

No news came for a while. Shortly after the men had left, we'd heard that Louis XIV of France had died. With his death came the possible demise of the assistance, and gold, that France had pledged to the Jacobite rebellion. France, now ruled by a youngster, was said to be at best a faint ally. Now, however, the rumors said all manner of things. France had sent ten thousand troops. Or none. James Stewart had landed with French troops and gold. The French had joined the English. Spain was at war with England. Spain was at war with France. Spain had allied with England. We waited for the truth.

I wrote to my aunt Louisa, my mother's sister, and

her husband, my uncle Randolph, in London, and my brother Will and his wife, Betty, of what had happened, telling them not to come for their usual visit at Christmas. No letters came in reply and I had no assurance that they had ever received mine. The post, always uncertain, was not usable now. We had in the past relied on the brigs' travels to bring us news, but now the *Mary Rose* and the *Katrine* sat idle in the loch, and the *Margaret* and *Gannon's Lady* were gone with the men.

I had not expected to miss receiving letters as much as I did. Louisa always relayed the most recent news and gossip circulating in London, while Randolph kept me abreast of the political affairs, often throwing in some tidbit for Alex, a new thought on raising horses or the latest changes in carriage design. That his items rarely interested Alex was beside the point. Randolph's thoughtfulness had been much appreciated by both of us. My brother wrote of my childhood home, Mountgarden, of its inhabitants and the rhythm of the seasons in that lovely place, which always made me nostalgic for what I'd left behind in Warwickshire. And he wrote of his life with the frivolous but beautiful Betty. My brother's marriage was very happy. The letters from my best friend, Rebecca Washburton Pearson, though much more infrequent since they must cross the Atlantic, told me of her everyday life in the Carolinas, and of her adjustments not only to married life, but, like me, to an entirely different people. She wrote also of her daughter, and sometimes of her boredom with the unvarying order of her life. The boredom was something I envied her almost as much as I did her daughter. I had realized long ago that I would never be bored while I was married to Alex MacGannon. I had treasured her letters, reading them over and over, sometimes even reciting parts aloud to Alex. How different our present lives were from what we'd imagined when we were little girls. Becca had married Lawrence and had gone to his plantation in the colonies; and I had married my Scotsman and come to his castle in the Highlands. We had always assumed that we'd grow up as our mothers had, neighbors and friends for life. But, I reflected, my mother had died at an early age, leaving her sister Louisa and her best friend, Eloise, now the Duchess of Fenster, to go on without her. My aunt and the Duchess had remained fast friends with each other, and with Becca's mother, Sarah, and I was determined that no matter the circumstances, Rebecca and I would do the same. But how? I wondered in the depths of my loneliness and fear. How would we remain friends?

It was a glum household that upheld the traditions of the season. Christmas was somber and although we celebrated New Year's with as much tradition as we could muster, none of us was in a rejoicing mood. I think we breathed a collective sigh of relief when we could stop the charade.

In the early hours of January first I wrapped Alex's old plaid around me and gave in to the tears that were never far away. I sobbed as I remembered last year's holidays. *"Je suis content,"* Matthew had said, and risked the teasing that had followed. I had agreed. I was content. And now, twelve months later, my life was in tatters, my husband far away with his men, defeated rebels running for their lives.

I slept at last, but my dreams were so vivid that I woke with the sound of Alex's voice still in the room. I had been remembering the day he'd first called me Mary Rose. We'd visited Duncan of the Glen's home and as we left one of his sons had handed me a beautiful white rose, diminutive and very fragrant. A wild rose, Thomas had told me. "It is small and easily bruised, but it will grow back again and again. Once it has taken root, ye cannot budge it for all the effort ye'd give," he'd said. And Alex, laughing, his eyes very blue, had asked the men, "Who is small and verra beautiful and easily bruised?" When they had all turned to see my reaction, Alex had grinned and said, "We'll call it the Mary Rose." Later that night he'd said the name suited me, and he'd called me that ever since. I woke to hear the echo of his voice still lingering. "Yer body is verra tender, Mary Rose," he'd said. I closed my eyes again, hoping to summon him close for just another moment. But he was gone and the night stretched long before me.

1716 was upon us, the weather cold and brutal. Ellen and I spent our evenings in the library with the boys or in the hall, where more and more often the women of the clan would gather with the children. It was one such evening, with the snow falling outside and the wind wailing at the windows, that the first of the Kilgannon men came home.

We heard a cry from the courtyard and one of the boys, for that's all who was left for such tasks, burst through the door shouting, "Lady Mary, riders approaching the glen, Kilgannon men, about twenty of them. They'll be here shortly." I had risen when he burst in, and I nodded, my heart beginning to pound. *Dear God*, I prayed, *let it be Alex*, but even as the thought was formed, I knew that if only twenty were coming home, Alex would not be among them. Unless the others were all dead.

We spilled out onto the steps as the men entered the

courtyard. Around me women called joyously as they saw their men, running to them with sobs and delighted greetings. Ellen and I stood with Thomas Mac-Neill's wife Murreal and watched the reunions, then exchanged somber looks and turned to go into the hall. Alex's cousin Dougall, his arm still around his wife Moira, struggled through the people, calling my name. The huge man looked twice his age, his face gray with fatigue, his cheek scarred with a wound that still looked fresh even though Sherrifmuir had been weeks ago.

"He's no' with us, Mary," Dougall said, his voice cracking with emotion. "But he's alive." Dougall enveloped me in an embrace while I struggled with my emotions, unable to speak. Dougall did not notice my state as he stepped back and fumbled in his plaid, pulling out a tattered letter that he handed to me. "It's from Alex," he said unnecessarily as I looked at the familiar writing and tore the letter open. Ellen ushered me inside the hall and the rest of the clan poured in behind us. I stood to the side and read my husband's letter while the people surged around me.

Mary Rose, Alex wrote. *I'm sending this home with Dougall. He'll tell you of Sherrifmuir and its aftermath. This rebellion is a worse nightmare than anything I could have imagined. We have no responsible leadership and half our force is fled. We wait while the English re-arm and reinforcements from the Continent arrive daily. If we could not win when we outnumbered them, what will happen when the forces are equal?*

The countryside is full of English troops taking reprisals, and we have retreated to Perth and do little to stop them. Mar and the others do nothing but talk, and I am disgusted with the lot of them, as are the MacDonalds and Macleans and many others as well. We should be camped outside London and King George should be begging for a truce instead of us sitting here on our hands. Unless a miracle happens, we are doomed. All that I ever said about the clans uniting or being destroyed is true here, and I wish I could not see it. Scotland and the MacGannons will pay dearly for this.

"Mama," Ian said, tugging at my skirt and bringing me back to the present. It took a moment for me to stop hearing Alex's voice, and I looked around in surprise at the clansmen waiting for me. "Come and sit with us. Dougall's telling what happened," Ian said. I nodded at Alex's son and, folding the letter, joined him at the table across from Dougall.

"Alex sent us home," Dougall said as he ate with one hand, his other arm wrapped around Moira, large with child. Their Alasdair, not quite two, sat on his father's lap, sucking his thumb.

"Why? What of the rebellion? Is it over?" I asked.

Dougall looked uncomfortable. "No. But nothing's happening, so Alex sent those of us with the youngest children home. We left the others in good health, Mary, although I must tell ye that Alex was hurt in the battle."

I nodded. "I have heard that. How is he now?"

"Better. It was no' a bad wound at first, but it kept bleeding because Alex wouldna stay abed." When I asked why, Dougall laughed and took a swig of whisky. "He was too busy arguing with Mar. Alex caused such a ruckus that Mar wouldna let him in the war councils. The MacDonald said that if Alex were no' there, neither would he be, and the Macleans did the same, so Mar finally let him back in." Dougall laughed again. "I dinna think Bobbing John Erskine, the mighty Earl of Mar, cares overmuch for our Alex."

"What were they arguing about?" I asked.

"Courage," he said and the other men nodded.

"Or the lack of it," said one. "Mar wouldna press his advantage and Alex and the others were vexed by it."

"I ken what Mar was thinking," Dougall said, "but I dinna agree with his conclusions. After the battle many men dinna have their plaids. They'd thrown them off before the battle and fought in shirts and it started to snow just after, so there were many men without proper clothing. Some left to go home then, more when the news came o' the loss at Preston. The roads were clogged with those leaving." He sighed and lifted his chin, looking around at the people gathered behind me. "Ye'll be happy to ken that we won our position in the battle. We were fearsome, we were, and the Clonmor men as well. The right dinna break, even when both the left and the middle did." Dougall sat back, his voice hushed now. "But I'll never forget the battle. When I looked up and beyond the next man in front of me, I couldna believe what I saw.

"A sea of red. Red blood, red plaids, red coats, red hair. I've never seen so many shades of red in my life. And mud, that had been dirt, moistened with blood until ye could hardly move with it sucking at the horse's hooves." Moira put a hand to his cheek and he kissed her palm, then looked at me. "It's then Alex was wounded. He was afoot, like Angus and me, and three of the enemy were bearing down on him. Angus charged in and I did the same but then four more of them were there. I thought we'd die the next minute but Gilbey came up on Alex's right and we all met in the middle. Who woulda thought the damned tutor would save Alex's life? All those swordfighting lessons from Angus paid off." He laughed, then continued. "When we looked up we realized that the battle was over. Then Alex fell to his knees and Gilbey shouted that Alex was hurt. He was bleeding so much we thought we'd lose him, but he wouldna leave the field until we found the others." He took a large gulp of whisky and stared into the distance for a moment.

"And the rest of it was as ye'd think, men dying and dead aready, the crows waiting in the trees for us to leave the field." He wiped his eyes and many of his listeners did the same. "We pulled back to Perth then and the talking began. I still think, and so did Alex, that we should ha' acted. We could ha' won then, if we'd attacked at once. I dinna think we can now unless something else happens." He shook his head. "And then we heard that Simon Fraser, Lord Lovat, the chief of the Frasers, had come back from France. Since he'd spent the last few years with the Stewart's court we expected him to join us, but no, the man turned tail and he took Inverness in the name of King George. So all the Frasers deserted and the Gordons as well, and then English reinforcements who had been in Holland came. Within two weeks they had three times our number and our advantage was lost."

He leaned forward, his voice solemn. "And then James Stewart came. We were there when he arrived at last from Peterhead, and we heard the news that the gold he'd brought, all the Spanish gold, had been lost at sea." Dougall's face darkened. "The king called us together and we thought he'd rally us, that maybe he'd thank us for our efforts and tell us what we'd all do next." He paused, his eyes narrowing. "He told us to continue. That was all the encouragement he gave us. 'Continue.' " He shook his head. "And then James Stewart told us how difficult his trip had been from France, and he complained about the food. He was making plans for his coronation as we left." He shook his head. "Our mighty leader."

Behind me someone asked a question about the battle, and I left them then, Dougall drawing the battle lines in the table as the boys and men leaned eagerly over them, Ian and Jamie in the thick of it. I went to the library and unfolded Alex's letter, my hands shaking as I found where I'd stopped reading.

James Stewart has arrived, Alex wrote, *and it is worse than before. We hear that English soldiers are walking the shore and picking up the gold we were to use to defeat them and to feed and arm our men. I will stay a little longer and see if our forces will rally, but I am sending the men who have small children or pregnant wives home with Dougall. He'll protect you, Mary, rely on him.*

Mar still expects men to leave their homes to aid us. He is a fool but I may yet be proved wrong. We are alive for the moment and healthy and I suppose I should take comfort in that, but, lass, how I miss you. I am not a man meant for warfare. I am so very angry over the mismanagement of this campaign that I can barely be civil. It is a disaster. If we are truly lost then Kilgannon may come under siege. If the news is worse when you get this or if you do not hear from me soon, then take the boys and go. Leave at once if you hear of troops moving west. Do not try to fight them or to defend the castle. Tell the clan to take to the heather and you take the Mary Rose *and go to England. Do this, Mary. I must know you are safe. I will come to Kilgannon as soon as we can.* Gannon's Lady *is here in Perth and we will come home on her.*

I miss you every moment, Mary Rose, and I will love you until I die. Keep yourself and my sons well and safe. Use whatever resources you can find and get yourself to safety with Will or Louisa and Randolph. The writing changed then, the last of the letter written in haste. *Worse news again. There's talk of surrender, of Mar turning over a number of us as hostages, to ensure no further rebellions. If that's true then I may not come home at all. I suspect I'd be among the first to be handed over, for Mar dislikes me greatly. If they take us I will be tried here and God only knows what a jury of Lowlanders loyal to the Crown would do. I am mindful of my peril and will do whatever I can to return home alive. I have no wish to die in Edinburgh. Forgive me, Mary. Take care of yourself and my sons and know I remain your loving husband, Alex.*

The days passed very slowly and I feared that the winter would never end, that we would always be imprisoned by the rain and snow, waiting. I tried to keep spirits up and keep everyone busy, but I was not Alex and I was not the leader that Kilgannon needed. I had never realized how effortlessly he led the clan, and how difficult it was to make the many necessary decisions with the sure skill and good humor that came so easily to him. Nor had I realized how invaluable Angus was. Alex's first cousin was Alex's war chieftain, responsible for the training of the men. Angus was several years older, but they acted like brothers, for they'd grown up together. Alex trusted Angus more than any of the other clansmen, and Angus, gruff, loyal, and a man of few words, returned the trust. Both had lost their wives in the last five years, Angus his Mairi to childbirth and Alex his Sorcha to illness, and both had been left with sons to raise alone. Angus's Matthew, grown now, was off at war with his father, and Alex's boys were with me. With both Alex and Angus gone, our lives could not hope to be normal. Dougall tried to fill the void and he did well if one did not look too closely. And none of us was looking too closely.

The news from the east was not good. The Loyalist forces far outnumbered the Jacobites now, and Mar's troops had retreated to Montrose. And then, the last day of January, Thomas MacNeill, Alex's factor, came home.

They arrived on *Gannon's Lady* and for a few splendid moments I thought Alex was with them. Thomas's son Liam burst in with the news of a ship in the loch, one of ours, and we all ran to see. *Gannon's Lady* came around the last bend, her rail in the water in the stiff wind, her decks crowded with men. A cheer rose from those behind me as we waited for her to land, and when she came closer the boys strained to see their father. Or Angus. Or Matthew. Ellen stood at Ian's side, her hand to her throat. As she drew to the dock we all realized who was missing.

"Da's no' there," said Ian, his tone hushed.

Dougall, standing on my left, let out a curse and then apologized as I looked at him. "I feared this would happen, Mary. Ye ken our Alex. He'll no' come home until everyone's safe. He's probably making sure the Clonmor men got home aright."

I nodded, understanding the words but not the reason why Alex would not let them go home with Malcolm. We waited in silence while the ship docked and the men poured from her, washing past me like a stream, flooding into the arms of their wives and children. The boys turned to me, their faces grave. Their father had not come home. Nor wee Donald, and at my side Ellen sobbed. I put an arm around her and waited. Thomas found me after only a few moments.

"Mary," he said, his tone quiet. "I must talk with ye."

I nodded up at him, noting how Alex's factor had aged, his face now lined. He met my look with weary eyes.

"Thomas, tell me. Is he alive? Is he well? Is he free?"

"Aye. Alex is alive and free and Angus and Matthew as well."

"And wee Donald? And Gilbey?"

"Aye. They are all well." Ellen took a ragged breath.

"And together?" I asked.

His eyes met mine. "Aye, Mary. They are together."

"Where are they?"

He shook his head. "I dinna ken. We saw them last at Montrose, standing on the dock as we left."

"I see." I took a deep breath. "Thank you. Go and see Murreal and your family, Thomas. It is enough for now that I know he is not with you. I know you will soon tell me the rest."

"Aye, Mary, and I thank ye." He pulled a ragged letter from his plaid. "From Alex. I will come to ye soon."

It was scrawled on the back of a map, filthy and torn. I took the letter and held it to my breast, then opened it there on the dock.

My dearest Mary, Alex had written. *I am sending this to you with Thomas as we part. I pray it finds you all well. We are truly lost here and I am trying to save as many men as I can. Take the Mary Rose and flee now. Go to safety in England if you can or Skye if ye cannot and ask Morag for shelter. Please forgive me for this disaster. Take care of my sons and tell them their father loved them. Flee now, before the English descend on Kilgannon. I love you, Mary. If I'm alive I'll find you. Alex.*

I will never ask Morag Maclean for shelter, I thought, remembering her lingering glances at Alex during our wedding celebrations at Kilgannon, and the furtive caresses she'd thought I'd not seen every time they'd

been together since. Alex had not responded to her,
but he'd have noticed. And no doubt had remembered
what had once been between them. Morag, then Morag
MacLeod, had been the girl Alex had fallen in love with
when he was sixteen and she fifteen, the girl he'd been
willing to defy his parents for and abandon the arranged
marriage with Sorcha MacDonald. Morag was the girl
he'd been sent to France for a year to forget. The first
woman he'd made love to. And Morag had waited
for Alex even after he'd married Sorcha, not marrying
Murdoch Maclean herself until Alex had made it abun-
dantly clear to her and to the world that ours was a love
match and a happy one. But Morag had never forgotten
their romance. Nor did I.

I read Alex's letter three times, holding the paper
against the wind that threatened to tear it from my
hands, then looked at the wedding ring gleaming on
my finger. No, I would not ask Morag for shelter, and I
would not go to safety in England. I would stay at Kilgannon despite Alex's instructions. We'd argued about
it enough before he'd left. "This is my home," I'd told
him when he'd asked me to go to France with his aunt
Deirdre and the MacDonalds. "If you need me, Alex, I
will be here. I can come to you. Anywhere in Scotland,"
I'd said, and then tried to explain that he was not the
only one who felt responsibility for the clan. I had been
raised with a strong sense of duty toward the people I'd
known at Mountgarden, and in the short time I'd lived
here I'd assumed the role of Alex's partner. The mantle
of leadership was not one I could shrug off when it
suited me. I would stay at Kilgannon as long as I could
to be with its people. And to be as close to Alex as I
could, for as long as I could.

TWO

BERTA, OUR CAPABLE HOUSEKEEPER, WELCOMED EVERY-
one inside with whisky and food. I sat on a bench with
the boys and Ellen while the greetings continued around
us. I comforted them as best I could, stilling the questions that flooded my mind. I had thought Thomas and
I would talk quietly while he told me the news, but the
men were full of stories and I sat with the others and
listened.

"Well," one of the men said, answering a question,
"I dinna think much of our James Stewart the now, not
after he left us to fend for ourselves." At the outcry he
looked around the room. "Have ye no' heard? James
Stewart and his special friends stole away to France in
the middle of the night. I canna believe the word has
no' come to ye yet."

"Aye, it's true." Thomas spoke quietly from behind
me and heads swiveled toward him. He moved to the
fireplace and sank down on a bench while the people
gathered around. "We never saw the king after the first
few days, and then we retreated once more, this time to
Montrose. Alex had us take *Gannon's Lady* there or we
wouldna be home the now." Thomas shook his head.
"We waited in Montrose while most of the Highlanders

walked to Aberdeen. Alex told us no' to leave with the others. He and Angus attended meetings that lasted half the night, and he was more angry every day. And then early one morning, in the wee hours, I heard all sorts o' noise from downstairs in the house we were staying in."

He leaned forward. "When I went down the stairs, there was the MacDonald himself and the Maclean brothers, filling the room, and Angus and Alex looking like murder. Mar had sent everyone on to Aberdeen and then he and the Stewart were about to sneak away to France. Someone told the MacDonald and Macleans and Alex, and they all went to see for themselves. I'm told that the MacDonald got on his knees and begged James Stewart to stay. But the Stewart wouldna stay. So off they went, James Stewart and Mar, in the dark of night. Sailed away, leaving us there. James Stewart sent a letter to be read to everyone waiting in Aberdeen: 'Goodbye, lads, fend for yerselves. I'm off to save my own skin. Thanks for the war.'

"Well, ye ken our Alex. He wouldna leave with the Stewart, though I would be surprised if Mar asked him, they were no' favorites of each other, especially after Alex all but called him a coward. Angus says he thought the two of them would end in blows and the king was just sitting in the corner, watching with a long face. Well, anyway, there we were, in that old house in the middle of the night, the MacDonald white-faced and furious and the Macleans screaming murderous things and Angus looking like he'd split someone. Then the MacDonald and Macleans took themselves off and Alex started waking our men, telling them to get ready. Alex thought he'd ride on to Aberdeen and warn those still on the road, and Angus thought he'd keep him company. They told us to leave and come home to be with ye here. And he was a mite forceful in his suggestions too." He smiled ruefully and laughed with the other men, who nodded. "He packed us off to *Gannon's Lady* and here we are. Argyll was moving into Montrose as we were leaving. We got out by a breath is all and I'm assuming the others got out as well." He took a long drink of his whisky. "The MacDonald's going to France, I'm told, and the Macleans took to the heather. Alex and Angus and the others are somewhere near Aberdeen, and the Clonmor men are with them. The land is full of English soldiers."

"How will they get home?" Ian's voice was loud in the pause.

Thomas's eyes met mine, then looked at Ian. "Yer da will find a way, laddie. He's a bonnie leader. He'll find a way."

"But you said the English soldiers are everywhere."

"Aye, so I did," Thomas said. "But what are a few English soldiers to a Gael who kens his homeland? Yer da kens the land there. He'll ken ways to get home that the English dinna. Never ye fear, Ian, yer da will be here soon." Ian nodded, his face expressionless as he looked at me. Jamie followed his gaze. I tried to smile, but I could only see the harsh winter and a handful of men, dressed in red plaids, running from soldiers in the snow.

Our waiting was full of work. We were preparing Kilgannon for a siege and we toiled constantly. All the stores we could find were brought into the keep, and the tunnel was readied in case we should need it. The *Katrine* was anchored in the outer loch, and the outlying areas were warned. Most of the men had gone to their homes, but they patrolled the perimeter of Kilgannon lands and runners kept us informed of what each village was doing. When Alex first left I had gathered all the things that he had told me to take with me, and the bags still stood in the library. The boys and I had packed our clothes. And Alex's. And I had packed Alex's box of sketches. We were ready to flee, at once if necessary. And then we waited.

The winter crept slowly on, cold and wet, and we worked until we dropped. The boys were very brave but they were afraid, and I spent much of my time cheering them on or leading them in their lessons. I kept my fears to myself. During the daylight hours I held them at bay, but at day's end they would reappear and the nights stretched interminably. I still roamed the house in the dark hours, pausing each night to look at the portraits that lined the stairs, asking Alex's image where he was.

I was in the hall at daybreak the morning the news came that a ship was in the loch, and said a silent prayer as I waited. My spirits sank when the word came that the ship was not ours, but they rose again with the news that it was a MacDonald ship, with Sir Donald himself on deck. But Alex was not aboard.

I waited on the dock with Thomas and Dougall as the ship approached, and waved in return when the MacDonald signaled to us. He climbed stiffly from the boat, his movements those of a man much older, then nodded at me and walked up the hill without a word. I followed the man who had enticed Alex to war, the leader of the MacDonalds. I had once been very fond of him, admiring not only his looks, still arresting though he was twenty years older than Alex, but also his wit and intelligence.

Inside the hall Sir Donald settled himself slowly at a

table and silently accepted the whisky I poured for him.
Dougall and Thomas sat to my right, their expressions
carefully blank. I kept my hand on the stone bottle, cool
under my grip, and felt my heart as cold. *But for you,* I
thought as I watched him, *Alex would be here with me
now.* He had difficulty meeting my eyes, but I felt no remorse for the chilliness with which I met his.

"Dinna look so baleful, Mary MacGannon," he said
at last. "I dinna mean to lead him to this." He glanced
around the hall, avoiding the gaze of the Kilgannon
men standing at a respectful distance but within reach if
I needed them. "I tried to convince him to come with
me, Mary. I am here now to ask ye to come to France
with us." I watched him as he leaned forward, his tone
earnest. "Mary, lassie, listen to me, when I left yer husband on the dock at Montrose, he was going to get
his men home and then join ye here. I dinna ken what
happened next." He sighed and rubbed his chin. "I
did try to convince him, Mary. I swear before God,
I did try. I wanted him to come with me. And that is
why I'm here. Most of my family has gone to France.
I'm here for the last of them. Come with us and bring
the lads. Come, Mary, and Alex will come after and ye'll
all be safe." I said nothing. He sighed again and looked
at his glass. When he looked up again, his eyes were
filled with unshed tears. "I tried, Mary," he said in a
choked voice. "And Alex tried. He was fair amazing.
But Mar would not listen and the others listened to
Mar." He took a deep drink of the whisky. "It broke my
heart when James Stewart left. It broke my heart. He
kent what it would mean and still he left." He stared
into the distance and I felt myself thawing. "Come with
us, Mary. Ye ken Angus's mother Deirdre and his sisters

are there? And yer sister-in-law Sibeal. Ye'll not be with strangers."

"Sibeal? Sibeal is there? And Malcolm?"

His gaze was level. "No. Hers is no' a happy marriage."

"I see," I said and studied my hands for a moment, then looked up at him. "You realize that Alex would not have gone if you had not persuaded him. He resisted Murdoch and the others."

"Aye, I ken that. I kent that day that he would come with us." We sat again and then he sighed. "Ye'll never forgive me for this, will ye?"

I met his eyes. Whatever I thought of this man, I had to admit he was courageous and honest. I answered him truthfully. "No."

He nodded to himself. "It was to the Gael in him that I appealed, Mary, and it was the Gael in him that answered. We would have won if more had heard the call and answered as well."

"Those who did not answer the call are safe at home, Sir Donald. And where are you?"

His fierce gaze met mine. "Free. Free, Mary. I am free."

"Not here, Sir Donald. If you stay here you will not be free. Perhaps in France you will be. But what about all the others? And Alex? He listened to you and you are off to France to protect yourself. And where is my husband?"

He looked at me for a long moment. "I asked him to come and I ask you now. If ye do no' join us, it is yer own choice."

"Like the choice you gave Alex? To join you or be burnt out? Would you have burnt us out?"

He blinked, startled, and some of the old fire appeared in his eyes as he smiled. And nodded. "Aye. We would have. Had it gone otherwise, aye. I wouldna have done it myself but I wouldna have stopped those who would."

"How could you?" I hissed.

He considered before he spoke. "In England, Mary, men dinna fight as we do here. They use words and laws to strike at each other's purses and careers. Here we use claymores and broadswords. It's much easier to understand."

I shook my head. "I'll never understand."

"Probably no'. But it's the Highland way. It willna change."

"Even when it ends like this?"

He leaned forward, his eyes gleaming. "It's no' ended, Mary MacGannon. As long as there is breath in one of us, it's no' ended. We may live under English domination for a time, but we never live comfortably. It always eats at us and the seeds of rebellion are always ready for sprouting. If we fail this time, we will live to rebel again. Wait and see, Mary. If Scotland is no' freed this time, we will rise again." We stared at each other.

"What will happen now?" I asked.

He shrugged. "We'll go to France and we'll try to get France's support again. If their troops had come we would have won."

"You outnumbered them four to one. What else did you need?"

He slammed his fist on the table. "A leader. We needed a leader. We needed a man who can lead men and who kens how to fight, who would ha' won the battles. Then we needed a man who can play the political games and win. Ye ken I'm no' the right man for the politics, and neither is yer Alex, but the right man could. With the support of France we could have won our freedom."

"But you did not."

"No' this time."

"So you will go to France."

"We will go to France and plan. Come with us, Mary. Come with us and Alex will come. We need him even more the now."

"Mar hates him. And James Stewart probably as well."

"Aye." He sighed. "Mar is at best a poor leader. At worst, a coward and a fool." He rubbed his hand through his hair. "Come with us, Mary. Keep yerself safe. And Alex's laddies. Come."

He met my eyes without flinching and I considered. What would Alex want me to do? No doubt he would want us away to safety. But Alex was not here and this decision was mine alone. The MacDonald was offering safety for the three of us. I looked around the hall. There were hundreds of people at Kilgannon.

"I thank you for your offer, Sir Donald."

His eyes narrowed. "But?"

"But I must decline. I cannot leave."

"Ye mean ye willna leave."

"I will not leave."

"Why? Alex will be here soon and he could join ye."

I waved my hand at the room. "And what of them? Who will keep them safe?"

"Is it no' better that ye leave for a bit and then return to lead them to freedom than to stay and perhaps perish with them?"

"No," I said. His chin lifted and he met my gaze with narrowed eyes. "I will wait for my husband and he will decide. I will not leave without him."

"And then ye will come to join us?"

"That will be for Alex to decide."

"If ye come now he will decide to come after ye."

I shook my head. "I will not go with you."

The MacDonald considered for a long moment, then stiffly rose and climbed over the bench. He stood straight and turned back to me. "Mary, think again."

"Sir Donald, I will not leave Kilgannon unprotected."

"What can a wisp of a girl do against the English army?"

I smiled. "Ask Joan of Arc."

He laughed then, a harsh bark, and turned to leave. Several steps away he turned back, his grin wide. "Mary MacGannon, I am glad to have met ye."

I rose and faced him. "And I you, Sir Donald."

"Come with me, Mary and ask Joan yerself."

I laughed then. "She's been dead for centuries, sir."

"The spirit of freedom never dies, just the bodies of those who attempt to win her. The spirit of freedom will live again."

I nodded. "I thank you for your invitation."

"But ye willna come."

"I will not come." He nodded and left us then. I looked after him as he went out the door without a backward glance.

The winter continued. I stood every night at the library windows or at the top of the keep, the boys often with me. We would stare into the distance as if by imagining Alex coming through the glen we could make it so. The storms continued, one after the other. I was so tired. I would work most of the night to avoid the dreams that haunted me, and often found myself falling asleep during the day. One afternoon I sank into a chair in our bedroom and closed my eyes, remembering when Alex had first come into my life. I was in London, on the steps of the landscaper's office, waiting for my aunt Louisa and sister-in-law Betty, when I saw him. Alex was walking toward me, unaware of me watching. His shoulders swayed with his firm steps, his hair, loose under the hat with the eagle feather, flowed to his shoulders, shining like a flame against the gray wall behind him. He turned his head and, seeing me, grinned as he moved toward me.

"Miss Mary, are you awake?" I opened my eyes. Ellen stood in the doorway. "Angus has returned on the *Margaret* with the men."

I stood immediately. "And Alex?"

Her eyes held an expression of pity. "No." At my start, she continued quickly. "They say he's alive. But not with them."

I was already moving past her. "Where's Angus?"

"In the courtyard."

"I'll go and talk to him." I started toward the stairs, then turned back to her. "Ellen, wee Donald? Is he here?"

Tears rolled down her cheeks and my heart stopped. *Dear God,* I prayed, *please, not Donald too. Let her have her love back, even if I cannot have mine.* She nodded and I breathed again.

"He's here." Her voice broke. "Praise God, he's here."

I embraced her. "I am so happy for you, my dear friend."

"Miss Mary, I wish . . ."

I stopped her with another embrace. "I know, Ellen,

and I thank you." I turned away before she could comment, but I could not still the voice in my head that asked questions and then answered them. The cloud of fear I had lived with for so long surrounded me and I stood, frozen, at the top of the stairs, terrified of what I'd find below. I was still there, staring downward, when Angus appeared at the foot, just removing his gloves. He looked up at me, his face ashen. My heart started thumping as I watched him. This was more than weariness.

"Mary." Angus's voice was grim. "We must talk."

"Where is he?" I asked as I descended.

Angus shook his head. "I dinna ken. He was alive when I left him," he said, his voice toneless. I felt the cloud of fear thicken around me.

"Angus? Where is he?" My voice was no more than a whisper.

"I left him on the shore of Loch Linnhe."

"Why?" I stood before him now and looked up into his eyes. "Why, Angus? Why is he not with you? Where is he?"

"Probably with Robert Campbell."

Robert. The name hit me like a blow and I swayed. I had known it. Somehow I had known that the two men, rivals so long ago for my affections, were destined to cross paths again. Robert would of course be with Argyll's forces. If the Campbells were fighting with the English troops and Argyll was their leader, Robert could be nowhere else. Alex had not mentioned him, but now I heard the echo of Robert's words years ago in London. "In Scotland we are enemies," he had said. Dear God, what had happened?

Angus folded me in a rough embrace and I clung to

him. Alex's cousin was a big man, larger even than Alex. Barrel-chested and huge, he could be very intimidating. He had cut his hair short, as all the men had done before they left for war, but it was the same silky golden blond as Alex's, his blue eyes a shade lighter and now, as he released me, filled with tears.

"Has Alex been taken prisoner?" I asked.

"I dinna ken, Mary. He was free when I left him."

I looked around the hall, now full of the men who had been with Angus, wearily sitting, shoulders slumped, women clustering around them. Gilbey, the boy's tutor and an ally for me before he'd gone to war, gave me a wan smile, but no other man would meet my eyes.

"Come and tell me," I said and Angus nodded, letting me lead him to the library, where he settled heavily into the chair. "Where's Matthew?" I asked, realizing I'd not seen him. Angus's son, tall, handsome Matthew, was never far from his father's side, nor Gilbey's, for they were fast friends. *Matthew,* I thought with a pang as I settled into the chair opposite.

"With Alex." Angus stared at the fire and I waited. I was sure Alex and Matthew had been taken by the English. It had been in my mind since Sherrifmuir and then Perth. For all the Kilgannon men to get safely home across a country filled with victorious enemies would have been a miracle. That so many had come home at all was a blessing. Why couldn't my husband have been among them? I struggled with my panic as the serving girl Leitis brought in the whisky and food. I poured a glass for Angus and he sipped it, silently watching the fire. At last I spoke again.

"I know Kilgannon's lost and I know there will be reprisals." I struggled to keep my voice from trembling.

"I know Alex is alive and Matthew as well and somehow Robert's in the middle of it. Now tell me the rest. It can be no worse than my imaginings."

His gaze lifted and met mine. "Och, Mary, yer right, and I'm sorry for my rudeness. I've been sitting here thinking my own thoughts and forgetting that ye dinna ken what happened."

"Dougall told us about Sheriffmuir and Thomas told us that James Stewart and Mar left for France secretly and that the rest of you had to fend for yourselves. And the MacDonald told me that you were going to Aberdeen and then trying to get home. Some of you got here. What happened? Where's Alex?"

"The MacDonald was here?"

I nodded.

"Why?"

I told him of the visit and my response and he nodded.

"Good."

"Angus, where is Alex?"

"Somewhere east of Loch Linnhe the last time I saw him." He took a sip of the whisky and met my eyes. "And my son went to be with him." His gaze returned to the fire. "We were in Montrose and James Stewart met with the chieftains. Alex was there; I was outside with Duncan Maclean. When Alex came to us, ye wouldna have known him. I've never seen him so angry. Now, mind ye"—he looked at me from under his bushy eyebrows, his eyes a steely blue—"many of the clans had been sent north to Aberdeen. We were only still in Perth because of our ties to the MacDonald, else we would ha' been north with the others." He shifted in the chair. "Where was I? Oh, aye. It seems the chiefs argued with the Stewart but he was set on leaving. And he left, leaving us on our own."

"And the MacDonald left too."

"Aye, after a bit. He asked us to come with him. He damn near begged. I've never seen the man so broken."

"Why did you not go with him?"

"Ah, well, Mary, there was not room for twenty-four more men, only four or five at best. I told Alex to go with them, but he wouldna leave us on our own. Or the Clonmor men. And we'd had word Clonmor was besieged. So there we stood, in the middle of an icy night, and we watched King James sail away from his country and leave us to our own devices." He shook his head.

"We headed north, telling those still on the road what had happened. Then we turned west and went to Clonmor." He sighed. "But we were too late. The house had been burnt and many were dead. We did what we could for them and the Clonmor men who had been with us said they'd be aright on their own, so we headed home. We thought we could get west by way of Inverness, but the troops were everywhere and the snow was astonishing, so we went south, staying high. But every time we went down into the glens we met more soldiers." He shook his head, remembering. "We had our share of skirmishes and we lost Finlay and Gabhan in one. We built cairns over their graves and moved on. I dinna think we'd make it through the snow. It was so bad that we couldna see four feet and even with the best we could do, we were making little distance each day, sleeping in caves, or a kind soul's barn or kitchen."

He gripped his glass. "There was one day when I thought we'd all die on the spot. Alex was in the rear, I was at the head. It was hard to see, what with the snow blowing so hard, and we looked like ghosts. It was hard to shout too, ye ken how yer mouth doesna work well when yer cold, so I turned to wave at Alex. I watched him stand there and he just faded away. I could see everyone else, lass, but Alex just faded away. And then he was gone." He gulped the whisky before meeting my eyes. "We searched for him until we could not go on, then found a cave and waited out the storm. If I'd been a different man I would have sworn the wee folk took him. He was there and then he was gone." He shook himself as if throwing off the memory. "We found him the next morning. He said he'd spent the night in an empty shieling, but he was as shaken as I." His eyes met mine. "He said he could see only me and then I just faded away. It was a warning, Mary, and we dinna heed it."

I wrapped my shawl around me as he continued. Hampered by the heavy snows and packs of English troops, they moved south and east, out of the mountains. By talking to those sympathetic to the Jacobites in the countryside, they learned that the north was solidly held by the Loyalists and that Inverness, held by the Frasers, would have been no haven even if they could have reached it. So they moved even further south and then west, avoiding the troops, who were everywhere. They headed for the *Margaret* where she was anchored in Loch Linnhe. Somewhere west of Stirling they became aware that they were being followed by a particular band of English soldiers. They moved even more cautiously then, leaving a man or two behind to see how quickly they were pursued, and going as fast as possible when weather permitted, choosing their way carefully through Flander's Moss, the bog-infested land of the MacGregors. And then they reached the lands of their cousin Lachlan, the one who had written to Angus months ago. They were planning to spend the night in his barn when a letter arrived, delivered by a young boy who said he'd been paid to come to Lachlan's and give the message to Kilgannon.

"We were in Lachlan's house," said Angus, "drinking a wee bit with him, feeling safe for a moment. Lachlan told us that the soldiers had not been by for a while. Ye can imagine what we thought when the letter came. At the first it mystified us, lass." He sipped the last of the whisky in his glass and I moved to refill it. "We dinna ken where we'd be that night, so how could the English ken we'd be in that barn? It had rained all day and Alex and I were the ones watching to see how closely we'd been followed. We kent no one had seen us approach, and unless Lachlan had become a different man and sent a runner, which he swore he hadna, how would they have known? We'd gone by a roundabout way and were heading east when we arrived. None of us had left the group, so we dinna believe we had a traitor amongst us. We were very worried." Angus sighed and closed his eyes. "When Alex took the note and read it he turned pale and he folded it up and put it in his plaid. He wouldna tell us what it said at first, just told all the men to pack up, we were leaving." He opened his eyes and looked at the fire grimly. "Then I asked him again what it said and he gave it to me." He swallowed a gulp of whisky.

"What did it say?" I asked, still standing in front of him. His eyes met mine and I was shocked at the rage in them.

"It said our route and where we would probably stop, what caves and what kinsmen were on the route. And where a ship would be most likely to be harbored to be waiting for us. It said that if Alex were to surrender himself to the English, the rest of us would be released unharmed and Kilgannon untouched. And you would be escorted to safety in England. If he dinna surrender, it said, we would be pursued until we were found and made prisoner. And if we were not found, you would be taken and held. Then Kilgannon would be torched and the people killed. All of them.

"And it was signed by Robert Campbell."

THREE

HE SPAT OUT THE LAST WORDS, THEN REACHED INTO his pocket and handed me the letter. I took it with a shaking hand. It was addressed to the Earl of Kilgannon and written formally and it said all that Angus had. But I knew immediately that it had not been written by Robert. I read it twice.

"This is not Robert's handwriting, Angus."

His head snapped up. "Are ye certain, Mary? Verra certain?"

"Yes. I've read his writing many times over the years. It's not his handwriting and it's not the way he words things."

He stared through me. "That's what we thought."

"Angus, was Robert pursuing you?"

"Aye," he said slowly. "We saw him. He was their leader."

Robert, I thought. It could not be a coincidence that Robert Campbell, of all the men in the English army, was pursuing Alex across Scotland. "This could have been written for him," I said, looking at the note again. "But it's not his signature." I rubbed my eyes wearily. "How could he know where you were? Could he have followed you, even when you were being so careful?"

"It's possible. Unlikely, as we're the ones who ken the countryside here, no' him, with all his years in England. But that's not what happened." He shook his head and rose stiffly from the chair, putting his glass on the table. He began pacing. "He dinna need to ken the land. He had information that could only come from a MacGannon. That's what Alex and I realized. We had left no one alone. Even when we left the men positioned behind, there were always at least two. We knew there was a possibility that someone could have been bought, but who and when? Or that Lachlan had given us away, but I dinna believe it. Nor did Alex."

"Then . . . ?"

Angus stopped moving. "Malcolm."

"Malcolm?" I had forgotten Malcolm. "But he was with you. I assumed you left him at Clonmor."

"With us? Malcolm was never with us. Except for the time in Perth, I have seen Malcolm once since I left this house."

I stared at him. "Not with you? But how? He was with you at Sherrifmuir . . . you went to help him—"

His voice cut across mine. "He was never with us at Sherrifmuir. Did Thomas no' tell ye what happened, did Dougall no'? Did Alex no' write to ye? Do ye no' ken?" I stood very still. "Mary," he said gently, "what did Thomas and Dougall tell ye?"

"That you met the rest of the army and went to Perth, then Sherrifmuir, and that when Mar withdrew for the second time Alex sent most of the men home. Alex sent me letters. . . ."

"He dinna tell ye what Malcolm had done?"

I shook my head, feeling sick. "Angus, tell me."

"Ye ken that Malcolm wrote to Alex begging him to help?"

"Yes. The MacDonald brought the letter." I could still see Alex and the MacDonald facing each other across the table.

"When we got to Perth," he said, "Mar was there and Alex threatened to split his head for threatening his brother. That dinna set well with Mar, as ye might imagine. Mar admitted that he'd used the tactic on many, but not Malcolm. He said Malcolm had already gone when Mar sent his men to fetch him at Clonmor."

"Gone?" I asked. "Where?"

"To the Frasers."

"To the Frasers? But when . . . ?"

"Apparently as soon as he heard we were on our way, he left his lands unguarded and fled. Mar took fifty Clonmor men into his army. When we arrived we discovered Malcolm was not there, nor was likely to be. Alex felt he had to stay and took the Clonmor men from Mar."

"So you stayed," I said. "Without Malcolm."

"I canna believe Thomas dinna tell ye." Angus stormed to the door, throwing it open and bellowing for Thomas. He turned back to me. "Malcolm joined the Frasers and was with them when they took Inverness. Ye remember our grandmother was a Fraser? He has been with them and they are now firmly Loyalist. Malcolm wasna at Sherrifmuir, but he came to see us in Perth, after we withdrew there. He thought . . . Och, who kens what was in the man's mind? Now I wonder that he dinna mean to hand Alex to the English then." My head snapped up at that, but before I could speak, Thomas appeared in the doorway. He glanced at me and then back to Angus.

"Here I am," Thomas said.

Angus spun around. "Thomas, why did ye no' tell

Mary about Malcolm? I told ye to tell her in case he came here. Why did ye no'?" I had never heard Angus use such a harsh tone to Thomas. Thomas's face grew red and he shifted from one foot to the other.

"I told her the most of it," he said, not looking at me.

"Why no' the whole of it? Did Alex tell ye nay?"

"No, Alex never said a word except to get safely home."

"Then . . . ?" The question was left hanging and when Thomas did not reply, Angus again spoke sharply. "What, man? Speak!"

Thomas's tone was calm. "I thought Alex would have told her in his letters or that Dougall had told her, and when I suspected she dinna know, I found I couldna tell her." His eyes met Angus's. " 'Tis a shameful thing when a brother betrays a brother."

Angus held his gaze for a moment longer and then sighed as he turned away. "Aye," he said, his anger replaced by weariness. "Aye. Yer right. 'Tis a shameful thing. Thank ye, Thomas. That was all I needed." Thomas left gratefully, closing the door behind him, and Angus sank into the chair opposite me, staring at the wall.

"Tell me the rest," I said. "Malcolm came to Perth. . . ."

Angus nodded. "He sent a message, asking to meet at an inn outside the town. At first Alex said no and sent that message, but Malcolm asked again and begged his forgiveness. So Alex agreed."

"And you went with him."

"We all went with him. We argued with Alex and said he shouldna go, but we couldna convince him. So we all went."

"What did Malcolm have to say?"

"I think he was surprised to have so many of us there. We arrived in the middle of the day and posted men all around, so by the time Malcolm got there, late as usual, we were long ready." He sipped his whisky. "He said just what ye'd think, Mary. It wasna his fault. He said the Frasers insisted he join them after he'd sent word to Alex, which we dinna believe, and that he'd tried to warn Alex, which we dinna believe. He said whichever side won, at least the brothers could help each other and that way Kilgannon would be safe, that Mar had left him no choice but to flee and he knew Alex would understand. He said his life had been a hell." Angus shook his head in disgust.

"And what did Alex say?"

"I canna use the same words to ye. Let's just say he told Malcolm that he dinna believe him."

"What did Malcolm say?"

"We dinna give him much chance to say anything. We listened to what he had to say and Alex told him only the one thing and then we walked out. It's only after everything else that I wonder what would have happened if Alex had gone alone."

"And after that you never saw him again."

"No," he said heavily and shook his head. "I saw him again. Ye remember we were at Lachlan's house and got the letter?" I nodded. "When we thought on it we kent it had to be Malcolm. No one else coulda kent exactly where we'd be. Only a MacGannon would ken we'd spend the night with Lachlan on that route. Only a MacGannon would ken where we'd harbor a ship. No one else would ken our habits, and there was only one MacGannon unaccounted for."

"You think Malcolm wrote the letter."

"It's no' his writing but I think he's behind it."

"And Robert was with him. Are you sure?"

"Aye. When the message came we questioned Lachlan and the boy who brought it. Lachlan swore he knew nothing and the boy said only that a man had paid him English money to deliver the message. A Scot, with soldiers."

"So you went to see for yourselves."

He shot me a sharp look. "Aye, that we did. We retraced our trail and found them about three miles from us in a small spot with a crofthouse. It was like a bowl, where they were, and Matthew, Alex, and I crept up to the edge and waited for daylight. And at last we saw him. With Robert Campbell. They were looking at a map and Malcolm was waving his hand off to the west. We crept back away and rode some miles away. Then . . ." His mouth twisted in a wry smile. "Then we argued. Alex wanted the rest of us to go on and he would go back and wait for them to find him. I wanted him to come with us to the *Margaret* and get home or else fight them there. We argued for a verra long time and heatedly." He sighed and rubbed his chin. "And then he said he was ordering me as my chief to go. And I laughed at him, Mary. I laughed and I told him that he was but Alex and he couldna tell me what to do. I told him I wouldna go without him. He was quiet then for a long time and at last he said, 'Angus, let's go home.'

"I believed him because I wanted to believe him. In the end I did what he wanted. Willing or no, wittingly or no, I did what he wanted and, I suspect, we all did what Malcolm wanted." He took a deep breath. "If no' for that letter Alex wouldna have thought of giving himself to them. Malcolm knew that Alex would do exactly what Alex did. So now I'm here, safe and he's . . ." His words trailed off as he rubbed his hand over his face. "I dinna ken what he was doing until it was too late. If I had known . . ."

"Why did you not fight Robert?"

His head sank onto his chest for a moment. With a visible effort, he lifted his chin. "Robert has over a hundred men with him, Mary. We had twenty-two. Alex dinna like the odds."

I nodded. Nor did I. "So Alex went back to the barn?"

"No. We were hours from the *Margaret*, back around the loch and then some. Alex said we'd all go to her. When we got to the eastern shore of the loch we . . . found . . . some boats. It took two trips to cross the loch. I went with the first group. Alex said he'd stay with the second and I dinna question it. We often split ourselves like that so one of us would be guarding each end of the group. And when they came without him I was furious." He stared through me. "He told wee Donald that I had agreed that he would stay. He knew Donald wouldna argue with him. I would have, and Gilbey would have, but Alex made sure we'd gone together. I should never have left him. I should have kent what he would do. And none of us knew where Matthew was." He rubbed his eyes. "So we went back looking for them. The English camp was all but empty. No Alex. No Matthew. No Robert. We looked for hours. We went back to Lachlan's house and found it burning and Lachlan gone, but no bodies, so we think Lachlan lives. Then went back to the English camp and back to the boat, but we couldna find a trace of them. So we came home. I dinna know what else to do."

He sighed heavily. "I left him there on the shore of the loch, Mary, and when we were halfway across I turned and looked at him. I dinna ken why I turned to

look, but I'll see him standing there, watching us, until
I die. When we got to the other side I realized Matthew
was no' with us. I thought he'd gone in the other boat.
I could have sworn I saw him getting into one as we left
the shore." He took a deep drink, then met my eyes.
"And now we dinna ken where they are. As soon as I
have ye ready here, lass, I'm leaving again to find
them."

I closed my eyes. *This is not true*, I told myself, but
the image of Alex standing alone on the shore of a loch,
planning to surrender himself, was too difficult to bear.
I opened my eyes and saw Angus's misery written plainly
on his face. "If you had all gone back with him, there
would have been a battle," I said. "If just Alex and
Matthew go, perhaps there will be no violence. Alex
knew what he was doing and Robert will honor the
terms in his letter. No one will be hurt. Robert is an
honorable man. It's not as though he's a stranger.
Surely Robert can't really mean to keep Alex."

"Ye canna really believe that, Mary."

"Angus, it's Robert. He'll keep his word."

Angus's expression was desolate. "Mary, we dinna
have Robert's word. We have Malcolm's word. Robert
dinna write the letter. We have no way of kenning what's
in Robert's mind."

"Oh, dear God," I said, understanding at last.

"Aye. And my son's with them too." I stared at him
mutely.

We had sent runners out to the edges of Kilgannon
land and the *Margaret* to Skye for news. We prepared
for the worst. We slept fully dressed with weapons at
our sides. *Alex is alive,* I told myself over and over, as if

by mere repetition of the words I could make them real. *And Matthew is with him and they will be home soon. Alex is alive. . . .*

Two days later, as the last of Angus's preparations were being finished, a runner came with the news that Matthew was coming home. I waited with the boys while Angus rode out with Gilbey to meet his son, so I did not see their reunion, nor hear what Angus had to say about his behavior, but when the three of them rode back into the courtyard Angus looked more at peace and Matthew remorseful. Matthew threw himself off the horse as the boys launched themselves at him, then met my embrace with a sad smile.

"I'm sorry, Mary," he said, his young voice harsh with fatigue. I froze in his arms and looked up at him. He nodded. "Aye, bad news. Alex has been taken by Robert's soldiers. And Robert's men are now coming to Kilgannon."

"Thank God," I said. "How can you call this bad news? Alex is alive. Nothing else matters. Alex is alive and Robert is bringing him home."

Matthew shook his head. "I dinna ken that Alex is alive for certain, Mary. There's a big man riding with them, covered with a cloak and hood. I dinna ken it's Alex."

I stared at him, trying to understand. Around me the voices rose as the people questioned him. Angus called for quiet, then gently took my arm and motioned for everyone to follow us to the hall. Matthew was fussed over and plied with whisky and food and asked a thousand questions while Angus stood next to me, waiting until his son had a bit of the liquor and a bite of the food. Then the three of us withdrew to the library.

"Tell her what happened," Angus said, settling into a chair. "Start from when ye deceived yer father at the side of the loch."

Matthew straightened his back and gave his father an unreadable glance before meeting my eyes. "Alex was no' himself, ye ken, Mary," he said. I nodded, wondering what was coming. "I dinna ken at first what he was planning but I had an uneasy feeling, so I got out of the boat and waited with wee Donald and the others. When Alex and Donald argued I realized Alex was going to stay and I hid in the trees with one of the horses we'd left there. I watched Alex watch the others row away. I kent my da would be furious, but I thought one of us should stay with Alex, and Da and Gilbey were gone. That left me."

"Brilliant thinking," growled Angus. Matthew glanced at his father and continued. "I followed Alex back to the clearing we had stopped in earlier. He had taken all the horses except for the one I had with me and he wasna paying close attention to anything, so it was easy to follow him. He dinna see me and I was careful. I thought if he kent I was there he'd send me back to my da."

"He probably would have," I said.

Matthew nodded. "Alex sat on a rock in the clearing for the longest time, just sitting and looking at the ground. I was about to show myself when at last he jumped up and leapt onto his horse, taking the other horses with him. I followed him to the English camp. First he rode close and dismounted and crawled up the hill where we had watched them before, then he went back down and got on the horse. He sat there for a bit, looking up at the crest. I guess he was judging when the guards wouldna be looking." He wiped his palms on his thighs. "And then he gathered up all the other horses, real loose, and he rode right to the top of the hill above the camp, right through their guards. I thought he'd go down there after Malcolm, but instead he rode above the hut, waiting there in full view so that they all saw him. I thought he'd gone mad. He was deliberately drawing their attention. And then, when they were all shouting and running for their horses, when Robert Campbell came out of the hut, Alex rode right down into the camp, right through the middle and he let the other horses go, so that they muddled everyone up. Then he spun around and jumped over a campfire and rode up the other side. He stopped at the top and waited for them to start after him."

I pictured it, Alex leaning low over the horse, his hair flying, his plaid a crimson slash against the horse's side. He'd known they'd follow him and he'd planned to lead them away from his men. *Alex,* I thought, *my love.*

"Did they follow him?" Angus asked.

"Aye. When they came to the top of the hill he was already in the trees, going toward Brenmargon Pass, with them like madmen after him. I rode to meet him at the other side of the trees and he saw me then." His mouth twisted. "He wasna pleased. He shouted at me to go. He was like a madman, too, and we rode toward the pass with him shouting at me. It's verra flat from the trees to the pass, all open moor and we kent they'd see us the minute they broke from the trees, and they did. We could hear them screaming. That's when we got through the beginning of the pass. There's a spot there that's wide and flat, with the rocks high all around, and the path is only wide enough for two horses. Alex told me to go ahead. He must have shouted it twenty times. He was spinning his horse around and looking behind us, telling me to go."

"Did you?" I asked.

He shook his head. "No' at first. Alex said he was a dead man already and that I had to go. He said my father would never forgive him if I were killed." We both glanced at Angus, who watched his son impassively. "I said I couldna leave him alone, but he smacked my horse's rump with the flat of his claymore and she jumped out of her skin and ran into the narrow part. By the time I had her under control again he was turning back into the first of the pass to meet them."

"To meet them?" I whispered.

"Aye." His worried gaze met mine and he nodded. "Aye. He went back. And that's when they got him."

I gasped. "What do you mean 'got him'? What did you see?"

"I was through that bit of the pass, so I went back over the rocks above to see what happened." He stared into the distance. "Alex was on the ground in the middle of a bunch of them, with Robert Campbell standing over him and shouting at the others. They were like a pack of wolves and Robert was holding them off."

"But Alex was alive?"

Matthew met my eyes. "I dinna ken, Mary. I couldna tell. Alex was on his back and there was so much blood I couldna be sure. Some was from the other man on the ground. He was dead for certain. But then Robert knelt down next to Alex and talked and patted his shoulder. I dinna think Robert would talk to him if he werena still alive. Then the others hauled Alex onto a horse and they were no' gentle about it. He was either dead or unconscious then. There was blood dripping on the ground from him."

"And then what?"

"They took him back to their camp. They never even came looking for me. I followed them but I never saw Alex again once they carried him into the crofter's hut. And I never saw Malcolm."

"He was not with Robert?"

Matthew shook his head. "I only saw him the once, that morning with Alex and Da. He dinna show himself after that. I dinna even ken if he was still in their camp. I waited and watched them for days until they started to move west. I was afraid to leave for fear they'd go east and I'd not ken, but I couldna tell if Alex was alive. And when they started riding I couldna tell if the man in the cloak and hood was Alex. Or Malcolm." He sighed and rubbed his eyes like a small boy. "They left men at the crofter's hut, so I couldna search it. So I followed them. I thought they'd kill Alex or bring him to Edinburgh. When they headed west I kent they were coming here."

I nodded but it did not make any sense. Why was Robert coming here? To claim Kilgannon? Would he march on my home with brutality in his heart? I shook my head in frustration. "And now Robert comes here," I said. "I don't understand that."

"Do ye not, lass?" Angus spoke quietly. When I turned to him his blue gaze met mine without censure. "Perhaps he wants to see ye again or to see Kilgannon. Even if Alex is alive, Robert kens there's a great chance Alex will be imprisoned or executed. And Robert Campbell will still be alive."

Matthew shook his head. "He could ha' killed Alex

in the pass, Da, and he dinna. The others were hot to kill him."

"Perhaps they did," I said, but Matthew shook his head again.

"I dinna think so. That's a lot of trouble to go to for a dead man. Why would Robert speak to him?"

"Perhaps Alex was alive then."

"And then died?"

"Yes," I said.

"They would have buried him. There were no cairns built, no graves dug."

"He may be alive in the crofter's hut or dead in the hut."

Matthew's eyes met mine. "Aye, but I dinna think so. Why no' bury him if he's dead? They dinna ken I was watching. Why would they stay there for days and then come here? And why would they leave men at the hut? No' to guard a dead man."

"Perhaps they left men to guard Alex and are coming here to give Kilgannon to Malcolm," I said. "Perhaps Malcolm's the man in the cloak and hood."

Angus shook his head. "I dinna think so, lass. If Alex has forfeited, it is unlikely they would give his lands to his brother. And Robert doesna have the authority. The English would sell the lands before they'd give them away to another Scot. No, Alex is with Robert or in that crofthouse and I think he's with Robert."

"If Alex is in the crofthouse," I asked, "why would Robert be coming here?" Angus looked at me from under his eyebrows, his blue gaze, like his voice, without expression.

"For ye."

FOUR

I STARTED, BUT I KNEW HE WAS RIGHT. WHY WOULD Robert let Alex come home? If it was an act of kindness then I was grateful, but if Robert thought I'd throw myself in his arms he was gravely mistaken. And, I thought grimly, if he is simply saving Alex now so Alex can suffer a traitor's death later, then I hate him. Under no circumstances would I be leaving with Robert Campbell. If he was coming for me he'd leave alone and in certain possession of my opinion of him. I sighed and looked at Matthew. "You're wrong, Matthew," I said. "Alex was very much himself. He knew exactly what he was doing."

Angus nodded. "Aye, he did. He led them away so we could get to the ship. He kent they'd follow him. Ye must have been in Brenmargon Pass when we went looking for ye." Matthew nodded.

Runners came just after dark to say that Robert had camped before Glengannon Pass. They would be here sometime in the morning. The man in the cloak had been escorted into a tent and was not seen again. Within an hour the torches had been lit and everyone within close distance of the castle had been gathered within its walls. Many of the women and children had gone to the shielings or to Glendevin for safety, but quite a few remained, mostly household staff who refused to leave. Angus and I had had a heated debate whether he should lead a group of men to meet Robert. I was firmly against it and won only because Kilgannon would be unprotected. Angus wanted me off with the boys. I refused to join them, but was grateful that they were safely tucked into Thomas's brother's crofthouse miles away. Only four of us knew for certain where they were, so no matter what happened here they had a chance to survive. That Duncan MacNeill would protect them with his life I had no doubt. I only hoped I had been unnecessarily protective.

Now I sat with Angus and Matthew and Gilbey in the library once again while outside the rain pounded the stones and the wind wailed, mirroring my mood. I had refused to join the women and children in the keep, and the three of them refused to join the other men in the hall. Every half hour they would walk the positions and talk to the men standing guard, but just now they sat here with me. We sat in silence, listening to the wind and the fire crackling in the grate. The man in the cloak had to be Alex, I thought. Nothing else made sense. Unless, said a voice in my head, unless it was Malcolm, who did not want to be recognized. But why would Malcolm be coming here? If Alex were dead, Ian would inherit, not Malcolm. Unless, said the voice, Malcolm thought he could be appointed as the boys' guardian, or unless he was coming to claim Kilgannon as a reward for his treachery. Would Robert do that? Did he have that power? And if he did, would he do that to me? Or was this his revenge?

"What have we forgotten?" I asked.

"Nothing," said Angus. "I would there were something else."

Gilbey nodded and Matthew looked from his father to me. Washed and in fresh clothes, he still looked worn and weary, but he would not leave us. We had taken every precaution we could think of. The *Margaret* was back from Skye and stationed in the outer loch, and a boat had been placed at the mouth of the sea cave. If we needed to, we'd go through the tunnel and be on the *Margaret;* Angus and I were agreed on that. If Alex was alive, I would do everything I could to persuade Alex to flee. If the enemy came by land, then Alex could leave by sea. Just how I would manage to whisk him away from under Robert's nose I had not determined, but if it was possible I'd be ready. If Alex could get to Skye, he could get to France. One man would be simple to hide. Or would we all go with him? I wondered. How could I leave the people to fend for themselves? If Alex were dead . . . Angus's voice interrupted me.

"Mary, will ye no' reconsider? I could ha' ye on yer way at once. I will tell ye what happens."

"No," I said. "Angus, I must be here. If Alex is coming here, then I must be here. If he is in the crofter's hut, I can distract Robert while you get Alex. And if Alex is dead, then what happens to me does not matter. Do not ask me to leave and not know."

Angus frowned, but he nodded.

Wee Donald burst in at breakfast the next morning, breathless and agitated, his arms flying as he skidded to a stop, shouting.

"They're comin'! They've just gone into the trees below Alasdair's cave." *Alasdair's cave,* I thought, remembering.

We rose as one from the table, Angus hurrying outside to make certain all was ready, Matthew in his
father's wake and Gilbey at their heels. Within a few
minutes we were ready, armed men lining the walls and
the top of the terraces. I walked to Angus's side as he
stood on the lowest terrace looking over the glen and
he gave me a fierce frowning look.

"I wish ye'd do as I ask and let Gilbey take ye to the
boys."

I shook my head. "I will not argue with you again,
Angus. I will be here to meet Alex."

"And if they mean violence?"

"Then they'd not be coming here with Alex. They
would have killed him or brought him to Fort William
and then swept down on us without him. Angus, I cannot believe Robert will harm us."

"And I couldna believe Malcolm would betray us,"
he said and I nodded, wondering how many times in
the last hours we had repeated the conversation. "Will
ye do me one thing, Mary?"

"If I can," I said.

"Will ye let Matthew take ye to safety if needed?"

"And where will Alex be?"

"If he's alive, in the middle. No' having ye to worry
about will free his mind. Dinna argue with me, lass.
Take my son and go to safety. If I am to die this day, I
would have Matthew alive. Will ye no' do that for me?"

Shaken, I nodded. I had only thought about Alex dying, not anyone else, I realized with chagrin. "I will,
Angus," I said. "But how will we know?"

"We'll ken the moment they break cover," he said
grimly. "Alex willna let them come upon us with drawn
arms. If he's over a horse I want ye to leave at once. If
he's astride we'll wait." He glanced at me sharply. "If I

tell ye to go, lass, dinna argue, just go. If Alex is lost, the boys must have ye. I have asked Matthew to take ye through the tunnel. Promise me ye'll go."

I met his look. "I promise. But Angus, if he is astride, I will stay."

He nodded and I walked slowly down the terrace to the beginning of the meadow, stopping at the small knoll that faced the end of the loch. It was from here that the prizes were given each year at the Kilgannon Games, Alex laughing and joking as he distributed them. How long ago that seemed. The others had followed me, and Angus now stood just behind me. I could hear the sound of his sword being drawn as he hid his arm behind my skirts. Matthew was on my right, his sword in his hand. Gilbey, Thomas, wee Donald, and Dougall came to stand behind us. The men shifted on the walls and terraces, and some followed us, standing between us and the castle. They would, I knew, jump in front of us at the first sign of trouble. I was the only woman visible. We waited.

Overhead the blue sky was filled with high clouds, and an icy wind ruffled the surface of the loch, stirring it into a frothy ashen mixture before coming to me and swirling my skirts around my legs. The pine trees at the beginning of the path to the pass swayed slightly in the breeze, green against the blue mountains behind them, and on my right the air rustled through the pine needles with the swish of silk. I closed my eyes. *When I open them*, I told myself, *Alex will stand before me, well and smiling, and I will tell him of the strange dream I had and he will laugh and hold me to him and tell me how silly I am*. I opened my eyes and saw the empty glen before me.

The first rider to emerge from the pines wore a red

coat that was a streak of scarlet against the green. He positioned his horse to the side and waited. A moment later a second soldier moved to the other side of the opening. After a pause, first one and then two additional men appeared, each stopping at the side of the path. They watched us watch them and we all waited. Slowly, slowly, from the trees came a solitary rider. He rode between the two pairs of soldiers, not giving them a glance. His head was bare, his shirt white against the green wall of the trees. He was a blond man in a plaid, his hair shining in the sun, and my heart stopped. At this distance I could not be sure. His horse moved forward at a sedate walk, and with each step I was more certain. The set of his shoulders as he rode, the angle of his chin as he saw us, surely no other man on earth had that same manner. I was about to step forward when I felt Angus's hand on my arm.

"Aye, it looks like him, lass, but many's a time I mistook Malcolm for Alex at a distance. Wait until he's closer. Ye would no' want to be running into Malcolm's arms just now, would ye?"

"No." I patted his hand and Angus released me. I could not draw a full breath and was only dimly aware that other riders had emerged from the shadows. When I could see the blond man clearly I drew a shuddery breath. "It's him, Angus," I cried, careless of who heard. "It's Alex! Oh my dear God, thank you. He's alive!"

My vision blurred as my tears came unbidden, and I held my hands tightly over my heart. As the riders grew closer I looked in vain for Malcolm, but Robert was behind Alex. The wind freshened, but I did not feel the cold. All I could see was my husband as he moved toward

me at that horrible walk. With each step I saw more of
the damage they had done to him. Blood stained his
shirt and his hair, and his right cheek was a battered
and bruised mass. He held himself stiffly, his eyes on us
except when his gaze rose to sweep the men on the
wall. From behind me there was a stir of excitement as
someone shouted the MacGannon war cry. Alex's head
snapped up at that and a crooked smile flitted across his
face. He raised his hands in the air and I stifled a gasp as
I saw they were bound together and then realized his
feet were tied as well under the horse's belly. The soldiers stopped with Robert at a distance and let Alex
come on alone. He stopped before me. Angus grabbed
the horse's bridle and I met Alex's blue, blue eyes for
the first time in months, an expression in them that I
could not read. I smiled at him and spoke in a clear
voice that carried to the soldiers.

"Welcome home, my love," I said and Alex's face
crumpled. He drew a deep breath as he struggled to
regain control. No one stopped them as Angus and
Matthew undid his bonds and Alex slid to the ground
and into my embrace. I could hear Angus sheathing
his sword. Alex and I clung to each other as the wind
strengthened. I closed my eyes and pressed my face
against his shoulder. He laid his cheek on the top of my
head and I tightened my arms around his waist, much
leaner than before. He was holding himself up, I suspected, only through the force of his will.

"Thank ye for that, lass," he whispered. "Thank ye. I
dinna ken if ye would welcome me home." I pulled
back and caressed his uninjured cheek, tears streaming
down my cheeks.

"Oh, Alex, my love, my love, how could you think

that? I love you. I will always love you. All these months, all I wanted was you home, and now, thank God, you're here."

He nodded, his eyes filling with tears that he blinked back. "Thank ye for that, lass," he said again and glanced at the soldiers waiting behind us, then at Angus and Matthew. He spoke to the three of us. "Robert Campbell and his men are here to take me to Edinburgh. I have only today and tonight. We leave in the morning." At my wail he tightened his arm around me. "Dinna cry, Mary Rose, dinna cry. I have no choice. I'll go with them on the morrow and then Robert will come back to take ye and the boys to yer family, lass. He has said he'll see ye there safely. I'm assuming that the boys are tucked away somewhere." Angus nodded.

"No," I said. "No! Alex, tell me this is not true! You cannot go with him." I glanced at Robert, motionless on his horse, and then back at Alex. "Alex, do not leave me again! Tell me you'll stay! Let Angus do whatever it takes to keep you here. You don't have to go. We can—" He interrupted me with a gentle finger on my lips, his tone weary.

"Hush, lass, hush. I canna stay. I have given my word." He wrapped his arms around me and held me to him, whispering that he loved me. The wind rose and the men around us shifted, but they all waited while he tried to explain it to me. I heard only that he was leaving and I sobbed in his arms, remembering my barter with God. *One night*, I'd begged. *Just one night*. His arm tightened around me, but at last he turned to Angus. "I have given my word that my conduct will be proper and that Kilgannon willna rise to free me. Tell me it will be kept."

Angus looked at his cousin without expression. "It doesna have to be. We could take them, Alex."

Alex's eyes flashed anger but his voice was calm. "Aye, and then the others would come and burn us out and rape the land and the women. I willna have it here and ye ken it well, we've discussed it enough times. It's my decision, Angus." Their eyes met and I felt Alex's heart pounding.

At last Angus nodded. "It will be as ye say, Alex."

"Thank ye," Alex said and added something in Gaelic that made Angus's face brighten. I stepped back as they embraced. Then Alex hugged Matthew and turned to the others behind us, greeting them before facing the men on the terraces and walls. He raised his arms and his voice as the clansmen roared at him. "I thank ye for yer welcome," Alex shouted. He gestured to Robert. "This is Major Robert Campbell. His men are my escort and I ask that ye welcome them to our home. I will be leaving with them tomorrow. Please receive them tonight as ye would any guests at Kilgannon."

The men bellowed in response and started moving off the walls and terrace toward him. I was lost in a sea of plaids as they reached us, and I stood back, watching. Alex was thinner and very drawn, his bruises startling colors, his shirt encrusted with blood from a wound hidden by his hair, a rat's nest of tangles and matted clumps. But he was standing and in one piece and he was home, still the Earl of Kilgannon.

I glanced at Robert and his men where they waited at a distance, not relaxing their guard. Robert's handsome face was a stone mask as he watched Alex, then turned to meet my gaze. He dismounted and came to meet me as I walked toward him. When we stood facing each other I extended my hand and he caught it in both of his. "Welcome to Kilgannon, Lord Campbell," I said loud enough for his men to hear. He bowed over my hand and met my eyes before looking away. It had been momentary, but long enough for me to see that Robert remembered as well as I all that had gone on before.

"Robert," I said, in a quieter tone, and his brown eyes found mine again. "Thank you for bringing him home. Thank you." I embraced him. At first he stood woodenly and then he clasped me tightly to him, holding me longer than was necessary. As if realizing that, he abruptly let me go and I swayed at my release. He grabbed my arm to steady me, then released me as though my arm burnt him. Puzzled, I glanced up at him but he was looking behind me and I followed his gaze. Alex had been swallowed by the crowd, appearing now and then as the men shifted position, but Angus stood apart, watching us with a grim expression. I turned back to Robert but he had gone back to his men. Both Robert and Alex had undergone a transformation and neither seemed the happier for it.

I fought my way to Alex's side and his arm went around me.

"Mary Rose," he whispered in my ear, then kissed me gently on the mouth. "Mary Rose, I love ye, lass." I clung to him as we moved up the terraces and into the courtyard. Someone had told the women it was safe and they swarmed forward now, greeting Alex. Wee Donald, Ellen at his side, thumped Alex's back, then released him as Ellen embraced Alex and nodded happily at something he said to her. *How can she smile,* I wondered, *when Alex will leave again? How can they all be smiling and laughing? Do they not understand?* And if they did not, I agreed. I did not understand it all. I felt as though I watched them from afar.

Most of the clan arrived in the next hour to welcome Alex home. Berta, Ellen, and I were hard-pressed to arrange food and drink for all, and it was quite a while before I found myself standing at the side of the hall next to Robert. Alex's eyes had found me wherever I was, and now was no exception. He smiled at the clansmen before him but he watched Robert and me standing together. And at the edge of the crowd around him Angus watched us as well. If Robert noticed he gave no acknowledgement of it.

"You'd think he was home for good, not one night, Mary," Robert said quietly. "Do they always greet him this way?"

"Yes," I said and then took a deep breath. "Robert?" He turned to me with a blank expression and I thought of the many times I had stood companionably next to Robert Campbell. How strange life is, I thought, to bring the three of us together thus. "Robert, why are you here? Why did you bring Alex home?"

"I am to bring Alex to Edinburgh for trial." His voice was toneless. Whatever he was feeling was well hidden.

"Then you went the wrong way." Something flashed in his eyes, but he said nothing. "I understand that you are bringing Alex to Edinburgh, Robert, but why did you come to Kilgannon?"

Robert looked at Alex and then at me. "He agreed to go with me without a battle and I agreed to spare Kilgannon. When we leave here I will bring him to Edinburgh and he will be tried for treason." He lowered his head to speak very quietly. "Mary, you must understand that if he escapes tonight, troops will come and take Kilgannon by force and then many will die."

I raised my chin, willing my voice not to betray my emotion. "Robert," I said coldly, "did you not hear what Alex said to the men today? He asked that you be welcomed as our guests. He will not breach his promise, nor will the men of Kilgannon. If Alex told you he will go with you tomorrow, he will go. He has given his word. Alex does not make vows lightly." Robert nodded, his movements tight, but before he could answer there was a commotion at the door. I labored to see and then heard Ian and Jamie calling to Alex. The crowds of people moved aside to let them throw themselves at their father.

"Are those his sons?" Robert asked in a strained voice. We watched the boys leap into Alex's arms. Alex clutched them to him, his head bent over theirs as they kissed him.

"Yes," I said. "Those are our sons, Robert." I left him then and went to stand next to my husband. *My husband*, I thought. For how long? No matter how bravely I had answered Robert, I wanted Alex to run, to escape, to live. But as I brushed the hair from his shoulders and listened to him laugh with the boys, I knew what he would do. I had known all along what could happen. When Thomas and the other men had come home and told their stories, I had realized that it was in Alex's mind to save as many MacGannon lives as possible, even if Kilgannon itself was lost. If he had to sacrifice himself to keep these people safe, he would think it a necessary sacrifice. But I never would. If I could keep him alive and with me, I would risk anything. With that thought still in my mind, I looked across the sea of faces

turned so trustingly to him. Perhaps, I admitted to myself, perhaps in his position I would do the same. He
had been raised with the sacredness of his responsibilities trained into him. They were as much a part of him
as his coloring and height. I stroked his shoulder and he
turned with a smile and patted my hand.

"The people want to have another ceremony to
mourn the men we lost, Mary Rose, and I canna do it
this dirty. Will ye have a bath prepared? And will ye
bring the boys up with ye too? I'll be with ye shortly."
He kissed my forehead as I nodded. "I would talk with
ye, lass, but first I must get clean and talk with my sons.
We may have to wait until later to be alone." I nodded
again and reached for the boys, who were reluctant to
leave him until I explained that he would come to us
upstairs. I called for hot water and asked Berta to see to
rooms for Robert and his men and then I left, knowing
she would take care of everything.

We waited in our bedroom. I spent the time trying
to think of words persuasive enough to convince Alex
to escape and stared out the window, wondering how
many more times in my life I would be waiting for him
to join me. When the door opened, the boys jumped up
from their seats and ran to him and he met my eyes
above their heads. I'd forgotten how he filled the doorway, how his form was masculine but graceful, how his
hair traced the corner of his brow, and how very blue his
eyes were. And how he made my body ache for him
with just a glance.

"I'm home, Mary Rose," he said quietly. "For one
night at least. I just never imagined it would be like this."

"Nor I, but I'll take whatever we can get," I said. "I
love you, Alex." I felt my chin tremble and struggled to
control it.

"And I ye, Mary."

"And I love ye, Da," Jamie said, throwing his arms around his father's waist. "But yer verra dirty."

Ian laughed. "Aye, Da, ye are. Did ye no' bathe off at war?"

Alex laughed, then grinned slowly, picking up a boy in each arm and rubbing them against his sides. "Now we're all dirty, eh, lads? And now we'll all get clean." He hauled the giggling boys into the adjoining room, where a tub of water waited for him. He dropped them into the tub fully clothed. It got worse then, as the boys splashed their father until he surrendered, leaving all four of us and most of the room wet.

I shooed the boys out of the tub and Alex shed his clothes quickly and climbed into it. I insisted on washing the blood and grime out of his hair and tried not to comment on the bruises that covered him and the new long scar that ran from his breast to his waist, jagged as it crossed his ribs, the healing barely begun. And he tried to ignore my tears and compressed lips, but he saw them and he kissed my hand as I gently sponged his battered cheek. He joked and teased the boys until they were giggling again.

In our room Alex dressed quickly, his mood growing sober. When he was dressed he kissed me and then sat on the edge of our bed, gesturing the still-damp boys to him. I sat next to him, suddenly reluctant to hear anything he had to say. *Think of something,* I commanded myself. *Think of something to convince him to leave.* Alex looked from one boy to the other.

"Ye ken we won the battle at Sherrifmuir, lads?"

"We heard no one won, Da," said Ian.

"We won," Alex said firmly. "We won." Two little

heads nodded solemnly. "And then we lost in a different way. The Stewart ran away, leaving us to fend for ourselves." My heart sank at his words. *He will not even try to escape,* I thought. *He will never run away. I have known that all along.* I patted the dripping ends of his hair with the towel.

"Thomas told us," whispered Ian.

Alex nodded. "Aye. James Stewart called us all to fight for him and we did and then he ran away and left us to take care of ourselves. So the English won the war after all."

"Ye lost the war?" asked Jamie.

"Aye. We lost it when the Stewart ran away. And now the English king and his soldiers are in control of Scotland once again. We had to come home from a long way away and we got separated from each other. That's why Angus and the others came home first." His eyes met mine over his sons' heads as he continued. "But I canna stay. I have to go with the soldiers tomorrow." The boys exclaimed.

"Where, Da? Where will ye go?" Jamie tugged at Alex's sleeve while Ian watched with troubled eyes. "Ye just got home!"

Alex ruffled Jamie's hair. "I ken that, lad. Do ye remember when we talked a long time ago about giving yer word?" The boys nodded. "Well, I gave my word to Robert Campbell. I dinna wish to go, but I must. If I go with them no one here will be hurt and if I dinna go many people will die. So I will go with them."

"Where will ye go?" Jamie asked.

Alex's tone was quiet. "The English will put me in prison."

"Prison!" Ian cried. Alex nodded.

"Da," Jamie said in horror. "They'll hit ye again."

Alex smiled wryly and put his hand to his bruised cheek. "Do ye mean this?"

Jamie nodded.

"They might." Alex suddenly grinned. "But, Jamie lad, I knocked the man who gave me this senseless, so perhaps they'll think twice before trying that again, no?" Both boys nodded and I rose and walked to the window, unable to bear another moment. I traced the lead of the window with a finger. I knew Alex watched me but his voice behind me was calm.

"Ye must understand something else as well. I may no' ever come home again. I made an agreement that I would do as they asked." The boys cried out and I turned and met Alex's eyes.

"Will they kill ye?" Ian whispered.

Alex looked at me over Ian's head. And then he looked at his oldest son and nodded. "Aye," he said slowly. "It is most likely."

"No!" Ian shouted, pulling on Alex's arm. "No, Da! Don't let them kill ye!" Next to him Jamie wailed. Alex hugged them fiercely to him and sank his face in their hair as they cried.

"I ken it is hard to understand what happened," he said. "I hardly understand it myself. But ken this, lads: I made this decision. It was my choice, and it is the correct thing to do. If I go to prison, even if I die, and everyone else here at Kilgannon lives, that is a good thing. If I run away like James Stewart and leave the people behind me to fend for themselves, then I would be a coward, and no MacGannon is a coward." His voice was gruff and he raised a fist. "We're brave! MacGannons are brave!"

"Brave!" Two small voices echoed him hollowly. I turned away, my hand at my throat. He would not even try to escape. And he was teaching his sons to live by the same code. I felt sick.

"And we don't run away," Alex said. "Never."

"Never," said Ian, and Jamie echoed him.

Alex's voice was normal again. "Even if ye are afraid. Especially if ye are afraid."

"Are ye afraid, Da?" Jamie asked.

"Aye, Jamie, of course I am, but I gave my word and I will go. Now, promise me to be good for yer mother and do as she says."

"We will, Da," Jamie said.

Ian threw himself in his father's arms. "Don't go, Da! Can't we go somewhere where they canna find you?"

Alex patted his back and kissed his hair. "Aye, I could, Ian, but I won't. I gave my pledge. I must go with them." He slapped his thighs. "And now, my laddies, ye must come with me while I tell the people what will happen. When I leave I willna be laird anymore and they must ken that."

"What will happen?"

"I dinna ken. The English will decide what happens to Kilgannon. Ye and yer brother will go to Mary's family."

"We have to leave too?" Ian cried. "Can we no' go with ye?"

"No," Alex said. "I wish ye could. Or, I wish I could go with ye. But we canna go together. Now go, lads, and change yer clothes and meet me downstairs. We must be clean when we talk to everyone. Go on with ye now. I'll be with ye shortly."

With a glance at me they started for the door. Halfway there Ian turned. "Da, do ye really have to go?" he asked, his voice wavering.

Alex nodded. "Aye, Ian. I wish it were not so, but I do."

"And we have to leave too?"

"Aye, but ye'll be most brave, aye?"

Ian nodded solemnly and left us, his brother behind him.

We were alone.

FIVE

WE STOOD APART, STARING AT THE CLOSED DOOR.
Alex moved to it and locked it while I tried to master
my emotions. I could not decide if I was sad or angry
or just numb, but when Alex came to stand in front of
me I opened my arms and he stepped into them. When
he kissed me my reserve melted and I half-sobbed,
half-moaned, running my hands along his cheeks and
through his hair. "Alex," I said, as my fingers explored
his shoulders and neck. He laced one hand through my
hair and held my mouth to his while the other held me
tight against him.

"My lips aren't bruised," he said when we paused. I
laughed breathlessly, remembering when I had said that
to him. So long ago.

"Alex," I said, but he bent to kiss me again and I
closed my eyes, savoring the feel of him against my
mouth. And my hips.

"Mary Rose," he whispered. "Mary Rose, how I've
missed ye."

"And I you, my love," I said, pulling his shirt loose
from his belt. He flinched when I tugged at the material, and I paused, the linen still in my hand. "That
hurts, doesn't it?"

He nodded. "It doesna matter. I'm just battered a bit, but all the parts work, as I'll show ye." He reached for me again but I stepped back, my hand on his unbruised cheek.

"The last thing I would do is hurt you more. We'll wait."

He shook his head. "We havena time to wait. Come to me."

"Alex," I began, but he shook his head again.

"Make love to me, Mary Rose," he said quietly. "Now. And later. And later again. Make love to me, Mary."

I did then, pulling his shirt free the rest of the way and undoing the belt he'd just buckled. His kilt fell to the floor and his shirt followed it and he stood before me, bruises and new scars livid against his skin. With a sob I ran my fingers lightly over his ribs and then kissed each shoulder, then his chest, and when he pulled me to him I kissed his mouth while I caressed his back. He undid my lacings with the ease born of practice, and within moments I stood naked before him as well. I closed my eyes and leaned against him, running my fingers along the length of him and feeling his response. "Alex," I breathed. "You are perfection."

He laughed in his throat and bent to kiss my neck and along my shoulder, then raised his lips to mine again and I kissed him fully, feeling him explore my mouth with the touch that always drove me mad. He lifted me then, carrying me easily in his arms and to our bed, where we changed rhythm, frantic now in our haste to have each other. And then it was over and I lay in his arms and stared at the ceiling, savoring the still-lingering taste of his mouth on mine, pretending that this was just a stolen moment in our ordinary life.

"Mary Rose," he said, rising to one elbow and tracing a finger from my collarbone to my navel, then moving to smooth his hand along my hip. "Yer so beautiful. I need to memorize ye, lass."

"Don't go," I said, surprising us both, and hearing the echo of the countless times I'd said that to him before he'd gone to war. "You don't have to go."

He looked over me, staring across the room, then abruptly let his eyes fall to meet mine. "I must. Ye heard what I told the boys." He leaned to kiss my shoulder, then my breast.

"They don't believe you're leaving forever. They don't understand." I felt my mouth tremble.

"No," he said, kissing my forehead. "But perhaps later they'll remember me talking of it."

"I don't understand either."

"Mary," he said, lifting his head, "can ye forgive me?"

"For which decision, Alex? Why will you not escape? We could go through the tunnel and be out of the loch before Robert ever knew. You could be in Glendevin before they even missed you. Robert won't let them burn Kilgannon. The English have more important places to burn than Kilgannon. It's too far from everything to be important. Why can't we try, Alex? I know you could get away! The MacDonald came to beg us to go to France. They would welcome—"

He interrupted me gently. "The MacDonald came? When, lass?"

More controlled now, I told him of Sir Donald's visit. He listened quietly, then nodded. "Ye did right, Mary Rose."

"Alex," I continued, "we could join them and you could help James Stewart from there. Oh, Alex, say yes, tell me you'll go. We could leave now. I have our clothes packed, but we don't even need them. We could get . . ."

His expression stopped me, his eyes cold and angry. He rose from the bed then and put his shirt on with abrupt movements. "Lass, I want ye to understand. I'll never help James Stewart do anything except step into an early grave. We would have been better if he'd never come. At least then we would have had illusions."

I scrambled out of bed, pulling the blanket with me, to stand before him. "Then we could go to Will. He would welcome us."

Alex shook his head. "No, Mary Rose, I willna run away like a coward. Dinna ask it of me." He pulled me to his chest, his tone softening as he continued. "I ken yer right, lass. We probably could sneak away, but then what? Where would we go? I would have traded my life for my honor. What would I have?"

"Your life!" I cried. "Your life with me and your sons! Does that mean nothing to you?"

He looked at me evenly. "It means everything to me, Mary. I've had months to think on this. I kent when James Stewart left that all was lost. I will foreefit my title and lands, and my sons will have nothing to inherit. Nothing, lass. If I escape and live they will have nothing."

I leaned back out of his arms. "They will have a father!"

"They will have a father who saved his own skin instead of his people! The English will burn Kilgannon. They will kill and rape and steal. I canna save myself and offer my clan in my place. I willna do that. Do ye no' understand? Robert Campbell has given me an amazing gift to let me come home to say goodbye. If I break my word to him I am nothing. If I escape I am alive, but a coward. Can ye no' understand? I have no choice."

I shook my head violently. "You do have a choice! And you are not choosing us!" At his stricken expression I burst into tears. "I'm sorry, Alex," I sobbed. "But, my love, I want you to live! I want you to be with me! That's all I ever wanted, was you and my home. You and your sons. It doesn't matter where we are, only that we're together. How can I live if you're in prison?"

"I won't be in prison long, lass," he said quietly and took my hands, his eyes full of unshed tears. "I love ye more than I have a right to, Mary Rose. I would give everything to spend my life with ye. Our time together has been far too short. But I must do this. If I save myself and lose my honor I have nothing. Ye, and the boys, and my word are all I have left." He swept his hand in a broad gesture to include the room. "All of this is gone. It's all gone, Mary. I have lost my sons, everything I was entrusted with. I lost my heritage for my children. There will be no eleventh Earl of Kilgannon. There will be no lands to give to Jamie. There will be no one to watch over the clan and see that they are safe. There will be nothing for my family, except my name and my word as a MacGannon. Dinna beg me to give that too!"

I wrapped my arms around him and sobbed, knowing I couldn't change his mind. "I love ye, Mary Rose," he said into my hair. "And I hope ye can forgive me. Can ye ever forgive me? All of this is my fault."

I looked up and into his blue eyes, so brilliant over the bruised cheek. "Alex, this is not your fault! How could you have known all this would happen? How could you know James Stewart would run away and that Malcolm would betray you like this?

How could you know the whole rebellion would be such a disaster?"

"Ye did," he said. "And ye were right, Mary. Ye were right in the whole of it and I should have listened. I should have listened to my own advice as well." He smiled ruefully. "I never thought we'd lose, lass. I never thought it," he whispered.

I brushed his hair from his forehead. "I love you, Alex," I said. "And I've known all along what could happen. But I hoped and prayed that I could convince you to leave."

"Aye," he said. I could hear this heart beating and took a ragged breath. *Remember this,* I commanded myself. *Remember how this feels, how he puts his arms around you, how wonderfully you fit together. It will have to last forever.* I fought a wave of hysteria and stroked his bruised cheek. "How did this happen?"

He smiled and shrugged. "Well, they were no' as pleased to see me as ye were. They're a rough bunch, the English."

"Do you hate them?" I asked softly. "Do you hate me as well?"

"No, lass, I dinna hate them. And never ye. Never ye. Do ye hate me for making war on yer country?"

"My darling man," I said. "You are my country." We looked at each other in silence, then I stepped back from him, trying to keep talking so he wouldn't leave. I'd talk forever if I had to. "Alex, why did you ride back into them at Brenmargon?"

He shrugged. "I was going to ride into their camp and let loose the horses and draw their troops away into the pass. And then, there's a place I ken well, where I was going to let the horse keep going while I climbed to the top of an outcropping and waited to talk to them.

It's a verra narrow passage there and I kent I could hold them for a bit. I thought if I could talk to Robert I would discover what he meant to do. And I wanted to see if Malcolm was with them. The last thing I wanted to do was lead them home. Or have Malcolm bring them here." He smiled wryly. "Matthew showing up scared me witless. I had to change my strategy and still get him away. It seems I dinna do as well as I'd hoped." He touched his cheek gingerly. "When they knocked me off the horse and attacked me I thought I was a dead man, but Robert saved me. He saved my life, Mary. He stopped them from killing me. He even had their doctor treat me at their camp. He was very kind. Distant, of course, but then that's Robert. No' a man ye ever ken well, I'm thinking. After a day or so we talked. At length." He looked over my head. "Damned if I understand the man, lass, but I canna help but respect him. He is a man of his word." He sighed and looked at me. "And it is that as much as anything that holds me. How can I betray his trust when I ken what it feels like to be betrayed? I canna do it. I'm no' Malcolm."

"How could Malcolm do that?" I whispered. "To his own brother? How could he hate you so much?"

Alex gave me a twisted smile. "Perhaps I shouldna have been born first. He seems to have taken offense."

"Where is he? And why were you covered when they brought you here? We thought you might be Malcolm."

"Malcolm? No, lass, he was long gone. I dinna see him nor did we talk on him much. I agreed to be covered so that the clan wouldna attack Robert's men to rescue me."

"That was foolish. They almost attacked you to keep the troops from coming here."

"Aye, I kent that was a risk as well, but, to tell the truth of it, I wasna thinking too clearly. Robert was giving me a chance to come home, even if for only one night, and I would have given much more to have another night with ye, lass." He kissed me gently. "Come, now, Mary Rose," he said, his arms falling from me as he stepped away. "I must tell the clan goodbye before I lose my nerve. Come with me, if ye will." I lingered yet another moment.

"Alex, why has Robert brought you home?"

He shook his head. "I dinna ken, lass. I've asked myself that hundreds of times. I have my own theories, but the truth of it is I dinna ken."

The boys and I waited in the courtyard and Alex stood on the steps above us, his expression remote as the people gathered around quietly. He carried himself rigidly. I wondered how many of those waiting for him to speak knew what this control was costing him. Robert and his men stood to the side, silently watching the growing crowd. The boys leaned against me and I put an arm around each one. Angus stood next to us, Matthew and Gilbey just behind.

"What is Da going to say?" Ian whispered to me.

"He'll tell the people what's going to happen, that he's going to leave. They will be unhappy. We must be as brave as he is." Ian nodded, his eyes dark and serious.

Jamie wrapped his arms around my waist. "Is my da brave?"

"Yes, sweetheart," I said gently, looking from Jamie to Alex. "He's the bravest man in the world." Jamie nodded but I knew he didn't understand what was happening. I'm not sure I did.

"Yer da's a braw man, Jamie, lad," Angus said hoarsely.

I met his eyes over the boys' heads. "Have you talked to him?"

"I have," Angus said. "It made no difference, lass, but I talked. I couldna change his mind."

"Nor I." I sighed. "Angus, could we defend ourselves?"

He nodded. "Aye. At a cost, but aye."

"What cost?" I asked.

"Glendevin. Glengannon. All the outlying areas, lass. We couldna hold them. Alex kens that and so do the clansmen."

"He feels he has no choice."

"There's always a choice, Mary. And always a cost."

I nodded and turned to look at Alex as he stepped forward. His voice wavered at first, then grew stronger until it rang across the courtyard easily. He looked over our heads as he spoke.

"I have gathered ye to say farewell," he said. "I leave on the morrow and I willna be coming home again." He ignored the muttering of his audience. "Despite what ye might have heard, we were no' defeated at Sherrifmuir. We held our position and we defeated the enemy before us. Some of ye lost men ye loved in that battle and for that I ask yer forgiveness. They were brave lads and should be remembered as such. I take all responsibility for their deaths. Had I kent what I was leading us into I mightna have done it. And on the way home we lost Finlay and Gabhan, good men as well. They will long be mourned. For their loss I beg yer forgiveness again." He paused and took a deep breath, glancing at Robert. "There will be a new laird at

Kilgannon soon, I ken no' who it will be, but it willna be a MacGannon. Any MacGannon." He ignored the ripple of murmurs. "I will be escorted from here tomorrow and brought to Edinburgh for trial. Lord Campbell will return to give my wife and sons safe passage to her family in England. I ask ye again to treat Robert Campbell as my guest."

Dougall's voice came from behind me. "Ye ken what happened the last time a man named Robert Campbell was offered hospitality in the Highlands, Alex?" The crowd, remembering the Glencoe massacre, muttered its agreement. I did not look at Robert.

Alex glared at him. "This Robert Campbell is far different, and ye'll treat him with respect, Dougall." He looked across the crowd. "All of ye. Kilgannon is no' Glencoe and I would have our hospitality extended to a man who has been most generous to me. I willna have it said that Kilgannon abuses its guests."

"Dinna go, Alex," Dougall said. " 'Tis not necessary. We can rid ourselves of the Campbells with no difficulty." Men near him nodded. Robert did not move but his men reached for their weapons.

"Oh, aye, Dougall," Alex said, nodding. "We could do that. And then what? Ye've seen the strength of the English army, man. Ye saw the sights we all passed on the way home. Would ye have that here? Tell me, Dougall, look around ye and tell me, which man's home could ye have burnt and feel no sorrow? Which woman could ye have raped and feel no guilt? Which bairn thrown against a wall and no matter? Who can we call dispensable?" Murmurs sped through the people and men moved restively, looking from their wives to their children.

"No' ye, Alex," Dougall persisted. "No' ye. We can call for help. Surely the MacDonalds, or Clanranald . . ."

Alex shook his head. "The MacDonalds are dispersed, some to France. The rest are trying to survive. They have no force to aid us. Clanranald has asked us for aid. We have no one to help us."

"Then we fight on our own," Dougall said and men nodded.

"Oh, aye, Dougall," Alex said. "Ye and me and the hundred men we have left. We have bonnie warriors and the best war chief in the world, lad, but we canna hold off the English army and all the mercenaries they have arriving daily. And if we do try and fail, Dougall, then I'll be alive and I can watch with ye from the hillside as they burn Glengannon and Glendevin and then march into my home. We can watch as our women are raped and our children murdered and our ships burnt. Did ye no' see what I did as we came home? Did ye no' see what they did and what was left? I willna have that here. No, Dougall, it's better that one man is imprisoned or executed than that many die for the one."

"Alex, if ye go, who will lead us? Ye've been a braw leader."

"I thank ye for that, cousin, but I'm easily replaced, I'm thinking. Dougall, ye ken that if I stay and if we fight, there will be nothing and no one left to lead."

"We can take to the hills."

"Aye." Alex nodded. "For a bit. But what about winter? How can ye raise children when yer running, with no homes and no cattle? Men can do it but look around ye. Look at the faces of these women and children. Would ye have them starve and die for me, so that I can live? Dougall, I ken what yer thinking and I thank ye for it, but it makes no sense." Alex looked across the now silent crowd. "What has a better solution? Can any of ye think of a better way out of this? Have ye a plan that would leave Kilgannon intact and the English away from our door? For if ye have, I'd be glad to hear it. I have no desire to leave ye and go east with the Campbell but I canna think of another way to assure Kilgannon's safety. If ye have a better solution, tell me. If no', then let me go and bring what peace I can buy for our home."

"There must be something else," Dougall said.

"If there is I dinna ken it," Alex said. Next to me Angus closed his eyes and hung his head, his fists clenched. Dougall nodded, his face plainly showing his despair. The clouds above us had melded into a gray dome and the breeze freshened further. I wondered if it would rain before dark or perhaps snow. And if it did, would the window in the library leak again? I felt myself swaying. Ian wrapped his arms around my waist and buried his face in my side and I came abruptly back to myself. Alex was speaking again, his hair lit brilliantly now by a shaft of light. I hugged the trembling boys to me and rubbed Ian's back.

"I thank ye for yer help through these troubled times and for the faith ye had in me, but I canna keep this from our door. I led ye into this disaster and this is the only way I ken to get ye out." Alex foundered, his pain visible. He opened his mouth and then closed it again and looked at me in desperation. Behind me men were muttering and a woman sobbed.

"Dinna blame yerself, Alexander MacGannon," called a harsh voice. I turned to see Duncan of the Glen shouting, his face flushed. "Ye were betrayed, we as well. Ye did nothin' wrong. Ye've been a good laird and I'm happy to have fought wi' ye."

Alex leaned forward. "I thank ye, Duncan, but . . ."

"Nay, Alex," cried Thomas, his voice raw with emotion. "We'll ha' none of this. We went willingly enough. And 'tis not us payin' this price, 'tis ye and yers. It should be Malcolm and Bobbing John on trial and maybe dying, not ye." He turned to the others and roared, "We will avenge ye!" The crowd blared its agreement and behind me Matthew and Gilbey raised their fists, shouting with them. Angus opened his eyes. Alex struggled for control before he held up his hands. I was crying now, the boys sobbing into my skirt. Alex raised his hands higher, his voice strong, the Earl of Kilgannon again, giving orders.

"Do not, Thomas MacNeill," he said firmly. "If ye avenge me more will die. I will come ba' from my grave and haunt ye, man." He smiled a twisted smile and his tone softened. "I coulda brought English vengeance on us easier ways than this. Dinna avenge me, Thomas. Ye must help me bring what peace Kilgannon can have or it's all been in vain." He looked from man to man. "Give me yer word. All of ye." Silence greeted him. Alex looked across the crowd slowly, paused and waited. I thought for a moment that he was lost but he stepped back, crossed his arms and tapped his foot impatiently as he threw back his head. "I am waiting!" He shouted to the sky. "And I dinna have much time." There was a pause and the roar of laughter that followed was mixed with rage and fear. Ian and Jamie watched their father, fascinated.

"Alex," said Angus, his voice clear and calm. "We'll do as ye ask." He turned to the others. "Won't we, lads?" A murmur of agreement went through the men. Alex nodded and met Angus's eyes.

"I thank ye for that, Angus. As always, cousin, I thank ye. And I'll hold ye to it. Now, come," he said to the crowd, "we have our kinsmen to mourn. Let's have at it."

Alex jumped from the step and swept the boys and me along with him. We did not speak as we walked to the cemetery, but he grabbed Jamie with one arm and wrapped the other around Ian. The boys clung to him and I walked behind the three, with Angus, the clan, and Robert and his men following us up the hill behind the castle. I remember little of the ceremony that the priest held, only that the sky descended and a fine mist enclosed us as the pipers began. Alex's arm went around me and we huddled in the wet grayness, listening to the mournful eulogy.

Seamus MacCrimmon started the piping alone and the others joined in and then died away, leaving Seamus alone again. I felt the music soothe my soul as always and tried not to realize that we were mourning not only the men lost in the rebellion but the end of the MacGannon line at Kilgannon, for life as we had known it. For Alex. The boys wrapped their arms around him and he held me close, but he seemed beyond our reach. He had withdrawn into himself and I felt a wave of loneliness. *He has already gone from us,* I thought, but even as the thought formed, he kissed my hair. I closed my eyes for a moment and wished us anywhere else but here. The priest said one last prayer and the crowd moved down the hill, followed slowly by Seamus and the pipers. Alex, the boys, and I stayed behind, standing silently over the graves for a long while, with Angus, Matthew, Gilbey, and Dougall. And Robert. And then Alex led us back to the castle.

I'm sure that somehow food was on the tables and that we were cordial to our guests. I vaguely remember talking with Robert about the rose garden that we had planted, but what else we said and what we ate I don't know. All I remember clearly is Alex's leg next to mine throughout the meal and the glow the candlelight brought to his hair. Like spun gold, I thought. I'm not sure I spoke intelligibly at all. After dinner Alex called for music. Murreal and Thomas sang and for a moment I forgot why we were gathered and leaned against Alex as I listened. But when they sang about lost love I had to fight my hysteria again. I'm sure that somehow the boys were put to bed and Robert and the others shown their rooms, but I don't remember any of it.

SIX

ΛLONE AGAIN IN OUR ROOM MUCH LATER, ALEX AND I stood together before the fire. Our last night together, I thought, trying to still my hysteria. I stole a look at him as he studied his hands, and realized with a start that tears were trickling down his cheeks. I wrapped my arms around him with a sob of my own, and he pulled me close. *I'll never feel his body against me again after tonight,* I thought, and lifted my mouth to his kiss. He found my lips and breasts and I pulled the clothes from him as he did the same to me. When we were both naked again he held my arms away from me and studied me. "I'm memorizing ye, lass," he said. "Look at yer skin in the firelight. Look how yer curves cast shadows, Mary." He leaned forward to kiss my shoulder, then worked his way lower. "I'm memorizing ye, lass," he murmured. "My lips need to memorize ye too."

I watched him and sobbed, my tears falling on his hair as I pulled it free of its binding. He stood then and kissed my tears away, his mouth at first gentle, then more insistent. I put my hands on his hips and pulled him against me, luxuriating in the feel of his skin against mine from my shoulder to my toes, in the leanness of his body and its response to mine. How long we stood in front of the fire or how we got to the bed I don't know. Our lovemaking was fierce and wordless. Afterward I lay next to him, his heart steady in my ear, and I slept at last.

I woke sometime in the night and he was gone. The fire had dwindled to embers and as I gathered the bedcovers around me to ward off the cold the thought came unbidden and unwelcome: *It will ever be like this. You'll always wake alone.* I threw a nightdress on and, wrapping my cloak around me, stole from the room. All was quiet as I crept down the stairs, and at the bottom one of our men-at-arms nodded at me. "Where is he?" I whispered.

"In the library, Lady Mary."

I laid my hand on his arm in thanks and went down the dark corridor, listening to the sounds of Robert's men snoring in the hall. The library door was open and I stood in the dark doorway watching Alex at his grandfather's desk, writing in the glow of the candle. From this angle his face seemed uninjured. Without raising his eyes, he spoke quietly, his voice calm. "Come in, lass. I'm finished. Angus just left." He looked up at me. "He had a few comments. And suggestions."

I closed the door behind me. "He wanted you to leave."

"Aye," he said, carefully putting the pen away.

"Did you sleep at all?"

I moved to stand before the hearth and he joined me. "I'll sleep in prison," he said and stirred the fire, rubbing his hands on his thighs while I watched him. *I'll never feel those lean legs next to me again,* I thought, and closed my eyes. *This is not possible. At any moment someone will rush in and shout that it is all a mistake or a dream and all will be well again.* I opened my eyes to find him watching me. He extended his arms and I flew into them. "Ye've been a good wife, Mary," he whispered into my hair. "I've been proud to have been yer husband. I'm sorry that I ruined everything." I looked into his face, opening my mouth to speak, but he put a finger to my lips. "Hush, lass," he said softly. "Get warmed now. Then we have something to do."

We stood silently by the fire until at last he took a candle and my hand, then walked through the dark house wordlessly while he looked at everything slowly. I watched him memorizing the house as we moved through the rooms and finally into the chapel, where he put a candle on a pew and took both my hands. His expression was carefully blank as he faced me but his eyes were very bright.

"We were wed in this very spot almost three years ago, Mary Rose. Do ye remember?" His voice was serious but remote. He might have been talking to a stranger.

"Yes, Alex," I said softly. "I'm not likely to forget it."

He sighed and looked over my head. "Mary, I am releasing ye from those vows. I've written to the bishop asking for an annulment. We have no children together, so it is . . ." His eyes met mine. "Ye do no' have to be the widow of a traitor. Ye can go to England again. Ye could have yer life back. . . ." My face must have shown my feelings, for he faltered and stared at me.

I was so angry that at first I could not speak. I ripped my hands out of his grip as I whirled away. My entire body shook with rage and it was with difficulty that I faced him. "I will not do this, Alexander MacGannon," I said fiercely. "You cannot cast me off as you would a . . . I will not be annulled! How dare you ask me to wed you and be your wife forever and at the first sign of trouble throw our marriage away! I became your wife willingly and I will die your wife, you huge fool!" I glared at him. At first he stood watching me with a startled look, then he laughed. The fool laughed so hard that he had to sit down. I crossed my arms until he stopped. Wiping his eyes, he looked at me again and drew a deep breath.

"Of all of the responses ye could have made, Mary Rose," he said, "I dinna expect that one." His expression grew sober. "But, lass, this is no' exactly the first sign of trouble. We're in a barrelful of trouble." He shook his head ruefully and extended his hand. "I dinna mean to make ye angry, lass. I am sorry to be such . . . to have gotten us in this." He took a deep breath as I took his hand. "I am sorry ye married such a huge fool."

I knelt before him and put my hands on his arms. He looked down at me wordlessly, his eyes very blue. *You'll never see these eyes again,* I thought and pushed the thought away. "Alex, my darling man," I said gently. "I have loved you for so long. I will always love you. You cannot protect me by releasing me. I married you in this chapel, and when I said my vows in front of witnesses and your sons, I meant every word. How can you ask me to retract that now? How can you ask me to let you go when we have so little time together? The greatest joy I have ever known has been as your wife, Alex. Do not take it from me. I will die your wife. And I will live as your wife. Proudly."

He searched my face, then gave me a shaky nod as he pulled me up and stood facing me. He took both my hands in his. "Mary," he said, "I will love ye until I die." His voice was steady and sure, as it had been on the day we wed, and he lifted my hand to his mouth, kissing my fingers while I watched.

"Alex, I will love you till the end of the world, beyond death." He kissed me then, a bittersweet kiss, and I wrapped my arms around him. *The last night, the last night,* my thoughts roared. At last he leaned back and looked into my face.

"Mary, will ye care for my boys? Or would ye have Angus take them off yer hands? Ye ken he will if I ask."

"They're mine now, too, Alex," I said softly. "I'm losing my husband. Don't take my sons."

He nodded. "Will ye tell them when they're older the truth of it? I wouldna have them think their father lost their land for lack of sense. Well, that's true enough. I did lose their land for lack of sense but I dinna mean to." He laughed ruefully. "Perhaps ye can tell them so I sound a bit brighter than I feel the now."

"I'll tell them the truth, Alex. I'll tell them their father was a man of courage and honor who was betrayed."

He kissed me softly, lingering, then leaning back to look at me. "I was afraid of yer opinion of me when we returned," he said.

I stroked his uninjured cheek. "Alex," I said, "I never had any doubt that you did what you thought best. Always. You acted out of a sense duty and honor and love for your people. Your only sin was that you trusted the wrong men. Theirs is the wrong here, Alex, not yours. Not yours. To ask men to risk all and when they do, to leave the job half done is a cruel thing. It's James Stewart and the Earl of Mar who should be asking your forgiveness. And the MacDonald. And Malcolm. Not you of me. I admit I was very angry when you left and hurt that you didn't choose mine above all other claims. All this Gaelic pride and clan duty seemed so very unnecessary to me then. But I've had a lot of time to think these months you've been gone. I never doubted that you would do the right thing as you saw it. Never."

"Ah, lass," he said. "Thank ye for that. Ye have no idea what a gift you've just given me." I kissed him again and he returned it and for a moment the world went away.

After I made sure the letter to the bishop had been burned, we returned to our room again. Alex stirred the fire, then came to me by the window while we waited for dawn. He stood behind me, his hands slipping forward to cup my breasts, and when I turned to face him our desire ignited once again. We made love before the fireplace in a frenzy and then climbed into bed to lie together dozing. After a while he sat up and stared across the room. In profile he looked unbattered and I savored the moment to watch him. Few men were so handsome and this one was mine. For another few moments.

"Tell me about Malcolm," I said softly.

He looked at me in surprise. "Do ye not ken?"

"I want to hear it from you."

He nodded. "So ye will, then." He told me the same story I'd heard before, but paused when he talked about Malcolm arriving in Perth. "I realized then that we will never be reconciled." He looked into the distance, his voice quiet. "It's as though I saw him for the first time, lass. I've been making excuses for him for so long that when I saw him again, smirking and lying and manipulating as he does, I was shamed that we had the same blood and I could see him for what he was, for what he's always been. I couldna stay longer. I dinna ken how long I could control myself, so I left." He spread his hands before him and stared at them, his voice a whisper. "I was afraid I'd kill him." He looked at me in horror. "My own brother. If he'd opened his mouth with one more lie I might have killed him. So I left."

"Angus was furious."

Alex nodded. "Aye. Angus was ready to murder him. I never should have agreed to meet him." He stared into the flames. "I dinna think he'd hand me to them, though." Blue eyes met mine. "I dinna think it true until I saw it for myself."

"How did they capture you, my love?"

"Well, ye ken we were at Lachlan's house?" I nodded. "We got that damned letter and something dinna ring true. I thought perhaps Malcolm had written it but I dinna want to believe it. I preferred to think it was Robert." He paused, then met my eyes evenly. "But Robert wouldna have asked a boy to deliver his terms. He wouldna risk a child's life." Alex rubbed his chin as he stared across the room. "Mary Rose, yer Robert Campbell has been most generous. When I saw him in the glen with Malcolm I assumed he wanted my death and that was why he was after me. But he could have killed me many times and he dinna. He has been a gentleman. I dinna understand why he brought me home to ye, lass, but I'm grateful. In another time I would have been proud to call him friend." He smiled wryly. "Except that he wants my wife."

"Alex," I said quietly, "he has been my friend, nothing more."

His eyes met mine. "On the surface, aye," he said. "But, Mary Rose, it's no' yer friendship he wants."

"I have a husband."

"For the now."

"Forever," I whispered. He stroked my hand and stared into space while I watched him in the flickering light from the fire. *The last time,* I thought, *the last time you'll lie with him in bed and talk.* "What if they'd killed you in the pass, Alex?"

"Lass, what were my choices? We could have fought them, but I had twenty-two men and Robert had a hundred. We were hungry and weary and Robert's men went to bed with full bellies. If we fought them we'd lose. No matter how well we fought, eventually we'd lose and we'd all be dead or captured. I thought that if Robert would take me and let the rest go, then it was the only sensible choice."

"So you turned back and let them decide to kill you or not?"

He shook his head. "My horse was wearying. I knew if I faced Robert's men with my sword drawn they'd kill me on the spot. I felt I had to talk to Robert but I couldna get to where I'd planned, so I turned around to meet them."

"And they attacked you?"

He nodded. "One did. Robert was shouting at his men to stop but one man dinna listen. He came at me with a claymore and by then I had my own out. I killed him, but he'd knocked me off the horse and the rest jumped on me. I dinna remember anything else until I woke up in their camp."

"Matthew thought you were dead."

"Aye. Well, when that man came at me, so did I." He stroked his chin, fingering the stubble on it. "It might have been better if I was."

"What happened in the camp?"

"Robert and I talked and he told me his terms, which were for the most part the same as the letter, though he dinna write it. Malcolm did, ye ken, and Malcolm sent it with Robert not kenning of it. I agreed to the terms and then Robert said he'd take me here before going back for the trial. I dinna argue and here we are."

"So you bartered your freedom for ours."

He met my gaze solemnly. "Would it be better for Kilgannon to be in ruins, Mary Rose? I've been a dead man since Sherrifmuir, or at least a marked one. The English have no choice, lass. If they dinna punish the rebels, the movement will grow. If they chop off the head, eventually the body will stop fighting. All of us who joined will pay. I dinna ken how dearly. Do ye remember the Treason Act? I've no illusions. Nor should ye, lass. I'll no' be coming home again."

How could he be so very matter-of-fact about it? *Dear God,* I prayed, *let me be as brave as he is.* "You are very direct, sir," I said, trying to keep my tone light.

He looked at me for a long moment and then a smile played around the corners of his mouth. "Aye," he said, nodding. "I've told ye. It saves time." I was unable to speak as he leaned forward to kiss my shoulder. I pulled him down to me and kissed his mouth and we made love again, slowly and gently, lingering deliberately as though we had years, not moments left.

It was dawn when I woke again. Alex stood at the window, looking across the glen. I wrapped my robe around me and went to him. He put an arm around me and kissed me, his voice husky. "I dinna deserve ye as a wife, lass, but I'm damned glad I had ye."

"There's more than one way that can be interpreted,"

I said and felt the rumble of laughter in his chest as he held me tighter.

"Then I mean all of them," he said and smiled.

The door burst open then and the boys tumbled into the room and into their father's arms. By the time I was dressed and ready to go downstairs, they were laughing and punching each other. Ellen came to the door asking for instructions, and Alex looked at me over the boys' heads. "Go on down without me, lass," he said. "I have a few things to say to my sons. We'll be down soon." The boys looked at me, waiting to take their cue from my behavior. *I must be as brave as Alex,* I thought. *If I can be.* I nodded and followed Ellen.

The hall was crowded, so crowded that I stopped at the top of the stairs, taking in the scene. Most of the clan was here and watched me descend. Some of Robert's men lined the walls but they were being ignored and made no move to join the clanspeople. Angus moved from the crowd to meet me at the foot of the stairs.

"Are ye aright, lass?" he asked kindly. I nodded, fighting the tears that threatened. "Robert Campbell is no' down yet, but the important people are here. And Seamus has his lads outside. They'll pipe him away properly." I nodded shakily and managed to thank him. His eyes filled with tears and he turned away abruptly with a squeeze of my hand.

I was surrounded then by the people who wanted to express their sorrow and anger. I heard their comments with nods and thanks but I understood none of them. A deep roaring filled my ears and I felt as if I was looking through a tunnel. And then the room hushed and I looked up through my fog and saw Alex and the boys standing at the top of the stairs. Alex wore his best plaid and a white shirt under the green doublet, his plaid over his shoulder. He looked as he had the night I'd met him. He met my eyes with a nod and I watched him descend, his sons' hands clasped firmly in his own. A pale Ian wore his great-grandfather's brooch. Alex's sword was tucked in Jamie's belt and dragged on the ground. Above them Robert stood without expression.

At Alex's appearance a clamor had erupted from the people and they pressed toward him. Robert and his men made no move toward Alex and I relaxed for a moment. Whatever their plan, it was not to tear him from us yet. Alex was enclosed by the clan and eventually was ushered to a table and handed food. The boys left his side for a moment or two, only to return immediately. His hand was always on one of them, touching a shoulder or holding a hand, and Angus was next to him constantly. But Alex's eyes kept finding mine and I moved closer until I was by his side and his arm was around me. It would be easy to imagine he was setting out for a voyage or a visit to family, not to his trial, I thought. His trial and possible death. What would they do to him? I felt again the paralyzing wave of fear. If the court declared it, he could be given a traitor's death. Hanging, disemboweling, and quartering. I drew a shuddering breath and felt myself swaying. Alex's arm tightened around me. *Dear God*, I prayed, *grant him mercy. No man should have to suffer so and not this man who was no traitor to anyone*. He squeezed me to him as he whispered in my ear, ignoring the crowd around us.

"Dinna fear, lass. Take the boys and go to yer family and be safe." I looked into his eyes. It was impossible that those blue eyes could soon be empty of life. He stroked my hair. "I love ye, Mary MacGannon. Never forget that. I love ye and I'm sorry."

"I love you, Alex," I said, "and I'm not sorry you love me."

He laughed shakily and kissed my forehead as Ian and Jamie squeezed between us, pointing to Robert standing with his men at the door. "Da," Ian said. "They say ye must go now. Can ye no' tell them no?"

Alex bent down until he was on a level with his sons. "When a MacGannon gives his word, lads," he said, "he must keep it. I gave my word that I would go with Robert and he gave me his that no one at Kilgannon would be harmed. Do ye remember me tellin' ye all that yesterday?"

Ian nodded. "Aye, Da, but I dinna want ye to go."

"I dinna want ye to go, Da," echoed Jamie.

Alex looked from Ian to Jamie and back. "Nor I, lads," he said, "but I must. Promise me one thing. Promise me ye'll take care of each other and yer mother."

"Aye, Da," said Ian.

Jamie nodded. "Aye, Da."

Alex gathered them to him, kissing their cheeks. "Yer verra braw lads. Ye make me proud to be yer da. Dinna forget me, no?"

"No, Da," they said, small arms winding around his neck.

"Now go tell them I'm ready," Alex said quietly as he stood. We looked after the boys as they scurried away, and the crowd pushed between us saying their farewells. The faces before me blurred and cleared and I felt the roaring in my ears again. I took a deep breath, willing myself to be calm as Alex led me toward Robert.

Just before the door Alex stopped and wrapped his arms around me.

"Kiss me once more, lass, and . . ." His voice broke and he pressed his face into my hair. "I love ye, Mary." He paused for control and when he continued his voice was calm again. "I'm sorry, lass, that it ended this way. Take good care of yerself and my sons. Dinna let them forget who they are. Tell them I tried." I kissed him one last time.

"I love you, Alex," I said, careless of who heard. "I'll take good care of your sons. God keep you, my love. I will be waiting."

Tears filled Alex's eyes and with a squeeze of my hand he left me, then embraced Angus, speaking for a moment. Angus patted his shoulder then stood back while Matthew and the others said their goodbyes, many openly weeping. We followed them out into the courtyard and I stood on the steps with Robert and the boys as Alex climbed onto a horse. One of Robert's men started to bind Alex's hands and a roar came from the clan. Alex said something to the Campbell, who jumped back as if struck and looked at Robert for direction. Robert nodded the man away and the people quieted. Robert turned to me then, his eyes glacial, his voice cold.

"Three days, Mary," Robert said. "I'll be back for you in three days. Be ready." I nodded, unable to speak.

The crowd stirred again as Robert made his way down the steps and leapt onto his horse, but no one moved to stop him. Angus had been busy, I realized, for that was the only way these people would have let Alex leave without a struggle. Alex looked at us as the pipers began, and I felt Ian straighten stiffly as he put his chin at a ridiculous height, Jamie following suit. Alex nodded at them, the ghost of a smile playing around his mouth, and then met my eyes for a brief moment before Robert moved to his side, blocking my view.

We stood at the outer gate as they moved slowly toward the end of the loch. Alex rode away with his back straight, surrounded by guards but unbound, his blond head a beacon among the dark ones of the soldiers. The music swirled around us as Jamie held my hand and Ian wrapped his arm around my waist. Angus put a hand on my shoulder. The pipers followed the riders, the crowd just behind them. At the edge of the trees, Alex turned and waved, his white shirtsleeve brilliant against the green behind him, just as he had waved that morning when The MacKinnon had come to persuade him to join the rebellion and I'd experienced my first feeling of foreboding. And the day he'd left for war.

We waved until the last horse was gone and there was no one to see and then listened as "MacGannon's Return" echoed hollowly from the forest.

SEVEN

*T*HREE DAYS, ROBERT HAD SAID. THREE DAYS PASSED,
then three weeks, and still no word from him. Angus,
worried about our safety, stayed with me, while Matthew
and Gilbey followed Robert's troop. They returned
with the news that Alex had been brought to Fort
William, then to Campbell territory, where he'd joined
an ever-growing group of Jacobites being marched to
Edinburgh. Hundreds were being held, lairds and chiefs,
tacksmen and crofters, herded together in makeshift
confinement, guarded by Campbells and English soldiers. Matthew and Gilbey had stayed close to the prisoners but they'd never seen Alex again once Robert had
joined the larger force. They'd followed the prisoners
to Edinburgh and then come home.

Their other news was more surprising. Argyll had
been dismissed as commander of the English troops.
Rumor had it that the Crown had feared he would be
too lenient with the rebels. Angus and I spent hours
speculating what Argyll's dismissal meant to us. Combined with no word from Robert, it seemed ominous
indeed. Matthew also brought stories of acts of English
reprisal. And of chiefs who had been taken or who, like
Alex, had surrendered themselves to save their people.

For some the sacrifice had proved futile, for their lands had been stripped and burnt and the people scattered without regard to prior agreements.

On some days it seemed as though the storm might pass by us and leave us overlooked in our isolation, and on others I was certain troops would arrive momentarily. We heard no news of Alex, nor of Robert. No one seemed to know when the trials would begin, for the courts were in disarray and we were told that King George did not know what to do with all the rebels his army held.

But we did not wait in idleness. Kilgannon prepared once again to withstand a siege. And Angus's absence. He planned to go to Edinburgh and I wanted to go with him. I could not bear to stay at home while Alex was imprisoned across the country. I had no idea what we might find in Edinburgh, but I didn't care. Alex was there and I was determined to join him. I had expected resistance from Angus, but when I explained my stratagem he had readily agreed, and I suspected he'd had the same idea. Before we left, though, we must be sure Kilgannon was prepared. While Angus worked, I was busy with the other half of our plan. I gathered everything worth selling, all the silver, all the jewelry, the gold dishes, everything of value that Kilgannon held, even the furniture, and I inventoried and packed them. When the *Katrine* returned from France with her latest cargo, we would take her to Edinburgh and sell the cargo and Kilgannon's treasures and then we would sell the *Katrine* herself. We would use the money to buy Alex's life, if possible. And if not, at least his comfort. Angus argued at first that my plan would leave the boys and I with no money, but I waved his protests away. If I lost Alex, money would be the least of my concerns. I was more worried that Robert might arrive before the *Katrine*.

In the end all the discussions proved unnecessary. Robert did not return and after eight weeks we all agreed he probably never would. The *Katrine* arrived after a successful voyage, and soon the castle was prepared and the *Katrine* was loaded with Kilgannon goods. But the boys and I did not leave with Angus after all. Runners reported that the country was in turmoil. Reprisals were sporadic but widespread, and Angus and Dougall worried that Edinburgh might be dangerous for us. Better, the men all told me, that I stay here in safety with the boys. Angus would arrange for the sale of the Kilgannon things and the *Katrine*, then return for me as soon as he could. I knew he was relieved, and puzzled, when I agreed to stay behind with no argument and no explanation, but he did not quiz me and I volunteered nothing. He bid me farewell on a miserable day with the wind blowing the rain sideways, and entrusted me to Dougall's care. And then the *Katrine*, heavily laden, left us, taking Angus and Matthew and Gilbey with her.

I had watched her sail away with a quiet resolve, but soon the enormity of the changes in our lives washed over me. The isolation which had saved us from reprisals now oppressed me. I walked the halls and haunted the gardens, waiting for news from the outside, and I read yet again the letters that the *Katrine* had brought.

Angus's mother, Deirdre, had written that she and her daughters were well and that there was talk that the court of James Stewart would be leaving for Italy. Since the rebellion had failed and France was at peace with England, France would no longer shelter the Pretender. I had often wondered where Sir Donald and the rest of the MacDonalds were and where we would have been if we'd accompanied him. Safe, I had thought earlier, safe with James Stewart holding court in freedom, but when I read Deirdre's news I congratulated myself for not having gone to France. As unsettled as our life was here, we were in our own home and surrounded by those who cared for us, at least for a while. *This is better,* I thought, *but so lonely.*

Ellen was, as always, a comfort. The only bright spot in that long spring was her marriage to wee Donald. I gave my approval readily, although I had explained to them both that Ellen was free to make her own choice. They were married in the chapel and we held a celebration afterward in the hall. I sat with the boys, smiling at the festivities but hearing the echoes of my own wedding and the missing voice of the man who should be with me. Ellen was busy with her husband now and I spent many hours with Berta and our cook, Mrs. M., who did their best to comfort me. We were not the mistress and staff these days, simply three women with an uncertain future and a dismal present.

I had one solace. No, three. The boys, although aware of the changes in our lives, never believed that their father could die. They were sure that Alex would return soon. Ian had given me Alex's brooch and Jamie his sword to hold safe for their father's homecoming. They gave me a reason to rise each day and I treasured their youthful optimism. My other solace was very private and was the reason I had not insisted on being on the *Katrine.* I was with child again. The baby would be born in late autumn or early winter, which meant that I had conceived on the one night we had spent together. Perhaps our last night together. I'd intended to keep my secret to myself, but Ellen and Berta and

Mrs. M. soon discovered that my lethargy and queasy stomach had quite legitimate reasons. Spring arrived and brought with it the promise of new life.

And then, three months after he'd left Kilgannon with Alex, on a cool and breezy May morning, Robert returned. When wee Donald found me and said that a ship was in the loch and that it looked like Lord Campbell, English soldiers, and Campbell men with him, I took a deep breath. I'd lost my gamble. Angus was still gone and Robert was coming for me after all.

The news of Robert's approach spread quickly and the clansmen began to gather. At my request, Thomas again brought the boys to his brother's house, where they would be safe. When I knew Robert's intentions I would decide whether to bring them home, but in the meantime Alex's sons would be well guarded. Thomas pressed me to accompany the boys and Dougall agreed, fervently arguing that I was risking my life unnecessarily. But I was resolute. I would talk with Robert. He might have news of Alex and certainly of Scotland at large. Thomas was not pleased, but he agreed. The boys, who had gone with reluctance, had begged to stay with me. I promised to come to them as soon as I could and sent them away with hugs and kisses and a heavy heart. They left at last, the dogs at their heels, Ian's hair a brilliant gold against the dark colors of his plaid, Jamie's redder hue a contrast, his head almost to his brother's shoulders. They took the last of the sun with them. *Dear God,* I prayed, *keep my boys safe. And let Robert not have vengeance in his heart. Or his orders.*

Dougall was not as easy to manage. He was visibly displeased and put my fears into words when he explained yet again that Robert might intend to claim Kilgannon for the Crown or to lay siege to it. Or to take me with him against my will. Or worst of all, Robert could have orders to take the boys with him and not me, as hostages to ensure Alex's compliance. I listened to all he had to say, privately agreeing that he could be right, but shook my head.

"If Robert were coming to lay siege to Kilgannon," I argued, "he would not sail into the loch with one ship and with himself blatantly on deck. He knows we're armed and ready for attack. He's met all of you. He knows you would not be easily outmaneuvered."

Dougall glowered at me, his sandy brows knotted. "Unless," he said, "we were convinced by a gullible woman that he meant no harm. Or unless he thought his presence would gain him admittance. For the love of God, Mary, will ye no' go with the boys?"

"Dougall," I said softly, looking into his eyes, "I have known Robert for years. I cannot believe he wishes me harm. Alex trusted him enough to leave with him, and enough to make Robert promise to see me safely home to my family. Do you question Alex's judgement?"

Dougall frowned and looked over my head. "Say what ye will, Mary. If the man makes one untoward move, he's a dead man."

"Dougall," I laughed shakily, "if the man makes one untoward move, I shall assist you."

He nodded unhappily and stood next to me on the dock as we waited. I watched Robert's ship approach with trembling knees, remembering his icy manner when he'd left with Alex. Why had he taken so long to return? Why had he returned at all? Why now? *Dear God, protect us,* I prayed, and then turned to Alex's cousin.

"I have a favor to ask," I said.

"Ask away, Mary," Dougall said. "It is yers to have."

"Hear me out before you agree, Dougall," I said.

"It is yers to have, Mary," he said again, meeting my eyes, "If it's in my power to assist ye, it's yers to have."

"I will hold you to that." I took a deep breath. "If Robert takes me, you must take the boys to my brother at Mountgarden or my aunt in London. And then find a way to tell Angus. If I am dead or imprisoned, Angus will find them. If Angus is dead, Matthew will find them. And if all of us are dead, you must raise them yourself. Will you promise me, Dougall, a solemn promise?"

There was no pause. He lifted his chin proudly and nodded. "It is a promise I gi' ye wi' my heart and all my honor."

I took another deep breath, blinking back my tears. "Thank you, Dougall. And, please, tell no one where they are. Malcolm's allies are still amongst us and we don't know who they are."

"I shall protect Alex's sons wi' my life. Never doubt it."

"And, Dougall, there's more."

He nodded.

"I will not go to England with Robert. I'm going to go to Edinburgh."

"Oh, aye? And how will ye do that?"

"If Robert will not take me, then I'll escape and hide until Angus comes back to get me."

Dougall nodded. "But, Mary, what if Robert Campbell willna leave without ye? Or the boys? Do ye trust his word if he says he'll take ye to Edinburgh? Do ye trust him wi' Alex's sons?"

I nodded. It was my fear as well. I was well aware that I might be putting Alex's sons at jeopardy if I agreed to take them with me, but I feared being separated from them even more. "I cannot believe that Robert would harm me and I cannot believe that he brought Alex back to us only to butcher his sons later. The boys represent no threat to anyone," I said bravely.

"I hope yer right."

"So do I," I said and watched Robert's ship advance.

Next to me Dougall gave a grunt of satisfaction and I followed his gaze. Kilgannon men were pouring down the glen's sides and approaching us, their faces grim and weapons ready. I smiled. *This is for Alex,* I thought. *We'll face them together.* The ship drew alongside the dock, and Robert, on its deck, nodded at me, his face stern. I struggled not to show my fear. From somewhere behind me, silent men came to catch lines and assist the landing. And then Robert was in front of me. I extended my hand and met his eyes. His expression was remote but not cold.

"Lord Campbell," I said coolly, acutely aware of the clansmen listening behind me. "Welcome again to Kilgannon."

"Mary," he whispered as bowed over my hand. And kept it in his grasp for a moment too long. "Madam," he said in a clear voice that carried to all the men. "Your husband still lives."

"Oh, thank God!" I cried, clasping my hands at my throat and bursting into tears. "Oh, Robert, thank you! Thank you!"

He patted my arm awkwardly and turned to his men, gesturing them off the ship. I wiped my eyes and tried to collect myself while they filed into Kilgannon's dock and waited. None of Alex's men moved for a moment, then Dougall extended a hand to Robert.

"Welcome to Kilgannon, Lord Campbell," he said and nodded as Robert shook his hand and thanked him.

"Come inside, Robert," I said and led the way up the terraces.

* * *

Eventually the English soldiers and the Campbells were installed in the hall, without arms, watched by silent Kilgannon men. Robert and I went to the library, where I had whisky and food brought, and then sat facing each other in uncomfortable silence. I had closed the door, but was aware, as no doubt Robert was, of the man pacing outside. *Dougall,* I thought, *still on guard.* I found it comforting.

"I wondered if you would come," I said. Robert nodded and stared into his whisky, turning the glass in his hand. "Thank you for the news of Alex. Where is he?" Robert's eyes met mine, unreadable. *Tread carefully,* I told myself, suddenly chilled.

"In prison in Edinburgh," Robert said, his tone detached. "He has not been tried but many have been. And there have been some hangings already. All peers who were in the rebellion have or will soon forfeit their lands and title, even before they are tried. Kilgannon is gone, Mary."

I nodded. "It is as we expected," I said softly. We sat in silence for several minutes. "Robert," I asked at last. "We've heard that Argyll has been removed from office. How is it that you are able to be here?"

He shrugged. "I'm naught but an errand boy. I was sent to find the MacDonald and you. MacDonald has gone to France, but I'm told that he burnt his castle at Sleat so it wouldn't fall into our hands."

I surprised both of us by laughing. "I never thought of that," I admitted and Robert gave me a weak smile, then leaned forward, his voice thawing.

"How are you, Mary?"

I folded my hands in my lap and met his eyes. "I am well, Robert. But I am fearful of the future."

He nodded and took one of my hands in both of his. "Mary, I have come to take you away from here. If you or your men defy me, I am to use force. I am to subdue any rebellion or any attempt to resist." He paused. "Do not resist." *How warm his hands and how cold his message,* I thought, as I withdrew my hand from his and rose, going to the fireplace before turning to face him. What I had seen in his eyes made me cautious.

"We will not resist, Robert," I said. "I am ready. Will and Betty will welcome me." I would, I thought, escape through the tunnel and hide with the boys until Angus came.

Robert watched me as he drummed his fingers on the arm of the chair for a long time. At last he spoke. "Mary, you are not going to England."

My heart lurched. "No?"

"You have been placed under my jurisdiction for the moment."

Robert's jurisdiction? What did that mean? "For what reason, Robert? You promised Alex safe passage for me to my family." I spoke mildly but my heart was racing and I heard the familiar roaring in my ears.

"The situation has changed. You are safer with me." I stared at him while wild thoughts raced in my head. Had I misjudged the man all along? He spoke earnestly, leaning forward again. "I cannot get you to London, Mary. I have told my superiors that you and I are childhood friends, and as a result you have been placed under my protection. But I must return to Edinburgh, not England." *Edinburgh,* I thought. Robert was going to Edinburgh. I tried to hide my excitement as he continued. "I cannot accompany you elsewhere and I will not let you go without me. I cannot entrust your safety to English soldiers. As the wife of a Jacobite, you are suspect. And his sons would be considered the devil's spawn."

I looked at him with narrowed eyes. "They are children, Robert. They represent danger to no one."

"Feelings are running very high. Kilgannon's sons are forgotten for the moment, but if he is executed they may be remembered." He rose and paced, then turned, his voice not as controlled now. "The country is in upheaval, Mary. You would not be safe if who you are were discovered and I was not there to protect you. In any event, there is no one to send with you. You must go to Edinburgh. I will endeavor to get you to England eventually, but not now." He came to stand in front of me. "Mary, what I have seen has frightened me. Scotland is bleeding. You will be safe with me but I cannot protect you elsewhere."

I lowered my eyes. I wanted to go to Edinburgh, for that's where Alex was, and, God willing, Angus and Matthew and Gilbey. But I did not want to go as Robert's ward or prisoner. I glanced at the man waiting so patiently for my answer, then away as I considered. Robert had never lied to me. His worst vice was his caution. Was this his desire or his duty? Dear God, I did not know what to do. How could I hope to aid Alex if I was Robert's prisoner? If I went with him, was I going willingly into my own prison? And taking Alex's sons? Could I trust this man?

"You are here to bring me to Edinburgh?" I asked, stalling.

"Yes." He took my hands in his again, his eyes glowing. "I will protect you, Mary. With my life. All of you."

"Just me, Robert."

He shook his head. "No. Kilgannon's sons come as well."

"The boys? Why?" I withdrew my hands from his. "Why not leave them alone? They are safe here."

His surprise and hurt was visible. "Do you think I'd harm Alex's sons, Mary? Or leave them behind? Do not imagine I will leave without them. These lands are not safe." He turned from me and paced again, stopping in front of the desk. "Alex was not as I had thought," he said, the words coming reluctantly. "We talked much on the journey." He stared at the floor and then looked up at me. "I cannot hate him. I hate the fact that he won you, but I cannot hate the man. Especially now."

"Especially now," I whispered. "What does that mean?"

He met my look without hesitation. "It means he will probably die. He'll be tried and executed as a traitor."

The roaring in my ears grew louder. "And if that happens?"

He lifted his chin. "I will be waiting."

"You will be waiting. For what, Robert?"

"For you, Mary."

"For me," I said, watching him in growing despair. And anger. "Have I no say in this? Did you and Alex discuss me on your journey? Did he agree? Was I part of an agreement, a bargain?"

He met my look unflinchingly. "Alex asked me to keep you safe if it were in my power. Nothing more. And I agreed."

I searched his face, looking for his intent. "I took vows, Robert," I said slowly. "I will never break them. Not out of fear, not out of gratitude. I want you to understand that. I am not to be bartered. There is to be no misunderstanding of our relationship if I go with you."

He straightened his shoulders. "Mary, you have no choice but to go with me, and I will not leave without all three of you."

"Why? Why not leave the boys here?"

He shook his head. "You do not understand. I have been sent here to remove Kilgannon's family. All of it."

"Then take the whole clan."

He whirled away and then back. "Damn, Mary, do you have to be so difficult?"

"Yes," I said and surprised a smile from him that faded as soon as it had blossomed. I moved from the fireplace and circled the room, moving behind the desk. He watched me silently. At last I paused and looked up at him. "Why did you let Alex come home, Robert? Why did you bring him here and not directly to Edinburgh or to meet the others?"

"Malcolm."

"Malcolm?" I could hear the surprise in my voice. "Malcolm?"

He nodded. "I despise the man. He sold his brother, Mary. He got paid for his information. Not by me, but he got paid. When he told me of the letter he had written, supposedly from me, I was sickened. He led his brother into a trap and used my name, knowing what effect it would have on Alex." His voice was raw now. "The countryside was in chaos. What difference did it make if I let him come home to you when we were so close?"

My tone was wintry. "I thank you for your kindness."

He leaned over the desk. "I wanted to see what you had left me for."

I took a step backward, shaking my head. "I was never with you, Robert, so I could not have left you."

He withdrew. "No," he said, his voice bleak.

"How fortunate that you were there to find Alex on his way home," I said coldly. "Of all people, it was you. You."

He shook his head. "It was not fortunate, Mary. It was no accident. Malcolm came to find me in Stirling and told me where Alex would be. It was a simple task to get permission to hunt down the Earl of Kilgannon and bring him back for trial."

I struggled to keep my calm. "I see. Thank you for not killing him when you had the opportunity."

"I was under orders to bring him back. The English want the Highlands subdued permanently. His will be a very public trial."

"I see."

"Do you, Mary? You do not know what's happening in the rest of Britain! How can you when you're out here with no contact?"

My anger exploded. I could hear my voice getting louder as I spoke but I could not stop the torrent of words. "I care not what is happening in the rest of Britain, Robert. I only care what is happening to my world, and my world has collapsed! And you aided the process. How do you feel now, now that you've brought Alex to prison where they will put him on trial as a spectacle for the masses? Where they will probably torture him and kill him as an example? He went with you even though he could have escaped. I begged him to escape, but he wouldn't leave, nor would he let his men kill you. Instead he treated you as a favored guest. He went with you because he is a man of honor and he said he could not betray your trust in him. You knew all this and still you tore him from me! To die, Robert! You took him from me so that he could die but his blood wouldn't be on your hands. How do you feel, Robert?" I glared at him.

He met my look evenly. "I feel that I did my duty."

"To whom? Your king? Or to your own desires? You had your chance to marry me and you did not take it. How is it that now that I belong to Alex I am suddenly the most desirable woman on earth?"

We stared at each other and Robert was the one to turn away. He waved his hands in the air and shook his head as he moved to look out the window. When at last he spoke it was calmly, but he spoke to the window. "Do not be stubborn, Mary. I will not overstep the bounds you set." He turned to look at me over his shoulder. "I simply want you safe. As does Alex. Please come with me. For now." He moved to stand in front of me, his voice soft at first. "Mary, I know you love the man. You must believe me that I did what I could to save him, to make this easier, not more difficult. If I were really only trying to please myself, I could have killed him in that pass and no one would have been the wiser. I could have come to you after that and forcibly removed you. I did not do either. I will not force you in Edinburgh. I love you, Mary, but I don't come to you now and ask you to break your marriage vows. For God's sake, what have I ever done that makes you so distrust me?" He threw his arms up and paced the room, shouting, his control suddenly gone. "I could have had Alex's life snuffed out, several times! And believe me, I thought of it! I spent hours wrestling with the idea. There would have been no one to gainsay me. But I did not. I saved him. More than once." He spun around and faced me, his face twisted in agony. "I saved him for you! For you, Mary! And I brought him back to you. Do you have any idea of what I felt being under this roof with you with him, with you looking at him as if he were a god and I nonexistent? Do you remember even speaking to me? Do you not think I knew I was under his protection? But pray remember, Mary, I had kept him from death myself and he owed me." He looked down at his hands and then up at me, speaking this time in a low voice. "I did what I could to let him have his last farewell to you and his sons and to this place. It was no joy to me to know you were with him, but it was for you that I did it. For you, Mary. Always. For you."

He walked to the other side of the room and looked at the books on the shelves. "And for him, damn it. When we rode to meet the others in Edinburgh, we talked as we never have. We talked of you, of course, but we also talked of duty and honor and Scotland. I respect him. He is a good man. I had hoped that there was nothing under the arrogance, that he was nothing but a handsome shell. But I was wrong. I can understand why they follow him. And I understand why you love him." He took a deep breath. "But, Mary, I do not think that he will live through this. I think that at best he will be imprisoned and then tried and put to death. And you're right, it will be as an example. And it will be horrible. I have never thought of myself as primarily Scottish, but, what I have seen, it stirs my blood with anger. I am at the brink of rebellion myself. I can understand . . ." He turned from me to stare at the wall as his words trailed off. He was silent so long that I wondered if he would continue, and after a very long pause he did. "If he does live, so be it. He is your husband and I acknowledge that. Perhaps . . ." He looked at the ceiling and then at me. "All I ask is that you come with me now peaceably and be in my care. You and the boys. You cannot leave them here, not in these uncertain times. I can offer you my protection. All I'm asking is to let me guard you from those who would destroy you. Come with me and be safe and we'll think of the future later. Come with me for now, Mary. Only for now. Please."

He turned away and I stared at his back, searching his words for traces of deception. And found none. *Dear God,* I thought, *I cannot distrust this man.* I'd had no idea that there was so much passion in him. Why had he never let me see it before? And I believed him. *God help me,* I thought, *I believe him. Alex,* I cried silently, *if I am wrong, forgive me. I do not know what else to do.* Robert turned, waiting for my response. I met his eyes and nodded.

"For now, Robert."

EIGHT

WE LEFT THE NEXT MORNING. NO PIPERS FOR US AS
we pulled slowly away from the dock, only a small for-
lorn group waving silently, Ellen and Berta at the front
of them. I looked one more time across the glen toward
the mountains. Somewhere beyond them Alex was in
prison. Somewhere beyond them Angus and Matthew
and Gilbey were working to free him. And now we were
going to Edinburgh as well. But how could I help if I
was under Robert's supervision? The boys were quiet,
standing with me on deck, watching the castle grow
smaller. I could not bring myself to tell them to bid Kilgannon goodbye for the last time. It had been with
great reluctance that I'd asked Thomas to bring them
home last night. And now, on this cold, crisp morning,
I looked at Kilgannon and put my hand on my middle,
reminding myself of my responsibilities. No matter
what, I must keep these three children safe.

I had walked through the house last night, just as
Alex had done, and said a silent farewell to my home. I
would probably never stand in these rooms again, never
sit before the fire in the library, nor join the clan for a
meal in the hall. My child would not be born in the bed
where I had known such happiness. *You have no choice*, I

told myself, but in my head I heard the echo of Angus's words. "There is always a choice, Mary. And always a cost."

Ellen had tearfully offered to come with us, but wee Donald had stood behind her and I'd looked over her shoulder and shook my head as I thanked her. It was a generous offer and one I would have gladly accepted, but I could not separate them and told her as much. Berta cried, asking if I wanted her to keep the house as always.

"Keep yourself safe, Berta," I had said as I embraced her. "Keep yourself safe for me. The house will keep itself if need be."

"It will be spotless when you return, madam," she said, weeping, and I thanked her as she handed me a large bundle. "Plaids for the laird, Lady Mary, and for the new bairn," she whispered, "so he'll grow up wearing the proper clothes."

Dougall, who had hovered nearby, put a hand on my shoulder, and I fought my tears as I looked up into his plain, honest face. "Please thank everyone for me, Dougall," I answered, embracing him quickly. "And you, Dougall, thank you for everything."

"I've done nothing but let ye do as ye wish, lass. I hope Alex agrees with the both of us."

I nodded and we looked together at the castle, so beautiful in the still morning air. "I'll always remember this," I said softly.

"Dinna say goodbye to Kilgannon, Mary," Dougall said gruffly. "Ye'll be back. I ken it. My Moira has the sight and she says ye'll be back. And Alex."

I met his clear blue eyes. "I hope she's right."

"I ken she is," he said. "We'll keep Kilgannon safe and we'll be here to welcome ye both back home."

"Thank you," I said, ignoring the tears now streaming down my cheeks.

He shook his head. "There's no thanks necessary. Yer a MacGannon now, Mary, and this is the home of the MacGannons. Haste ye back, lass," he said hoarsely and stalked away as I stared after him. *Haste ye back,* I thought. *Would it were so.*

I turned then to Thomas and Murreal at my side. "Thank you," I said, "for all your kindnesses to me. And for your loyalty." I smiled sadly. "And all your songs and stories. We will miss them terribly." Thomas waved my words away with embarrassment.

"I wish ye would ha' let us spirit ye all elsewhere as I've offered, Mary," he said and patted my arm. "Take care of yourself, lass. I do no' trust the Campbell. He has lust in his eyes for ye."

"I will be careful, Thomas, but Robert is taking us to Edinburgh and Alex is in Edinburgh. . . ." I looked east across the glen before turning back to him. "We will find a way to free Alex."

He nodded as he patted my arm again. "Yer a brave lass, Mary," he said, his eyes filling with tears.

I thought of that moment now as we slipped around the first bend and Kilgannon was lost from sight. I did not feel brave. In three short years Kilgannon had become home, and for the first time I realized how very much I had been searching for just that. Home. Alex and home. What would happen to Kilgannon, left unprotected? Dougall and Thomas would stay, and Berta and Ellen and wee Donald, but with only a handful of trained men left, how would they hold off the predators? I wished I were not powerless to change it.

And what would happen to us? I wondered as I looked at Alex's sons. Robert moved to Jamie's side and caught my eye. His expression was bland, but I felt a tension, an excitement in his bearing. What man would protect his rival's sons? And yet I could not imagine Robert harming these boys. He'd sworn to protect them and I believed him, but, I reminded myself, at one time I'd thought that Malcolm, however unpleasant, would be faithful to his brother.

Robert swallowed a curse as Jamie's dog, William Wallace, forced his way to the rail, pushing Robert aside with a wet nose, and I smiled to myself. Robert had not been pleased with the amount of my luggage, nor the dogs, but I had been firm. Everything went, I said, or I didn't. I stood at the rail now, watching us pass the bare hills of the outer loch. This land, I knew, would always hold me in its thrall. It was almost as though I could hear the bagpipes as I had the day I had arrived with Alex, I thought, and then realized with a start that I *could* hear them. I looked around wildly. Ian, next to me, pointed to the headland. Following his gaze, I saw Seamus MacCrimmon silhouetted against the sky, playing "MacGannon's Return." As we watched, Seamus was joined by scores of others, waving and shouting. We waved back excitedly and Robert frowned as Kilgannon's sons were piped out of MacGannon territory. Or what had been MacGannon territory. It would still be ours if not for James Stewart, I thought. And the Earl of Mar. And Malcolm. May they rot in hell. I put my hand on my waist and faced the sea.

The trip to Fort Williams was uneventful. I was so busy caring for the boys and the dogs that I had little chance to talk to Robert, but what could we have to say to each other? Although he was being kind, and despite his protestations to me, I had no illusions that he would risk all, or anything, to protect us. Not Alex's sons and possibly even me, when it became evident I was carrying Alex's child. I nursed the boys through the worst of their fears, and when we docked they were cheerful again. I nursed my own hopes as well, that by the time we arrived in Edinburgh, Alex would have been freed. Or, at worst, be still alive. My heart leapt at the thought that I would soon see him, but I chided myself every time. Let it come as it would, I had decided. I no longer wanted to know what the future would bring.

At Fort William we were ushered into the main building, and Robert reported to someone while we waited in a dreary parlor, guarded by two armed and uniformed men. The boys sat on either side of me, their eyes enormous and their mouths firmly closed, unhappy that the dogs had been left outside. The fort was little more than ruins, and I wondered at the English army keeping their men in a hostile land in such conditions. At last Robert returned to us, saying that the captain wished to speak with me. We followed Robert into the office and were politely greeted by a middle-aged, balding man who looked somewhat familiar. As he bowed over my hand, I remembered that I had met him at one of the Duchess's parties several years ago, and said a quick prayer of thanks for the recollection, and for my aunt's friend's thoroughness in introducing all who attended her evenings. Eloise Barrington, the Duchess of Fenster, had never overlooked anyone and now I reaped the rewards of her courtesy.

"Madam, my compliments," said the officer. "I am Captain Charles Jeffers. I hope your journey has not been too exhausting." I murmured something vaguely polite. He gestured for me to sit, and as I did so he sat down behind his desk. The boys stood on either side of me, and behind us Robert leaned against the wall by the door. "I am sure you do not remember me," he said.

"Indeed I do, sir," I said, grateful that I had. "You were with the Duke of Fenster in France and we met in London."

His brown eyes lit with pleasure. "How kind you are to recall a simple soldier." I smiled at him. "I am sorry for your present situation, madam. Are these Kilgannon's sons?"

"Yes," I said, introducing them. The boys bowed perfectly.

"Fine-looking boys, madam. They look just like their father."

"Yes," I murmured, aware of Robert's sharp movement behind me.

"And you have been well cared for thus far?"

"We have been treated very well, sir."

"Good, good. Lord Campbell is, of course, an old acquaintance of yours, I believe," he said with an inquisitive glance at Robert.

"Yes," I said mildly. "I have known Lord Campbell forever."

His nods were rapid. "And you are now going to Edinburgh?"

I said we were.

"I'll be there soon myself," he said. "If I can be of any service while you are, please do not hesitate to tell me."

I thanked him as he ushered me to the door. At the threshold, Captain Jeffers took my hand. "Madam," he said earnestly, "I was once able to thank your husband for a service he rendered for the Duke in France. I stand ready now to repay his kindness in any manner I can. If there is anything you desire that is in my power to deliver, you have only to speak and it shall be yours."

I looked at him and smiled sadly. "Sir, I wish my husband to be released and allowed to go home. Is that within your power?"

His kind expression clouded. "Alas, no, dear lady," he said. "But I will send a letter to Edinburgh commending him and I will do the same in person when I arrive. Perhaps it will help."

"You are very generous, sir."

"It is nothing," the captain said. "I only wish I could have offered you safe passage to England." A vision of Louisa and London, with all its comforts and safety, rose in my mind, but hard on its heels came the image of Alex in a jail cell in Edinburgh.

"I thank you for your kindness, sir," I said, "but my husband is in Edinburgh and my place is with him." The captain nodded and bowed. Over his head Robert met my look with a somber expression.

In the morning we were mounted on fine English horses. Fifty armed men traveled with us, Robert at their head. Each boy was seated on a horse with a soldier, for which I was grateful, since they were far too young to handle a horse on their own in such country. The land quickly turned into bogs and moors interspersed with lovely meadows, or what had been lovely meadows, for we began to see signs of the reprisals. The journey branded pictures into my memory. Each mile that brought us closer to Alex showed us more of the devastation. We passed house after house that had been burnt out, some months ago, some still smoldering, some with bodies still in the yard. Men in plaids lay

dead at the side of the road, their corpses long ago food
for the crows. I took Jamie onto the horse with me and
tried to answer his questions. Robert took Ian with him
and I wondered what he was saying to Alex's son.

Women were rarely seen, and when they were, they
usually were hurrying away from us in their tattered and
filthy clothing, their expressions haunted, their children's frightened eyes huge as they watched us pass. I
remembered Robert saying "Scotland is bleeding" to
me. He had not said the half of it. Scotland was hemor-
rhaging and there was no one to staunch the flow. For
the first time in my life I was ashamed of my English
blood. How could soldiers who had been raised on the
same prayers as these people butcher them and burn
them out? This, then, was what Alex had feared for Kilgannon and why he had sacrificed himself. He had been
correct in fearing this for his own. My mind became
numb as we rode, mile after mile, passing the ravages of
defeat. How could this country ever recover? Robert,
his expression remote, watched me silently.

Our first night after Fort William was spent in a
moldy tent on a rainy hill, but we were so tired that it
did not matter. I answered the boys' questions the best
I could and calmed their fears before they fell asleep in
their clothes, the dogs piled on top of us. Ian had night-
mares and I held him to me, my tears falling for this little boy and the thousands of others whose sleep would
always be haunted by the images of war. When at last I
slept myself, I dreamed that the boys and I were one of
the families running through the mud from the soldiers, me with a baby in my arms, wrapped in his father's torn plaid.

The rest of the trip melded together in misery. It
rained constantly and the horses slowed as they picked

their way carefully through the mud. The only comfortable night was in a Campbell castle owned by one of Robert's cousins, and it was there, tucked in a featherbed with the boys asleep next to me, that I felt Alex's third child move under my hand. I looked up at the carved panels of the ceiling and cried. "Alex, my love," I said to the comfortable room. "Alex, where are you?" But there was no answer and I had to find my own consolation.

Edinburgh was the filthiest city I'd ever seen and I was horrified by it. The contents of chamber pots and all manner of garbage lay in the street. I quickly learned to be leery of the cry from above which meant someone's refuse, or worse, was about to be thrown upon the unwary from a window. The more prosperous lived in separate houses or on the upper floors where the smells and sounds from below were muted. We were soon ensconced in Robert's comfortable town house, the top three floors of a tenement on a quiet street. Robert left us there without a word of explanation, simply telling us to rest. We spent the first night getting clean and fending off the questions of Robert's inquisitive aunt, who kept house for him. She was quite relentless in her quest to discover exactly what my relationship to Robert was until I made it very clear that there was no relationship. She was, however, also a source of ready information, and I quickly discovered that there were two places that Alex might be imprisoned, in the castle itself with its extensive walls or at a temporary outpost holding Jacobites just outside the city.

For the next three days, on the pretense of seeing the city, the boys and I combed the streets searching for information. And for Angus and Matthew. If we were visible enough, I reasoned, they would find us. We were, however, accompanied at all times by at least two of Robert's men, Highland Campbells, who tolerated us silently, and I knew it would be difficult, if not impossible, to be approached with them there. Still, I felt I must try, and anything was preferable to sitting within walls and waiting while Robert's kind but witless aunt presided over us and the Campbell men waited below. The men barely spoke to me, although they were always polite and never interfered with my roamings. I did my best to get what information I could from the few people who would talk with me. Robert himself I did not see, for he did not live in the house and I knew nothing of his whereabouts. I wrapped my anger and my sorrow around me like a plaid and withdrew into my own world, peopled only by the boys and Alex.

On the fourth day of my stay in Edinburgh I was in a foul temper. I had not found Angus or the others, and I was out of patience with waiting for men to do my bidding. I wanted to see Alex. Now. I bundled up a change of clothing for Alex and dressed the boys in their finest. Then, to the horror of our Campbell guards, I marched the three of us to the castle, demanding a visit with my husband. The soldiers at the gate did not know what to do with me and put us aside. We waited for thirty minutes while my anger grew. At last, with a deep breath, I walked boldly through the gate, the spluttering guard at my heels. After ten feet another guard stopped my progress by blocking my way. I summoned a goddess look and imperiously demanded to see someone of authority. At once. We were led into a small room off the gate, where we waited yet again. I was about to find someone else to take my message when the door opened and a uniformed man entered. He stood, watching us, and I gave him an icy look. And then recognized him.

"Captain Jeffers," I said, rising. "Thank God. I thought perhaps no one here spoke English." He bowed over my hand and met my eyes with a warmth that surprised me. I felt my restraint melting before this greeting and willed myself to be icy again but it was too late. I could meet disdain and confusion with aplomb, but friendliness disarmed me. I felt dangerously close to tears. He smiled sadly and gestured to the walls that surrounded us.

"I am not surprised to find you here, madam," he said.

"I did not expect you to be here already, sir."

"Nor I, madam. I have only just arrived. I will be stationed here until provisions can be made for all the prisoners."

"I see," I said. *Provisions for the prisoners,* I thought. What exactly did that mean?

"You wish, I understand, to see your husband," Jeffers said.

"Yes, Captain. I have been told that he is here."

"He is indeed, madam. But"—he looked at the boys—"I am sorry to tell you that he is allowed no visitors." His warm manner and unwelcome message undid me. I could think of nothing to say and sat down on the bench. And burst into tears, alarming every male in the room. I had not planned it, but it certainly had the effect I desired. The boys hovered over me and the Campbells shot worried looks at each other. Captain Jeffers looked at me with consternation, offered me his handkerchief, then ran out of the room, muttering something about seeing what he could do.

We waited another hour. At last Captain Jeffers returned with the news that I could see his superior, but the boys must stay here. I paused, afraid to leave them behind. Captain Jeffers assured me that they would be watched by one of his men, but one of the Campbells stepped forward.

"We'll be with them, Lady Mary," he said kindly, quite astonishing me. "We willna leave them for a minute." The other Campbell nodded.

"We'll be fine, Mama," said Ian with dignity, taking his brother's hand. Jamie echoed him and I smiled.

"Thank you," I said to each of the three men and followed Captain Jeffers. The halls were damp as I was led down two flights of stairs and into a small, dark room where a disgruntled man sat behind a desk. Captain Jeffers introduced us, but Colonel Porter did not stand. He was at least ten years older than I, the ruddy blotchiness of his complexion ugly above his red collar, his gaunt chest making the buttons of his uniform sag. He watched me with small blue eyes that narrowed as I entered. I steeled myself.

"Mistress MacGannon, is it?" His tone was imperious.

"Yes," I said and sat without bidding on the chair opposite him. Captain Jeffers stood behind me.

"Your husband is a prisoner here." Porter's tone bordered on disrespectful and I measured him. English. Smug. His mother had bought his commission, no doubt, I thought. This man would have no cause to be partial to me. I was a member of that class to which he believed he correctly belonged but knew he did not. And he now had power over me. And Alex. I tried my best goddess look, but I was trembling inside.

"Yes," I said evenly. "And I have come to see him."

"Kilgannon is the man who aided the Duke of Fenster in France, sir." Captain Jeffers's tone was politely persuasive.

"Yes." Porter did not even glance at Jeffers. He studied me. "I believe you are someone's niece," he drawled.

"I am the niece of the Duke of Grafton and of Lord Randolph."

"Tories."

"Peers."

"Your husband is Scottish. And a Jacobite."

"My husband is Scottish."

"Interesting that you would marry him." I was silent. "And now he is held for trial."

"Yes."

"For treason." He smiled unpleasantly. "He will die, madam."

"My husband has not yet been tried, sir."

The briefest of smiles touched his lips and he nodded. "Of course, madam. But he will be. And he will be found guilty."

"We cannot know that for certain."

"Actually, madam, we can."

I lifted my chin. "I am here to see my husband, sir."

"Men under my authority who are accused of treason are not allowed visitors. You must leave."

I struggled to control my temper. "I have never heard of such a thing. I have come to see my husband and I will see him, sir."

"You speak as though it were your decision to make. Alexander MacGannon is not allowed visitors. That is *my* decision. The man has been charged with treason." Porter leaned forward, licking his lips. I fought the wave of revulsion that washed over me. "Do you understand the word, madam? It means one betrays one's country. Perhaps it runs in the family?"

I ignored his gibe. *Be calm,* I ordered myself and took a deep breath. "I understand the word, sir. But under English law the prisoner has certain rights."

"We are in Scotland, madam."

"English law is still enforced, I believe."

"Madam, I think you do not understand your position here. You are the supplicant, not the bestower." I did not trust myself to speak. "You threw away the ability to claim your English blood when you married this . . . Scot. You are now Scottish, madam, and the wife of a traitor. And traitors can only be controlled in one fashion. It is very simple." He slumped back. "You are not allowed to see him. Do not ask me again."

I felt my fury climb. "Why?" I asked coldly.

"Why?" His anger was immediate and very visible. He rose and leaned over the desk. "Why? You ask me why? Who are you to question my decision?" Our eyes met, his enraged and piggish.

"An English citizen. And his wife. Why can I not see him?"

"Because I have decided that you will not. MacGannon is a very difficult man. You will not see him."

"Why?"

"I have decided it is so, madam." He sank back in the chair.

"I would like to see your superior."

"I have no superior," Colonel Porter said.

I almost laughed. *You have many superiors,* I thought. *Every man who has been kind to us is your superior.* But I was silent. If I inflamed him further, who knew how Alex would pay for my anger? I could not risk it. I rose and brushed my skirts, trying to think of an appropriate answer. Behind me Jeffers cleared his throat. It was hopeless.

"Thank you for your time, sir," I said and turned to the door.

"Easily dissuaded, eh?"

I froze and met Captain Jeffers's sympathetic eyes. *Do not let this disgusting man anger you,* I commanded myself, *or Alex will pay.* I turned back to Porter. "Sir," I said quietly, "I am at a loss. What is it that will persuade you? Money? I will gladly pay to see my husband."

"Are you bribing me, madam?" The colonel's tone was menacing.

"No, of course not," I said evenly, "but I would be delighted to contribute to the cost of maintaining troops in Edinburgh."

He watched me through narrowed eyes. "You may ask me again in four days, madam. I will consider your request then."

"Thank you, sir," I said and sailed out the door, trembling with anger. I was halfway down the hall when Jeffers caught me.

"Madam, I am sorry he was so difficult. We will try again."

I took a shaky breath. "Is it me? Or does he treat all visitors like that?"

"It is you. Or, actually, it is your husband."

"But why?"

"Kilgannon has been . . . unrepentant."

I laughed then, my heart suddenly lighter. Unrepentant. An understatement, no doubt. *Good for you, my darling man,* I thought. "I'm sure he was," I said. "Well, we will try again. I thank you for your help, Captain. You are very kind." I held out the bundle of Alex's clothing. "Do you think there is any way to get these to him?"

"I will see to it," he said, taking the bundle from me.

"Thank you, sir. You are kindness itself." I turned to leave.

"Madam." He took my elbow and turned to me. "I have thought of something. Come with me." He led me down a hallway I had not noticed before. "And pray be quiet," he said over his shoulder. We made two turns and then climbed two flights of stairs. I was feeling quite disoriented when at last we stopped in a hallway, one side filled with windows that overlooked a tiny courtyard two stories below us. I turned to the captain with a curious look.

"From here, madam," he whispered, "you may see your husband. In just a few moments some of the prisoners will be brought outside. He may be with them."

"Thank you," I said, my eyes filling with tears. "Thank you for being so very considerate."

"It is my pleasure, madam." He looked down at the still-empty courtyard and then back at me. "I am simply repaying a debt. Your husband risked his life, Lady Mary, to aid the Duke. I was supposed to be with Duke John that day but had been reassigned at the last moment. I would have been devastated if he had met with harm, but thanks to your husband the Duke was untouched. What I can do here to repay his courage is very little."

"It is very appreciated."

"It is very little," he answered, embarrassed.

We stood in silence then. The hallway overlooked one small part of the courtyard, and soon a group of people had gathered at a balcony to our right. Several women, fashionably dressed, were accompanied by men in uniform. They chatted and gaily pointed down as though they were at a party. I followed their gaze. Below us a group of prisoners were being led by soldiers into the courtyard. It took me several moments to recognize Alex and the man next to him. Murdoch Maclean. They were filthy and chained at wrist and ankle, but the two of them talked cheerfully to each other and gazed insolently up at the watchers while the soldiers prodded them to form a line. Alex had a beard now, copper against the blond of his hair. I strained to see his face and tried to open the window.

Captain Jeffers spoke quietly. "The windows are fixed, madam, and just as well. I must ask you not to try to get your husband's attention. It will go very badly for me if we are discovered. And perhaps for Kilgannon."

I nodded and let my hands fall to my waist. Alex looked healthy. His clothing was grimy, his bonnet crooked on his head, but his stance was defiant. The group on the balcony was calling jeers down to the prisoners, one woman waving her handkerchief tauntingly while the men with her laughed. The prisoners watched her and some called comments. Alex and Murdoch talked to each other, looking at the visitors, and then Alex leaned over to his friend, saying something that made Murdoch grin. The two exchanged a look and began singing. After a few lines the other prisoners joined them. I could not distinguish the words, but the group on the balcony stepped back as if singed. The woman who had been waving her handkerchief now clutched her throat. The soldiers in the courtyard grabbed Alex and Murdoch roughly and dragged them away. Alex was laughing. I pressed my forehead to the window and tried not to cry.

The next few days were a miserable blur. The smells of the city assailed me and I spent much of my time with an uneasy stomach or worse. For two days after the visit

to the castle I was so sick and despondent that I could
barely get out of bed. I kept telling myself that the sick-
ness was a normal part of my pregnancy and would pass,
as I had been told. But surely it should be over by now?
Perhaps something was going wrong with this pregnancy as it had all the others. The thought paralyzed
me. Since I'd arrived I'd accomplished nothing, but I
could not think what else to do. I waited for the fourth
day to come. It was on that morning, when I was feeling too queasy to face the world, that Angus marched
boldly up to the front door and demanded to see me.

NINE

I RAN DOWN THE STAIRS, HAPPIER THAN I'D BEEN IN weeks. Angus stood in front of the fire in Robert's parlor. When he turned to me, I threw myself into his arms with a cry, bursting into tears.

"Angus, I'm so happy to see you!" I wailed.

"So it would seem," he said coldly, then sank into the chair opposite me, stretching his legs to the fire before turning an angry blue gaze to me. "Mary, what in the name of God are ye doing roaming the streets of this place, dragging the lads with ye and ye with child? What are ye thinking?"

I stared at him. "How did you know, Angus?"

"We saw ye. First, of course, we heard about the English woman who wore a MacGannon plaid over her skirts and had two boys with her and two Campbells to guard her. I'm surprised ye did no' bring the dogs as well. Did ye not think we'd find ye on our own?"

"About the child."

His expression softened. "I was wed, lass, and fathered three children. I ken when a woman is breeding. Ye look puny."

"Thank you, Angus," I said. "It's nice to see you too."

He laughed and shook his head, then turned serious again, his tone softer now. "Mary, what in God's name are ye doing here in Edinburgh?"

"Robert brought me," I said and told him.

He listened quietly, then nodded. "I feared as much. Matthew saw ye first and followed ye back to this house. And we've been following ye ever since. Including to the castle two days ago. What were ye thinking, going there, lass?"

"To see Alex. What else?"

"But ye dinna see him, did ye?"

"I did see him, Angus," I said and related my visit.

He almost smiled, then nodded again. "Aye, that's our Alex." He met my eyes. "I saw him this morning."

"Angus, how is he? Is he well? Is he mistreated?"

He shrugged. "He's well, as well as can be expected. They are no' treating him like an honored guest but he's no' abused."

"How did you manage to see him?"

"How do ye think? Money. We used the money from selling all the Kilgannon goods. I have brought it for ye," he said, fishing a purse from his plaid and handed it to me. I refused to take it. "Take it, Mary. Ye may have need of it. And it's yer money, lass. I have only been safeguarding it for ye. I have used a bit of it to see Alex and some to bribe the jailers to give him things." He reached into his shirt and pulled out a packet. "Like paper. Here. I have a letter from him." I saw the familiar writing through a blur of tears. *Alex,* I thought. Angus turned to watch the fire. "Go ahead and read it. It's no' long. I'll wait." I unfolded the dirty paper, my hands shaking.

My dearest Mary, Alex wrote. *I am told that you and*

the boys have arrived in Edinburgh with Robert. Why are
you here and not safely in England? How are you, my
lady? And my sons? We do well enough here and await
our trials. I am housed with Murdoch and Jamie Ramsay
so I am in good company. I am fortunate that Angus was
allowed to see me. Do not try to visit me in this place. It
will have to be enough that we are in the same city. They
tell me that prisoners are allowed a visit from family be-
fore trial, so I will wait for Angus to bring you to me then.
I love you, Mary. Keep yourself and my sons safe. I remain
yours, Alex.

I looked up at Angus. "Do you know what he says?"

He shook his head and I passed him the letter, which
he read quickly, then returned with narrowed eyes.
"Put the thought from yer mind, lass. I'll no' take ye to
see him. It's a hellish place and no' fit for a woman."

"No one would harm me. I'm English."

"Ye've already seen what respect that earns ye here.
Yer married to a man who is to be tried for treason,
lass."

I felt my chin go up of its own accord. "He is still an
earl and I a countess until the trial. Surely that makes a
difference."

"No."

"Then we will use the money." He looked at me from
under his eyebrows and began to argue, but I waved his
protests away. "I will see my husband, Angus."

"Mary, Alex asks ye not to try to see him."

I continued as though he'd not spoken. "And I will
not stay in this house a moment longer. We will leave
immediately. I'll get our things together." I rose, ready
to depart. "We will come to where you are staying.
And, I assume, Matthew and Gilbey."

"Ye canna stay where we are."

"Wherever you are will do. Or we will go to the *Mary Rose*."

"Ye canna. She's no' here. I sent her to Kilgannon."

"To Kilgannon! Why?"

"For men." He met my eyes. "If there is a way to spring Alex out of yon prison, we will do so, and if we do, I canna promise to be able to deliver all of ye to safety. We might get the brig away, we might no'. If we dinna, then we divide and flee, and one man, or a handful, I can spirit away, but a pregnant woman and two boys and the blasted dogs, that's another matter. No, Mary, I came to see how ye were and to tell ye to stay here and no' cause a fuss about seeing Alex. If ye go to visit him and then he escapes, the soldiers will be beating down yer door in a moment. Better that ye disappear here in a Campbell's home for a bit. I can think of no place yer less likely to come under suspicion. As soon as the *Mary Rose* returns I'll send ye to England overland with some of the men. 'Twill be a tricky business, the timing, but I canna see another choice." He sighed. "Everaone in the city kens who ye are and what ye do, Mary. They all talk about ye. So become invisible for a bit, will ye, lass? Stay here with Robert."

"Angus," I said crisply. "I am not staying here *with Robert*. He does not live here and he does not visit. His aunt and the boys are my only companions."

"Aye, I ken that. All of Edinburgh kens he does no' stain yer honor. It is the only reason he is still alive." He paused. "He brought ye here because he had to be here. And for his own reasons, which ye ken as well as I."

"Robert has been courteous to me, Angus. And nothing more. He said that we had been placed under his jurisdiction."

"Aye, well, true enough, I've been told. But I suspect that was only to get ye out of Kilgannon." He smiled wryly. "Perhaps we could get Alex placed under Robert's jurisdiction."

"Angus, how will you do it? How will you free Alex?"

He shook his head. "I canna tell ye, as we've no' figured it all out yet. But the Macleans are willing. Murdoch's brother Duncan has been to see me, and Ramsay's brothers are coming from the south to assist." He sighed. "Ye being here is a complication I'd no' anticipated. I thought ye safely on yer way to England."

I nodded. We were silent for a long time then, each lost in his own thoughts. How I longed to see Alex. It was not enough to be in the same city with him. Why could I not have an hour with him, just one hour? How would that change anything? I sighed.

"Angus, do we not have anyone else we can turn to? I would rather not stay here. Is there nowhere we can go?"

Angus stared at the floor for a long time before answering. "I have nowhere safe to put ye, lass." He shook his head. "If ye'd arrived a few days earlier, I could have sent ye home on the *Mary Rose*, but I have no men to spare to take ye to England or to Kilgannon and I dinna think Robert does either. Ye canna travel on yer own, that would be foolish." He sighed. "I think this is the safest place for ye in Edinburgh. And at least here ye can still try to free Alex by writing to the judges and the court. Just stay here in this house. No one who kens ye are with child would think anything of that. And it is obvious ye are no' the Campbell's . . ." He paused, his face flushing.

"I hope it is obvious," I said tartly. "If it is not, then

they all think the worst of me already and any plea on my part for Alex would only appear to be the worst hypocrisy."

"The word abroad in town is only that Robert Campbell is giving ye safe harbor since ye were childhood friends. Nothing more. Robert has been most considerate of yer reputation."

I nodded. "But, Angus, if that's the case, then the most logical thing for me to do is to see Alex. If I were here as Robert's . . . companion . . . I would not attempt to see the man I was unfaithful to, would I? But if I am a faithful wife, which I am and you know it, then the only sensible thing for me to do is try to see my husband. And I've already begun the process. Today, in fact, is the day that I am to return to the castle and contribute money for maintaining troops in Edinburgh."

Angus watched me with narrowed eyes. "Mary," he began, then shook his head. I laughed, knowing I'd won a point.

"Angus, what can it hurt if I see him? Or at least try? It's the only thing that will actually defer suspicion from me. If I do as you suggest and stay hidden in this house and people continue to talk about me, then I will appear more guilty of adultery, or of plotting Alex's release, than I am. It would be unnatural for a wife to not visit her husband. Please, Angus, let me go see him. Just once. And then I'll stay here. And when the *Mary Rose* comes I'll go anywhere you like and not be in the way. But the only way I'll agree to stay here in this house is if you help me see Alex."

He frowned at me. "We're no' negotiating, lass."

I laughed and rose to stand before him. "No, Angus, we've finished negotiating." I leaned to kiss his cheek.

"Thank you," I said softly and he didn't pretend to misunderstand.

"Once, Mary," he said. "Only one visit."

I nodded.

It was not so easy to arrange. Angus accompanied me, and when the Campbell soldiers understood that I was leaving the boys behind in Robert's house, they did not insist on joining us. At the castle we waited in the same anteroom as before, I with my hands in my lap while Angus paced. Eventually a soldier came to bring us to Colonel Porter, but Angus had insisted that I not see him again, and he went alone to talk with the officer, a bag of money hidden in his plaid. It was another hour before he returned, his color high and his manner abrupt. He nodded at me.

"It's arranged, Mary," he said, gesturing me to follow the soldier who waited behind him. "I'll be here when yer finished, lass." He crossed the room and settled himself on a bench.

I thanked him breathlessly and hurried to follow the soldier, who led me without a word to a dingy room overlooking the same courtyard that I'd seen Alex in on my last visit, holding the door open for me to enter.

I looked across the tiny room. And saw Morag Maclean with her arms around my husband's neck. Morag, I thought, bristling. I fought my anger.

Alex, with his back to the door, did not see me at first, but Morag did, and she smiled slightly, then ran her hands down Alex's chest, letting them linger at his waist. Alex's arms were at his sides and he lifted them now and moved her hands from him as he stepped back from her.

"Morag, dinna . . ." he was saying as the door

slammed shut behind me. He turned with a surprised expression, dropped Morag's wrists, and moved toward me. "Mary Rose!" he cried, his cheeks flaming above his beard. He swept me into his arms and kissed me soundly. "Mary," he said. "Lass, it's good to see ye."

"Alex," I said stiffly, not returning his kiss, nor his embrace. I left my arms at my waist where they'd been. He ignored my coldness and kept his arms around me. "I see you have a visitor already. Hello, Morag."

Morag smiled her cat smile. "Mary. We dinna expect ye."

"Obviously."

"If we had kent ye might be coming, we'd have been more discreet," Morag purred.

Alex released me then and faced her, his tone bitter. "Oh, no, lassie," he said to Morag heatedly. "Dinna play that game. No' with me, no' with Mary. Ye ken better than that." He turned to me, his eyes blazing. "It's no' what yer thinking, Mary Rose. Morag only just arrived." He threw her a baleful glance. "To see her husband. Ye do remember yer married, aye, Morag? It's Murdoch ye came to see."

"And ye, Alex," Morag said, apparently unscathed by his anger.

"Then yer fooling yerself," Alex said. "We've naught between us and ye ken it. Dinna be causing trouble in my marriage."

"There's a lot between us, Alex," Morag said, coming to stand before him. "A lifetime between us. Or do ye choose to no' remember all tha' has been between us?"

"That was a long time ago, Morag."

Morag tilted her head and watched Alex with a smile flitting about her lips. "No' so long ago, Alex. Have ye forgotten a visit to Dunvegan after Sorcha's death? A very . . ."—she reached out and traced a hand along Alex's jaw—". . . memorable . . ."

Alex reached for her wrist and drew her forward, his tone menacing. "Morag, for the love of God, will ye stop this charade? This is no' the time to be playing games with my marriage. Or yers." He looked over at me, then back at Morag. "Tell her the truth of it, Morag. Tell Mary there's naught between us."

"I would be lying, Alex," she said quietly.

He loomed over her and shook her wrist. "I'm in no mood to be trifled with. Tell her."

Morag met his eyes. "I have kent ye all yer life, Alex. I was the first . . ." She stopped as Alex backed her to the wall.

"Morag, if ye think this is amusing, or that somehow it'll bring me to ye, yer sadly mistaken. I married Mary, not ye, though God kens I kent that's what ye wanted; ye made it plain enough. But, Morag, I dinna want it. I dinna want ye. Nor do I now. Ye satisfied my body, but ye had nothing for my mind. No' then and certainly no' now. It's Mary I love and she was good enough to marry me. And ye married Murdoch, if ye'll remember, of yer own volition. I dinna remember a gun to yer head." He spun away from her, then back, his fists clenched. "Dinna do this, Morag. Ye'll wreck two marriages for naught and break Murdoch's heart in the bargain. If this is yer revenge on me for no' marrying ye, it's falsely conceived. Ye've naught to gain but my contempt. I wouldna be wi' ye even if I were no' married, Morag. Ye've naught for me. It makes ye look foolish to be playing these games the now. Go see yer husband while ye can and pray I dinna tell him what ye are."

"Murdoch loves me," she said, raising her chin.

Alex nodded. "Aye, the more fool he. Why can ye

no' go and comfort him, Morag? We're headed for trial and we willna be coming home, lass, no' him to ye, nor me to Mary. Stop the playacting. Go. Dinna shame yerself further."

"Ye promised me, Alex," she said.

"A long time ago," he said quietly. "A verra long time ago. Ye canna hold me to that. If I had wanted to marry ye I would have after Sorcha died. Ye'll notice I dinna."

She turned her head away and began to cry. Alex closed his eyes and shook his head and I wished myself anywhere but here. After a moment Alex opened his eyes.

"Morag," he said, his tone quiet now. "I'm sorry yer sad, but I canna help ye now. Go see your husband and leave me with my wife." Morag wiped her eyes and left us without a word.

When the door closed behind her Alex sighed and looked at me. "Mary . . ." he began, then stopped. "*Mo Dia,* lass, what can I say to ye? I dinna encourage her. I dinna want her, Mary; I dinna want anyone but ye. And what a time to choose, when I have no' long to be with ye at the best of it." He crossed the room, taking me in his arms, and this time I returned his embrace. And when he kissed me I raised my hand to his jaw and erased Morag's touch.

His kiss was desperate and bittersweet, his anger still palpable. But his arms were strong around me and for just a moment I pretended that we were not here, that the ugly scene with Morag had not just happened. "Mary," he breathed, then bent to kiss my neck and I arched back to receive his touch. "Do ye love me, Mary Rose?" he asked hoarsely. "Even now, lass, do ye love me?"

"Yes," I gasped as he kissed me again, this time more insistently, backing me against the wall and searching my mouth with his until I couldn't breathe. "Oh, yes, Alex! Yes and yes and yes!" I wrapped my arms around his neck and pulled him tighter against me, feeling his body's readiness for mine.

"Then love me now, Mary Rose," he said, leaning back to look into my eyes. "Love me now."

I felt my cheeks color. "Here? Now?"

"Here. Now." He traced a line of kisses from my temple to my shoulder. "Now, lass, for perhaps the last time."

"But, Alex, there are men just outside this door. They could hear us. Or someone could come in. . . ."

"Then let them, lass. We're doing naught wrong. I'm making love to my wife. Let them listen and envy me."

I shook my head, then smiled as Alex leapt away from me to pull the table, which had been in the corner, to block the door.

"Now, lass, they canna interrupt without us kenning beforehand." He stroked my cheek and gave me a hopeful look. "Mary, love me. Come, lass, let's have one more memory."

"Alex . . ." I began, but he stopped my protests with his mouth as his hands roamed over my clothes, loosening laces and undoing sashes.

" 'Had we world enough, and time,' " he said quietly as he pulled my bodice from my shoulders and bent to unfasten the waist of my skirt. " 'This coyness, lady, were no crime.' "

I laughed a throaty laugh and stepped back as he spread my cloak to the floor and, a moment later, laid his now-discarded kilt atop it. He reached for me again, clad now only in his shirt, and slowly undid the lacings of my shift. "Alex," I said, and pulled his mouth to mine. "I love you."

"Aye," he said, "and I ye, Mary Rose." He put a hand on each of my arms and leaned to kiss my forehead. " 'An hundred years should go to praise thine eyes, and on thy forehead gaze.' " He slowly pulled the shift free from my body and I stood before him naked and smiling. " 'Two hundred to adore each breast,' " he quoted, and kissed each breast in turn, then ran his hands lower. " 'But thirty thousand to the rest.' " I inhaled sharply as his hands found their target and began to caress me. " 'An age at least to every part, and the last age should show your heart.' "

It was his turn to gasp as I reached for him and ran my fingers along his length, teasing and drawing him closer. We sank to the floor, still caught in our embrace, and kissed as he gently laid me back on our makeshift bed, then hovered over me, his eyes dark and his lips finding mine again.

" 'For, lady, you deserve this state, nor would I love at lower rate.' " He smiled as I readied myself and reached for him. " 'But at my back I always hear Time's winged chariot hurrying near,' " he said, and sank into me.

"I love you, Alex," I said, holding him to me with a desperate grip. "You're mine. Mine. I love you."

"And I ye, Mary Rose. Only ye. And ye forever."

We did not speak for a while.

Afterward, he helped me dress and laughed as I fumbled with my clothes, unable to do the simplest fastening. And then I watched him shrug his shirt on and calmly sling his kilt about his waist, both of us pretending not to hear the men outside the door. He took a deep breath and met my eyes as the door was tried and bumped against the table. Alex reached to pull the table away, then faced the soldiers who entered.

"Kilgannon!" one shouted, reaching for him with a drawn sword.

Alex took a step backward, pulling me with him in the circle of his arm, then leaning to retrieve my cloak. "I'll be right wi' ye, sirs," he said calmly.

But they didn't listen, taking Alex's arms from me and yanking him toward the door. They ignored his protests and mine as they dragged him away.

"Mary Rose!" he cried as he went through the door. "I love ye, lass. Only ye, Mary. Only ye."

"Alex," I sobbed. "Alex. I love you. Forever, Alex."

"And I ye, Mary." And then he was gone.

It was not until later that I realized I'd not told him about the baby.

We were a quiet group at our evening meal, the boys displeased that they'd not been allowed to see Alex and I lost in my own thoughts. Even Robert's aunt was quiet, her incessant chatter stilled for once. Angus had left with a promise to return the next day, and I went to bed when the boys did.

The morning dawned gray and cold, yet again, and I sat before the fire and thought as I waited for Angus, thinking about my visit to Alex. His face, when he'd been torn from me, haunted me. As did the pitiful sobbing of Morag. I closed my eyes. What a morass.

I opened my eyes as the maid announced Angus. He was gray-faced and somber and filled the room with his mood. After our greetings were exchanged he sat heavily on the chair opposite me and stared into the fire. "What is it, Angus?" I asked at last.

His blue eyes met mine with reluctance. "I've heard rumors, lass." He frowned and rose to pace before me.

"What do the rumors say?" He paused before the window and stood staring out at the house next door while I waited, my heart beginning a slow thumping. I put a hand to my throat to still it. "Tell me, Angus," I said, my voice deceptively calm.

He turned to me with another frown. "I'm hearing some of the prisoners are to be sent to England for trial." I sat back against the chair, his words a blow. "Alex doesna ken this."

"They were promised trial here."

"Aye. I ken that. They ken that. All of Scotland kens that. But what good does it do if the English decide differently?"

"Angus, this cannot be! He would be tried fairly here."

He snorted. "I dinna think fairness is their chief concern."

"But to be tried in London! This is terrible, Angus! London courts are controlled by the Whigs. You know what will happen!"

"Aye, lass, I ken what will happen. And Alex will ken as well when he hears." He stared at his hands, then looked up at me. "There is a faction that is arguing for clemency, even amnesty. Many think the reprisals have been too harsh. Robert has been one of them, one of the loudest."

I felt my eyes widen in surprise and answered his unasked question. "Robert is a good man, Angus." I sighed and studied my hands. "I always knew he was a good man." I looked up at Angus. "But he is not Alex, and for me no one else exists."

Angus mulled over my answer, then nodded. "Aye."

"We must free Alex now, Angus. You must finish the

planning and act. And if you need me to be gone so I don't hamper you, I will be. Say the word and I'll be away. But you must get Alex out of Edinburgh. Now."

He met my eyes. "I canna be sure we can get him out, but I will try, Mary. Ye can be assured of that. I will do everything in my power to free him. Or die trying."

"What do you have planned?"

"I'll no' tell ye, lass, and then ye can tell the truth if asked. I want ye to stay here for the now and I'll come myself or get word to ye if I need ye to do aught."

"How can I reach you if I need you?"

He shook his head. "Ye canna. If ye have news or an emergency, put a plaid out a front window. One of us will see it and get to ye." He stood then and leaned to kiss my forehead. "Dinna fret, Mary. It's no' over yet, lass. While Alex lives there's hope, and we are no' without our resources, ye ken."

I nodded, thinking how very powerless we were.

"There's another thing, Mary," he said. "We must be careful no' to involve Robert. He has been most kind to ye and it would be a sad way to repay the man for his generosity by casting doubt on his loyalty. We must be careful of him as well as ye. Do ye agree with my thinking?"

"Yes, of course, Angus. Robert must not come to harm because of me. It would be a dreadful way to repay his kindness."

Angus stayed for a few moments more and then left with promises to stay in touch when he could. After he left I sat with my hands in my lap for a moment, thinking. Alex would go to London for his trial. God help us. I looked up when the door opened again, thinking Angus had something else to say. But it was not Angus who entered. It was Robert.

I greeted him cautiously, wondering if he had passed
Angus on the stairs. He must not have seen Angus, I
decided, for he seemed very calm. Robert seated himself, his hands loosely in his lap, and when the serving
girl arrived behind him with tea we wordlessly watched
her set up the table between us. This was the first time
we'd been alone together since our arrival in Edinburgh, and I wondered what he had to tell me. After
the girl left, Robert poured a cup of tea and handed it to
me, his eyes at last meeting mine.

"No harm could ever come to me as a result of you,
Mary," he said quietly. "But I thank you and Angus for
your consideration." My heart stopped and I paused,
my hand halfway to the cup, as I stared at him. "I heard
Angus's last remarks and your answer," he said. "I am
pleased that you are both grateful to me and that you
are considering my safety. But I am not a fool. I know
you are in Edinburgh because Alex is here. I know Angus has visited him, and I've heard all about your visit
yesterday and how upset Morag Maclean was. The castle is buzzing with the topic. It has, for once, replaced
you and me as the topic of choice." He sipped his tea
and looked at me over the rim, then carefully put the
cup and saucer down and wiped his hands on a napkin.
"I have seen Alex myself. I saw him this morning." I
looked at him openmouthed as he continued in that
mild tone. "It is now definite that Alex will be taken to
England for trial. That is what Angus came to tell you,
is that correct?"

My voice was a whisper. "Yes."

"I told Alex the news. Those imprisoned in the castle
will be taken to England. Those at the outpost will be
allowed to return home with no further punishment. It

was the best we could do. The soldiers who were at the outpost will be moving back to the castle to guard the prisoners, and there will be no further visitors allowed. This will be common knowledge by morning, so I expect Angus will know soon. If you like, I will send a runner to his lodgings to tell him."

"I do not know where he is staying."

"But I do." I searched his face, my thoughts turbulent, but his expression told me nothing. *Who is this man?* I wondered. If his desire was for revenge, it was now thoroughly within his grasp. If he did not know for certain what Angus had planned, he suspected it. Of course, only a fool would not suspect that those imprisoned would not attempt to escape and that their men would not aid them. Why had Alex not disappeared when he had the chance? Why had he not gone with the MacDonald? Why was he not safe in France? And what would Robert do now with the knowledge he had? Or what had he already done? I took a deep breath and willed myself to be calm.

"How do you know these things, Robert?"

"I am a soldier, Mary. I am an officer and an English peer. I have access to information that Angus can only guess at. Do not look at me so wildly. Calm yourself. I will not endanger Alex further. But Angus must be warned that he is watched and that the Ramsays have been . . . prevented . . . from arriving in Edinburgh with a company of men. Angus must be told that any attempt to free Alex will meet with disaster and more danger for Alex. Or for Angus. Or Matthew. Or for you, and I will not allow that."

"Danger from you?" I cried. "You would harm them, Robert?"

The hurt flashed in his eyes and was gone. "No," he said quietly and looked at his hands. "No, Mary, I would not harm them." He paused. "I am here now to tell you what is known at the castle about their movements. They have been betrayed by their own. I believe it was Morag, but I don't know that for certain, nor do I care. If it was her, she has taken quite a revenge on you all. I am here to tell you what I know."

"Robert, why do you do this? Why warn us? I don't understand."

"Why do I do this?" His mouth twisted and he looked away. "Why do I do this? I cannot tell myself why, Mary. But I do. You must let Alex go, Mary. And tell Angus not to interfere or it will not go well with him." He turned to the fire while I watched him and thought furiously. The baby moved within me and I placed my hand on my middle just as Robert turned back to me. He glanced at my hand and then away again. "My aunt told me about the child," Robert continued, his tone harsh. "Alex's child. I didn't know, didn't even guess. I should hate you both. But I don't. I don't even hate Alex. I went to see him because . . ." He stared at the floor before looking up at me, then spread his hands in a futile gesture and rose, pacing in front of the fireplace, his movements agitated. ". . . because I am somehow bound to you both now, and as absurd as it is, I wanted him to hear about going to England from someone who would tell him . . . in a civilized manner. Does that make sense?" He shook his head savagely. "No, it makes no sense. Not to me either. And I went to tell him that I . . . that you . . . would always be cared for while I lived." He fingered a candlestick on the mantel. "And he was grateful, Mary." *Grateful,* I thought. *Alex was grateful.*

"Robert," I said, "you have no reason to hate either of us. Neither Alex nor I has ever done anything to you." When Robert raised his eyebrows as if to dispute me, I threw away all attempts to calm myself. "I appreciate your kindness and your generosity and I am grateful for the restraint you show in not acting upon your knowledge, but I will not accept that Alex or I have ever intentionally harmed you."

He stared at me. "No," he said hoarsely. "You are correct, it was not intentional. But you do not know what I . . . you do not know what it feels like to have something precious taken from you."

I laughed harshly, my voice unrecognizable. "No? I suspect I know far better than you ever will what it feels like. I have lost my husband, perhaps forever. I have lost my home. I have already lost both of my parents and now I do not even have a country. Do not speak to me of loss. If you have suffered, it is only because you did not act in time. I was available for years and you did nothing. You chose your fate."

We glared at each other for a long moment, and then, to my surprise, he laughed, a genuine laugh. "Mary," he said, smiling ruefully, "you do amaze me. Only you would find a way to be angry because I love you. Do not look at me so. You are perfectly correct. Please accept my apology." He bowed to me and smiled again and my anger ebbed away as quickly as it had come, leaving me exhausted. I blinked and shook my head.

"Robert," I said, but could not say more.

"Do you forgive me?" he asked.

My eyes filled and I nodded, very close to hysteria.

"I imagine you would like to know how Alex took the news."

"Yes," I said.

"Alex was not surprised." Robert spoke quite calmly now. "No doubt he suspected it long ago. He is grateful to me for bringing you here. I told him that even now I am unable to get you to England, especially in your condition. Which he did not know." Robert gave me an appraising glance. "I told him about the child."

My head snapped up at that. Robert had told Alex that I was with child? This was too absurd. I stood suddenly and started to speak, but the room swam before me and I felt Robert catch me as I fainted.

TEN

I WAS ON THE COUCH WHEN I WOKE, ROBERT HOVERING over me. His face showed his relief when I opened my eyes. "Mary," he said, his voice hoarse. "I'm so sorry. I should not have told you like that. Forgive me, please."

"Of course," I said hoarsely, and he stepped back from the couch and studied me while I straightened my clothing and tried to straighten my mind as well.

"I have sent for Angus," Robert said.

I sat up and looked at him in surprise. "You would do that?"

"I have done that. But I have one condition: that you do not, nor do you allow Angus . . . An attempt to free Alex or the others is suspected and planned for. It will fail. And then . . . Mary, you know you'll be suspected. Troops will come to this house. I cannot always be here to protect you. I have come here today because you might be in danger."

I tried to keep my voice level. "A threat, Robert?"

"A warning."

"What could I be planning?"

He made a sharp gesture, his anger apparent. "Do not play with me," he growled. "You would give your right arm to free him."

"I'd give my life to free him but I do not have the means."

"Do not attempt it, Mary."

Robert's aunt and the boys burst into the room then. Mrs. Campbell fussed over me and made me recline again while the boys ducked under her arms into mine. She clucked at them but I held them even closer, finding comfort in their embraces.

"Lord Campbell said we were to come to ye, Mama," Ian said worriedly, perching himself next to me. "He said ye needed us."

"I always need you, my love," I said, clutching him to me. "Both of you." I soothed them and met Robert's eyes over their heads.

"You've had a spell, Lady Kilgannon," Robert's aunt said, waving Robert away from the couch. "You are doing too much. You should be in bed, lass. Come now."

I protested and we had a short discussion, but I was firm that I would stay where I was, which annoyed her thoroughly. She withdrew and, with a toss of her hand, said she'd go and spend her energies on those who appreciated them. *I've lost her as an ally,* I thought, amused. My diversion was short-lived, however, for when she left, the maid announced Angus, and our wretched situation became very real again.

Angus, his face white with worry, stepped into the room, looking from me to Robert and then back to me. "Mary, lass, what's wrong?"

"I'm fine, Angus—" I said, but Robert interrupted me.

"A word with you, MacGannon," he said brusquely, taking Angus's arm and leading him into the hallway, closing the door behind them. The boys turned to give me a confused look.

When the door opened again, only Angus walked in. "Mary," he said, "I have agreed to Robert's condition." He waved aside my protests. "Two days," he cried, his voice raw. "He leaves in two days, lass. I canna hope to do anything with only a handful of men. I needed just a little more time, just a few more days. Damn Morag. Damn her. Now the Ramsays are held and I'm no' sure of the Macleans. I dinna ken where Duncan is and I'm leery of using the same methods we used before. Morag kent everything about our plans. Damn her. And the *Mary Rose* has no' returned." He ran his hand wearily over his forehead. "*Mo Dia,* I have failed." He shrugged off my attempts to comfort him and patted the boys absently, ignoring their questions. "I must go now, lass. I must warn Matthew. And move our lodgings. And find Duncan. And try to warn the others on the *Mary Rose*. Stay here, Mary," he said as he left us, his voice thick with emotion. "I'll come to ye tomorrow. Do nothing until then." We stared after him as the door slammed.

The boys had a thousand questions for me then, and I had to judge what was best to tell them. In the end I told them an amended version of the truth and they bore the burden with me.

The day dragged on, but finally passed. I could not sleep that night and passed the time by packing all of our belongings. I would stay in this house no longer than necessary. When Angus came to me I'd be ready to go. I didn't know where, but I had some money now and at worst we'd find an inn somewhere.

The next day was the longest day I'd known. No news came, no Angus, no Robert. I thought of every possibility but I knew nothing for certain. By evening I could not sit still and I paced the rooms, the boys haunting my footsteps. Where was Angus? And what had Morag done? Obviously she'd been aware of the plans afoot. If this was her revenge on Alex, it was hurting many more people.

Well after our evening meal one of the Campbells brought me a letter from Robert. He wrote that Alex and the other prisoners would be taken to ships bound for England the following afternoon. If I wanted to see Alex pass as he was marched with the others down to Leith, Robert would arrange a spot for us. There was to be no misunderstanding of his offer; his condition still applied. I told the messenger that I would accept Robert's offer and asked him to thank Robert for me. And then I told the boys that Alex was leaving the next day.

Morning came at last and the boys looked at me with huge eyes, silent for once. They dressed quickly, with none of their usual bantering. And then we waited. Breakfast was a quiet meal. Even Robert's aunt was subdued and I wondered what she had been told. I sat in a chair and watched the clouds gather in the sky, big gray clouds, full of threats, but no rain yet. I read to the boys but kept missing words and drifting off into my own thoughts and they did not correct me. Luncheon was impossible to eat. I sat watching the boys and watching Robert's aunt watch them. And then, at last, Robert was at the door with his Campbells, looking as though he'd not slept since I'd seen him.

"Alex leaves in an hour," he said without preamble. "Come with me now. All of you. Let's go."

I sprang from my chair. "Robert, where is Angus?"

He shook his head. "I don't know where he is," he said flatly.

"Oh, my dear God, Robert! What has happened? Something has happened to prevent him from coming to me. Do you know anything?"

"I don't know where Angus is."

"I don't know what to do! What will I do now?"

He looked at me gravely, then gestured to the door. "You'll come with me, Mary. We'll find Angus later."

I took a deep breath and tried to be calm. And then I nodded.

We followed Robert downstairs and through the streets toward the castle, his Campbells at his heels. The boys had asked no more questions. They knew their father was leaving again and that we were powerless to prevent it and that was all that mattered. At last we reached a spot close to the entrance to the castle itself. I was surprised to see how many others waited in the weak sunlight. It was a quiet crowd, its numbers steadily increasing as we waited. At least it did not have the air of a celebration, which I had feared. Those who had jeered at the Jacobites in the past were silent today, or they were elsewhere. I stood quiet, with my thoughts screaming in my head. Where was Angus? Had he been successful? But no, if Alex were free now, Robert would not have brought me here. *Dear God,* I prayed, *keep them safe. All of them.*

I do not know how long we waited, but I was very weary when we heard the drums from within the walls. The big doors swung open and a troop of soldiers, four abreast, marched forward. And then more. And more. They lined the narrow pathway above us, stationing

themselves every few feet, weapons at the ready. The
crowd stirred but was peaceful. The first prisoners were
led out, filthy men, chained at wrist and ankle, their hair
and beards unkempt, plaids and shirts tattered. These
were the men who had stayed behind when the leaders
of the rebellion ran to safety, and these the men who
would pay the price of their decision. That they knew
this well could be seen in their faces, their expressions
still defiant. I searched for Alex, as the people around
me erupted in shouts and calls and sobs, but he was not
there. The soldiers held the crowd back without violence and the group shuffled past us, their chains clink-
ing. Somewhere down the street I heard the drone of
bagpipes and near me a woman was keening.

There was a pause and I feared that no more prisoners were to come by us, but another group appeared
soon, Murdoch among them. He did not see us at first
but I waved and called and at last he looked our way.
His grin was wide as he shouted greetings to us and
pointed behind him, then waved as he was quickly
pushed past. *Godspeed, Murdoch,* I said silently, *may
God protect you, dear friend.* And I refused to think of
Morag and the havoc she had wrought.

A third group passed us but still no Alex. Around us
many had seen their loved ones, and shouts between
the prisoners and watchers filled the air. I craned my
neck to see over the soldiers in front of me and jumped
when I felt a hand on my shoulder. I turned to find an
ashen Angus behind me. Over his shoulder I saw a soldier talking quietly to Robert, gesturing to Angus.

"We have failed, Mary," Angus whispered into my
ear, his voice raw. "We were arrested in the night after I
left ye. They took Matthew away. And Gilbey. I dinna

ken where they have been taken. Two of Jamie Ramsay's brothers are dead and I dinna ken where the Macleans are. The *Mary Rose* was seized as she arrived this morning and the men on it are held."

I stared at him openmouthed as his words took effect. Some part of me had always believed he'd free Alex, and I struggled to let the dream go. "Oh, Angus," I said as the meaning sank in.

"They have my son, Mary," he said. "They have my boy and they're holding him to ensure my good behavior. They say they will release him, and Gilbey as well, if Alex sails on that ship. And kill them if no'. Mary, even if I wished to risk their lives, I have no one to aid me. We've failed. I've failed."

I clung to him, hearing the despair in his voice. It was worse than I'd feared. Somehow I'd always thought the only risk we were taking was in freeing or not freeing Alex. I'd not taken it the next step and thought how much more we had to lose. *Matthew,* I thought. *And Gilbey. Dear God.* "And the others?" I asked.

"I dinna ken. I wasna in a position to ask many questions."

"Oh, Angus. What happened?"

"We were taken two nights ago, after moving to what we thought was a safe place. The soldiers burst in on us in the wee hours. There were just the three of us and we tried, but it was over as soon as it was begun. They held us in some garrison rooms, all separated, and they questioned me. I dinna ken what they did to Matthew or Gilbey. They let me go about two hours ago. That's when I heard of the *Mary Rose*'s seizure. Mary, we are undone."

"We had very little chance of success at best, Angus.

We knew that. It's all right. We'll try another way later."
I leaned back and looked into his face. "We'll find another way. Let's get your boy back. And Gilbey."

"It was Morag, Mary," he growled. "She betrayed us. She told the soldiers where we were and she told them Matthew was my son." He ignored the tears streaming down his face and I wiped them away, ignoring my own. Ian and Jamie wrapped their arms around him and he patted them as he fought his emotions.

"It's all right, Angus. It's all right."

He shook his head angrily. "No, Mary, it's no' aright. It'll never be aright again. If I ever find her . . ."

"Don't, Angus. Don't." I gestured to the boys. "We'll find another way."

He shook his head again tightly and pressed his lips together. I leaned my head against his shoulder and we huddled like that while we waited. I knew I'd convinced neither of us with my brave talk. *Dear God*, I prayed, *keep Matthew and Gilbey safe. And Alex.*

At last I spoke. "Angus, how did you find us?"

"Went to Robert's house. His men told me where ye were. Has Alex gone by yet?"

I shook my head and looked behind me at Robert. "Angus," I asked, "did Robert have you captured?"

Angus shook his head. "No, lass, I dinna think so. He wasna with the soldiers who came, and I dinna see him where I was held. He may have been told, but I canna think he had a part in it. No, it was Morag. For revenge on Alex. For revenge, lass."

I nodded and he turned from me, wiping his eyes, and then pointed to another group of prisoners approaching. But no Alex. And we waited again, this time in silence. I turned to look at Robert and met his eyes, his expression unreadable. He'd known. He perhaps had not directed the arrest, nor even known of it beforehand, but he'd known when he'd come to get me today. He was the first to turn away.

And then Alex was there, standing in the gateway blinking at the light. I held my breath as he paused for a moment and looked at the crowd below him. His hair was loose and floated above his shoulders, his beard a copper slash across his cheeks. His plaid was grimy but his shirt was clean, and his chin went up as he was pushed forward. I could not speak, but I raised my arm. Beside me Angus was shouting, his voice lost in the din. The boys squirmed between us, shouting "Da!" and before I knew what they intended they'd darted out into the pathway, heading for their father. I found my voice then and screamed, straining against the soldier's arm as he held me back, and Alex looked our way as his sons flew to him. The boys evaded the hands that reached for them and threw themselves into Alex's waiting arms. He lifted them to him, enclosing them in the chains and his embrace, and they clung to him. And then he had them point us out. He tried to push his way toward us, but was prevented from reaching us by the soldiers who massed in front of him. He put the boys carefully on the ground, but the soldiers did not harm them, only gently guided the boys back toward us.

"Alex!" I screamed. "Alex, Alex!"

"Mary!" Alex cried, fighting to stand as the other prisoners were forced past him. "I love ye, Mary Rose!" Hands were on my arms, pulling me back, and Alex was pushed into the crowd of prisoners behind him. Angus reached a hand past me and clasped Alex's for a moment before they were torn apart. He shouted at Alex in Gaelic, and Alex answered with the MacGannon war cry. Angus, his face ablaze now, bellowed it back to him as we were shoved against the wall.

Alex disappeared from sight. My arms went around the sobbing boys as they reached me, and Angus met my look with an agonized expression. Behind us Robert watched without visible emotion.

I do not remember much in detail after that. We waited until the rest of the prisoners passed by, and then followed with the crowd as it made its way to the harbor. We spoke little, watching in silence as the prisoners were herded onto the waiting ships. We never saw Alex at the harbor and could only guess which ship he'd been placed on. And then we turned away from the harbor to find a spot to watch the ships sail, and saw Robert, still waiting, with his coach behind him. I could not speak when he gestured to his coach. I shook my head and Angus did not even look at him. Robert followed us at a distance.

Hours later Matthew was released as promised and he found us as we walked east with the others, his eyes anguished and his shoulders sagging. Angus embraced his son without a word, the two of them united in their misery. Matthew said he'd not been mistreated, but his manner told otherwise and I held him to me with fresh heartache. I had no more success in consoling him than I'd had with his father. He said he'd been told Gilbey would be held until the ship sailed with Alex on it.

We stood on the side of a hill above the Firth with a small group of solemn people, the cold seeping into our bones. Behind me a woman sobbed relentlessly and a baby started wailing. The wind whipped the plaid from my head and lashed my hair into my face, but I barely noticed. Angus shifted and Matthew hoisted Jamie onto his shoulders. A man said it was so wintry it did not feel like June, but I thought the bitter wind appropriate. Our leave-taking at Kilgannon had been wrenching, but this one filled me with despair. *I might never see him again,* I thought. *He will go hundreds of miles away, without a friend to speak for him, alone in a country filled with those who cry for his blood. And his enemies will try to kill him while I wait in Scotland.*

How quickly our four years had flown by and how foolish we had been not to treasure each moment with each other. Had we known what a short time we would have together, we would have savored every day, every sunset, every night in each other's arms. *Alex,* I thought, *my love. How can they take you from me and leave me standing on this hill in the closing of the day?*

The ships started to move and one by one headed east toward the sea. My eyes never left them as they made their way down the Firth into the gathering gloom. The five of us were among the few left when the ships approached the headland and turned, and when the last ship disappeared, I sank to the ground and wept.

ELEVEN

THE MORNING AFTER ALEX SAILED HAD DAWNED sunny and warm, as though Edinburgh were at long last celebrating summer. But I paid no attention. Anguish and fear washed over me in alternating waves. I knew the overwhelming sense of loss would never leave me; I wore it like a second skin. Robert had brought us back from watching Alex's ship sail, wordlessly handing me and the boys into his coach. He then climbed in himself, sitting between Angus and Matthew in silence. I had not argued when he'd brought us to his house, but had retreated at once to my room, keeping the boys with me. Matthew slept across our door and Angus elsewhere, but Robert had left at once.

I'd not slept, but spent the night in a chair before the fire, trying to determine how I'd get to England. If Alex was going to London, I'd go there as well. Angus and Matthew left at dawn to see what they could find out about the *Mary Rose*'s seizure. To keep my sanity I kept myself busy. I had determined that I could not spend another moment in Robert's house and hurried the boys into packing, then harried the Campbells into bringing my luggage below. We were ready to leave as soon as Angus and Matthew returned from their visit to the ship. And to the lawyer. I'd reminded Angus, who had forgotten, that the *Mary Rose* was my personal property, not Alex's, bought with my dowry and kept in my name, as Alex had insisted years ago. I wanted Kenneth Ogilvie, Alex's lawyer, to confirm that she could not be seized as Alex's property, and Angus had gone to see him.

But neither Angus nor Matthew returned. Robert did. He arrived in the late afternoon and I was summoned to him at once. When I entered the room, he was standing by the window and turned a grim face to me.

"Mary," he said, "your luggage is downstairs. Are you leaving this house?" I nodded. "Where do you think you can find shelter in this city?" His tone was quiet but I knew he was very angry.

I sighed. "Robert, it is no longer proper for me to stay here."

"Why? Nothing has changed."

"Everything has changed." He turned back to the window. "Robert," I said, pleading. He did not respond and I moved to stand next to him, placing my hand on his arm. He watched me glacially. "Robert, please. I must go," I said softly. "I thank you for all your kindness and your generosity, but I cannot stay here. Surely you can see that. I must go." He was silent and I turned away, tears in my eyes. After a moment Robert turned to me.

"Where will you go?"

I met his eyes. "To London."

"How?"

"I don't know yet," I said, "but I will get there. I'm going to go to the *Mary Rose* now and get her released. And then I'll go to London."

"And then what?" He frowned and held his hands up

in anger. "And then what, Mary? What can you hope to accomplish?"

"I will continue to try to free Alex."

"Unlikely at best."

"Yes."

"You know what will happen. Why would you want to be there to watch it?"

"I no longer know what will happen. I could not have predicted that we'd be where we are now, and I have no idea of what the future will bring." I sighed. "But he's my husband and I love him. I must try." The silence stretched between us. "Robert," I said, "I do thank you. For everything. I am mindful of your sacrifices for me."

"But you are going to London."

"I am going to London."

"As you will, Mary," Robert said, and I heard the hollow echo of Alex's words. *It will be as you wish, Mary,* he'd said so long ago. *It will be as you wish if you go and get it,* I told myself. I thanked him again and he nodded, moving toward the door. "I'll call my carriage," he said. "Come."

I collected the boys while Robert waited, and then we followed him down the stairs, the boys and dogs making a terrible din behind us, William Wallace nearly knocking Robert over in his excitement. At the street Robert ushered us into the carriage and stood at the door. Robert the Bruce rose to nuzzle him, and Robert gave him an affectionate pat. His eyes met mine and I shrank from what I still saw in them. I extended my hand.

"Thank you, Robert," I said, "with all my heart, thank you, for your generosity and your kindness."

He took my hand in both of his. "You are welcome, Mary," he said, each word weighted, "you are welcome. With all my heart." We stared at each other for a moment, then he glanced behind him. "My men will take you to your ship." I thanked him again. He lowered his voice. "Mary, a long time ago I told you that if you ever needed me, I would be there. I have tried to be. But now I am considering my pledge fulfilled. I wish you well."

My eyes filled with tears and his expression softened as he saw them. I withdrew my hand. "Take care of yourself," I said.

Robert stepped back. "Godspeed, Mary," he said as the carriage lurched away. "Safe journey."

The *Mary Rose* was docked and guarded by armed soldiers, but we were not prevented from approaching her. Matthew stood by himself on the wharf while the men of Kilgannon hung over the ship's rails above him. As the carriage drew to a halt and the boys burst out, followed by the dogs, a cheer rose from the clansmen. And when I emerged the roar that greeted me was overwhelming. I smiled up into their faces, surprised by their welcome, and saw Gilbey just above me, Thomas and Dougall at his side, and many others, including Calum MacGannon, the *Mary Rose*'s captain. *Thank God,* I thought, *Gilbey is safe. They are all safe.* My vision blurred, but I smiled again and waved to them, calling my greetings while the soldiers watched us warily.

"Where is your father?" I asked Matthew. His expression was worried as he pointed to the small building on the dock.

"The English willna release the ship even with the lawyer."

"We'll see about that," I said and raised my chin.

It had been easier than I'd thought. I had walked into the building boldly and in my most imperious manner told the assembled men staring at me in astonishment that I was the Countess of Kilgannon come to claim my dowry. I said I wanted to go back to England and was claiming the *Mary Rose* as my personal property and had waved my receipts at them as though that would solve everything. The soldiers had scrambled to find me a chair while Angus crossed his arms over his chest and watched me from under bushy eyebrows, then introduced me to Kenneth Ogilvie, who I'd heard of for years, but never met. Alex's lawyer, a quiet man of medium height with sparse dark hair and startling blue eyes, had watched me with open amusement. When the English army officer argued that the ship belonged to Alex and had been forfeited, I waved his words away.

"Check with the shipwrights. My solicitor has already told you the same. She is my ship. It was my money that bought her, not my husband's, and it is my name that she carries. I am going on board now and then I am going home to England." I looked from the blazing face of the officer before me to his captain, who watched me cautiously. "Sir," I said to the captain, my voice full of the tears that were never far away, "I am an English citizen and the *Mary Rose* is my property, the only property I have left. I want to go home. Have I not suffered enough in Scotland?" Tears filled my eyes and spilled down my cheeks, but I ignored them as I continued. "The ship is mine, sir, and I want to go home." I wiped my cheek. I was not lying. I did want to go on board the *Mary Rose* and more than anything I wanted to go to England.

The captain's expression softened and he nodded slowly. "You may go aboard, madam, with your sons, but I'll have to have orders from the castle before I can release the ship."

"Thank you, sir. I will wait on board for your news."

The captain bowed. I turned from him and tried not to trip over the jumble of boys and dogs before me. I did not look back as I left the building, and when I came to the gangplank the soldiers there moved aside. I went on board the *Mary Rose,* followed by the boys and Angus and Matthew and Kenneth Ogilvie, and was greeted with a roar of approval by the clansmen.

Angus was not so pleased. He shook his head and frowned. "Well, lass, ye got us on board, for whatever good it will do. What have ye accomplished? We'll all be prisoners here the now."

I met his gaze evenly. "What do you think I've been at Robert's? At least here, prisoners or not, we are all together and that's a far sight better than where I've been. And we're going to London." I ignored Angus's raised eyebrows and turned to greet the men.

My luggage was brought on board eventually, amidst much amusement at the number of pieces. I ignored all the jibes and settled us into the big cabin. And at last found a quiet moment. *London,* I thought. *We will go to London.* I knew that we were not yet free to go, but legally the ship was clearly mine and Kenneth had told me it was within my rights to demand return of my property. I wanted more, though, and that could be difficult. I wanted all the Kilgannon men to be allowed to leave with me. Ogilvie warned me that here I was on shaky ground. These were the same men who had taken arms against England, and while they would not be imprisoned now, I could hardly expect beneficence from the English army while I was in their company.

London, I thought again. There, at least, we would have allies. Or would we? What would our reception be? I'd not heard from Louisa or Will since I wrote that Alex had joined the rebellion. Would they welcome us or would I be an unwanted burden? Had I embarrassed them, or worse, made their political situation more difficult? Would they be aghast at Alex's joining the rebellion? Would they despise him now? No matter, I told myself. If my family could not, or would not, aid us, I would at least be near Alex, and if I had no allies but the boys and the MacGannons, I would be content. I opened another trunk and for the moment ignored what lay ahead.

Whether Mr. Ogilvie was successful or money had been exchanged I never discovered, but we were not challenged further. Nor, however, were we allowed to leave. The ships blocking our path were manned and the sailors on them firm in their orders. The mood on board was quiet, but I often heard smidgens of plots to free us, hastily interrupted as I appeared, and I knew it would not be long before the rebellious attitudes turned into action, if for no other reason than that we were almost out of food. And then Kenneth Ogilvie, who had been visiting daily, brought unwelcome news. Jamie Ramsay had been hanged after a perfunctory trial. The men muttered amongst themselves, any pretense at calm gone.

On the morning of our third day on board, Ian and

Jamie burst into my cabin and, with excited grins, insisted that I go on deck. They grabbed my hands and I followed them, thinking that we must have received permission to leave. In the sunshine I blinked and let my eyes adjust. To my left a man in dark clothes moved quickly toward me and I turned to him, my hand at my throat.

"This is a fine welcome after we've combed all of Scotland for you, Mary! I expected a warmer welcome for the world's most wonderful brother!"

"Will!" I threw my arms around him with a sob. And eventually saw my uncles over his shoulder. "Randolph! And Uncle Harry!"

We settled into the cabin with tea and whisky, and Angus, Matthew, and I heard their story. My brother and uncles had indeed been all over Scotland looking for me. After the word of the rebellion reached London, they had been terribly worried about us. Both Louisa and Will had written, but of course I never received those letters. When Will and Randolph decided to go to Kilgannon themselves, no one would bring them by boat, and when the news of Sherrifmuir came they knew it was foolish to go overland. They got my letter telling them not to come for Christmas. And then silence. They wrote again and waited for news and when they heard that James Stewart had left Scotland and that many of the rebels had gone with him, they prayed that we had joined him.

In March, Will went to France. He found the Jacobite court and the MacDonald, who told him that Alex and I had refused to accompany them. Will returned to England then, and he and Randolph went to see my father's brother Harry, who had inherited my grandfather's title and estates at Grafton. Harry told them three things: that Will and Betty must come to live at Harry's estate at Grafton to learn to manage it for the day when Will would inherit from Harry; but that first, Will must find me and bring me to Mountgarden, which was what Will and Randolph wanted to hear; and that Harry would accompany them, which was not.

They told me of sailing to Kilgannon, where they found Dougall and the others defending the Mac-Gannon lands. "You don't have to worry about anyone taking over your home without a struggle, Mary," Will said, laughing. "There are not many of them, but they are very fierce. When we sailed into the loch they blocked our passage until we were recognized. We were given a warm welcome, but our English crew was asked to leave at once. They had to wait for us at sea, not even in the outer loch. Harry was most impressed."

I smiled, trying to ignore the pangs of homesickness. It was my turn then and I told them of all that had happened to us and of the child I carried. Randolph and Will exclaimed over my news and insisted that I lie down at once. I laughed at them and told them I was fine, while Uncle Harry watched me with a worried expression. And then Harry drew Randolph and Angus into a discussion of our best course of action while Matthew hovered near his father, and Will and I had a moment alone.

Giving me that special Will smile, he spoke quietly. "We're with you, Mary. You know that."

"Oh, Will, thank you," I said blearily. Then I glanced at the others still talking across the cabin and said, in a lower voice, "What does the family think of Alex now? Do they think he's terrible?"

Will's dark eyes were serious. "Louisa was furious

and ranted for days about Alex endangering you. Randolph was not pleased, but he, well, he's Randolph, so he thought about it for a week and then decided that he could understand Alex's position, especially after I went to France and brought home those stories. And Betty," he laughed, "doesn't have an opinion. We ordered three new dresses before I left, so she's quite content." He shrugged. "No one can be surprised. It's been brewing for at least eight years. Thirty years, to tell the truth. I don't know what your welcome will be in society, and you must be prepared for that, but in our family you are welcome. As always. All of you."

I took a deep breath and gave him a shaky smile. "Thank you, Will," I said. "I didn't know what to expect."

Will watched me appraisingly. "Mary, did you think we'd abandon you?"

I shook my head. "No, but I do know I may be putting careers and fortunes at risk by asking for your aid."

"The hell with that," Will growled. "We don't give a fig what society thinks, and they cannot touch our lands, so our fortunes are secure. Don't worry about any of that." My brother frowned. "But you must understand that Alex is considered a traitor," he continued. "No one is likely to forget that. Does Alex understand his situation?"

"Yes, Will, and so do I. We have no illusions."

"You should not. None of you. No one is fond of King George, least of all we Tories, and some people, at least in private, will admit that the Scots have been treated abysmally. Among those, you understand, who admit that Scots are human. But, Mary, it *is* treason." I nodded and Will frowned again, looking at his hands.

"You do know what can happen to Alex?" He glanced up at me.

"Yes. I have known from the first, but now that Alex is to be tried in London it is much more serious than before."

"You believe he would have been freed if he was tried here?"

"It was more likely. There is still much sympathy for the rebellion here, even among those who did not join, especially since the reprisals have been harsh and Argyll has been replaced. Even among the Campbells there are those who sympathized."

"Was Robert one who sympathized?"

"He was distraught. It must be very difficult to see your country at war with itself and being ravaged."

Will leaned forward. "Mary, what of you and Robert?"

I frowned at my brother. "There is no me and Robert, Will. He has been a kind friend, that is all. No one should think anything else." I met his eyes and after a moment he nodded.

"But they will, Mary. Like it or not, they will."

"I know that. But it doesn't matter. None of that matters."

Will picked up his glass of whisky and looked at me over the rim in a gesture that reminded me of Alex. *Alex,* I thought, *where are you?* Across the cabin the men rose as one, moving toward us.

"Well, young lady!" boomed Randolph. "We are going to London." I looked up at him and then at Uncle Harry, who stood at his side. "Angus has told us all of the nonsense about keeping you and the ship here, and Harry's about to remedy that."

"Do you think you can?" I asked my uncles.

Harry laughed. "What good is it being a duke if one cannot have one's way? We will see it done, Mary. I will send for you if I need to, so be ready to weep and appear pale." He studied me for a moment. "You won't have to feign being pale, dear. Just weep."

I nodded. "Thank you. Thank you both for all your efforts."

"Nonsense," Harry said briskly. "We'll be back soon. You can thank us then for our success." He left with the men and I waited.

In the end our departure from Edinburgh was uncomplicated. Uncle Harry proved immediately successful. The military, it seemed, had far more respect for an English duke than for a former Scottish countess, and the impediments to our leaving melted away. I smiled as Harry told the story, and even Angus laughed, for Harry mocked the Lowlanders and their accents. He had apparently asked for someone who could speak English, to the chagrin of the Scottish army captain who thought he did. Back on the *Mary Rose*, Gilbey explained to Harry that Highlanders learned English as a distinct language from Gaelic and spoke it with much less accent than the Lowlanders, who had changed the pronunciation of English words and added their own to the language over the years until it was a separate way of speech.

"Well," said Uncle Harry, surveying the listening Kilgannon men on deck, "give me a Highlander any day. He is someone I can understand. Now let's get out of here." The men cheered him.

We left with the tide, the *Mary Rose* silently gliding out of Leith as Captain Colum took us to London. And to what? I wondered, watching the Firth fall away as we entered the open ocean. The men had made it clear that they were ready to go to London and storm the Tower if need be. I was grateful for their loyalty, and if in truth I thought they'd have had any success, I would have cheered them on or led them myself. I knew that it was hopeless to try to free Alex by force and foolish to encourage these men to go to London and die trying. But, oh, how I wanted to try.

Alex, I thought, *we're coming.*

PART TWO

Western wind, when wilt thou blow?
The small rain down can rain.
Christ, that my love were in my arms
And I in my bed again!

"WESTERN WIND" ANONYMOUS, SIXTEENTH CENTURY

TWELVE

LONDON. THE LAST TIME I'D SAILED INTO THE Thames, Alex had been with me, and we'd been burdened with our worries of having children and the loss of the *Diana*. Two years, almost exactly. How long ago that seemed. Next to me Angus moved restlessly, but I did not turn to him. I needed a moment's quiet. Our trip south had been wet and uncomfortable, but mercifully short. Uncle Harry had been relentlessly cheerful but a great comfort to me. The boys were delighted to be with Randolph again, and the three of them took up where they had stopped at Christmas in 1714, the boys listening to his often improbable adventures for hours, which had helped pass the time.

Now we were nearing London, and the enormity of the task we faced washed over me. I stole a look at the silent Angus at my side, ignoring the rain beginning to fall. We stood together at the rail, but so far apart in opinion. We had argued for most of the journey and had just finished another round. Angus wanted me to go to Mountgarden and had pressed his point. I had refused and he'd asked me scornfully what I would do. I told him I planned to besiege the king and Parliament and any official who would listen.

"It will likely be for naught," he'd said and I'd glared at him, icily asking him what he planned. He'd met my gaze with a cool look of his own. "I mean to bribe and threaten and kill if necessary, lass. If I can, I'll go in the dead of night and spirit him away. And when the morning comes they'll come looking for ye. That's when I would have ye at Mountgarden, guarding my cousin's unborn child and his sons in safety, so that neither Alex nor I have to worry about protecting ye." He'd paused and continued in a calmer tone. "Mary, can ye no' see? Ye have no chance to persuade them to free Alex. Words willna sway them, nor tears. If yer in London I am as hamstrung as I would have been in Edinburgh. Even more so, for I canna tell yer family what I plan, and they will be well-meaning but they'll still be obstacles."

"As I would be," I'd said bitterly.

He'd continued as though I'd not spoken. "Mary, I failed to keep Alex from being captured at Brenmargon. And I stayed my hand when we could have freed him at Kilgannon or on the trip east with Robert Campbell, because Alex asked me not to act, only because he asked me. Then I failed again in Edinburgh. And I will be impeded here if it means ye or the boys would be harmed because of my efforts. Mary, will ye no' get yerself to safety and let us wage this war? Lass, if aught were to happen to ye, or to the babe ye carry, I couldna live with it." His eyes had met mine with sadness and that undid me. I'd burst into tears while Angus patted my shoulder.

"Angus," I said when I'd calmed myself, "at least let me try. Let me try and if I fail, I will retreat and give you the field."

"We may miss an opportunity while yer trying."

"Then don't miss it," I'd said. "Angus, I spent years in London society. I know it well. I know the people in control as you will never know them. Let me try my way."

He'd shaken his head. "Lass, ye ken the people who were in control, but no more. New people are playing the game of London politics. Whigs are in power, not Tories, and ye dinna ken them. Yer weapons will prove ineffective."

"And yours outdated and dangerous, especially for Alex. What if you try and fail? What will they do to him then? And what of the Kilgannon men and your own son? You are a warrior and a good one, yes, but your skills have no place in London. Do not let men I love die attempting the impossible. We were fortunate that you and Matthew and Gilbey were freed in Edinburgh rather than killed. You cannot seriously think to try to free Alex from the Tower without losses." He'd closed his eyes and rubbed his hand through his hair, then gave me an icy blue stare.

"Mary, ye undo me. Ye willna leave me the field to move without endangering ye, and ye insist on trying things that I dinna believe can succeed. What would ye have me do, sit on my hands or perhaps pray for the judge to have a change of heart? We canna take the chance. Ye must let me try my way first. I ken no other."

I had watched him watch me, this dear man who had been so faithful to us, and my anger faded as quickly as it had bloomed. "We're both trying to do the same thing, Angus," I'd said. "We just have different weapons in our arsenals. I cannot use stealth or force, and you cannot use social ties and influence. Why can we not both try? Say the word and I will not see you again.

I will be careful not to even let anyone know that I know you. But I will not leave London without trying. I have my family to protect me."

He'd made a derisive sound. "They dinna ken the first of it."

"It is their town, Angus, not yours. Do not sneer at their power here. You may have contempt for London politics, but those politics will determine Alex's fate. I intend to wage war with all my weapons. There is no one more affected by what happens to Alex than I, and everyone is trying to get me to leave the field. I will not. Let me try! I will fight in every way I can, with or without your help. Do not join the others in banishing me."

We scowled at each other and he was the first to turn away, swinging from me with a weary gesture, then smiling wryly at me over his shoulder. "What will I do with ye, Mary MacGannon?"

I smiled. "Let me have my way and I am most docile."

"No, lass, docile yer no'. Let me think on it and we'll discuss it the more later."

But we did not discuss it later. There was no time. By the time we arrived in London the rain had turned from an annoyance to a furious rainstorm, and Calum needed every hand to help. Eventually we landed at the proper dock and my family and I hurried to a coach. Angus and Matthew had not joined us, saying that they would stay with the brig. When we left, Angus nodded at me but said nothing. We'd not had another moment alone together, and I suspected that he still was not sure what to do with me. As for me, I knew exactly what I would try. Everything. But first I needed a good night's sleep and a dry change of clothing.

The boys' eyes were huge as we rolled through the wet streets. London had intimidated many much older than these two, I thought, and watched Randolph point out sights and calm their fears. I gave him a smile of gratitude and leaned back against the cushions of the coach, remembering London when Alex had been courting me here. When we passed the landscaper's office, I remembered Alex stealing me away for two hours. We'd talked over a meal, then visited Westminster Abbey. The words came unbidden. *"I felt like celebrating,"* he'd said that day, showing me the gold watch he'd bought himself, looking up at me with those amazing eyes. And with his heart in them as well. *Part of us will always be here in London,* I thought, *for this is where we started. And where will we end?*

Louisa welcomed us with smiles and uncharacteristic tears, her embraces fierce. Ian and Jamie clung to her. Over their heads she smiled at me and for the first time in weeks I felt consoled. But the next morning Randolph told me that the *Mary Rose* had left the dock where she had landed and no one seemed to know where she or the crew had gone.

I was immediately swept up in the circle of my family and the unfamiliar demands of Uncle Harry. I soon suspected that one of the reasons he stayed on his estates was that he enjoyed being king of his tiny domain, and here in London, even in Louisa's house, he tried the same techniques. I watched Randolph struggling to be polite, but underneath his annoyance was growing. Even sweet-tempered Will found Uncle Harry tiresome, as I did. But I was grateful to my uncle, for he was proving to be a most able ally. Uncle Harry had an opinion about everything from architecture to shoes. He considered himself well versed in the law, as in most subjects. He wrote long drafts to Kenneth Ogilvie, instructing him to send Scottish laws and precedents. And Harry explained at length to me that English law was based on tiny details, many of which had been the undoing of the prosecution.

"I need to know what has been used before and with what success," he said to me. "Then we may choose to use a specific approach with some confidence in its outcome. Of course, my dear, we do have a monarch and he has undue influence over the courts. As does Parliament. If it is determined that your husband is dangerous to the careers of members of Parliament, he will not have much chance. Our best strategy is to make his release in the best interest of the members of Parliament, and that means money. You will require my aid. I will take lodgings in London immediately."

"Thank you, Harry," I said. "I will repay you. Every cent."

Harry looked at me with annoyance. "No, Mary, you will not. You will accept my assistance without a quarrel. You have only to wait and rest, my dear. Do nothing. You really should go to Mountgarden. Yes"—he nodded to himself—"I'll speak to Louisa."

I shook my head. "No. I want to see Alex."

Harry looked at me blankly, then blinked and nodded again. "Well," he said. "Well. Of course. Of course you do. I should think that could be arranged. But I would rather you withdrew."

"I will not," I said and watched his eyes widen.

"Well. Young lady, you might have to if we deem it necessary. And where have all your Scots gotten themselves to? They certainly made themselves scarce. Can we rely upon them?"

Randolph, who had entered the room with the boys

as Harry had spoken, put an ample hand on my shoulder. "Yes, Harry," Randolph said. "Of course you can. If I know them, and I do, they will not stand idly by while Alex is tried. Mark my words, they have something planned."

Harry looked at Randolph and then at me. "How can we reach them?" he asked. "Where are they lodging?" Randolph shrugged and Harry turned to me. When I said I didn't know how to find them, Harry frowned.

"I know where they are," said Ian. "They are with that woman that Angus knows." We all turned to look at Ian.

"What woman?" I asked.

"Elizabeth," said Ian, looking from me to my uncles.

"And who is Elizabeth?" Harry asked, not unkindly.

Ian frowned. "I don't know. He just calls her Elizabeth. He was talking to Matthew and Gilbey."

"What did he say?" I asked.

"That he was going to visit Elizabeth and pay his respects."

"Oh." I laughed, remembering Angus, in the hall two winters ago, after too much to drink, saying that he would go to London and dance on Queen Elizabeth's coffin. "I shall pay my respects to Elizabeth," he had said. And we'd laughed with him. I looked at my uncles. "Randolph, where is Queen Elizabeth buried?"

"In Westminster Abbey," Randolph said. "Yes, of course. Westminster." He looked at me in puzzlement and I explained. Randolph chuckled but Harry remained pensive.

"So neither of you knows where to find your Scots?"

I bristled. "I know they are here. I just do not know where. But Angus will find me if he has need of me or if he has news. I know these men. They will be loyal to Alex until they die."

"Truly they will," said Randolph. "I've spent much time with them, Harry. They have not disappeared. They are planning."

Harry pondered. "That may not help us. We do not need them rampaging around London. I dislike this loose end." He drummed his fingers on the chair arm. "Well. Well. It cannot be helped. I will set my men to find them. Surely a handful of men so noticeable can be found quickly. I want them found."

"Why do you want them found, Harry?" I asked, trying to keep my tone light. Surely he did not mean to betray them. Surely Harry would not do that. Harry glanced at the boys, then at me.

"If we cannot be successful one way, Mary, we will try another. They would be helpful in the 'another.'" He smiled at my expression as he rose and walked away. "Randolph," he called over his shoulder. "I am taking lodgings nearby. I have trespassed on your hospitality long enough."

Randolph glanced at me with eyebrows raised. "Harry, you are most welcome here," he called as he hurried after Harry. The two of them disappeared down the hall, still arguing. I looked into the boys' puzzled faces.

"How," I said, smoothing Jamie's hair and smiling at Ian, "would you two like to see Westminster Abbey?"

The Abbey was cold and damp on this dreary July day. I showed the boys the Musician's Aisle and the Choir and the Lady Chapel, where Queen Elizabeth and her sister Mary Tudor were buried, and farther on, her cousin Mary Stuart, Queen of Scots. It seemed only weeks ago that I'd stood here with their father on another rainy day. Alex had been merry until we entered the Lady Chapel and he had looked at the queens' tombs thoughtfully. I'd had no idea then what he had been thinking, but now I felt I could guess. His sons looked at the tombs with little interest.

I was quite unprepared for the emotions that overwhelmed me when we reached the poets' alcove. I knew I'd recall my visit here with Alex, but had not expected the memories both of that time and of our last visit in Edinburgh to cascade over me with the force of a tidal wave. I closed my eyes now, as I had then, and heard Alex's voice echo in my mind. " 'Had we but world enough, and time,' " he'd said as he'd recited Andrew Marvell's poem. And set every inch of me aflame with the words and his tone. " 'An hundred years should go to praise thine eyes, and on thy forehead gaze; Two hundred to adore each breast.' " I clasped my hands to my mouth to keep from sobbing, my body responding to the memory of his touch. I opened my eyes, half-expecting to see him, tall and intent, standing before me. " 'But at my back I always hear Time's wingèd chariot hurrying near. . . .'" And the echo died with my fantasy. *Alex, my love,* I thought. *I hear the chariot.*

We did not see Angus, though we tarried much longer than Louisa's coachman wished. At last, defeated, I bundled the boys into the coach and rode home.

A week after our arrival in London, Uncle Harry came to us with the news that he had arranged for me to visit Alex the following day. I don't believe I heard anything else he said. The boys were very disappointed not to be included, but Harry promised that they would see their father soon, and I watched him with narrowed eyes, hoping he was not raising false hopes in them. Harry caught my look and nodded. "I was told they could see him soon. And so they shall, I promise. What's the good of being a duke if one can't have one's way?" I hardly slept that night.

The Tower of London. Not one tower, as I had thought when I was a girl, but a collection of rooms and corridors. They circled the White Tower, built six hundred years ago by William the Conqueror, the Norman who had supplanted the Saxons and brought my ancestors to these shores. And around the inner courtyard another gray stone wall, and another, defending the tower amply from attackers. No, I thought, as I was led through the battlements, Angus could not hope to besiege this fortress with success. I paused at the foot of the courtyard and thought about all those who had spent their last hours here, then followed my guide to a tiny stone room, square and unfurnished, with one heavily leaded, small-paned window that looked as though it had been there for centuries. It probably had, I reflected, moving toward it. Behind me the door closed softly. I was alone. I could barely see through the glass, but I could make out the river below. I was almost directly above Traitor's Gate, I realized, and pushed the thought away with a shake of my head.

I tried to think of the last time Alex and I had had a simple conversation. I could not count the words we had shouted as he was marched to Leigh, nor our fleeting visit at Edinburgh Castle. We had not really spoken since Kilgannon, and I'd been in no frame of mind then to talk of simple things. I could not remember when we had talked without rancor or anguish. I pressed my forehead against the cold glass and closed my eyes. *Perhaps we are fated not to be together,* I thought. *Perhaps I have already had all the happiness I ever will have in my life. Perhaps Alex will die here and I will grow old alone, a widow raising a child who never knew his father.* I smoothed the cloth over my middle and waited.

When the door opened again, Alex was led into the room by two men who did not even glance at me. With rough movements they pulled him to the side of the door and unlocked the chains around his wrists and ankles while he stood without expression, looking at nothing. He was pale but clean-shaven, his hair tied back neatly, his clothes tidy. He wore the kilt I had given Captain Jeffers in Edinburgh and a clean but stained shirt. The men left us, slamming the door behind them without a word, and Alex looked at me at last.

"Mary," he said, his voice hoarse, and I answered the question in his eyes with a sob, all my attempts at self-control lost as he pulled me to him. "Oh, lass, I have longed for ye so." I sobbed into his shirt, calling his name over and over. "I love ye, Mary Rose. I love ye so much it hurts. I love ye, lass."

"And I you, Alex, my love. Forever." I kissed him again and again and cried anew as I saw the raw circles around his wrists where the chains had cut into his skin. He smiled wryly.

"That's what's left from Edinburgh and the trip here, lass. I've no' been mistreated." I could not answer and he wrapped his arms around me again until I grew calm again. "Mary," he said at last, kissing my neck. "Thank ye for coming to see me."

"Oh, Alex, as if I would not."

"Lass, I would no' have ye see me like this."

I deliberately misunderstood him. "You look better than you did in Edinburgh and than you did when you came home to Kilgannon."

"That is no' what I meant."

"Well," I said, trying to keep my tone light, "I would not have you see me like this." I put a hand over my middle and he took a step back from me, appraising me with a long look.

"Yer still the most beautiful woman in the world, Mary Rose, and more so now. Never think that yer not." He kissed my forehead and I tried to smile. "Thank ye for that welcome, lass." He stroked my hair. "Are ye well? And my sons? Are they aright?"

"For the most part. They do not understand what is happening, but they are healthy. And optimistic. And you, my love?"

He shrugged. "I am well. They are decent to me. Perhaps it is better to be considered a serious danger to the Crown as I am here, than to be one more Highlander in Edinburgh. But, lass, ye dinna answer my question. Are ye well, Mary Rose?"

"I am, my love." I smoothed the material of my skirt. "Almost five months. The babe has moved within me." His eyes flickered over me and returned to my face as I continued. "Your child, Alex. Your son." The baby fluttered then more strongly than ever before, and I stepped back from him, putting my hands on my stomach.

Alex's eyes grew wide with fear. "What? What is it, Mary? Is something wrong?" He put a hand next to mine and stared at my middle.

"Your child . . ." I laughed breathlessly as the baby moved again. "I am fine. Did you feel that?"

"Aye. I felt it, lass. I felt it." He bent down and looked anxiously at me. "Is it amiss?"

I laughed and stroked his cheek. "No, Alex, it is a mister."

He blinked, then shook his head. "You will amaze me until the day I die, Mary Rose," he said and turned abruptly away as his words echoed against the stones. We stood in silence and at last he spoke, his voice very controlled. "I pray that I still live when the child is born, Mary. I canna believe ye conceived that one night." I stood frozen, looking at him.

"Alex?" My voice sounded strange to me. Alex turned to me with a puzzled expression. "Do you think that this child is not yours?"

He paled and blinked. "No," he said in a strangled voice as he moved to me. "No, Mary, I'm no' suggesting that. No."

"It is your child."

He met my eyes. "Lass," he said, his voice hoarse with emotion. "I have never doubted ye. Never. I did wonder how ye could still love me, Mary, but I dinna think ye'd go to another man's bed. Not even Robert's. Nor, God help me for believing good of him, did I think he'd ask ye while I live. No, lass, all I'm thinking is how strange it was for ye to conceive that night when we tried so often earlier. And now I willna be there to see this child grow up, or perhaps even born."

"I am trying to be as brave as you, but, Alex, if you doubt me, I cannot go on. I have never been unfaithful. Never."

"Mary." He gripped my arms. "Lass, I never doubted ye. Put it from yer mind. I was only in wonder at the timing. *Mo Dia,* Mary, do ye no' think I ken ye better than that? I asked ye to trust me that there was nothing between Morag and me and ye've asked me to trust ye about Robert. That's what a marriage is, lass, is trust and love." He released his grip and ran his hands up my arms as he shook his head. "No, Mary, I'm just having a hard time being in here. I kent that prison was a possibility, but I dinna ken how it would feel to be here." He smiled. "I've never lost before. 'Tis a harsh lesson. I wake each day thinking it could be my last, and every moment I'm haunted by wondering what ye and the boys are doing and kenning I canna help ye. I must rely on others, including the man who wants to take my place, and every part of me says I should be caring for ye and my sons. But I canna, and to see ye like this, carrying my child all that time without me even kenning . . ." He shook his head. "Well, lass, let's just say it doesna sit well with me." He stroked my hair. "But I love ye truly, Mary MacGannon, and when I'm in my right mind I never doubt that ye love me as well."

I looked up at his face. "And when you're not?"

"Well, lass, then I think on Robert Campbell waiting for my death and I go mad for a bit."

"I will love you forever, Alex. Only you. Only you."

"And I ye." He held me to him fiercely.

"Alex," I said to his chest, "we're trying to get you freed."

"Dinna bother, lass. It's no likely they'll release me. I dinna think the Pope could free me now."

"Alex, we will try to free you." I told him of selling everything from Kilgannon and the sale of the *Katrine*. He listened quietly and nodded, releasing me and pacing the room.

"Ye did well, lass, but I would prefer that now ye use

the money for yer own needs. Ye will have many in the months to come, though it is good that yer family came to rescue ye. I'm glad they're in yer camp. I would no' have ye be alone. Now, tell me, where is Angus? Where are my men?" He listened quietly while I told about my last conversation with Angus, then sighed. "I feared as much. Ye must find him, Mary, and tell him no' to try to free me here by force. It canna be done; I dinna want them to end up in here with me, or dead."

"I will. But, Alex, he says he will die trying to free you."

Anger washed over his face. "Tell him I want no more deaths, and no' Angus's, of all people. If he dies, Mary, then my sacrifice has been for naught. We could have sat down in the snow last winter and let ourselves have a peaceful death. I dinna struggle to return home and then let Robert capture me so that Angus and the men could die trying to free me from here." He waved his hand in an abrupt gesture. "Ye see this place, lass. They have no chance to free me from here by force." He took a deep breath. "But there are other ways to get out, lass, smarter ways, and we need to discover them. I need ye to tell Angus that I've been told I can have a valet. Have him send Gilbey to me as soon as he can. I thought of Matthew, but he doesna look like a manservant, nor Angus, so Gilbey will have to do. Tell him to look servile." Alex laughed. "We'll see what a playactor he is. He'll be our means of communication, lass, and we must have someone we can trust. Ye must find Angus and tell him these are my orders. He mustna try to free me yet. I want other things taken care of in my absence, like Clonmor. Do ye remember it? The property that I gave Malcolm? Well, it's still legally mine. The papers are at Kilgannon. If someone can get there and find them, we can sell it, or at the least get him off my lands. Ask Kenneth Ogilvie, the lawyer. He'll do it." He frowned. "If it's no' included in the forfeiture. I dinna ken. They have no' given me the papers yet, but I have been told I've forfeited."

"Clonmor? Your mother's lands are still yours?"

"Aye, we always meant to deed it over to Malcolm, but we never did." He went to the window and looked out. "We must discover if it's included in the forfeiture. If it is, then it's gone and Malcolm canna have it either, but if it is no', then perhaps the wisest would be to let everything settle and then ye can claim Clonmor after . . . later. If we act on it now without kenning its status, the court will discover the truth and we may claim it only to have it seized. We must discover what the law says. And I need Angus and Kenneth Ogilvie to do that."

"I will try to find Angus."

"Someone will have to go to Kilgannon and get the papers."

"We don't need to, Alex. I emptied your desk, I brought all of your papers with me. Would Clonmor's have been among them?"

"They were in the desk."

"Then I have them at Louisa's."

He grinned at me. "Remind me to marry ye again."

"I will hold you to that," I said and leaned against him. He laughed as my arms went around his waist.

"Mary Rose," he said, "I missed ye so." And bent to kiss me. I closed my eyes and concentrated on his soft lips. He threaded his fingers through my hair and pulled me closer, tilting his head to kiss me more fully while I stroked his back, tracing my fingers down his ribs to his waist, and smiling to myself when I felt his body's response. We were lost in our embrace when the door opened. I put my head on his chest and did not turn as the guard told Alex politely that it was time for me to go. I could hear Alex's heart beating steadily as he thanked the guard, and waited until the door closed. I closed my eyes for a moment and tightened my arms around him, willing time to stop. Alex was calm as he leaned back and looked into my face.

"Ye must tell Angus what I've said and what I need him to do. And tell my sons that I love them. Will ye do that?"

"I will," I said, fighting for calm. He kissed me again, then stepped back, his arms falling to his sides.

"Go now, lass, while I can let ye leave."

I nodded, my tears beginning again. "I love you, Alex."

"And I you, Mary Rose. Until the end of time."

"Until the end of time," I said. At the threshold I turned back for one last look. He stood very still, his face pale against the gray stone. He raised a hand to wave and behind me I heard the clink of chains as his jailers waited to return him to his cell.

The boys were allowed to see him the next week, but I was not. I told Ian to tell his father that I'd not found Angus, despite several visits to Westminster. Alex sent word that he needed a valet as soon as possible. I discussed it with my family and in the end, to my chagrin, my aunt's butler, Bronson, never one of my favorite people, was the one chosen to act the part. And then Harry's requests for visits were denied. We were not given an explanation but we soon discovered why.

THIRTEEN

WE'D KNOWN OF THE MAXWELLS, BUT HAD NEVER met them. William, the fifth Earl of Nithsdale, Jacobite to the bone, had joined the rebellion early on and had traveled south with one branch of the rebel army. He'd been captured at Preston, after the defeat there, summarily tried, and found guilty of treason. Imprisoned in the Tower after being sentenced to death, he had been allowed frequent visits from his wife, Winifred. The night before his execution, the same day I'd seen Alex, Lady Nithsdale had visited her husband one last time. And stood at his door saying her farewells, sobbing and being comforted by her maid. She'd left the Tower at once, still inconsolable, her maid bending over her. It was not until the guards came to take Nithsdale back to his cell that the real maid was discovered huddled in a corner. We heard later that the Maxwells had escaped to Rome.

As a result of their deception, Alex was allowed no visitors but his valet. Bronson, coached in his part by all in Louisa's household and endlessly instructed by Uncle Harry, went to the Tower every day seeking admittance. And on the third day he gained it. He reported that Alex was well, not mistreated, and in good spirits. And that he wanted Gilbey to come at once. Money, Bronson reported, would gain all sorts of special favors, and he'd been able to smuggle some whisky in, for which Alex was very grateful. I watched the self-satisfied butler, knowing I was indebted to him for his efforts, and thanked him as graciously as I could. On my own, I redoubled my efforts to find Angus, and that night I hung a MacGannon plaid out my bedroom window in the hope that someone was watching.

I was very frustrated. I had written to the king and ministers and every member of Parliament that I had ever been introduced to, to no avail. Most never even answered my letters. I had asked my uncles to contact anyone who could assist us. With their intervention the officials listened more often, but nothing had really changed. I'd trudged from apartment to apartment, from office to office, waiting for hours to finally see some minor official who listened with boredom. Occasionally I would receive a cordial welcome and an introduction to the next level of official, and while that was always welcome I'd seen no results from my efforts. Nor my money, though I was lavish in my "gifts."

Will and Betty had returned to Mountgarden and I missed my brother terribly. Louisa was always at my side, and Randolph and Harry had been kind and generous, but what I wanted was news from Angus. It was as though London had swallowed him. And then, two weeks after I'd seen Alex, on a warm, late summer evening, I received an invitation written in the Duchess's bold hand. The Barringtons were having a party. Almost all of London had retired to the country for the summer, and the Duchess's affair heralded the new season and the return of society. I shook my head, but Louisa told me firmly that I would be going, saying I could not refuse her dear friend's invitation.

No one had visited me since my return to London except for the Duchess and for Rebecca's mother, Sarah, both as kind and welcoming as ever. While I was grateful to them for their friendship and loyalty, I was sure I would prove unable to spend a social evening in London. I held the Duchess's invitation in my hand and then threw it on the table. "I cannot. I will not."

Louisa retrieved the invitation. "Mary," she began, her tone threatening, but we were interrupted by a maid, who handed me a letter. She did not know who it was from, nor who had brought it, and said that no one was waiting for a reply. I held the note in my hand, my heart pounding as I recognized Angus's handwriting. He asked me to pay my respects to Elizabeth again tomorrow afternoon.

I went alone. And waited for two hours, anxiously walking around the Abbey, watching everyone who entered. I heard no voices this time as I wandered past the queens and the poets, merely my own turbulent thoughts, and I asked myself how I, Mary Lowell Mac-Gannon, had ended up pacing in Westminster Abbey, waiting for my husband's kinsman to tell me of his plans to free my husband from the Tower of London. My husband, who I loved more than my life; my husband, considered a traitor to my country. How does one define loyalty? I waited another few minutes before dispiritedly walking outside, my head bowed, and almost bumped into a tall man at the door. I quickly stepped aside, then looked up at him in alarm as he grasped my arm. He wore English clothing and for a moment I did not recognize Gilbey. His whispered welcome was warm and I looked up into his smile.

"Gilbey," I said, embracing him. "Where is Angus? And Matthew? How are you all? Why haven't I heard from you?" Gilbey smiled down at me, but said nothing as he guided me to the street and into a coach which began moving as soon as the door closed.

Angus, seated opposite, gave me a subdued greeting as we sped along the bumpy streets. He looked drawn and weary and out of place here, and despite being dressed in English clothing, very much the Highlander. He nodded when I chastised him for not contacting me. "I apologize for all the secrecy, Mary, but ye ken we were betrayed in Edinburgh and I've no desires to repeat the incident. Ye've heard about Nithsdale." At my nod he continued. "Several of the English prisoners have been 'released' with help from friends and well-placed money. But the Scottish prisoners are going to be used as examples of what happens when a mere Gael defies the Crown." Our eyes met, his angry.

"I've seen Alex," I said and told them of my visit and of Alex's messages. Angus nodded but made no comment. Gilbey's face had lit when he'd heard that Alex had requested him as his valet, and he'd started asking questions, but Angus silenced him with a glance, then asked about the boys and my family. I told him they were all well, of Harry's interest in "another" plan and his insistence on seeing him. And then of the Duchess's invitation.

"Well, lass, it seems as though yer making more progress than we. Ye should go to it and see what ye learn."

"I don't want to go."

"And I dinna want to have my son drinking with English soldiers to hear the gossip, but it needs to be done," he growled. "Go and discover what ye can, Mary, and meet with me after and we'll see if it changes anything. Will ye do that?"

"Yes," I said and he nodded. We sat in silence as the coach leaned around a corner. "What are you going to do?" I asked him.

"I canna tell ye." At my exclamation, Angus continued in a patient tone. "I asked ye here, Mary, to tell ye that we are alive, that we have no' abandoned Alex, nor ye and the boys. It is no' going well, but we are still trying. And to tell ye that ye need have no fear of recognizing me if we meet. I ken ye said that ye would pretend no' to know me, but it willna be necessary."

I nodded. "Why?"

"Enough of the English ken who I am to render me useless in secrecy, but I have Matthew and Gilbey to do what requires it. Even if Gilbey becomes Alex's valet, I still have Matthew."

"Angus, what are you doing that requires secrecy?"

"Nothing alarming. Ye need no' look daggers at me, lass. We canna spring Alex out of the Tower by force without an army, and even with the men from Kilgannon I still dinna have an army. Even if the Macleans arrive I still willna have one. So dinna fear that we are to lay siege to yer Tower."

"It's not my Tower."

"It's more yers than mine."

"No. Not anymore." His eyes met mine and he almost smiled. "Angus," I said, "why don't you three come and stay with Louisa and Randolph? They told me to tell you that you are all welcome. Come and join us and at least we'll all be together. The boys would love to see you. And I would love to have you with me."

Angus leaned forward into the light, his expression softened. "I canna do that, Mary. If we are successful, then the trail would lead right back to ye and to yer aunt and uncle. The English already ken I'm yer husband's cousin, but it's no' the same as if I'm living with yer family. It's no' wise, lass. I canna have any of ye come to any grief because of what I do."

"Angus, please, remember that Alex does not want this." He looked at the floor for a moment, nodded, and asked me to ask Harry to arrange a visit with Alex. I agreed and he thanked me, then lifted the curtain and glanced out the window.

"Matthew would like to see ye. If yer willing?"

"Oh, yes, of course." He leaned out to say something to the driver. We rode in silence for a few moments and then came to an abrupt stop. The door flew open and Matthew propelled himself inside, breathless and grinning, smelling of ale, and the coach hurtled forward. He was dressed in the clothing of an English peasant, no more convincing than his father in his outlandish dress, but passable. His energy filled the coach.

"Mary, I knew Gilbey would find ye! How are ye?"

"Matthew." We embraced awkwardly in the cramped quarters.

Angus watched his son. "Did ye discover anything?"

Matthew shook his head. "No' much. The trial is to begin in a month or two. No' much help, is that?" He frowned. "But, Da, something more important has happened. The Duke of Grafton has sent for ye. His footman came to our rooms an hour ago, acting as if he kent who I was. He said the Duke wishes ye to visit with him. I told the man that I would deliver the message. I could see no use in dissembling." Matthew looked at me. "Do ye ken anything of this, Mary? Why would yer uncle wish to talk with us?"

"I don't know. Harry said that he wanted to talk to your father, but I thought I was to deliver the message. He is very discouraged with you all disappearing."

"Is he now?" Angus's tone was mild, but I knew him better. "Well, we canna travel in the same circles as a duke, can we?"

"What do ye suppose he wants with ye, Da?" Matthew asked.

Angus shrugged. "Probably to tell me what to do. I've not spoken to him since we left the *Mary Rose*." Angus met my eyes. "Mary, lass, let's go and see yer uncle."

"Now?"

Angus nodded. "Aye. Let's go." I nodded.

Harry welcomed us warmly, then offered Angus brandy and retreated with him to his study, leaving Matthew and Gilbey and me waiting in the parlor. When they returned, Harry would tell us nothing except that he would arrange for Gilbey to replace Bronson as Alex's valet, and then began badgering me to retire to Mountgarden. Angus watched Harry's performance without expression. On the defensive again, I went home.

When I told my aunt and uncle of my visit with Angus and Harry, Randolph left at once to see Harry. When he returned he closeted himself with Bronson, then joined Louisa and me, but reported only that Harry seemed to have several plots in mind, all legal maneuverings, which Randolph thought absurd.

"He tells me that he is trying to use tactics used by the Scots after the rebellion of '88," Randolph said with a shake of his head. "He won't elaborate. He's very stubborn, have you noticed? But he's arranged to have Gilbey as the valet, and he'll try to get you to see Alex again." Louisa sighed and Randolph nodded at her. "Harry worries me. I wish he'd just tell me what he's hatching."

"Probably nothing of note," I said. "Harry does not always seem to have a clear grasp of reality." Randolph laughed.

Gilbey went to Alex the next day and reported to me later, saying that Harry had been there, talking with Alex about lawyers. Alex, he said, sent his love. The next day Gilbey told us that he'd not been allowed to see Alex, and a moment later the maid announced that Angus waited for me in the library. Louisa, Randolph, and Gilbey hurried behind me to join him. Angus was pacing when we entered, his color high, his movements agitated, and my heart fell. I did not bother with a greeting.

"What has happened?"

Angus met my eyes, then looked behind me at the others. "I saw Alex. Murdoch's been tried."

I gasped. "But how? I thought the trials were to be public."

"Aye," he said, looking down at his hands, then up at us. "They took Murdoch to Westminster this morning. They tried him before three judges, and his lordship Edgar DeBroun found him guilty on the spot." He shifted his weight.

"Edgar DeBroun?" Randolph asked. "The peer?

He's trying the prisoners?" I glanced at him. Something in Randolph's voice made me know he knew much more of DeBroun than I did.

Angus nodded. "Aye. Alex's been questioned before by DeBroun, the bloody bastard. Forgive me, ladies, but I truly hate the man."

"You've met him before," Randolph said.

Angus met his eyes and nodded. "Aye. I've met him before. And taken his measure. And he's met Alex before." He looked at me. "DeBroun had an offer for Alex."

I could feel my heart's lunge. "What is the offer?"

"Comfort. Visits from ye and the boys. A possibility of freedom or at least life in prison. In exchange they want Alex to recant publicly, to get on his knees before the king at Westminster and beg for forgiveness." Gilbey made a disgusted sound and Louisa shook her head. "And to tell them where the ones who have gone to the heather are hiding. Murdoch was given the same offer and he told them . . . well, let's simply say he was rude. That was yestere'en, and today he was tried. Alex said they asked him the same this morning."

"What did Alex answer?" I whispered, afraid to hear his reply.

"Alex was rude as well."

"Oh, Angus."

"Aye." He looked at all of us, then turned away. "It looks like this is the end of it."

"What will happen now to Murdoch?" Gilbey asked.

"I dinna ken. Alex doesna ken." Angus sighed again. "Ye can expect to hear that Alex was tried tonight or in the morning."

I felt a wave of desperation. "I'm not Winifred Maxwell, Angus. I cannot spirit Alex out of the Tower. What can we do?"

"We pray, Mary. Pray, lass, as ye never have before, and then get yerself to the Duchess's party. It might be yer last chance to get the ear of someone who could make a difference. Make sure they ken who ye are and what ye want." I nodded, numb, and sank into the chair while the others talked.

But Alex was not tried the next day, nor the next. And we were not told why, nor what would happen. And the third day was the Duchess's party.

My first social evening in London in years and I felt as though I were seventeen again. It had been so long since I'd worn fashionable clothes or paid any attention to how women were dressing their hair that I felt quite incapable of coping with the details of preparing. Not that it mattered. How could I laugh and chat with strangers while Alex was in jeopardy? I'd said I would do this, but now I wasn't sure I could. I smoothed the material over my middle, noting the bulge of the baby at last. *I will do this for you, sweet child,* I said silently, *and for your father. But I don't know where to begin.*

With a cursory knock, Louisa breezed into the room and marched toward me. "Mary, you will not be a coward!" she cried, coming to a stop before me. I looked down at her wordlessly, knowing that I must master my emotions before I spoke. Her expression softened and she patted my cheek.

"What difference will it make?" I asked. "I have seen everyone in London who will receive me."

She arched her brows. "Mary, my dear, you are one of London's own. If society rallies behind you, Alex will benefit. If you hide at home, they will assume you are convinced of your husband's guilt. You must go into the lions' den and charm the lions."

"They will not accept me. They will only watch me and talk."

"They have been talking about you for months. Years, actually. They've been talking since you met Alex. Let's get you ready and they will say that you looked radiant and healthy and overly proud." She threw open the doors of my closets. "What shall you wear? I think the rose with the low neckline. Do not give me that look, miss. It has been a long time since you were in London and now you are a married woman. You're very beautiful, Mary. Use what weapons you have."

In the end I wore what she selected, and her maid had my hair looking perfect. I had no more excuses. My body might be ready, but long before my mind was, we were off. I huddled in the carriage, trying to steel myself. Randolph patted my hand.

The Duchess's house glowed with lights and danced with music. The halls were full of crowds and I ignored the curious looks thrown at us as we slowly made our way to the ballroom. Several people that I knew, some I would have thought I knew well, turned away before meeting my eyes, and no one spoke to me, although they greeted Louisa and Randolph. *So be it,* I told myself. My chin was at the same absurd angle Ian and Jamie used. *I must look ridiculous,* I thought. A hush fell over the ballroom when I was announced as the Countess of Kilgannon, and the sea of faces turned to watch us enter. I fought the urge to run away. *Damn them all. I am the granddaughter and the niece of a duke, and the wife of an earl. I am the Countess of Kilgannon.* I lifted my chin even higher and tried to look haughty. *I must look as though my dress pains me severely,* I thought, and smiled to myself as I descended into the crowd.

The Duchess, bless her, rushed over to welcome us at once. After the initial greetings she squeezed my hand and led me away from my aunt and uncle to group after group of London's elite. I was greeted with politeness but little more, and I was well aware that every detail of my costume and bearing was being noted for later dissection. At last the Duchess brought me to a group of gentlemen in the center of the room, whispering to me on the way.

"I am so proud of you for coming, dear. The Duke was worried that you would not be able to able to face the crowds, but I told him you were made of sterner stuff."

"The Duke is correct."

She patted my hand. "I understand, but you can face a bunch of gossiping fools with good grace for your husband's sake." She never heard my inane answer, for we had reached the men and she introduced me gaily to several of them, then was called away by a friend. I faced the men alone with a fixed smile. Some of them I had known for years and they greeted me cautiously, but they did greet me and I took some comfort in that. One man I did not recognize watched me with avid interest but said nothing. We talked banally of the weather, then the man to my right gestured to the silent man. "Madam, may I introduce Lord Edgar DeBroun. He will be one of the judges at your husband's trial."

What little composure I had disappeared and I stared, totally at a loss, into the dark eyes of Edgar De-Broun, Earl and Peer of the Realm, with family lines that reached back to William the Conqueror. DeBroun bowed over my hand and let his eyes roam across my face and body. *Edgar DeBroun,* I thought. *The man who pronounced Murdoch guilty. One of the men who will judge whether Alex lives or dies.* He was, surprisingly, just a few years older than Alex, tall and dark, a handsome, self-assured man, quite accustomed to having his needs met. His eyes were warm and his expression pleased. I must have gone very pale and possibly swayed, for he reached out for my elbow and held it for the briefest of moments before releasing me.

"Madam," he said. "I am delighted to make your acquaintance. I did not anticipate seeing you here to-night. You are as lovely as I'd heard. What an agreeable surprise."

"Thank you, sir." I tried to smile. "It is a surprise."

He smiled a slow smile that did not reach his eyes, and I stared, feeling like a mouse the cat had just discovered. The Duchess rescued me by returning to my side and moving me away. I turned from one last look at Edgar DeBroun's saturnine face. And found myself in front of Janice. Once a close companion, she was now even more uncomfortable than I, and I smiled genu-inely, if maliciously, watching her struggle. *Poor Janice,* I thought. To recognize me as an old and dear friend could be hazardous to her social ambitions, and yet here I was at the Duchess's elbow. Janice must be most discomforted. To my right, Jonathan Wumple bowed. I groaned inwardly as I faced my old acquaintance.

"Madam," he said, "as beautiful as ever. What a delight to have you back with us despite your recent troubles."

"Sir, you are gracious to welcome me," I said, surprised.

He simpered. "How could we not, when Her Grace

threatens us with transportation if we are not kind to you?"

I forced a smile.

"Lord Wumple," said the Duchess with asperity, "I have done no such thing. I merely said that the Earl and Lady Mary are my dear friends and you must treat my dear friends with courtesy."

Jonathan gave a bark of laugh in reply. "What a pity your husband is not here to be treated with courtesy." With a sidelong glance at me, he turned to Janice. "You remember our Janice, Mary."

I met her eyes and I smiled, holding my hands out to her. "Janice, how lovely to see you again."

"Mary," she said, but did not take my hands. I folded them at my waist. Her tone was strained, her eyes anxious. In her position I would have embraced my old friend for all the world to see. *How I wish Becca were here,* I thought, as Janice's sister Elizabeth gaily greeted me.

"Mary," she said, "it's lovely to see you again. Did you know that Jan and Lord Wumple are engaged? They have set the date at last." I looked from Jonathan to Janice, who frowned at her sister.

"What a perfect match," I said.

"I agree," said the Duchess, her eyes dancing. "Just as I thought you and Lord Kilgannon were perfect for each other, both so very handsome and intelligent and well-bred." She looked at the engaged pair. "Yes, our Miss Janice and Lord Wumple are perfect for each other. Very well suited." The Duchess was already moving me on. "Come, Mary," she said and I followed.

The next hour was a blur of faces, some cautious, some cold, several most gracious to me. It was the Duchess's doing, I knew, but some of these people had been at my wedding and remarked on that, as well as

Alex's situation. A few were bold enough to express dismay at the harsh treatment of the Scots and to tell me they believed that Alex and the others who had not run to safety in France had been ill used by both the Stewarts and the English victors. I was quite surprised. For English voices, so often disdainful of anyone else, to be raised in protest of cruel treatment of another people, let alone the uncivilized Scots, was truly amazing. I smiled, agreed, and asked them to speak to the Court on behalf of the prisoners, knowing that they never would. Still, it was comforting to at least hear the sentiments, and my smiles grew less forced. The Duchess left me alone for the first time that evening, assuming, I supposed, that her chick had had enough time under her wing. Louisa and Randolph, who had never been far away, were in the group behind me, the men discussing horses as usual. I stood on the edge of their group, not drawn into the conversation, until I felt a hand on my arm and turned to find Edgar DeBroun at my side.

"A word with you, madam," he said, taking my elbow and leading me away, his head lowered to my ear so that only I might hear him. "I must speak with you," he said. "Will you come with me?" As I hesitated he paused and turned to me fully. "Madam, it is about your husband."

The room faded from my view as I turned to him, keeping my tone quiet, but not caring who watched or overheard. "Sir, you will soon try my husband for treason. You have very recently found a dear friend of his guilty—"

He put a finger to my lips and spoke quickly. "Exactly. Please come with me, madam." He took my hand and led me through the crowd.

FOURTEEN

I WAS ASTONISHED AT HIS ACTION, BUT WHEN HE CON-
tinued to lead me from the room I followed peaceably.
We went down a hallway and into a sitting room. He
bowed again and when he raised his eyes to mine I felt a
thrill of fear. That this man wanted something from me
was obvious, and that he was very pleased was apparent
as well. I wondered where Randolph was.

"Madam," said DeBroun. "I wish to convey to you
my sorrow at your situation. It is imperative that you
understand my position. We in the court have a responsibility to uphold the law and the orderly transition of
the Crown. When the Jacobites rebelled they threatened this transition and therefore had to be quelled.
Lawlessness, whatever its form, cannot be tolerated,
and all possible sources of rebellion must be destroyed
with the most effective means. It is imperative that we
thread a fine line between justice and reprisal." He
paused and his eyes ran down my body. And up again,
lingering at my low neckline. He glanced at the door.
"My message is simple. I will arrange for you to see
your husband. And in return you will ask your husband a simple request. I am sure you will find a way to

convince him. He could not remain unmoved by you. Be sure to tell him you have met me."

"What do you wish me to ask him to do?" I asked quietly.

"Ask him to beg our king for forgiveness. If Kilgannon publicly recants and gives us the information we require, I am in a position to make his situation much easier, which, I am sure, would please you."

Beg for forgiveness, I thought. A flash of memory came, of Alex standing in Robert's house four years ago, telling me that he loved me but could not beg me to love him in return. "I do not beg," he'd said, and I'd believed him. I looked up at DeBroun's impassive face.

"And if he will not?" I asked. DeBroun shrugged. "Will you give him the same sort of trial you gave Murdoch Maclean?"

"Maclean has no land and no title. He is of no consequence."

"No consequence. Murdoch Maclean is of no consequence."

"None. Your husband, however, has both land and title. We will try him publicly very soon. Unless he recants now."

"I see." I paused while I struggled for control. "Sir, the prisoners were promised trial under Scottish law. I beg you to return my husband to Scotland for his trial."

"That is out of my control," he said, the subject obviously dismissed. "You are in a position to change your husband's mind, madam. I have tried, but he is reluctant to accept my offer. Change his mind. It is not the goal of the court to be so very harsh that we instigate in Scotland any feeling of resentment."

I tried to keep my tone mild. "Then your court is tardy, sir. You are already the targets of resentment."

DeBroun's eyes narrowed. "In what manner are we too tardy?"

"I can only speak from my own experience, sir. In Scotland the people are understandably resentful, but I have been surprised to find that many people in England are also unhappy with the situation. Even tonight I have been told so. The reprisals have been very harsh and the barbarity of the treatment of Scottish civilians has aroused popular sentiment. Even English popular sentiment, sir. Your court only adds fuel to that fire, and I would ask you, on behalf of all the prisoners, to declare an amnesty for those now in custody. It is the most prudent course. Or, at the very least, return them to Scotland for their trials."

He watched me for a moment, his expression unreadable. Then he straightened his back and spoke in a patronizing tone. "Madam, of course you hold such views. But consider. Those who joined the rebellion committed treason. This cannot go unpunished. Many of those imprisoned are English, and we will be harsher with them than with the Scots."

Of course you will be, I thought. *You assume the Scots to be by nature unruly and dangerous. The English rebels are the true traitors. Theirs is the worse crime, for they know better.* I swallowed my anger as he continued.

"I urge you to visit your husband, to convince him. If he were to have a sudden change of heart, it would go far easier upon him. If he could give us information on the remaining rebels, his situation would be much simpler to discuss with the other judges. If he were to recant, it would be a simple matter to spare his life. May I assume, madam, that you will speak to your husband?"

I tried to keep my tone civil. "Sir, I thank you," I said, "and I am grateful to you for your information. I will certainly speak with my husband. I cannot, however, promise any change of heart on his part. He is a most determined man."

DeBroun's eyes were on my neckline again. "I entreat you, madam, to do what you can to alter his position."

We both turned as the door opened and Randolph walked into the room without knocking. I let out the breath I did not even know I was holding. "What's all this?" My uncle's tone was cheerful enough, but his smile did not extend to his eyes as he came to stand next to me, his hand comforting on my arm.

"Lord DeBroun wants me to ask Alex to recant and beg publicly for forgiveness, and to give whatever information he has on the whereabouts of any Jacobites who are not held prisoner," I said, as though I was telling him about the last dance we'd had.

Randolph nodded, then asked if DeBroun could reduce Alex's sentence.

"I will endeavor for that result in any event, sir, but it would be much simpler if I had information in return for leniency."

"There is a difficulty with your plan," Randolph said.

"And that is?"

"Everyone knows that James Stewart and the Earl of Mar and many of the others went to France. This is no secret."

DeBroun nodded. "That is what Kilgannon told us. But that is not our primary purpose in questioning him."

"You want the whereabouts of the rebels still in Scotland?"

"Exactly. They must be brought to justice."

"But, sir, you must know that Kilgannon would have

no way to know where they are. He was captured shortly after the Stewart's flight and escorted to Edinburgh."

"Where he was housed with several men who have now escaped. We believe Kilgannon will know where to find them."

Randolph and I exchanged a look. This was news to both of us. "They escaped from the Tower?" Randolph asked.

DeBroun shook his head. "No. They were held in Edinburgh and escaped from there. With assistance, of course. We believe Kilgannon will know where to find these men, or will be able to persuade Murdoch Maclean to tell us." Randolph drummed his fingers on his chin as he regarded DeBroun, who continued in that same quiet tone. "We are seeking Duncan Maclean. And Joseph MacDonald and Alexander MacDonell."

Joseph MacDonald and Alexander MacDonell. Both brave men that Alex knew well. And Duncan, Murdoch's brother. One of our dearest friends. Alex might indeed have an idea where they would be, since each man's clan bordered Kilgannon land, and since he knew Duncan so well. Alex was being asked to betray them to gain his own freedom. My heart sank. Alex would never do it.

"Lord DeBroun," Randolph said, his tone mild, "it is unlikely that Kilgannon would have this information. Even if some of the men had talked about their plans in Edinburgh, it is obvious that they know Kilgannon is here. They will have changed whatever they might have discussed with him for fear that he would do exactly what you are asking him to do. Any prudent man would. It is more likely that they are tucked away in France than that they would continue to endanger themselves by staying in occupied Scotland."

I knew Randolph was wrong but I kept my silence. If he knew he was wrong he did a wonderful job of disguising it. Duncan and the others would never run away now. They would take to the heather and try to hold their clans together. I knew the type well.

Edgar DeBroun was studying Randolph. "Then it is most unfortunate, sir, that he does not have this information."

My uncle spread his hands. "Can you not think of another way than for him to deliver information which he does not have? Can we, perhaps, further his cause in another manner?"

DeBroun shook his head. "None occurs to me, sir, nor to the other judges, especially in light of Kilgannon's dismissal of my suggestion that he throw himself on the king's mercy. His answer was most inappropriate. And unfortunate for his cause. Indeed, two of the judges, after hearing what Kilgannon called us, are adamant that he and all the rebels be put to death immediately as a deterrent to others of their kind. I have been arguing for a simple hanging rather than the traditional traitor's death. Unless something changes, I think that would be as merciful as we could be in these circumstances." I gasped and Randolph tightened his arm around me while DeBroun leaned toward me, his expression distressed. "I apologize, madam. I forgot you were listening. I will arrange for you to see your husband tomorrow."

I took a deep breath and nodded. "I thank you, sir, for whatever you can do for us. I will most gratefully accept your offer to see my husband." He bowed again and left the room. I looked after him and then turned to meet Randolph's eyes.

* * *

Angus and Harry were waiting for us as planned when we returned to Louisa's, and listened with worried eyes to our story.

"I dinna trust him," Angus said and Louisa nodded.

"Nor I," Randolph said.

"Trust him or not," Harry said, "he is arranging for Mary to see Alex. That much is good."

The men nodded and although we discussed it for an hour no one had any plan cleverer than that I go to see Alex the next day.

I went to the Tower in the morning, but it was afternoon before I saw Alex. I was kept waiting three hours in the captain's quarters. The captain, who I'd seen be brusque with others, fussed over me with tea and pillows and told me that Alex's trial would begin the first week of October, and that Alex and I would have several hours undisturbed. His kindness confused me.

Eventually I was led upstairs, not to the little stone room where we had met before, but to a comfortable room in Beauchamp Tower, overlooking the courtyard, furnished with couches and a table laden with food and whisky. And in the corner, a bed. I wandered to the window, wiping the glass clean, but there was nothing to see this cold gray day but the courtyard where Anne Boleyn and Catherine Howard and Lady Jane Grey had been beheaded. Small comfort to know it had been almost two hundred years ago. I left the window and waited in a chair, my hands folded in my lap. When at last the door opened and Alex was let in I leapt up.

He was pale and wary, but alone and unchained, and I threw myself into his arms. But I didn't kiss him. His lips were bruised. He held me to him as he said my name over and over. I smiled at him, my smile becoming rigid as I noted the circles under his eyes, the bruises creeping up his neck, the dried blood in his hair and the stiff way he moved. I stepped back from him, afraid of doing more injury. *Damn them,* I thought, and struggled to keep my tone mild. "How are you, my love?"

He smiled gingerly. "I am well, Mary Rose, all things considered." He held me at arm's length as he examined me. "How good ye look, lass. How are ye? And the babe and my boys?"

"They are well. We are all well." We talked first of the children, then of my family, and of Angus and Matthew and Gilbey. I told him I'd heard about Murdoch's trial. And then of my meeting Edgar DeBroun and everything that he'd said. Alex nodded.

"He told me he'd seen ye. He said ye defended me strongly."

"I simply told him the truth."

He gave me a wry smile. "They're no' interested in the truth, lass, only in revenge. Especially DeBroun. He tells me I can buy an easier death if I tell them what they want to ken."

"Do you know where Duncan could be? Or the others?"

Alex shrugged. "Any fool kens they're in hiding. I dinna ken where. Why does DeBroun think I would tell them even if I kent?"

"To ease your suffering."

"I'm no' suffering. My body is taken care of well enough."

"Alex, how can you say that? Look at you. You look as though . . . Alex, how do they question you? Are you . . . ?"

"Tortured? No, lass, they dinna torture me." He touched his jaw gently. "Well, sometimes, aye, when they're frustrated, they batter a bit." He grinned. "And sometimes I bring it on just to stop their questions. It willna kill me. By the trial naught will show. They'll see to that."

"Can you not tell them something?"

"Tell them something?" His voice was tight. "What I suspect is not what I ken. What I ken is of no value to them."

"But you do know something."

"Mary, I ken what I'd do if I'd taken to the heather, but I ken nothing that could benefit the English. We have heard nothing from the outside except for what ye and Angus and Gilbey have told me. No, lass, I have nothing to bargain with even if I had a mind to bargain."

"And you would not bargain in any case."

He grinned at me. "I can see ye do ken me well."

I was silent as he roamed the room and stopped in front of the table, looking at it and then pouring a glass of whisky. He turned to me with a wry laugh. "Whisky," he said, holding the glass up to the light as he always did, then draining it in one gulp. He poured another. "Ye understand why they allowed ye to see me, lass?"

"I am to convince you to tell where Duncan is, or the others."

"Aye, but ye were no' successful, despite the enticements." He took a sip of the whisky. "Mary, dinna waste yer worry on me. 'Tis Murdoch in the most danger here. Duncan is his brother and there's not a spot Duncan could be but that Murdoch would ken. What I canna figure out is why they care so much about Duncan. He's no' a large part of this. I canna help but think it's naught but another of DeBroun's tricks."

He paced the room again while I watched, then

turned to the window and wiped the glass as I had done, telling me over his shoulder that DeBroun supervised the questioning and that hardly a day went by that he did not visit. The questions had expanded as the Crown prepared its case. Now they asked him about events that had no relation to his joining the rebellion, including the man he'd killed in Brenmargon Pass, the man who had attacked him the day Robert had captured Alex.

"Is treason not enough?" I cried "Why are they doing this? The other has no relevance here."

"Tell that to the lawyers."

"I cannot. The court will not tell me who will defend you. And Kenneth Ogilvie cannot practice here because he was not educated in England. I still don't understand that. He's a solicitor so he can handle your business matters—"

"But he's no' a barrister, lass," Alex interrupted, "so he canna defend me in court. And he's no' English, so he wasna welcomed at the Inns of Court. It's an effective way of keeping the power in English hands."

I agreed. "Oh," I said, remembering a message Angus had asked me to relay. "Kenneth arrived yesterday."

Alex nodded. "Good. He wrote me from Edinburgh when he agreed to come. It's verra good of him. Ye ken that Harry has a scheme to keep Kilgannon from being seized by the English?" When I shook my head, Alex smiled wryly. "It's good of Harry to try. And ye ken Harry's paying all of Kenneth's expenses? Yer uncle's been most generous, Mary Rose."

"What is his scheme?"

"Convoluted, lass," Alex said. "It will come to naught, but nothing ventured . . ." He waved a hand in the air and sighed. "I'll do what Harry wishes. Perhaps Kenneth will try to help Murdoch as well."

"How is Murdoch?"

"They now question him every day. And Morag hasna come to see him. Damn her!" he said viciously. "I dinna think she'd desert him like this."

"It's her revenge, Alex."

He nodded. "Aye, and verra thorough too. She kens what she does. She should be revenging herself on me, no' Murdoch."

"She knows this will hurt you, Alex."

"Aye. I should never have been so harsh with her."

I raised my eyebrows. "No. It would have been much wiser to let her kiss you in front of your wife. Or more." I surprised a laugh from him. "And if you'd sacrificed yourself and married her, none of this would have happened."

He grinned at me. "What could I have been thinking, to marry ye instead, Mary?"

"A weakness of mind, no doubt," I said, then jumped as the baby moved strongly. "Alex, we have to name this child. We can postpone it no longer. It is a boy."

He laughed, startled. "How can ye be so certain, lass?"

"I have no idea, but I am."

"You're a one, Mary Rose." He laughed again and then considered. "Why not after yer father? What was his name?"

"Robert." It was as though I had conjured Robert Campbell into the room, and Alex's face fell. After a moment he met my eyes.

"Aye. I'd forgotten that." His voice was toneless.

"What about William?"

"Well, no offense to yer brother, lass, but no child of mine will be named after King William. It's bad enough that you two were William and Mary. What's yer brother's second name?"

"Robert."

The corner of his mouth twitched. "Of course. Well, what about yer uncle Randolph? What is his given name?" I smiled and he groaned. "Dinna tell me. Robert, aye?" I nodded and Alex blinked. "Damn! I canna believe it." We bantered names back and forth for a long while and at last, defeated, stared at each other, then decided on a girl's name in case I was wrong.

"Margaret for yer mother and mine, both Margarets," he said and I nodded, pleased, for I'd had the same thought. "Margaret Rose MacGannon. Bonnie name. She'll be a bonnie wee lass." He nodded, satisfied. "Aye. That's simple. Now just have a girl."

"And if she's a boy?"

"Then you decide, lass," he said softly. "I won't be there." He looked at the whisky in his hand and slowly put the glass on the table before raising his eyes to look at me. *So blue,* I thought. "We have a bed, Mary," he said quietly. "Will ye share it with me?"

I nodded, unable to speak, and rose to meet him, pulling his mouth down to mine. He tasted of whisky and tears and I clung to him, then slipped my hands under his shirt and slowly peeled the material away, and then repeated the process with his other clothing until he was naked before me. As his skin was revealed I saw the bruises and welts on his chest and back and the burns on his thighs, and I cried with new distress. Alex dismissed the marks with a shrug. "I've been . . . what did they tell ye in Edinburgh? . . . unrepentant? Aye, that's it, I've been unrepentant and they're no' pleased with me. Now kiss me, Mary."

"Your lips are bruised," I said softly.

"So they are, lass, but having ye kiss me is the best medicine I ken." He sat on the edge of the bed, pulling me down next to him.

"Then, my love," I said, pushing him horizontal, "let me heal you all over." He smiled and lay back and I kissed his shoulders and neck and traced my fingers across his skin. "Do you remember, Alex?" I asked, pausing and lifting my head from across his chest. "Do you remember after the attack in the coach, when you brought me to your ship, that you offered to heal each bruise I had by kissing it?"

He laughed softly and ran his hands through my hair, loosening the pins. "No, lass, I dinna remember. Did I do that?"

"Yes." I breathed on his skin and kissed my way across a rib. "And even when I was so angry with you, even later when you'd brought me back to Louisa's, I remembered you doing that, kissing each bruise on my neck, and what it did to me."

"Rather like what yer doing to me now?"

I laughed. "Not exactly," I said and bent to my task.

Somewhat later he pulled me against him and kissed me soundly. "Your lips," I cautioned but he laughed.

"Healed, lass. Quite healed. And now, Mary Rose, it's yer turn. Come, lassie, let's get these clothes off ye. I've some healing to do, I'm thinking." He helped me remove my bodice and skirt and he wondered at how little my body had changed with the pregnancy. But when he moved to let me lie next to him, he winced, and I paused, knowing he was in pain, and that my remedy was inadequate for what he was facing. I began to cry then and he held me to him gently, his caresses gradually growing more insistent.

Our lovemaking was silent and gentle, as if we were each afraid that the other would break. Afterward I lay in his arms and looked at the ceiling, telling myself to memorize the feel of his body stretched next to mine, the sound of his heart beating, the silk of his skin as I caressed him from hip to thigh, finding an unbattered spot. And when he slept I watched him, feeling both father and son against me, separated only by a thin veil of skin. And at last I slept as well, wondering how much longer we'd have before we were separated. Moments, perhaps, I thought, and drifted off.

Sometime in the middle of the night we found comfort in each other again and then lay in gratification in the dark, talking of inconsequential things. Then he paused and smoothed a hand over my hair. "This might be the last time we're together talking like this, ye ken." He pulled me closer. "I love ye, Mary Rose. Ye've made me verra happy and I'm no' afraid to die. When they lead me to the platform I will have yer face in my mind."

"How can you talk so calmly of this?" I whispered.

"How can I not? Do ye no' think I live with it every minute? I faced it long ago, lass. After Sherrifmuir I kent I was lost." He sat up and lit the candle, facing me in the dim light. "I kent the risks when I joined the rebellion, Mary. Like it or no', it's right that I am here the now. I ask my clan to obey the law and if they dinna, to suffer the consequences. How can I no' see the comparison with this? I dinna choose to have lost a rebellion and now be considered a traitor, but it is what happened. I see the correctness of this." He raked his hand through his hair. "But I wish they would get on with it.

If they're going to kill me, I wish they'd just do so. The waiting is far harder than I imagined." He sighed. "But so be it. This is where we are. And soon where I am will matter to no one."

I sat up and faced him, pulling the blanket to my throat. "It will always matter to me, Alex."

"It will fade," he said quietly.

"No."

"Make it fade, Mary."

I shook my head furiously. "No. Never. Never, Alex. I will never let you go. You promised to be with me always."

"I canna change that I am to die."

"Then come to me after death. If it is possible, come to me. Promise me. Promise me!" I heard my shrill voice ring against the stones. His mouth twisted and he reached for me again. I could feel his ragged breath as he held me and I tightened my arms.

"I'll never deny ye anything, lass. If it is possible, I will come to ye." I nodded then, satisfied with what little I had.

The boys were allowed to see Alex the next day, brought by Gilbey, who met our questions as to how long I'd be staying with shrugs. And he brought me fresh clothes and toiletries. "DeBroun suggested it, Mary," he said quietly to me while Alex sat with his sons across the room.

"Do they mean to allow me to remain?"

He shrugged. "Louisa is very troubled, but Harry says ye'll come to no harm here. They all say to tell ye the boys will be fine and no' to worry about them. And yer brother promises to no' cause a stink as long as yer well. Have the people here told ye nothing?"

"No. When they brought more food they would not talk. What can this be?"

Gilbey looked at my dishevelment and gave me a quick grin. "I'd say you were a persuasion, Mary, for good behavior." I smiled wryly, ignoring my flaming cheeks. Gilbey looked over at Alex and then met my eyes. "Enjoy this time. Ye ken Alex will tell them nothing." I nodded.

We had a week. Gilbey visited each day and brought us news. And more. He brought maps and charts and sat with Alex at the table, poring over them when they thought I slept in the afternoon. I lay in the bed, shielded by the hangings, and listened.

"Here, Gilbey," Alex said, and I raised myself up on one elbow and watched through the gap in the hangings. Alex was pointing to a spot on the map before them. "This is the best place. They'll bring me past here if I'm to hang on Tower Hill, so ye'll have to be hiding among the crowd right here. Any further and the soldiers will be able to be more abreast. But right here they'll have to narrow down to one or two on each side. Tell Angus."

"Aye," Gilbey said. "If it's Tower Hill. What if they decide not to hang you there? What if they bring ye to Newgate?" They both looked up at my gasp, and Gilbey took a step back from the table as I clambered from the bed and approached them.

"What are you doing?" I asked.

"Planning how to be rescued, lass," Alex said evenly. "On the way to my execution." I sank into a chair and looked at the map before us, then nodded at them. Alex looked up at Gilbey. "Aye, lad, we'll look at that as well." He met my eyes. "Mary," he said, "I'm trying to plan for any eventuality. When they take ye from me, and ye ken they will, I want ye to get out of London. Yer being here will give the English a target. They ken yer our weakness, ye and the boys. Get yerself out of the line of fire." When I didn't respond he frowned. "Mary . . ."

"They may not hang you, Alex," I said and he frowned again.

"What d'ye mean?"

"What if they give you transportation to the colonies or Barbados? How will Angus rescue you then?"

Alex laughed. "We'd no' thought of that, lass," Alex said and glanced at Gilbey. "Next time bring the charts of the Thames and offshore."

Gilbey nodded.

The fourth day of my stay, Alex was taken for "questioning."

FIFTEEN

I SAT IN A CHAIR BY THE WINDOW AND TRIED NOT TO think of what could be happening to him. How could Edgar DeBroun talk to me so smoothly of "persuasion" at the Duchess's house and be the same man who oversaw the batterings that Alex had endured?

He was gone for two hours and when he returned walked stiffly into the room and waited while the guards closed the door behind him. I'd risen to go to him, but he shook his head and limped over to the table, sinking into a chair and staring into the distance. I sat opposite him, watching the new weals on his neck grow redder.

"Alex," I said at last and his eyes shifted to meet mine. "Tell them. Tell them what you know, or what you suspect. Tell them, for God's sake!"

He shook his head and winced. "No," he whispered, his voice a croak. I went to him then and knelt before him, pulling the neckline of his shirt away from his skin. It was as I'd suspected.

"What have they done to you?"

He almost smiled. "Practiced, lass."

"Practiced? Practiced what, Alex? This looks like they tried to hang you."

"Aye," he said. "Perhaps they're no' sure of the procedure."

I rose and stepped back from him. "It's not amusing, Alex."

He shook his head and smiled. "No, lass, no' amusing at all."

"Then why do you smile?"

"I win when I resist them, Mary. I win."

I crossed the room, heading for the door. "Then I'll tell them, Alex. I'll not allow them to do this to you. I'll tell them what I know."

He was to the door before me, his eyes blazing as he drew himself to his full height. "Ye'll tell them nothing, Mary. Ye'll tell them nothing. This is unimportant."

"Unimportant," I gasped. "Unimportant. They 'practice' hanging you and it doesn't matter?"

He shook his head. "Do ye no' see, Mary? If I tell them nothing they'll kill me. And if I tell them what little I ken, or guess, they'll use that information to kill the others and then they'll kill me. I'll no' be a party to it. I'll tell them nothing and neither will ye."

I collapsed against his chest. "Alex," I sobbed. "I cannot bear to see you like this. Tell them. I cannot bear it."

He wrapped an arm around me and kissed my hair. "Dinna fret, Mary Rose. It willna be much longer."

The next day Gilbey smuggled in the sea charts, and the three of us studied them for possible sites appropriate for ambushing ships headed out to sea from London. And later that afternoon Alex was taken for questioning again. When he returned, barely able to stand, I pleaded with him again that he should tell them what he knew. He shook his head and wouldn't answer me, merely crawled into bed and closed his eyes. It was a very long night.

We were left alone then for two days, without "questioning," without Gilbey. We knew it was a ploy, that Alex was being shown his choices quite explicitly. Life in the Tower of London could be confining but comfortable, or it could be hell. We'd also had no news of Murdoch with Gilbey's absence, and Alex brooded about that. I prayed for Murdoch, feeling guilty that Alex was here with me.

And on the seventh day of my visit the man who brought us our breakfast also brought the news that I was to leave by ten. He would tell me nothing else. I had packed my meager possessions and Alex and I were together on the edge of the bed, hand in hand, when they came to escort me out. I rose, determined to appear calm, and, as we'd practiced, kissed Alex lightly and smiled as I bid him farewell. It was pride, we'd decided, that was the only thing they could not take from us.

But it was not pride I felt when I followed the guard to the courtyard and then to the streets, leaving the Tower behind me. I felt sickened, unable to face what would come next. I retreated to Louisa's and to the comfort of her sympathy and the cheer Alex's sons brought me. It would have to be enough.

Three days after my return, Angus sent a note asking me to meet him. We followed the same pattern as before. I wandered around the Abbey until Matthew found me, and then we rode in a coach while I visited with Angus. But this time Angus was not alone. Duncan Maclean was with him.

I embraced him with joy but Duncan did not return

my smile. He was an embittered man and snarled as he told me his story. The Maclean clan had rallied after Alex and Murdoch had sailed to London and, with the help of ready coin, Duncan had been allowed to "escape" from Edinburgh. He had stolen across Scotland with his kinsmen and eventually returned to Maclean territory, where they found the burnt remains of their home and the graves of Morag and his mother. Both women were murdered, they'd been told, by English troops. *Morag,* I thought.

Since then Duncan had been on the run, living on the charity of Jacobite sympathizers and plotting the escape of his brother. Upon his arrival in London, he was told of Murdoch's conviction and he now swore vengeance on DeBroun. I did not know how to respond to his bitter manner and sad story, but I told him how sorry I was. He asked about Alex and listened carefully when I told him what had happened during my stay, of DeBroun's interest in him and the others, and Alex's refusal to tell him anything. I told them of the trial date and everything else I could think of that would be of interest to them.

Angus, who had spent most of the time moodily staring out the window, met my eyes then and I knew I did not need to ask how he'd been. His silence was tangible and it was with a heavy heart that I stepped down from the coach. Angus followed me. "Mary," he said. "I ken yer distraught about DeBroun's treatment of Alex."

"I am," I said, guessing what was next.

"And . . ." He looked over my head at the coach behind us. "And now ye ken where Duncan is."

"Don't insult me by saying it, Angus," I said heatedly.

"I was going to tell ye . . ."

"That I now have it in my power to go to DeBroun

and tell him Duncan's in London. And barter the information for Alex. I find your suggestion insulting."

He shook his head, then laughed. "I was going to warn ye to be extra careful, lass. Ye may be being followed and if they find ye've seen Duncan ye could be back in the Tower as a prisoner yerself. Yer in danger as well as us, Mary."

"Oh," I said, chagrined. "Well. Thank you for the warning." I smiled. "And for your faith in me."

"I took yer measure long ago, Mary MacGannon. Ye'll do."

"Thank you, Angus," I said, and he laughed again as he climbed into the coach.

"Take care, lassie. Ye have the future of the MacGannons in yer charge. Take good care of the four of ye."

"I will," I said and turned to follow Matthew to Louisa's coach.

A moment later, outside the Abbey doors, Matthew paused. "Mary, I went to Kilgannon to check on things," he said. "And to Edinburgh."

I fought the longing to be home that swept over me. "How is everyone? Ellen and Dougall and Thomas and Murreal, and Berta?"

"They are well. All are well. Ye ken Dougall. He'll no' let anyone approach the inner loch or through the pass, though both apparently have been tried. The people are doing well enough, all things considered. Ellen sends her love and the message that she is with child."

"Oh! How wonderful!"

"Aye." He smiled at my expression and then glanced around. "Mary, I saw Robert Campbell."

"Robert?" I looked around us. "Where?"

"No, no' here. In Edinburgh. Robert told me to tell

you . . ." He looked over my head. "He said to wish you well."

"He is still in Edinburgh?"

"For a bit longer. Then he is coming to London. He said he'll be here for the trial."

My anger was immediate. "Why? Is he coming to gloat?"

Matthew looked at me for a long moment and then a slow smile blossomed. "And I feared he had some hold on you."

I took a deep breath. "Robert was a friend when I needed one, Matthew, nothing more. And despite all his kindnesses I will never forget that he was the one to take Alex to Edinburgh."

"So he was and I'll no' forget it either. Care for yourself, Mary," he said as he ushered me into the coach. "I must be gone."

I bid him farewell, then leaned back against the cushions with the growing belief that I was not going to be able to stop it, any of it, not the trial, not whatever Angus, Duncan, and Harry were planning, not DeBroun, nor Alex's headlong plunge to his own death, nor Robert coming to London to watch it. These men, all of them, were going to persist and I was powerless to prevent whatever was going to happen. I closed my eyes and let the coach bring me home.

At Louisa's I had intended to slip upstairs quietly but was caught with one foot on the first step by Ian and Jamie and the dogs. I sighed to myself. The solitude and quiet I had sought would not be mine now, but then Jamie threw his arms around me while Ian showed me the sums he had worked on all afternoon

and I forgot my exhaustion and tumbled emotions. I let
them lead me to the library, where we had tea and the
boys filled the room with their chatter while the dogs
nudged against me, looking for attention. *This is what is
important, Mary,* I told myself. *Nothing else matters but
these two boys and the baby. And their father. And the
blessed dogs.* Robert the Bruce knocked a teacup over
with his tail, and Jamie scrambled to clean up the mess.
William Wallace decided he needed to see what had
happened, and I sat back against the cushions and
watched the uproar as boys and dogs met porcelain and
silver. Fortunately we had the disorder straightened before Louisa and Randolph joined us, followed by Uncle
Harry talking over his shoulder to Kenneth Ogilvie behind him. The boys leapt to their feet to greet everyone,
and the dogs began barking. We all shushed them at the
same time. Kenneth Ogilvie watched the chaos and met
my eyes, his full of amusement and warmth, and I felt
a wave of comfort. *Harry was right to bring him here,*
I thought. Kenneth radiated common sense and good
cheer. I didn't think he could change anything, but at
least we would have tried everything.

I was not allowed to see Alex again, nor was anyone
else. Gilbey told us only that Alex had been left alone. I
spent my time in enforced idleness. After months of
simply looking pudgy, I was suddenly noticeably with
child, my expanded middle impossible to disguise. As a
result, I had to curtail my visits to officials and members
of Parliament for fear of offending them. I felt fine,
much better than earlier in the pregnancy, and I reflected again how very strange it was that society viewed
a woman having a child as unsuitable for its company.

Adulterers, liars, and thieves could be welcomed under the guise of politeness or hospitality, but a woman bearing her husband's child was someone to stash away until she was again fit for society.

Gilbey visited every night with the tidings of the day. There was little to report. DeBroun seemed to have lost interest in his diversions, for neither Alex nor Murdoch were "questioned" again. Alex was usually cheerful, but occasionally pensive, Gilbey said, recounting how Alex had once asked him to have Seamus pipe him home if he "took the low road." Gilbey, himself rarely emotional, had been distraught, and I had comforted him while I tried not to imagine Alex facing his execution.

The days passed sluggishly, but October arrived at last. We expected each day to hear that Alex's trial would begin the next.

It didn't.

Suddenly all of London seemed to be talking about us. Several of the small journals spent the week discussing, as they labeled it, the "Scottish problem," personified by Alexander MacGannon, the former Earl of Kilgannon. I was grateful that I was sequestered in Louisa's home and did not have to face the curious hordes. The Duchess and Sarah came to see me, but no one else. Louisa's friends were shying away from her, and I told her and Randolph that we must leave their home now or they might never be received in London society again. Louisa laughed and Randolph assured me that there were worse fates than not being received by the Mayfair Bartletts.

The hardest part was not seeing Alex. I'd known that every visit might be the last, but I had never really believed it. I smoothed a hand over my middle and tried

to summon some strength, telling myself that Alex
would be thankful to have the trial begin and the waiting end. But I wasn't thankful. While he had simply
been imprisoned I could fool myself that one day he
would be freed and we could go home, but I could pretend no longer. Alex would be tried and when the farce
was over, he would be executed. I tried to remember
the feel of his arms around me.

Will wrote that he would return for the trial and told
me to keep smiling. I knew he meant well, but the
words rang hollow and I put his letter in a drawer without a second reading. And I had other worries. I was
dangerously low on funds. I had little money of my own
left and wondered how long we could live on charity.
All that money that I had thrown to uncaring officials
was gone. It seemed poorly spent now. The boys and
the baby were my only real comfort. Louisa and Randolph tried to be reassuring, but I knew them too well
not to see that they did not believe their optimistic
words any more than I did. And I'd heard nothing from
Angus.

The journals were revisiting the events of the rebellion now, calling it the "Final Defeat of the Stewarts," listing in lurid detail the dissolution and rout of
the Jacobites, lingering on the lack of leadership and
Stewart's ignominious flight from Montrose. Alex was
described as devilishly handsome, an imprudent and
violent man, and I was called by one writer "the innocent English gentlewoman that Kilgannon carried away
to his lair in the wilds of the north," as though Alex had
stolen me away against my will.

I was not allowed to write to Alex nor he to me. It
seemed unnecessarily cruel. No one seemed to know
when, or indeed if at all, his trial would begin, though

we asked everyone. At last I wrote to the court, asking the schedule and when I could see my husband. I did not expect the answer I received.

Two days later, on a bright and breezy October afternoon, when I was walking in Louisa's gardens with the boys and dogs, Bronson hurried down the path to us.

"Madam," he said in a solicitous tone that amazed me, "Lord DeBroun is here. He asked if Lord and Lady Randolph were gone before he asked for you. Do you wish to see him? Do you wish me to stay with you? I will happily do so." I stared at him but before I could answer, Edgar DeBroun strode up the path toward us.

"Thank you, Bronson," I said, watching DeBroun approach. "I'll be fine. I will send for you if I need you."

"Madam, I will not be far," he said and bowed, his troubled eyes lingering on DeBroun as they passed on the path.

And then DeBroun stood before me and I looked up into his dark eyes, remembering the weals on Alex's neck. I felt at a complete loss. The boys stood protectively at my sides, watching him with wary glances. *Tread carefully,* I told myself. *You brought this upon yourself by writing to the court. This man does nothing without a purpose. Find out what his is.*

"Madam," DeBroun said, his voice silky as he bowed over my hand. "How lovely to see you again. Do we not have a fine day? These are your sons? Or, I should say, Kilgannon's sons?"

"They are, Lord DeBroun," I said, introducing the boys, who bowed perfectly. DeBroun smiled, gesturing to the gardens. "I have interrupted your walk. Pray continue, only let me join you for a moment." I nodded stiffly and we started down the path again. As we walked he asked the boys a series of questions, his tone friendly. The boys looked to me for direction and I nodded and tried to smile. They answered politely. Yes, they both liked London, but Ian liked Scotland better. Yes, they had seen the river and the city and St. Paul's. Jamie told DeBroun that they had visited their father at the Tower. DeBroun nodded but did not comment further. And then, just as casually as he'd asked all the other questions, he asked them if they would like to visit his estate in Cornwall. With their stepmother, of course. It was, he said, on a cliff overlooking the sea and they could sail and fish. I stared at him over the boys' heads, the air suddenly chill. I felt a tremor of fear run through me and I struggled not to shiver. *Dear God,* I thought, *is he saying what I think he is? And this man will determine Alex's fate? Tell me no.*

"We can do that at Kilgannon, sir," said Ian politely, "but thank you for inviting us."

"Son, you cannot return to Kilgannon." DeBroun looked at me over Ian's head. "You'll be here in London or in Warwickshire, dependent on the charity of your stepmother's family. Perhaps you will miss the sea and want to visit. With a close friend." I stared into his eyes until William Wallace bounded away after a cat and Robert the Bruce followed, the boys chasing after them. I watched the boys until they were safely out of earshot, then turned back to Edgar DeBroun.

"What exactly do you mean, sir?" Anger made my voice tremble.

He smiled in a smug manner, mistaking my shock for fear. "Do not be afraid, madam. I meant only what I said. I would be most pleased to have you and your sons visit me in Cornwall when your . . ." He looked at my middle, and I took a shuddery breath, trying to master my rage. ". . . schedule allows it." He met my eyes again, his self-satisfied and amused. "Do not mistake me, madam. I ask nothing of you now. But one day, perhaps soon, you will find yourself with no home in Scotland and your brother's or your aunt's hospitality tiresome. One day you will be raising three children with no home of your own. One day you will welcome the attentions of someone who admires you despite your liabilities, and then you will understand that I was most generous toward your husband. I cannot change his fate but I can, possibly, persuade the others to be somewhat lenient with your husband. Perhaps hanging instead of . . . With the understanding, of course, that if I were to one day visit you I would be received as a welcome friend." I stared at him, quite incapable of speech. "I would be most kind to your children. All of them."

My voice trembled. "Sir, are you asking me to marry you?"

He laughed and looked after the boys. "It was not marriage that I was contemplating." He laughed again and stole a long look at my bosom before meeting my eyes. "Of course, I would not rule it out. It depends. Perhaps we could discuss it." I closed my mouth firmly before I could scream. *Mary,* I told myself as I looked after the boys, *remember who this man is. Remember the bruises on Alex. Say nothing.* The baby moved within me and suddenly I felt very alone. Tears of frustration ran down my cheeks before I could control them, and De-Broun's expression changed as he watched me and he sighed as I fumbled for my handkerchief.

"Very well!" he snapped. "We will discuss marriage." He sounded genuinely distressed and I stared at him as the absurdity of the situation overwhelmed me. "Madam," he said, his eyes drifting to my breasts again, "I am quite earnest. I will wait until you have recovered and then, despite your obvious political liabilities, I will have you. When all of this is over I will come to visit you and you will welcome me. I will give you back your place in society. You are very fortunate that I am so generous."

I took a deep breath and proved myself unable to think as I gaped at him. "Madam," he said as the boys and dogs returned to us, "we are agreed? Remember that generosity is a virtue and that one cannot help but be swayed today by promises of tomorrow's pleasures."

Be careful, I told myself as I met his eyes. *Alex will pay for your mistakes.* "I cannot think beyond my present circumstances, sir. I make no promises but I agree that generosity is a virtue."

DeBroun bowed and smiled. "One week, madam. The trial will begin in one week. And it will be over one week after that." He walked quickly away. I stared after him, my hands clasped at my heart. *Alex,* I thought. *Oh, dear God, Alex.*

"What did he want, Mama?" asked Jamie, watching DeBroun's retreating back. I took a deep breath and willed myself to be calm.

"I . . . I don't know, Jamie."

"Well, I'm not going to any place in Cornwall," growled Ian. "I don't like him and I'll bet his home is not like Kilgannon."

"No," I said, meeting his eyes. "It couldn't possibly be."

"Nowhere is like Kilgannon," said Jamie.

"No," I agreed, taking their hands in mine. "Nowhere is like Kilgannon. And no one is like Kilgannon."

SIXTEEN

I STRUGGLED WITH IT FOR DAYS. WHAT AN IMPOSSIBLE thing for DeBroun to have done. What a brainless thing for me to have done, to have written to the court. And what should I do now? If I told Will or Randolph or Uncle Harry, they would be outraged and feel they had to act, and I could not risk that. DeBroun was still one of the judges on Alex's case, no matter what else he was. What had I set in motion by writing that letter? Dear God, what had I done? If I did nothing, then DeBroun thought we had some sort of agreement. If I made him aware of my antipathy, Alex would suffer. If I let him think I would one day accept his proposition, would it help or hurt Alex? I knew I could not tell Louisa without her telling Randolph. Uncle Harry's reaction I could not begin to guess. Where was Angus? But no, it was out of the question to think of telling any of the Kilgannon men.

I wish Will were here, I thought, but reconsidered at once. Will would be outraged as well and he had his own problems just now. He had written to tell us that Betty was very ill at Grafton with fever and lethargy. He was very worried, for Betty did not care how she looked, which meant that she must be very ill indeed. I had written that of course he should stay with Betty. Louisa offered to go to them, but Will wrote that she should stay with me for now. Was there no end to our troubles?

Gilbey was allowed to see Alex daily again, but he said only that Alex had been sequestered and no one, not even DeBroun, had come to see him. I sent messages of my love and reassurances that we were well. They rang hollow even as I wrote them, and Alex's just as empty when I read his.

The morning the trial began I woke before daybreak. In a weak moment I considered not going, but the thought that Alex would arrive in the courtroom and not find me drove me out of bed. And Uncle Harry had been adamant that I be there. All of London would be watching to see if Mary Lowell MacGannon supported her husband, he'd said, and if I stayed home all of London would assume that I had forsaken him. I had agreed. But now, on this chill morning, I stood at the window staring into the street, trying to convince myself that this was real. Where was Angus?

I felt very alone. I had agreed to the coaxing and sent the boys to Mountgarden, despite their arguments, but my heart sank as I'd watched their coach drive away, both boys, and the dogs, hanging out the windows. Selfishly I wished them here now, to cheer me with their optimism and clamor, but was glad they would be spared this final misery. I moved as though in a nightmare, aware of the smallest things and numb at the same time. I could not have said what clothes I wore nor what day of the week it was. The butter on my knife seemed to glow bright yellow in the dim dining room, but I could not hear him easily when Randolph spoke to me.

"Mary, dear, I said that Angus has arrived. Shall he join us?"

I nodded. *Of course Angus should join us for break-fast. It would be rude to leave him standing in the foyer and he should eat,* I thought foggily, as though it were of vast importance that Angus be well fed on this of all mornings. And then Angus stood in the doorway and I gasped, halfway out of my seat. For just a moment, with him standing there, dressed in Highland clothing, his blond hair pulled back, I'd thought it was Alex and my heart had taken a wild leap. Just as quickly I knew my mistake and could feel the color drain from my face.

"Angus," I said, meeting him halfway across the room. I embraced him, feeling how rigid his body was.

"Mary," he said, his voice rough with emotion. "I couldna let ye go alone." He released me and looked at my uncle. "I mean no insult, sir," Angus said to Randolph, "but I would have Mary have a Highland guard with her. My men are waiting outside."

Randolph nodded. "I expected you, Angus. I am bringing several of my men as well. I've ordered two coaches."

We rolled through the streets of London, tucked safely in Randolph's coaches. The streets were clogged with people, and the street vendors called out their wares as the crowds passed on their way to this latest amusement. I tried not think of Alex's trial being of no more importance than something to discuss over a mug of ale, but I knew that was all it would ever be to most of these people. For a moment I hated them, the ones for whom Alex's trial was only a diversion. Angus sat opposite me, silent and withdrawn. When I asked him where Matthew and Gilbey were, he looked at me without expression. "They'll be there," he said.

"Is Gilbey with Alex?"

He nodded. "He was earlier this morning, for a bit. But they werena allowed to be alone. Alex says he's ready."

As we drew at last to the curb and I stepped from the coach, Angus and several men surrounded me, to my surprise Duncan among them. He winked at me as he offered his hand for my descent.

"We're here, Mary," he said, sounding for a moment like the Duncan I remembered from happier times. "And we'll be with ye throughout the trial. Never ye fear that ye'll be unprotected."

"I am not worried about myself, Duncan," I whispered and he nodded, but there was no time to speak further.

I raised my chin as I heard the cries of recognition around me. Some were speaking kindly, but I was called a traitor and a whore by others. The men pressed tightly around Louisa and me as we followed Angus and Randolph in a phalanx to the door.

Westminster Hall. Sir William Wallace had been condemned within these walls. Charles Stuart, once King of England, had been tried here and beheaded a stone's throw away. Sir Thomas More, Guy Fawkes, Perkin Warbeck, and the Duke of Somerset had received sentences of death in this room; Edward II and Richard II were deposed here. I wished I did not know my history. I needed no reminders of what happened when the Crown of England was challenged. I paused at the top of the stairs before descending into the hall itself, taking in the sight before me.

The massive room had been transformed since my last visit, a large section set aside for the public. The stone walls were glowing with light from the many chandeliers, and far overhead the carvings of dark hammered wood cast shadows on the spaces behind. The benches for the public were raised and separated by a railing from the floor of the courtroom, and behind the railing, facing the audience, was the dais where the judges sat. To the left and right were lower and smaller daises, with three tiers of benches cushioned in deep burgundy velvet. Above the judges' dais was a large wooden screen, decorated with a relief of blind Justice holding the scales. Blind justice indeed, I thought. Not with this trial. It was a travesty, a sham. A spectacle.

It was as public as Robert had said it would be. The crowds pressed against the doors outside, and the anteroom was filled with those hoping to get a seat. Inside the hall the benches were full, although the trial was not scheduled to begin for over an hour. I was grateful to sink down between Angus and Louisa and pleased to note the Duchess in the row behind me as she patted my shoulder and whispered encouragement.

But I was not afraid. I was angry. Angry that they had chosen to make an example of Alex, angry at Malcolm and the MacDonald, at the Earl of Mar and James Stewart, and Robert, and DeBroun. And Alex. Angry that there would be no one to raise a cry of outrage for him and no one to stop this farce. I knew they would find him guilty and that they would then sentence him to die. Part of me still hoped for a miracle, but I would be here, miracle or no. I put my hands in my lap and concentrated on the carving on the railings while around me the elite of London discussed Alex's chances of living as though it were a horse race. I tried not to see those I knew pass in the aisles before me, searching for good seats. Janice and Jonathan Wumple pretended not to see me, which meant they had to ignore the Duchess as well. Small price to pay for letting the world know they had no connection to me, I thought, and groaned inwardly as more faces from my past went by. Rowena deBurghesse hung on Edmund Bartlett's arm. She did not have to pretend not to see me as she simpered up into Edmund's face. And Rowena, whose only talent as far as I could tell was gossip, would spread the fate of this day all over London. *They were all here,* I thought.

We waited in silence until a voice droned from the floor that the proceedings would begin and asked us to rise. There was no one yet to see on the floor, then a side door opened and several men in uniform stepped into the hall. Following closely behind them were men in dark robes, the barristers, I discovered. They filled the benches on each side of the floor. The five judges filed in slowly from a door behind the dais, their robes gleaming satin and their wigs starkly white against the dark wood. It was difficult to tell what they looked like in the robes and wigs, but they were of varying ages. Edgar DeBroun sat to the left of the middle judge, his dark eyes scanning the crowd until he found me. He nodded almost imperceptibly and I turned my eyes away.

There was a pause during which all on the dais looked at something hidden from us, then a ripple from those in the crowd far to the left, where they could see between the dais and the benches into the doors that still stood open. The clamor grew as Alex was led in.

His hair was pulled neatly back, and he was clean-shaven but pale. He wore his green velvet doublet and the plaid I'd seen him in last, fixed at his shoulder with the old brooch. And he'd been correct; not a mark of abuse showed. He looked devastatingly handsome as he towered over the men who stood on either side of him, and seemed not the least intimidated by his surroundings. He looked, I realized, like a Gaelic laird, and I knew many would consider him the picture of the barbarian they'd like to believe him to be. *Dear God,* I prayed, *protect my love.* Alex's expression was carefully blank as he stood next to the raised benches, and he looked straight ahead until a voice rose from behind us, shouting a Gaelic phrase I did not know. Alex turned then and grinned, raising a hand in salute.

I had recognized the voice and craned my neck to find him. Next to me Angus did the same. "Is it Gilbey?" I asked and Angus nodded. "What did he say?"

"The MacIntyre war cry, lass," Angus whispered. "I'd say Alex kens Gilbey's here." He nodded then to the courtroom floor where two men led Alex to stand in front of the judges, then stepped back. One of the lawyers, a man I'd never seen before, came to his left, and I regretted anew that Kenneth was not allowed to represent Alex in England. I had no idea who this lawyer was or what he intended to do, for I had been barred from talking with him. The judges motioned for silence and I watched Alex's stiff back. As the crowd settled, the center judge, a thin man with a dissatisfied expression, leaned forward, speaking in a demanding tone.

"Sir, I am Lord Webster, your high judge. Are you Ian Alexander James Fraser MacKenzie MacGannon, the Earl of Kilgannon?"

No, I thought, *he is not Ian Alexander,* and said

as much to Kenneth, leaning across Angus to do so. I supposed it made no difference, but Kenneth Ogilvie wrote it down.

Alex's answer was clear and calm. "I am Alexander Ian James Keith Fraser MacGannon, the Earl of Kilgannon."

The judged nodded. "The charges against you are most serious, Kilgannon. There will be no further outbursts from the audience. Do you understand?"

"I am no' in control of the audience, your honor," Alex said, "but I understand English quite well." The crowd shifted in their seats and some laughed. The judges exchanged glances.

Lord Webster frowned. "Kilgannon, you will be read two charges and then asked how you plead. Answer clearly."

Alex lifted his chin. "I do no' plead, sir."

The crowd snickered and Webster leaned forward, his frown deepening. "Sir, you are accused of two charges. Do you understand that?"

"I understand yer trumping up charges against me, aye."

"These are not trumped-up charges, Kilgannon."

"One is, your honor, but at least yer saving the Crown the expense of two trials. I admire yer economy." The laughter that rippled through the stands was excited. They used to enjoy bearbaiting, too, I thought. The judge waited as the crowd settled.

"Kilgannon, do you understand the seriousness of the charges?"

"I understand the accusations, sir. Do ye understand that I dinna agree with them?" The crowd rustled again and some clapped.

"You are not asked to agree with them, sir." Webster

straightened his back and began to read in a stentorian voice. "To the charge of high treason, by your willful rebellion in Scotland, in September 1715, against His Majesty King George, King of all Britain, and by your willful participation with the Jacobite troops at the battle of Sherrifmuir against the forces of His Majesty King George, King of all Britain, in November 1715, how do you, Ian Alexander James Fraser MacKenzie MacGannon, the Earl of Kilgannon, plead?"

"I told ye, sir. I dinna plead. And I am no' guilty of treason against George of Hanover, for I am no' his subject."

Alex's lawyer stepped forward, bowing. "The Earl of Kilgannon pleads not guilty, your honor," he said in an obsequious tone.

Alex watched the lawyer with a sideways glance and then nodded again. "Aye," he said to the judge. "That's what I said."

Lord Webster spoke again. "To the charge of willful murder of Douglas Campbell, a British citizen, in Brenmargon Pass, Scotland, in February 1716, how do you, Ian Alexander James Fraser MacKenzie MacGannon, the Earl of Kilgannon, plead?"

"That was no murder and ye ken it well, sir," Alex said harshly. "It was war and if that's murder, then ye should include the men I killed at Sherrifmuir as well, aye?" Alex frowned while his lawyer stood before him, talking intently. Alex nodded and stepped back, crossing his arms over his chest, his anger evident.

Lord Webster glared at Alex. "Kilgannon, I will not tolerate this behavior. This is a court of law, not some Highland gathering. You will refrain from outbursts or I will have you removed. Do you understand?"

Alex glared back at him and nodded curtly.

"Do you understand, sir?" the judge repeated.

"Aye, your honor, I understand entirely."

"How do you plead?"

"Not guilty," the lawyer said before Alex could answer, and the judge sat back and placed both hands on the table before him.

Lord Webster explained the procedure at great length and then a clerk stood and read the additional charge against Alex. I was outraged. Apparently the charge of treason was not sufficient. They had added this second, absurd charge. Either was enough to sentence him to death, and the picture they presented together was of a dangerous and violent man.

A wave of conversation filled the time it took Alex to be led to the dock, where he stood facing us, searching the audience. He found us at last and nodded. Hundreds of eyes followed his gaze and when I forced a smile Alex winked at me.

"Kilgannon," Judge Webster said in a menacing tone, "I expect you to behave in a proper fashion as befits this courtroom. If you cannot, I will try you in absentia. When the witnesses come forward you will be silent and you will speak only when spoken to, or I will have you removed. Is that understood?"

"Perfectly," said Alex, raising his chin, and for a moment he looked so like Jamie that I caught my breath. "If I defend myself you'll find me guilty with me gone rather than with me here."

"The choice is yours, sir. I will not have my court turned into a circus."

"Then bring reasonable charges against me. If yer goal is to hang me, ye don't need more than the charge of treason. I will answer for what I've done, but no' more. Ye have the wrong charges, sir, and the wrong name. Yer court canna even get my name correct."

"The choice is yours, Kilgannon."

"Can ye hang me in absentia, your honor?"

"I think not."

"Then I will be here to see this through."

"As you wish, Kilgannon. But remember my terms."

Alex nodded grimly. "I'm no' likely to forget them."

The morning was spent hearing several witnesses, all English or Campbells, who swore that Alex was at Sherrifmuir and had been in the company of the rebels. Alex had watched the witnesses in stony silence, leaning gracefully against the back railing of the dock, his arms crossed over his chest. The witnesses continued into the afternoon, and by day's end it had been determined that Alex had been with the rebels, with the added information that he had been said to attend the war councils of the Earl of Mar and that he kept company with such known rebels as Sir Donald MacDonald and the Macleans.

The crowd had grown bored with the proceedings, and there had been fewer of them in the afternoon. The testimony continued, officer after officer claiming to have seen Alex at Sherrifmuir, in the Jacobite troops led by General Gordon. As the last officer stepped down, Alex leaned forward and caught the judge's eye.

"Sir, I have admitted that I was at the battle of Sherrifmuir, leading my men. Can we no' have done with this part of it? We've wasted a whole day proving what I've never denied. I took arms against yer king. No' mine, but yers."

"Sir, you have been warned."

"Aye, but, your honor, let's get on with it. I took arms against yer Geordie. But I will never agree that it is treason."

"You claim James Stewart as your king?"

"No."

Lord Webster's voice was harsh. "You do not claim James Stewart as king of England and Ireland and Scotland?"

"I do no' claim James Stewart as my king. I have no king."

"You must have a king. You must declare yourself for one or the other. You have chosen James Stewart."

"I did once declare myself for the Stewart, sir, but no more."

"Then who is king of your country?"

Alex leaned forward as he and the judge stared at each other. They might have been alone in the room. "I have no king, nor need o' one. I wish only to be left alone to live my life without interference. Leave me and mine alone and I willna bother ye. I've no desire to fight your army, nor do most Scots. Take yer armies home and leave us be. Get out of my country and I will stay out of yers. But if ye come to dominate us, we'll resist. As ye would. I was only defending my homeland." The crowd muttered and the judges exchanged glances. De-Broun watched Alex.

Lord Webster spoke slowly. "You admit that you took arms against King George, King of all Britain."

Alex shook his head. "No. I took arms against King George, King of England. Not King of all Britain. Just England. I do no' deny that George of Hanover is King of England, and that I fought his troops. I fought men who would dominate my country against its will. I fought troops occupying my homeland. And I would do so again. But I do no longer seek to restore James Stewart."

"Why?"

"Because he is unfit to rule. But"— Alex smiled—"at least he can speak English." The crowd laughed and the judge frowned. He pounded on the desk and declared the day over.

SEVENTEEN

WE WERE A SOBER GROUP AT LOUISA'S THAT EVE-
ning, even Harry made quiet by the day's events. Gilbey
and Matthew snuck in to join us and we revisited the
day over and over. After dinner we sat in the library, discussing it yet again. Kenneth Ogilvie was reading his
notes, and Angus withdrew to the window. I joined him
and after a moment met his blue eyes, so like Alex's.

"Lass, do ye trust me?" he asked quietly.

"Always," I said and he nodded with the ghost of a
smile.

"Then promise me one thing, Mary," he said. "If I
tell ye to stay or to go somewhere, will ye do it without
questions?"

"No," I said and watched the anger flash in his eyes.
"No. I'll still ask questions. But you don't have to answer them."

He shook his head at me, the anger replaced by
amusement. "Fair enough. At least yer consistent, lass,"
he said, then moved away to withdraw with Randolph
to a corner while Louisa talked with Matthew and
Gilbey. I returned to the couch, and sat staring into the
fire, looking up when my view was blocked. Kenneth
stood before me with a quiet smile.

"A very interesting beginning," he said.

"A disaster already, sir," I answered.

"No, no, not at all, Lady Mary," he said, sitting next to me. "Quite the opposite."

"What do you mean?" I asked as the others gathered around us, Angus and Randolph standing with folded arms before us.

"Well," said Kenneth, "you pointed it out yourself, Lady Mary, and it may yet be important. Alex's name was incorrect."

"Yes, but what matters—"

"What matters is that the indictments were brought against a man who does not exist."

I stared at him. "Does that make a difference?"

Kenneth waved a hand. "I believe Alex's lawyer can apply to the court for dismissal of the charges. It's unlikely they will be dropped, but Alexander Ian James Keith Fraser MacGannon was not indicted this morning. If Alex is found guilty, perhaps we can prove that the man who is guilty of treason does not exist. Stranger things have happened. After the rebellion of '88, several rebels were let free because of stupid errors by clerks. We'll make note of it and see what happens."

"We ken what will happen, Ogilvie," growled Angus.

"Not for certain, Angus," said Kenneth, unperturbed. Angus shrugged. I looked up at the lawyer, fearful of hoping.

"I will speak to the barrister in the morning," said Randolph.

Tuesday was little better. Alex's lawyer had agreed to discuss our concerns about the name with the judges. When the time was right. I made no comment when Randolph told me. The day in court, a very long day, was spent determining that Alex had been seen with Jacobites. Alex appeared bored, but I watched with a growing terror. It was true. They would convict him. At the end of the day, as he was led out, I tried to smile, but I'm sure my face showed my thoughts. Alex lifted his chin and waved.

That night I dreamed of being in his arms in the Tower, of him next to me, about to kiss me, his hair falling about his shoulders as he moved. I could feel the hair on his chest as he leaned against my breasts and his quiet chuckle when the baby moved and we could both feel it. I woke, cold and alone, to feel the baby move again, and I stared at nothing, trying to conjure Alex back to me.

Wednesday morning London buzzed with a new topic. Richard Steele, one of the authors of *The Spectator*, had taken up Alex's cause in his journal. Steele, notorious for selecting those of questionable virtue in society and raising them to a pedestal where they were endowed with every quality desirable in a member of a civilized society, had declared Alex the "New Scotsman," a breed of man never seen before. Alex, Steele stated, embodied the courage and intelligence necessary for a leader, even for a leader of an unknown and unaccomplished group of Scots on the border of beyond.

"We are forced, once again, to consider that cold land to our north," wrote Steele. "What to think, when an uneducated man such as Kilgannon, though fair of form and face as he is, raises the very issues that so many of us have discussed behind closed doors? That the Scots, long a thorn in the side of the royal personage and those that sit in Parliament, should be unhappy in the union so swiftly imposed upon them, is of no surprise to any thoughtful Londoner. But that a man such as Kilgannon, on trial for treason against that very union, can express his discontent not only with our royal leader but with the other claimants of that position, is of the utmost interest. One scarcely knows how to address such a situation. If the Scots view themselves as not of this union, then this latest insurrection will not be the last, but only one in a continuous series of rebellions designed with only one purpose, the annihilation of that aforementioned and despised union, and without complete direction as to the desired leader in the resulting void.

"Kilgannon refuses to be cowed by our courts. He is of a breed apart from us, a breed both civilized and violent, which will take arms over ideas and asks to be left alone with its own kind. It will be a futile attempt to fashion these Highland lairds into English gentlemen. Perhaps we should follow the pattern of the Romans and leave them to their northern climes. Perhaps we would be better to let those not of us be separated from us, lest we all perish in the attempt for affiliation. Why not leave the barbarous Scots to their own devices rather than to pretend that we can fuse in peace? We would be better to have them as allies than subjects."

Steele's essay was so well received that the other papers joined him with their own flourishes and even the more prosaic suggested that perhaps the Union should be reconsidered.

That day at the trial it was determined yet again that Alex had fought with the Jacobites, and he met my eyes with a shrug as he was led away at the end of the day. Nothing, it appeared, not even boredom, would hurry these judges.

That evening Louisa's maid came to my door, her eyes huge. "Lady Mary," she said, wringing her hands, "Lady Randolph requests your presence in the library at once."

I rose, alarmed. "What is it?"

"I don't know, madam, but the Duke of Grafton has just arrived as well. Please hurry."

In the library I found Louisa and Randolph, and Uncle Harry. And Bronson. Their expressions were serious and Louisa seemed distraught. Harry was agitated as he paced the room, rubbing his arm. When he turned to me I could see that he was angry as well.

"Mary," Harry said in a tight tone before anyone else could speak, "I've heard a very strange story this evening."

"What is it, Harry? What have you heard? Is it news of Alex?" But Harry did not immediately answer me. I looked from Harry to Louisa and saw that she had been crying. "Is it Alex?"

"No," said Randolph, shaking his head. Harry broke in before Randolph could continue.

"I realize we have not always been close, Mary," Harry said. "But I hope you know I am very fond of you and your brother."

"Yes, Uncle Harry," I said, confused, "and we of you."

"I had assumed that. So, you can imagine my surprise upon hearing tonight that you have not told us something so very important. Or is it perhaps not true?"

"What? Is what not true?"

"Mary, my dear," said Randolph, "Bronson told me this evening that Lord DeBroun came to you shortly before Alex's trial began and asked you to marry him sometime in the future. Is this true?"

I looked at Bronson, despising him for his meddling. He looked away. I turned to Randolph again. "Yes," I said.

"You may leave us, Bronson," said Randolph.

The butler moved to the door, meeting my eyes as he passed me. "Lady Mary," Bronson said, "I told Lord Randolph because I felt that Lord DeBroun had acted most unwisely and that he put you in a very difficult position. I thought it was for the best."

I nodded coldly. I would deal with Bronson later. The look of hurt in Louisa's and Randolph's eyes lacerated me, and I wondered for the first time if I had been right to conceal DeBroun's visit. When the door shut behind Bronson, Harry whirled around to face me.

"How did you answer Lord DeBroun, Mary?" he demanded.

"I didn't, Harry," I said and told them of DeBroun's visit, my answer and my concerns.

Harry nodded, chewing his lip and rubbing his arm thoughtfully, his anger visibly dissipating. "You understand that you should have told me?"

"Or me," said Randolph.

"Or me," said Louisa faintly and my heart sank. I had not meant to hurt any of them, and I said as much.

"You should have come to your family," said Harry. "What's the use of being a duke if your family doesn't come to you with its problems? I am not without power. You should have come to me."

"I was afraid for Alex, Harry. I thought if I was harsh in my refusal then DeBroun would be hostile to Alex."

"And you thought that if you were pleasant to him, he'd be lenient to the man whose wife he covets? Surely you cannot have thought this?"

"I did not know what to think. It was unexpected and unwelcome and it caught me off guard. I still am not sure what I should have said."

"You should have burst into tears and driven him away."

I smiled wryly, remembering. "I did burst into tears. He had not asked me to marry at first." Harry gaped at me, his face now florid. Randolph rose to stand before me.

"He asked you to be his mistress?" asked Randolph, his voice hoarse with indignation.

"I'm not sure, Randolph. I was so stunned that I started crying and then he told me we would discuss marriage. He might have intended that all along." The men exchanged glances and Louisa wiped her eyes with her handkerchief. "I did not know what to do. I did not tell you," I said, looking at each of them in turn, "any of you, because I was afraid of what you might do. Anything that you do now to DeBroun will jeopardize Alex. Can we not simply pretend it never happened? I have made no agreement with the man. After . . . after the trial, I will tell DeBroun my true feelings, and when I do, believe me, he will not trouble me again."

Harry came to me then and patted my arm while Louisa and Randolph exchanged a look. "My dear," Harry said. "One cannot expect a woman to understand a man like Edgar DeBroun, but I understand him. What a turn of events. Actually, though, it plays into our plans. I still say you should have told me."

I nodded. "I was afraid you'd feel you had to avenge my honor. I did not consider his proposal for a mo-

ment, Harry, but I was afraid to tell him so because of
Alex."

"Of course. Well, well, my dear. This is an interesting
development."

"What will we do?" asked Louisa.

"What can we do?" Randolph answered, looking to
Harry for agreement. But Harry just smiled, taking his
leave soon after that, saying he would think of the best
course of action overnight.

Alone with Louisa and Randolph, I listened with
remorse as they chided me for not telling them. We discussed it into the night, Randolph growing more furious with DeBroun as the hours passed. They wanted
me to leave London immediately. But where would I
go? Betty was ill at Grafton, and Mountgarden was too
far away. I refused to leave until the trial was over. Then,
I told them, I would surely be allowed to see Alex again.
I would not leave London before that and asked them if
they wished me to leave their house. Louisa embraced
me then and Randolph told me that I would be going
nowhere.

On Thursday morning, the city still abuzz with
Steele's essay, the trial was the place to be seen and I was
one of its chief attractions. People talked behind their
hands as I passed, but I tried to ignore them all, though
I heard laughter behind me and felt my color rise.
Damn them all, I thought. *Ghouls, every one of them,
happy to feed on my grief.*

The testimony that morning determined that Alex
had never signed the two letters that had circulated
the Highlands, one acknowledging Sophia as the Elec-
torate, the other welcoming George as king. Alex had
never sworn his loyalty, to George or to Sophia, argued

his lawyer, and had never been asked to recognize the succession. "Nor," he said, "was Kilgannon among those Scottish nobles who accepted English money to assure that their clans would not rise in rebellion and then did so."

But the judges were not listening. They talked among themselves, except for Edgar DeBroun, who watched Alex constantly. The others listened only when Alex's lawyer told of Alex's trip to France in 1710 as an emissary of Scotland's goodwill toward Queen Anne and brazenly mentioned that Alex saved Duke John's life. I watched Alex stare ahead as all of this was discussed, knowing that he would never have suggested the topic himself, and wondering who had told the barrister. The Duchess beamed when curious glances came her way.

That afternoon the examination of Alex's treason was put aside for the discussion of the second charge. Several witnesses discussed the "murder" of Douglas Campbell in Brenmargon Pass. The absurdity of the charge made me angry every time I thought of Alex, outnumbered and thinking he was doomed, facing Robert's men and striking down the one who attacked him. Next to me Angus muttered to himself. Several Campbells, two of whom had testified earlier that they had seen Alex at Sherrifmuir, told the same story, that they had been pursuing Alex to bring him to trial in Edinburgh. In the pass, they said, he had faced them appearing to surrender and then striking Douglas Campbell, who had approached Alex to talk.

Alex's lawyer questioned the men and brought out the facts, that Alex was one man against the fifty pursuing him and that he had only lifted his sword when the Campbell was bearing down upon him with weapon raised, but the impression of Alex as dangerous lingered and I knew Alex's lawyer had not sufficiently swayed the judges. I only half-listened to Alex's lawyer's request to call only one witness on this charge and to Lord Webster's agreement.

The bailiff cleared his throat and announced that Lord Robert Campbell would take the stand. I met Alex's eyes across the room. He gave me a crooked smile and drew his hand across his throat.

EIGHTEEN

ROBERT STEPPED BOLDLY ONTO THE COURTROOM floor dressed in his military uniform, with a Campbell plaid thrown over his shoulder. He looked tall and powerful. And very handsome. The crowd stirred as he crossed the floor and nodded to Alex. Alex watched Robert approach with a stony expression, then he looked for my reaction and I met his eyes as hundreds watched.

Robert was sworn in as Lord Robert Duncan Campbell, Major of the Campbell Brigade, formerly in the command of the Duke of Argyll. Alex's lawyer questioned him about his military experience and stressed how very distinguished Robert's career had been. No taint of disloyalty had ever touched Robert, which made his answers to the questions all the more compelling. He'd been promoted, it seemed, after the battle at Sherrifmuir, to major. With a comment that the men who had testified earlier might not have seen all that had happened, he declared that Alex had had no choice but to defend himself and that to his regret, and in complete defiance of his orders, Douglas Campbell had been the aggressor.

"I would have done the same in Kilgannon's position, sir," Robert said in his clear voice. "Indeed, my own arm was raised to stop Douglas when Kilgannon did. I would advise the court to dismiss this charge, your honor. We were at war and cannot consider every death to be murder. Kilgannon defended himself well and bravely and if anyone caused Douglas's death, it was himself."

The crowd erupted with discussion, and the judge, obviously as surprised as the rest of us at Robert's testimony, had to call for order several times. During the fracas Robert turned to gaze at Alex. When their eyes met in a long look, Alex raised a hand in salute and Robert nodded, then turned away as the judge spoke.

"Lord Campbell, we will consider your remarks," Webster said and cleared his throat. "Now, as to the charge of high treason, have you ever seen Kilgannon in the presence of Jacobites?"

Robert nodded. "At the battle of Sherrifmuir, your honor."

"And where was he, Lord Campbell?"

"Across the field, fighting under General Gordon."

"Have you any doubt he was fighting for the Stewart cause?"

"He was with the Jacobites, your honor. I have no doubt that Kilgannon was fighting for the Stewarts."

"Fighting the forces of the King of England."

"I am sure he felt he was fighting for the freedom of Scotland," Robert replied.

"Thank you, Lord Campbell," Webster said. "That will be all."

Robert stepped down and as he passed, Alex leaned over the railing and spoke quietly to him. Robert nodded up at Alex and then both looked at me.

London buzzed again. I did not sleep that night.

* * *

Friday was interminable. I spent it in a state of alarm. Angus had been at my side throughout the proceedings, silent for the most part, but I'd found comfort in his presence. But this morning Angus had not arrived to come with us, nor was Duncan with our escort. Randolph and I had asked the men when they arrived where Angus and Duncan were, but had received no answer. My uneasiness grew with every moment as we traveled to Westminster.

When we were seated, Randolph talked to Harry in a quiet voice, but when he straightened I could tell he had gotten no information. Randolph gave me a glance, shaking his head, and I battled another wave of fear. Harry, Angus, and Duncan were plotting something, and if they had not taken Randolph into their confidence it was very likely that they were doing something which neither of us would approve. Harry rubbed his arm and kept his silence.

After a long delay Alex was led to the dock and the judges filed in. Lord Webster announced without preamble that the charges against Alex of the murder of Douglas Campbell had been dismissed, but I barely heard him. Only four judges were seated on the dais.

Edgar DeBroun was missing.

The morning was spent in yet again bringing witnesses who had seen Alex at Sherrifmuir or in the company of Jacobites, but there was nothing new and the crowd and I grew restless. No mention of DeBroun's absence had been made, and I found myself looking at his empty chair as if it could explain where he was. Just before noon Lord Webster dismissed the witness and leaned forward to silently stare at Alex. Alex met his look with a wintry expression of his own. The moment went on for far too long and at last the judge straightened and spoke, his tone mild.

"Lord Kilgannon, are you aware that the Jacobite cause has several symbols affiliated with it?"

Alex nodded. "If ye mean the Stewart crest and badge, I ken them."

"There is a white cockade that Jacobites wear in their hats."

"I've seen it, your honor."

"It is a symbol of a flower, I'm told. A rose. And the rose, a white rose, can also thus be considered to be a symbol of the Jacobite cause." He paused. "Can you tell me why you call one of your ships the *Mary Rose?*"

Alex raised his chin. "The *Mary Rose* is named after my wife, your honor."

"Your wife's name is Mary Rose?"

"My wife's name is Mary."

Lord Webster appeared bemused. "Yet you named your ship the *Mary Rose*. You added the name Rose to your wife's name?"

Alex looked across the room to me and smiled. "I did."

"After the Jacobite cause."

"No. After the flower," Alex said calmly. "There are wild roses in Scotland, sir, and white ones grow near our home."

"White roses. The symbol of the Jacobite cause."

"To some. In my home it was only a very beautiful flower. And a wild rose, your honor. I dinna plant it. God did."

"Do you not think it strange that you call your wife a

name that also symbolizes the cause for which you later fought?"

"No." He paused and then smiled. "The rose has been used for centuries to describe beautiful women, and it has been used as a symbol by many causes. I do not call my wife or the ship Mary Rose to back the Jacobite cause. Nor to back the York or Lancaster causes either. Ye have heard of the War of the Roses?"

The crowd laughed and Alex grinned at the judge, then turned to me. I smiled in return, but the judge was not amused. *Alex,* I thought, *tread lightly.* Webster appeared to ponder.

"Why do you call your wife Mary Rose?" he asked.

Alex's cheeks flamed, but his tone was as mild as the judge's. "It is a beautiful flower, sir, and a splendid name for a beautiful woman. And it is no concern of this court."

Webster merely nodded and announced that the trial was in recess for the day. How the gossips loved it.

We had little to say at luncheon except to ask each other over and over where Angus and Duncan were. And Edgar DeBroun. My fears rose that evening when only Kenneth Ogilvie joined us at dinner. Harry and Angus had come every night, but tonight neither appeared nor did they send messages, although when we had parted at the courtroom Harry had said he would see us this evening. We did not know where Angus was lodging and had no way of reaching him. I hung the plaid from my window but it did nothing. And our notes to Harry went unanswered. At last Randolph went to Harry's lodgings himself, but Harry was not there, nor did his staff know where he was. It was a very long evening and my nightly letter to the boys was stilted.

Will had written that Betty's condition was the same and asked Louisa to have Dr. Sutter visit them. Louisa wrote to the doctor at once and wrote Will with the news that Dr. Sutter would go to Grafton as soon as possible. I wrote as well, telling him all that had happened and sending my love and prayers for Betty. I didn't tell him my fear, that we both could lose the people we loved.

On Saturday afternoon the Duchess arrived, her usual bustle replaced with tight-lipped anxiety, and my heart sank as I saw her mood. She dropped into a chair next to me. *What now?* I wondered.

"Where is Louisa? Oh, Mary, my dear," she said breathlessly. "All of London is talking. How can you be so calm?"

I blinked at her, mystified. "What, Your Grace?"

She interrupted as though I had not spoken. "This morning the court reconvened to discuss it, and even the king has been told. What shall we do? What shall we do?" She fluttered her hands before her face and pulled her gloves off with jerky motions. "Oh, this is dreadful! Oh dear."

"Your Grace, please, what is it you mean? What has happened?"

"DeBroun asked you to marry him! Or be his mistress! What a villain! What a to-do this has caused! The Duke is most distressed! And your uncle Harry has challenged him to a duel!"

I leapt to my feet. "Harry has challenged the Duke to a duel?"

She shook her head violently. "No, child, not the Duke. Harry has challenged DeBroun to a duel."

I stared at her, incredulous. "Tell me this is not true!"

"You had not heard?"

"No, Your Grace. No one visits us now but you and Becca's mother. Oh, where is Louisa?" I ran for the door.

A few moments later we'd found Louisa and Randolph, and the Duchess told her story, punctuating it with her comments. Harry and Angus, she said, had gone to DeBroun's house on Friday night, where they had burst into his dinner party. With Angus holding pistols at the ready, Harry had delivered his challenge before the stunned assembly and then left as DeBroun raged at them.

Randolph departed at once to find Harry. Louisa sat with me, pale and worried, as the Duchess argued for me to leave London. I refused. At last, defeated, she sat back against the cushions and looked at me with displeasure, announcing that she had asked her husband to plead with Harry and DeBroun to reconsider. I nodded and asked her to thank the Duke for me. Privately I did not think he'd be successful. My faith was with Randolph. I was sure he would find Harry, and when he did, Randolph, and I, would be able to talk Harry out of this harebrained scheme.

But Randolph returned without having found Harry, and we discussed what to do in a growing mood of gloom. We had few options. Duke John joined us and, with the Duchess, tried again to convince me to retreat to Mountgarden. I only shook my head and once again braved the displeasure of the Barringtons.

On Monday we were told, with all of London, that Alex's trial would be postponed indefinitely. I wrote to the boys and told them some of what had happened. The days dragged and while I was grateful that, to our knowledge, no duel had taken place, it was difficult to keep our spirits up with no news. And no Alex.

Will wrote that Dr. Sutter had visited and said Betty would recover. I read his joyous letter, finding solace in his relief, and spent the afternoon lighter of heart than in weeks. But when night came again my own worries returned. I tried to care for myself for the sake of the baby, who was growing despite all, but it was exhausting. And on Thursday the soldiers came.

I was alone that cold snowy afternoon, standing by the fire in the library, when Bronson burst in, bringing a gust of icy air with him. *How appropriate,* I thought, and lifted my head from the eagle stone, the talisman against pregnancy Alex had given me which I held in my hand. I gave Bronson a cold look of my own. My eyes widened as I saw his face and the red uniforms behind him.

"Yes, Bronson?" I asked, as though it were my habit to find soldiers in my aunt's house every day.

"Madam," he said, his distress obvious, "this officer would have a word with you. I did ask them to wait, but . . ."

"Won't you come in, sir?" I asked, summoning a goddess look as the soldier filled the doorway. I folded my hands before me, hoping that my shaking knees would not give my fear away.

"No, thank you, madam," the soldier answered, his tone stiffly polite. "We are not here to visit. We are searching the house."

"Oh? An exercise, perhaps?" In the room above us we could hear booted feet moving about. He gave me a cold glance. "Sir," I said. "Do you have my uncle's permission to search his house?"

"I have the court's permission and the Crown's. That is sufficient. We are searching for Edgar DeBroun, madam."

"Edgar DeBroun? Surely, sir, he would not be here. Of all people who would not be welcome in this house, he is among the foremost."

"DeBroun is missing, madam, and his staff says he was kidnapped by Scots. Big blond Scots. And your uncle."

"Randolph? That's ridiculous. He's been here with me."

"The Duke of Grafton, madam."

I felt my eyes widen. "Harry? My uncle Harry? Kidnap Edgar DeBroun? Why on earth would he do that?"

"Why on earth would he challenge DeBroun to a duel, madam? I think we both know the answer." He watched me impassively. "Where are your husband's relations, Mistress MacGannon?"

"I do not know where they are, sir," I said coolly, refusing to acknowledge his rudeness. "They are not here."

"We shall soon see," he said.

I nodded as though I were calm, and sank to the chair behind me. My knees had given out. "Shall I order tea?" I asked.

"No, thank you, madam," he said, and watched me while his men searched every room, including the servants' quarters and the storerooms. Eventually they left, leaving half the rooms in disarray and me with a shaken staff and a butler who was apologizing yet again to me.

"I know it's not your fault, Bronson," I said for the tenth time. "There was nothing else you could have done. Now go and set this house in order before my aunt returns."

"Yes, madam. Thank you, Lady Mary. I am so very sorry. . . ."

I waved him away and tried to gather my thoughts. Randolph and Louisa arrived before long and the staff told them of the soldiers' visit before I did. Randolph was furious and it was all Louisa and I could do to keep him from calling on the captain of the Guard that moment. We reminded him that it was the Guard who had searched the house, and he assuaged his anger by writing to the king and the court, complaining about the soldier's treatment of us. But I knew it would do nothing.

The next day Louisa and I were in the library when Randolph abruptly entered the room, grinning, leading Angus behind him.

"Angus, what have you done?" I cried shrilly.

"We've been busy," he said, settling himself into a chair and accepting whisky from Randolph while Louisa and I watched him.

"Did you kidnap DeBroun?" I demanded.

He nodded. "Aye, we have the bas . . . him. Sorry, ladies, I've no' been in polite company for some days now." I waved his apology aside. "We've got Matthew and Gilbey and a handful of others laying false trails all over London. That should keep the soldiers busy for a bit." He looked at me as he sipped the whisky.

"Angus, what were you thinking? Let DeBroun go. Let him go!"

Angus paused and watched me with frosty eyes. "Revenge, Mary. We were thinking about revenge."

"You must let him go! For God's sake, Angus, release him!"

"No." The word hung in the air with something that I could not identify, something that chilled me. Next to me Louisa stiffened.

"Then at least tell us what happened," I said as frostily.

Angus nodded and told about going to DeBroun's house to deliver Harry's challenge, his expression lightening as he talked. DeBroun, he said, had been enraged. "Of course," Angus said, grinning, "perhaps I should have stopped yer uncle from issuing a challenge at a dinner party. What do ye think, Randolph, were we rude?"

Randolph laughed. "I'm sure DeBroun was delighted to see you."

"It'll be an evening not soon forgotten," Angus continued. "One of yer favorite people was there, Mary, that Rowena woman. She's a powerful gossip, so it's all over London by now. It's a pity that yer Duchess could no' have been there as well. We could have used her abilities." He took a sip of whisky. "When we left DeBroun's, we went to Harry's house to discuss it. We were thinking that maybe we'd just take DeBroun when he showed up for the duel and then we thought, well, why not the now? He might not show up for the duel at all. So back we went to his house in the wee hours with the Macleans and our own men." He took another sip and sighed appreciatively. "When we got there DeBroun was gone. Left in the night, just flown away. He's brave with women and a coward with men."

Randolph and Angus shared a laugh and Angus continued his story. After returning to DeBroun's house and finding him gone, Angus, Harry, the Macleans, and the Kilgannon men had separated, determined to find DeBroun. It was Harry who eventually captured him, on the road headed north from London, and Harry who told the others where to hide him in a small cottage he owned just north of there. They deposited DeBroun at the cottage, under Duncan's heavy guard, and Angus and Harry had returned to Harry's town house only to find it full of soldiers.

"We went out the back door as they went in the front," Angus said. "They dinna see us. It must have been the day before they came here."

"And what now?" I asked.

Angus shrugged. "Now we wait. We've sent word from me, of course, not from Harry, who cannot be involved in such dealings, that DeBroun will be held captive until Alex is released."

"And if they won't release Alex?"

Angus's expression darkened. "Then we'll send them one piece of DeBroun at a time until they do."

I stared at him, horrified. "Surely you don't mean that."

Blue eyes met mine. "Surely I do."

"Why are you doing this? You are risking Alex's life!"

"Mary," he said in a low voice, "Alex's life has been forfeit for quite a while, lass. I'm not a fool, but DeBroun's been one. He's given us an opportunity we canna ignore, and he deserves whatever happens to him. Surely ye can understand that? Ye dinna expect me to sit on my hands? What did ye think was going to happen? Ye were there when Gilbey brought the maps and the charts. I thought ye kent we'd try to free him any way we could."

"But this, Angus!" I struggled to my feet. "Why can you not all leave DeBroun alone? Let the man be." Something flashed in Angus's eyes that I'd never seen before and I moved backward, holding my hands at my heart as Angus rose to stand before me.

"Are ye defending DeBroun? Do ye believe he's a right to revenge himself and we dinna?"

"What does that mean?" I demanded. Randolph moved to stand next to me and we faced Angus together. Angus glowered at me.

"It means DeBroun wants his revenge on Alex to be complete and yer part of it," he said.

"Why?" I whispered. "Why does DeBroun want revenge?"

"For something that happened a long time ago."

"And you think DeBroun still remembers?"

"Oh, aye, I ken he does. That's why he hates Alex."

"Please, Angus, let DeBroun go. Now. Let him go. For me."

"Are ye asking me to spare him for ye?" he roared. "Is it him ye want alive instead of Alex?" His eyes blazed with outrage and Randolph stepped between us. I lifted my chin, as angry as Angus.

"I will ignore that, you damn fool," I said coldly. "How can you ask me that? Don't you see what you're risking? DeBroun is one of the men in control of Alex's fate. If DeBroun is killed or injured, Alex will pay the price, not you, not Harry not Duncan! How can you gamble with Alex's life for your damn pride?"

"It's no' pride, Mary. Something must be done."

"Oh yes, and killing DeBroun is just what the other judges need to persuade them to be lenient," I sneered. "Alex will pay the price for this folly. Why could you not leave DeBroun alone?"

"If we did nothing they'd hang Alex, Mary. Or worse."

"You don't seem to understand how delicate this balance is!" I cried. "You've put Alex at risk with this scheme. I don't care for DeBroun, only for Alex, and you have played dice with his life. *He'll* pay if you're wrong! I am trying to keep him alive and you've just made my task much more difficult! How could you do this? Angus, how could you do this?" We glared at each other and in the silence that stretched between us I could hear the slow ticking of the clock in the corner. I don't know what he had intended to answer, but the baby moved just then and I put my hand on my middle. Angus's gaze followed it, and I watched his anger fade and his expression soften. He took a deep breath.

"I dinna play dice with Alex's life," he said slowly. "I love the man, as ye do." He looked at the ceiling and then back at me. "Mary, I beg yer pardon for doubting ye even for a second. Forgive me, lass, please. But with or without yer permission, we have done this and we will see it through. We had to do something."

"What if it doesn't work? What will they do to Alex?" I whispered. "What if something happens to you as well? Do you not see that you have put all of you at risk with this? If something were to happen to you, or Harry, or Matthew, or Gilbey, I could not bear it. Angus, I could not bear it." I wiped the tears from my cheeks and Angus leaned to wrap his arms around me.

"Nothing will happen to us, lass. Nothing will happen."

"It already has," I said to his chest. "Angus, I'm so afraid. Please. Please, let DeBroun go."

He released me. "I canna, Mary. It's too late for that now."

I clung to him then and sobbed while Louisa patted my back protectively. Eventually I quieted and stepped back from him and we all sat down again, discussing what next to do. Louisa told Angus she agreed with me, and Angus nodded but said the deed was done. Randolph poured Angus more whisky.

"Angus," Randolph said, handing him the glass. "Why does DeBroun want revenge on Alex?"

Angus waved a hand. "It was a long time ago."

But Randolph persisted and the story came out slowly. When Alex was twenty, before he'd married Sorcha, Angus said, he and Angus had stopped in London after a successful trading journey.

"We played cards at the home of a friend, and DeBroun was there. He and Alex were at one table, I at another, when Alex accused DeBroun of cheating. Now, mind ye, we'd done a bit of drinking, but false accusations are no' like Alex. I believed him, but others dinna. Alex threw the table over and lunged at DeBroun and found cards stashed in his waistcoat. DeBroun was humiliated before all his fine friends, but the worst of it was when the woman who had been DeBroun's favorite . . ." He paused and met my eyes. "She went home with Alex."

"I see," I said, remembering DeBroun saying what an agreeable surprise it had been to meet me. I'm sure it had been.

"I thought ye might," Angus said.

"But it's been ten years," Louisa said.

"He's no' forgotten," Angus said. "Nor have we."

My instincts had been correct, I thought. DeBroun was neither overwhelmed by my beauty, nor a man in love. I had been a tool, a means to wound Alex further;

I was to be part of his revenge. I shook my head as my hatred of him grew. But now I understood.

"What will the court do now?" I asked.

"Harry's back," said Randolph. "He'll find out. The court won't talk to me, but they will to him."

My head snapped up. "What do you mean, Harry's back? Where is he?"

"Harry said he'd invent a story about having been at Grafton to see Betty. His staff will confirm that," said Angus. "I left him this morning at the cottage; he should be in London by now. He said the best thing to do was brave it out. No one would dare to accuse him of kidnapping DeBroun."

"They all but have," I said and told Angus of the soldiers' visit to Louisa and Randolph's house. He nodded and I realized Randolph must have told him already. "What will happen now?"

"The court will have to continue the trial with or without DeBroun," Randolph said, looking from me to Louisa. "There's more news. The papers have been busy again. Steele has taken DeBroun on as the scourge of humanity, and so have the others. Much of London has rallied for Alex, which the judges cannot have helped but hear. DeBroun will not be able to show his face for a long while. Whether it will change anything for Alex, I do not know."

Angus left us then and Randolph went to see Harry at his town house. But Harry was not there.

The next night, Matthew came to visit, creeping in after dark through the kitchens. He stood before us in the library with an unhappy expression. "My da wants ye to go to Mountgarden," he said to me. "That's why

I'm here. He said ye may have questions but I dinna have to answer them and that ye'd ken what that means."

I thought of my promise to Angus, and I nodded. "I'll leave in the morning," I said. Randolph and Matthew both sighed with relief.

But I didn't go to Mountgarden, for the next morning we discovered that Harry was dead.

NINETEEN

ʜARRY DIED ON HIS WAY HOME, ALONE, IN HIS coach on the London road. He'd told Angus he would return to London, but instead he'd stolen another visit with DeBroun and they had quarreled bitterly. Duncan, who had been guarding DeBroun, had helped Harry when he had grasped his arm and fallen to his knees. Harry had rested for a while, then assured Duncan he was fit to travel. When Duncan had implored him to wait until Angus or Matthew returned, Harry had refused and climbed into his coach. And died on the journey.

When his driver had discovered that Harry was dead, he had returned to Duncan, who had told him to go to Grafton, as though Harry had been there all along. Will brought the news himself, arriving in London in the early morning hours. Betty was recovering nicely and he thought we should hear about Harry from him. I'd stared at my brother as he told us, and tried to believe it. *Oh, Harry,* I thought, *I am so sorry.*

By the next day the news that Harry had died was all over London. Randolph spread the tale that Harry had died at Grafton, and there was no one to dispute it. Harry's staff at his estate had confirmed the story and so had Betty, who said he'd been visiting her. She was apparently quite convincing, for the soldier who had questioned her did not return, and we were not bothered by any officials as we prepared for Harry's funeral.

We buried my uncle Harry with great pomp, as he had wished, at Grafton. Most of London's elite was at the funeral. Draped in black, a veil over my face, I stood as inconspicuously as possible while Will, now the Duke of Grafton, was addressed as Your Grace. Will was a duke, I thought, and Betty a duchess. We had known that this day would come eventually, but we could never have imagined that it would come about in such a fashion. Few guests spoke to me at all, and Will and Betty had no time, but I was not alone. Angus was with me, and Kilgannon men hovered uneasily at the edge of the crowd, dressed as Englishmen. Gilbey rarely left my side. Kenneth Ogilvie, who we now discovered had been recently acting as Harry's solicitor, was never far away. And I had my guilt for company. But for me Harry would be alive now. But for me.

At the graveside I stood with my brother and thought of my father's family. Only Will and I were left of the Lowell line. And the baby I carried. It was with a great sense of family loss and the passage of time that I threw my handful of dirt into my uncle's grave. *Harry,* I said to the coffin, *I am so sorry.*

The trial was to resume the following Monday, when, it was said, the verdict would be announced. The funeral guests talked of little else than Harry, Alex, and DeBroun. Apparently the word had flown through the city that DeBroun was somehow responsible for Harry's death and that DeBroun's conduct toward me had been despicable. Many thought him to be in hiding, and the great weight of London's public opinion fell at last on Alex's side. If, the papers said, Alex had cravenly saved himself by going to France and I had joined him there, DeBroun would never have approached me and Harry would not have felt he had to avenge my honor. And Harry would be alive today. The masses loved it and Harry's status in London was approaching heroic. Harry would have laughed.

Three days later we were back in London. I withdrew from those who had accompanied us from Grafton, wishing that Will and Betty had not had to stay at Harry's estate to deal with the transition legalities, and retired upstairs. Late that evening, after all the guests had left, Randolph brought Angus to me and left us to visit. Angus kissed my cheek as I greeted him, then settled into the chair opposite me without a word. His presence was comforting, but I found I did not want to know what was happening in the outside world. I had no desire to know how he'd gotten here, or what he'd been doing with DeBroun. We watched the fire for a long time before Angus stretched and then put his clasped hands on his stomach.

"We still have DeBroun, lass," he said. "We've kept Duncan from him, so he's no' been harmed though he's a bit disagreeable these days." I nodded. "The verdict will be announced Monday, but ye ken that. No word has been sent to me. They still hold Alex."

"What will you do?" I asked quietly

"Whatever we have to, lass. Dinna ask me more." We sat in silence for a bit, each lost in his own thoughts.

"Angus," I said at last, "what is the low road?"

He blinked. "Where did ye hear that, Mary?"

"From Gilbey. Alex asked him to have Seamus pipe him home if he took the low road. What does that mean?"

Angus sighed and answered slowly. "Some believe that when a Gael is far from home, there are two ways of returning. One is aboveground, called the high road, and only the living can do it. The other is the low road and ye must be dead to take it. It's when the fairies take ye home. But yer spirit is restless sometimes then and it's best to be piped home as well."

"Alex said that if he dies, he wants Seamus to pipe him home."

Angus met my eyes and nodded. "Should that day ever come, Mary, we'll see that it's done. But I'm trying to prevent that." I nodded, unwilling to argue with him tonight. We sat in silence until he spoke again. "When is yer babe due, Mary?"

"Sometime mid-month November. About two more weeks." I met his eyes but could not tell what he was thinking.

"Mary, I ken ye'll wish to be at the verdict." I nodded. "But, lass, will ye leave London then? Will ye go to the boys and be with them? Ye ken I'm going to try to free Alex, even if it's on the scaffold, Mary, and I need a free hand to act."

I agreed without argument and he nodded in satisfaction. We sat for a moment and then he looked at me again. "Mary, ye ken, if the worst happens, ye might be raising the boys on yer own?"

"Yes. I think of it often and wonder if these brothers will be like Alex and Malcolm. Angus, why does Malcolm hate Alex so much?"

Angus considered as he stretched his legs before him. "Alex was never his father's favorite. Katrine was

Ian's darling daughter and when she died he was angry
with his sons for still living. Jamie, Alex's brother, dinna
count with his father, for he was afraid of most everything and Ian despised that in his son. Malcolm got
used to being the center of attention and having all that
he wanted." He shrugged. "I thought he'd grow out of
it, ye ken, and take the responsibilities of manhood
when it was time, but Malcolm never wanted them. He
just wanted whatever Alex had. I dinna ken what makes
the man so, Mary, but those are the things I saw. And
Alex never did see them, though I tried in my way to tell
him. I should have told him straight out." He sighed.
"And those are the things ye must avoid in raising his
children. If yer correct and this one yer carrying is a boy,
you'll have three brothers to raise, and it would be only
natural that ye'd favor the one who is yer own blood."

I met his worried look. "They will all be my sons,
Angus. I will never favor one. Each is as dear as the
other."

He nodded. "Good. And we will visit often, ye ken."

"Where will you be?"

"Alex gave us each a ship, so I imagine we'll be trading with the continent like always. I dinna ken what the
future will hold, but I have few regrets. I've had a good
life, except for losing my Mairi and my children, and if it
ends tomorrow the only things I'd sorrow for are no'
seeing my son full-grown and no' following my own
instincts and taking Alex from the English when we
could."

"That was his decision."

"And a poor one. No' all of his decisions are correct,
ye ken."

I laughed softly. "No."

He rose stiffly. "I'll be going now, lass." He paused

at the doorway. "I'm sorry about Harry. I was fond of him. He was a good man and I'll miss his company."

I nodded. "As I will. Thank you, Angus. As always, thank you."

He left me with a wave of his hand.

As late as Sunday part of me had not yet given up hope, and although I knew all reason said there could be only one verdict, I still thought it possible that public opinion might sway the judges and they might free Alex. But by Monday morning I was as resigned as everyone else. I sat in the dining room, staring through the windows at the gardens, waiting for the time to leave. At last Randolph touched my shoulder and gestured to the door.

Westminster was chaotic. Outside the Hall crowds milled, straining to get a glimpse of the proceedings. I saw no one I knew as we pushed my way to the guard, but I heard the comments as I was recognized. Inside it was calmer, although the same air of expectation filled the anteroom. They were better dressed indoors, but no less anxious for the news. I recognized many faces here, but no one would meet my eyes. I held my head high and tried to remember what a goddess look felt like, looking neither to the right nor left as I walked behind Louisa down the aisle they created and into the Hall itself.

We found seats in a row toward the front. Strangers moved kindly aside to let us pass, though I did hear whispers announcing who we were. It must not have been very long that we waited, but it seemed like an eternity. At last there was a shuffle of feet as uniformed soldiers, heavily armed, moved in to line the walls of the floor of the court, many more than had ever been present before. The judges filed into the dais, their faces unreadable. There was still an empty chair. The lawyers and clerks entered until the courtroom floor was filled. And the crowd waited, the tension palpable. Alex was brought in then, his back straight. He scanned the room once then focused on the gallery, nodding at someone. *He does not know I am here,* I thought. The crowd stirred restively and from somewhere on my left came the cry, "Set him free!" in English and then in Gaelic. It sounded like Matthew and I turned to see if it was but saw only a sea of faces. I turned back when a voice came from the dais.

"Kilgannon," Lord Webster said, "we will deliver your verdict and sentence this morning. Do you understand that?"

Alex nodded. "Aye, your honor. Let's have it done."

The judge nodded. "Sir, I must admonish you that I will tolerate no outbreaks from the audience."

Alex smiled grimly. "Your honor, I must inform ye I am no' in control of the audience. Ye might note I'm the prisoner here."

The judge ignored the laughs from the crowd. "You have been a difficult man to deal with, Kilgannon."

Alex raised his chin and grinned. "Thank ye, sir. It is at last a charge I dinna argue with."

Webster narrowed his eyes as he glared at Alex, then folded his arms before him and leaned over them. "It is the finding of this court that you, Ian Alexander James Fraser Mackenzie MacGannon, the former Earl of Kilgannon, Scotland"—he paused and glanced around the room—"are guilty of high treason against . . ."

The roar of the crowd drowned his words. Alex bent his head, his eyes closed, but a moment later his chin rose as he looked at the judge again.

"No!" I did not mean to scream nor to stand but I did. "No, no, no, no!" Hands reached for me but I fought them off, laboring to reach Alex. Someone was calling my name. Around me the crowd had erupted into chaos and someone was pounding on something.

"Mary!" I heard Alex's roar and strained to see him. He was out of the box, charging across the floor, and then he disappeared in the mass of uniforms that attacked him.

"Alex!" I screamed again and this time managed to get to the aisle. "Alex!" He came to the surface once, arms thrashing, but they subdued him at last and the hands pulled me to a seat.

"Quiet! Quiet!" thundered Lord Webster, pounding harder, as the crowd surged forward and the uniforms dragged my unconscious and bleeding husband out of the courtroom. Behind me I heard the MacGannon war cry and armed men spilled onto the floor. The judges, with fearful glances at the men closing in on them, rushed out of the room, Webster at their lead. The crowd filled the floor of the court and banged on the closed doors. I had the thought that I should simply walk across the floor of the court and go to Alex and that's what I tried to do, except that as I stood at the top of the stairs I saw, through the masses of legs and feet, blood on the floor. Alex's blood. And I fainted.

Hands must have caught me and put me gently on a bench, for I woke without a bruise, to look up into loved faces. But not his. Louisa and Angus bent over me, Angus turning his head to say something to someone out of sight. I closed my eyes again. Strong arms lifted me and I felt the wool of a plaid against my cheek.

"Make way," Angus bellowed as he carried me up the stairs. "Make way for the Countess of Kilgannon."

He carried me to the anteroom, down the stairs, and
outside, Randolph running ahead to call the carriage.
Angus put me on my feet with a pat on my arm and a
glare at the crowd. I stood shakily at the curb with
Louisa, Randolph's arm around me, and I stared into
the air and clung to my uncle. Louisa was murmuring
comforting things and brushing my hair back with gentle hands. *Guilty,* I thought. *Guilty of treason. Dear
God.* I closed my eyes again against the roaring in my
head. *Guilty.* Alex, unconscious, beaten as he tried to
reach me.

At Louisa's I lay in my bed while Louisa and Randolph hovered nearby. I stared at the ceiling. Angus and
Matthew and Gilbey leaned against the wall of my bedroom, silent, their mouths drawn in tight lines, but they
would not leave, even when Louisa reminded them that
they'd been seen and no doubt recognized.

"I have requested another audience with the king,"
Randolph said. We all looked at him in surprise. "I had
requested it beforehand, just in case. It cannot hurt.
The Duke and Duchess have sent word that they will do
the same."

"Thank you," I said hoarsely and watched Randolph's eyes fill with tears as he turned away. "We will
talk with everyone who will listen," I said. "There is still
hope." I met Angus's blue eyes, so like Alex's, but so
anguished now. "There is still hope."

Angus nodded grimly. "Aye, lass. There is still hope.
While Alex is alive there is still hope."

"Yes," I said and dared them to tell me otherwise.

It was more difficult to convince myself in the hours
between dusk and dawn when I haunted the halls of

Louisa's house wrapped in Alex's plaid, seeing his face when the verdict had been announced. *And what must he be thinking now, alone in his cell? The cruelest part was his isolation. As if they did not know that well,* I thought bitterly. It was nearly impossible to convince myself to hope as I stood in Louisa's ballroom and remembered seeing him for the first time. *Never again,* I thought. *We'll never stand together again, anywhere.* I whispered his name and then felt the first contractions. I put my hands on my middle and realized I was having Alex's baby.

TWENTY

OUR SON WAS BORN IN THE LATE MORNING. I NAMED him Alexander Robert Harold Lowell Keith MacGannon and I wept from exhaustion and sorrow and joy as he was handed to me, with thanks to God that he was whole, and with sorrow that his father might never see him. I wept for all our losses and then I slept.

The childbirth had proved the least of my worries, I reflected the next day. Unsure of what to expect, I had waited through the hours of labor with a growing fear of what lay ahead of me and a persistent worry that I might not survive and might leave Ian and Jamie orphans. I had woken Louisa in the wee hours when the pains had persisted, and she had roused the household. The midwife, cheerful despite being roused from her slumbers, had assured me that the labor, while not pleasant, was very routine. And hours later, as I lay exhausted, with the baby at my side, she told me that the delivery had been normal. Both the baby and I, she said, were doing fine. The details I chose not to remember, but the moment my son, solid and healthy, was put into my arms, I forgot the struggle to bring him into the world.

Will and Betty had raced to London and arrived the

next afternoon, bringing the boys with them. I sighed now as I looked at Alex's sons examining their new brother.

"He's very wrinkled, Mama," said Ian worriedly.

"Babies are like that," I said with a smile.

"And he's very red," said Jamie, his hair falling over his forehead. I brushed it back and thought of the night I'd met Alex. *My love, my love,* I thought, and kissed his second son.

Ian snuggled against me and I put my arm around him. "He's really small," he said. "Really small."

"He's a baby," Louisa said. "You two looked just like he does when you were first born."

"Yuck," said Jamie and the boys laughed. I met Louisa's eyes over their heads and she smiled, although her weariness and worry were apparent. I returned her smile and refused to think.

In the next few days Will threw all of his newfound political power into helping Alex's cause, but no one from the Court was listening and I watched the men all grow silent. Our requests to see Alex had been denied and no one could even tell me if my letter to Alex telling him of our son's birth had reached him, for Gilbey was not allowed to visit either.

Angus or Matthew visited us every evening. They still held DeBroun, they said, but had not harmed him, despite Duncan's wishes. They'd decided to wait until the sentence, for DeBroun had hinted that Alex might receive only imprisonment. And if Alex was alive there was always hope that Kenneth Ogilvie would be successful in his attempt to have the indictment overturned. I did not argue with them, though I thought their optimism misplaced.

The baby cheered everyone, though, and I smiled to see the big men hold Alex's son and gently touch his tiny hands and face. Angus cooed to him and smiled and more than once wiped a tear away when he thought no one was looking.

Twenty days passed and still Alex's sentence had not been delivered. Everyone insisted that I go to Mountgarden with the boys, and I did not argue. We needed two coaches, for there would be eight of us. Will and Betty went in the first coach with the boys, leaving just after breakfast. I was to follow with Louisa, the baby, and his nurse within the hour, but the coachman was not pleased with one of the wheels, and before we knew it, it was afternoon and snowing. We sent a messenger to find Will with a note saying Louisa and I would leave in the morning.

It snowed all the next day as well. Randolph did not want us to travel in this storm, and neither Louisa nor I were eager to do so. The day drew to a close, ending with clear skies and stars, and I knew we'd leave in the morning. I roamed the house with my baby asleep in my arms and stepped out onto the ballroom balcony, staring up at the darkening sky and remembering. I shivered at the cold, thinking that it was time to oversee the last of the packing and give the baby to his nurse. As I turned to go inside, I saw a man moving rapidly through the gardens toward the kitchen. A tall man. Without stopping to think, I hurried to the kitchen and found Matthew flinging off a cloak and handing it to Bronson. Both men turned as I entered, and Matthew's jaw dropped.

"Mary! Why are ye here? I thought ye'd gone to Mountgarden."

I shifted the baby and pointed at the window. "The

storm. The boys went ahead with Will and Betty. We were delayed and the storm hit and we stayed. We're leaving in the morning. Why, Matthew? What's happening?"

Randolph entered before Matthew could answer and stood next to me, a hand on my shoulder. "Hello, Matthew," he said.

"I would talk with ye, Randolph," Matthew said.

"Of course," my uncle said, gesturing me before him. He turned to Bronson as we left the room. "You've seen no one."

Bronson nodded. "No, sir, no one."

Randolph led us to the library. As soon as the door was closed, Matthew turned to us. "They've found us," he said. "We've had to move DeBroun."

"Where?" Randolph asked.

"He's at Harry's town house the now. We leave in an hour to bring him to the *Mary Rose*. I came to warn ye and to find out what ye ken. Have ye heard anything?"

Randolph shook his head. "No."

"Matthew," I said, "what news of Alex?"

"None. Gilbey wasna allowed to see him yet again. Ye need to go, Mary. The soldiers will be coming here. We barely got out of Harry's cottage."

"Your father? Is everyone all right?"

"Dougall took a shot in the shoulder but he'll survive. But the English are not holding back."

Randolph moved to the door as Matthew was speaking, and opened it. Bronson was, as I would have guessed, just on the other side. Randolph looked at him without a change of expression.

"Tell Lady Randolph to prepare to leave at once," he said and turned back to us, leaving the door open. "You're leaving now, Mary." I nodded and started to answer, then froze as we all heard the pounding on the front door.

"They're here already," Matthew said and started for the door to the hall, drawing his sword from its scabbard as he moved.

"No, this way," said Randolph, shutting the library door and opening the tall window next to him. With a quick glance around the garden, Matthew stepped through the window and turned back to us. The library door opened. I turned, fearful of what I'd see, but it was Bronson who entered, closing the door behind him.

"Soldiers are here to search the house again, sir," he said. "They wish to question Lady Mary and any Scots they find. Lady Randolph told them that Lady Mary has gone to Grafton with her sons. She says for you to get Mary and the baby out of the house while she delays them." He held out two cloaks, Matthew's and one of mine. Without a word, Matthew stepped back through the window, took his cloak and reached for the baby. Randolph sprang into movement, throwing the cloak around my shoulders.

"Go, for God's sake," said Randolph, bundling me toward Matthew. "And Godspeed. I'll see you at Mountgarden."

"Aye, sir," said Matthew and handed me through the window. Randolph closed it behind us before I had time to speak at all.

We raced through the dark streets, Matthew pulling me along and holding the baby, who was mercifully silent. We arrived at Harry's town house without incident, recognized at once by the Maclean who guarded the kitchen garden, and were led through vacant storerooms, the counters empty and windows shuttered. Only a candle or two glowed in each room, and none of

Harry's staff was visible. The Kilgannon men exclaimed to see me, not pleased, and Matthew met their curious looks with curt nods. "Where's my father?" was all he said, and we were taken to Angus.

Thomas was ministering to Dougall in the kitchen while Angus and others watched. Matthew entered first and Angus glanced up and then back to Dougall. "Took ye long enough," Angus said. "Did ye tell Randolph?"

"Da," said Matthew and Angus looked up again, his expression at first puzzled, then angry as he saw me in the doorway.

"Mary!" Angus cried. "What in God's name are ye doing here? *Mo Dia,* lass, yer supposed to be at Mount-garden. Matthew . . . ?"

"Soldiers, Da," Matthew answered. "They came to Randolph's looking for Mary. We only just got out before them."

"They're looking for all of you, Angus," I said, shifting the baby. I explained why we'd been delayed in leaving, and Angus shook his head unhappily and sighed.

"We have to get ye somewhere safe, lass, as soon as we can leave," he said and gestured to Thomas, still poulticing Dougall's shoulder. Thomas gave me a smile. When I offered assistance the men all looked askance and Dougall said he was fine, though I saw him favoring the arm. He said he wanted to see the baby, and I showed him Alex's son while the other men gathered around the child. Thomas pulled Dougall's shirt back over the shoulder and gave Dougall a pat.

"Ye'll do, laddie," he said and Dougall rose.

"Let's go, lads," Angus said. "The English will be here before long. We're off to the *Mary Rose,* lass, and we're staying close to London. I sent *Gannon's Lady* to

Bristol in case we needed her to escape, and I've sent men to Grafton and Mountgarden to warn ye there of the situation. I expected ye to be there by now."

I nodded unhappily. I had imagined the boys safe with Will and Betty, but now was struck with fear for them, picturing soldiers riding to the door. *I should never have let them leave without me,* I thought. *Dear God,* I prayed, *keep my boys safe.*

"Matthew," Angus said, "ye'll have to get Mary to Mountgarden and then find us. Go get the men moving and send the coach."

Matthew nodded and left us, Dougall following him. Thomas packed up the last of his doctoring tools as I turned to Angus.

"All of London now knows whose ship the *Mary Rose* is," I said. "Why not use the *Margaret?* No one will recognize her."

"I've sent the *Margaret* to Edinburgh with Kenneth Ogilvie and Gilbey. There's news there. Or there might be." I asked what he meant, but he never got to tell me, for Thomas's son Liam ran into the room.

"English soldiers, Angus! They've left Randolph's and they're coming this way. And Captain Calum just sent a man to say they're being too closely watched and ye canna get DeBroun to the *Mary Rose.*"

Angus nodded and barked orders, and men scrambled to obey. Angus took the pistol that Thomas handed him. "Gather the men," he said. "Send word to Calum to stay put. Meet me at Harry's cottage. If I'm not there in four hours, go to Bristol. Tell the others. Thomas, make sure Duncan has DeBroun on his way. Liam, put out all the candles in the front of the house and then get ye gone." The room cleared and Angus turned to me. "Stay here, Mary. I've got to see to our guest."

The house was rapidly emptying and within moments I stood alone in the dim kitchen with my baby, listening to the sudden quiet. And then Thomas and Duncan burst into the kitchen, holding Edgar DeBroun between them. He looked none the worse for his adventures, even if his shirt needed changing and his beard a trim.

"Mary," Duncan said gaily, as though we'd met at a party. "Watch! This is for Murdoch." I gasped as he punched DeBroun in the stomach. DeBroun grunted and doubled over. Duncan laughed and Thomas frowned. And Angus came into the room behind them.

"That's enough, Duncan," said Angus angrily. "We havena time for yer games. Thomas, go and see what's keeping the coach. Mary's coming with us. Make sure there's room for her. And no' next to this vermin." He gave DeBroun a push into one of the chairs. The baby fussed then and the three men looked at me.

"Alex's wee bairn, aye, Mary?" Duncan asked.

"Yes," I said, pulling back the blanket to let him see.

Duncan smiled at my child and at me, then looked at DeBroun. "Yer no' fit to be in this bairn's presence, ye filth," he sneered.

Angus frowned, pulling his pistol from his belt. He trained it on DeBroun. "Go, Duncan," he said with a nod at the door. "Yer in the devil's own mood tonight."

Duncan grinned and stepped in front of DeBroun for a moment. That was all DeBroun needed. He leapt at Duncan, pulling the pistol from Duncan's waistband. Before Angus could move, DeBroun held the pistol to Duncan's head.

DeBroun retreated with one arm around Duncan's

neck, his other hand holding the pistol, backing me against the wall behind them. I could see nothing but DeBroun's coat as he pressed against me, but I heard his ragged breathing and the scuffle of their feet as Duncan struggled against him. DeBroun smelled of fear and sweat.

Angus's voice was very calm. "Drop it, DeBroun. Let him go."

"Or? I am the one with the upper hand here, Mac-Gannon."

"Let him go."

"Show him mercy?" DeBroun scoffed. "The same mercy he would have shown me? I think not. I'll not go willingly to my death."

"Let him go," Angus said. His voice sounded closer.

I pushed DeBroun as hard as I could and he fell hard against Duncan. I toppled myself as well and fell on top of them, clasping my wailing baby to my breast. We went down in a tangle of legs and arms and my skirts. DeBroun was the first to his feet and stood over us, waving Duncan's pistol wildly. I scrambled to my feet, my arms cradling my crying child. Angus pointed his pistol at DeBroun but I was between them and he hesitated. Duncan was still on the floor. On the other side of DeBroun, Duncan grabbed for DeBroun's leg and DeBroun sidestepped, grabbing me around the waist with his left hand while he pointed the gun at Duncan with his right. Duncan and DeBroun stared at each other and then, with deliberation, DeBroun smashed the gun across Duncan's head. Duncan fell on his back, unconscious, blood streaming from the gash at his temple. Angus dove for DeBroun, but DeBroun pulled me back with him and Angus stopped abruptly. I looked from Angus's face up into DeBroun's and then down at the pistol DeBroun pointed at my baby. I stared into Angus's eyes, then took a deep breath and forced myself to look at DeBroun again.

"What is this, Edgar?" I asked, my voice remarkably calm. I drew strength from that, but I was trembling and I knew my bravado would not last long. Nor would his. The hand holding the pistol was shaking. I pulled myself back against him as far as I could, but the gun could still reach the baby.

"Your damned Scotsmen have held me long enough, madam," he said. "Call them off."

"I have nothing to do with it," I said and brought a hand up, gently pushing the pistol away from my child. DeBroun let me move his hand, but then brought the barrel to my neck.

"Of course not," he snarled. "And I had nothing to do with Maclean." He looked at Angus. "Back away," he said and Angus took two steps backward. "The soldiers will be here soon. You'd better go now, MacGannon." Angus watched as DeBroun shifted position, pointing the gun at my head.

"Let Mary and the bairn go and we can discuss this," Angus said calmly. The two men stared at each other with guns ready, and me in the middle with my baby, my skirts floating over Duncan's motionless body and dipping in his blood.

DeBroun shook his head. "What is there to discuss? Leave."

"Not without Mary," Angus said. The baby let out a wail as DeBroun tightened his arm around both of us and Angus's eyes narrowed. "Are ye aright, lass?" he asked, keeping his eyes on DeBroun.

"Yes," I gasped.

Angus nodded. "Good. Then let's have a talk about Alex."

"What about him?" DeBroun demanded.

"The same thing we've been discussing for a while, DeBroun. I want whatever ye can do for Alex in exchange for yer life."

DeBroun snorted. "I have Mary now. I'm not in jeopardy."

Angus's voice was very calm. "Ye canna shoot the both of us. Ye'll have to choose."

"I choose you, then," DeBroun said, pointing the gun at Angus.

Angus did not blink. "Fine. Let's talk about what ye can do for my cousin."

"I can do nothing," DeBroun said.

"Do what ye can to free Alex by writing to the other judges, and when he's free I will let ye go."

"How do I know I can trust you?"

"I've been fair to ye while ye've been here, DeBroun."

DeBroun nodded. "All right. Put your gun down and then we can talk," said DeBroun. Slowly, watching DeBroun all the while, Angus leaned down and placed his pistol on the floor.

"Now, let's talk like gentlemen," Angus said.

"You are no gentleman," sneered DeBroun and raised the pistol to the level of Angus's heart. Angus watched him impassively.

"I have put my gun down, DeBroun. Do the same and I willna have my men kill ye. They are just outside this door."

"But not in this room, MacGannon, you damn fool." DeBroun raised an eyebrow and sighted down the pistol's barrel. Without a pause, he shot Angus in

the stomach. Then, calmly, he stooped and retrieved
Angus's pistol and gave me a glance. He paused beside
Duncan, looked at me, and shot Duncan in the head.
Then he ran out the door.

TWENTY-ONE

THE KITCHEN WAS SUDDENLY FILED WITH MEN, TOO many men and too late. Matthew stepped over Duncan and huddled with me over Angus, trying to stop the bleeding, while around us the men milled without direction. Thomas took the baby from me, cradling Alex's son in his practiced arms while he and Dougall gave orders. I paid no attention as the men hurried to follow their commands, focusing only on Angus, who was conscious and in great pain. I pulled his shirts and jacket from his chest and wound a makeshift bandage around him, wishing we had a doctor. Dr. Sutter would come if we asked, I thought and said so, but Angus shook his head.

"No," he'd said, his voice tight with pain. "We havena time for it. Duncan?"

Thomas shook his head. "He's gone, Angus," he said and Angus nodded.

"Get the men gone, Thomas, and get Mary to safety."

Dougall knelt over Angus, his face twisted with anguish. "Let us get the doctor," he said hoarsely. "We'll make time."

"No," Angus said roughly. "It willna matter, lad," he

added in a kinder tone. "Take my place, Dougall. Lead the men. And leave no trail to involve Mary's family."

The whole world seemed to slow and shrink to Matthew's hands on his father's bandages, the blood soaking through the cloth and welling around his fingers. Behind me I heard the door open and a sharp cry, but turned only when a hand was placed on my shoulder. I looked up into Randolph's and Louisa's shocked faces.

"Get yer niece to safety," Angus said. "Someone will have heard the shots." Randolph nodded and then bowed his head as Angus coughed blood. I wiped Angus's mouth with a gentle hand. "Will ye promise to care for my son, Mary?" he whispered.

"Angus . . ." I could not continue.

"Promise . . ." Angus coughed again.

"I promise," I said and he gave me a weak smile.

"Dinna give up hope, lass. Our Alex is not gone yet."

"No," I whispered. "No. Angus, oh, Angus . . ."

"Aye," he said. "Aye, Mary, I ken." He turned to his son. "Yer a good son, Matthew," Angus said. "Ye've done me proud. I wish yer mother could have seen ye grown. Pipe me home, will ye? And tell Alex I'll see him soon enough and no' to hurry." He closed his eyes and opened them again with visible effort. "And Dougall." He looked from Dougall to his son. "Matthew. Get De-Broun for me. Kill the bastard." Matthew and Dougall exchanged a look, then nodded.

Next to us Louisa took the baby from Thomas and crooned to him. Maclean clansmen wrapped Duncan in a plaid and lifted him gently to their shoulders as though he could still be injured. I stared at the pools of blood left by each man and turned back to Angus, meeting his eyes above his son's bent head. He tried to smile, but as I brushed the bloodied hair back from his cheek he closed his eyes again.

Angus opened his eyes only once more, to ask Matthew to bury him next to Mairi, and then he closed his eyes and left us. I listened to Matthew sob, my heart too full for my own tears. I heard the echoes in my dreams.

It was a wild ride to Mountgarden that night. We arrived without incident, although exhausted and distraught, to be welcomed by Will and Betty. They were alarmed at our appearance and our story, having heard nothing of what had happened. I was relieved that they knew none of it, for it meant that no soldiers had come looking for me or the MacGannon men. Or the boys. The fear that been my companion began to ease and I went to find them. I held Alex's sons to me and told them the bare facts of what had happened, my tears mingling with theirs as they sobbed in my arms.

The next day we tensed at each noise outside, but we were unmolested by visitors. Or soldiers, though we expected DeBroun to have raised them. As the hours went on, though, we talked less of Edgar DeBroun and more of Angus and Duncan. At first Matthew stared silently into the distance, but as we sat with whisky and wine the talk grew easier and he joined in. I sat next to Louisa, her hand in mine, the baby between us, as Thomas told stories of growing up with Angus, and Dougall made us smile with his memories of Angus training him in the arts of war. We cried and laughed and when the sun rose Matthew said he would meet *Gannon's Lady* in Bristol and take his father home.

Despite pleas from my brother and aunt and uncle, I had refused to go with them. I would not leave England until we knew what would happen to Alex.

We bid Matthew farewell that evening just after sunset and waved as the Kilgannon men rode out of sight. I watched them leave with a heavy heart. *If only Angus were going home with them,* I thought, and then realized he would be. Randolph and Will accompanied Matthew for a short way and then went to London, despite my pleas that they stay with us. Will was adamant. His argument, which rendered me speechless, was that we had to know if DeBroun had raised a cry against the MacGannons. Or the Lowells. Or the Randolphs. Betty, Louisa, and I were poor company for each other until Will and Randolph arrived late the next day. They brought the news that DeBroun had not surfaced, that London still buzzed with his disappearance, but nothing else.

They brought Kenneth Ogilvie and Gilbey with them as well. Gilbey's eyes were haunted and though I tried to comfort him, nothing changed his conviction that he should have been with Angus and Matthew. We were a subdued group, except for Kenneth, who bristled with suppressed excitement. Whatever had happened in Edinburgh could not erase our loss, and I did not care what it was. I stepped away from the group, but turned to find he'd followed me across the room.

"Angus was a fine man and I will miss him," Kenneth said and I nodded. He took a deep breath. "Mary, I bring news from Edinburgh and you need to hear it. Good news. The Scottish Court of Sessions raised charges against Alex."

"Good news, Kenneth? How is this good news?" I asked dully, sinking into a chair. Kenneth handed me a sheaf of papers.

"I will tell you," Kenneth said. I took the papers with apathy. Will came to my side, Louisa sat at the end of the couch, and Randolph hovered nearby. "The English commissioners," Kenneth continued, "the 'Commissioners Appointed to Enquire of the Estates of certain Traitors in that Part of Great Britain called Scotland,' cannot lay claim to Kilgannon. The Scottish Court of Sessions has done so already. They have raised charges against Alex and he has been found guilty of those charges. As a result Kilgannon has been seized by the Scottish court. The English commissioners cannot take the land for Alex's forfeiture."

A hollow victory, I thought. I should ask him to leave. The man is an idiot and I am in no mood to listen to an idiot. I could not understand his mood. Angus was dead and Alex had been found guilty of treason and might soon face death as well. What did it matter to us who held Kilgannon if it was not MacGannons?

"What charges were brought by the court?" Randolph asked.

"The Scottish Court of Sessions was applied to by a creditor and his claim was held to be legitimate. Kilgannon cannot be claimed by the English commissioners when a creditor is recognized by the Scottish court as having a valid debt."

"A creditor? Who is it, Kenneth?" I asked, sure I would know of any outstanding debts. What had I overlooked? Who could be claiming a debt that I would not recognize? I could remember no outstanding debt, but even if I did, what difference would it make? I had no money to pay a debt. The vultures were circling.

"The Duke of Grafton."

"The Duke of Grafton? Will?" I met Will's startled eyes.

Kenneth shook his head. "No, Mary. This was before Harry died. It was Harry." Next to me Will exclaimed.

"My uncle Harry?" I asked stupidly. "I owe Harry a debt?"

"Yes." Kenneth smiled at my expression. "Harry claims that he loaned Alex money for a new brig and that the brig was never bought and the money never returned. Harry put it in writing."

"Alex never told me he borrowed money from Harry."

"Harry went to see Alex in the Tower and had Alex sign a note that admitted a previous debt," Kenneth said.

I was mystified. Why had Alex never told me he had borrowed money from Harry? What had he used it for? And when had Alex done this? The last time we were in London was in 1714, just before Queen Anne died. It would take the whole day to get to Grafton and back and Alex had never left me for more than a few hours. It made no sense. "Why does this make you so cheerful?" I asked the lawyer.

Kenneth smiled. "You still don't understand. What this means is that the English cannot take control of Kilgannon. The Scottish court has control of your lands."

I gestured sharply. "What difference does this make? If Alex or I do not have control of our lands, what difference to us who does?"

"A very large difference. If the English Commission held Kilgannon, it would sell the land to the highest bidder. That could be anyone. The Scottish court will not allow Kilgannon to be sold until the creditor has been paid. And the court has appointed a new factor for Kilgannon to safeguard its interests."

I closed my eyes. *The man is truly an idiot,* I thought.

I have misjudged him all these months. I opened my eyes and looked at him. "Let me understand," I said at last. "I have to pay my uncle Harry, or now my brother, for a debt I did not know existed. And in the meantime, there will be a new factor at Kilgannon managing our lands and doing God knows what to our people. Oh, yes, Kenneth, now I understand why you are so pleased."

Kenneth shook his head. "Mary, you are not asking the correct questions. Why did Harry go to the Tower and why did Alex sign the note?" He waited for my answer and when I gave none he continued. "To establish that a debt was owed. And where is the money that Harry supposedly lent to Alex?" He reached into his jacket and withdrew a purse, holding it out to me. "Here. Here is the money that Harry lent Alex. And more. Harry said you were to use it to pay the debt, but not just yet. He said you'd know the right time." I took the purse. It was heavier than I thought and it dropped into my lap where it lay as I stared at it.

"Uncle Harry had Alex sign a note admitting a debt but there was no debt previous to that?"

Kenneth nodded. "Correct."

"And this money is the same amount that Harry applied to the court for?" I looked up at Kenneth.

"And more. Harry said there might be some other expenses that you might encounter."

My head was spinning. "When did they do this?"

"Before the trial, Mary. Remember the research Harry had me do? Harry and I studied the previous rebellions. When his heart started paining him he feared he might not be here to direct everything as he wished, so he gave me the money. And his instructions. I have followed them."

"I see," I whispered, looking from Kenneth to the purse on my lap, remembering Alex telling me that Harry's schemes were convoluted. "They'll come to naught, but nothing ventured . . ." he'd said. *Oh, Harry, I thought as my eyes filled. How I misjudged you.*

"After the rebellion of 1708," Kenneth continued, "the same technique was used successfully to keep the lands of the Jacobites in their own hands or in the hands of their families. Many of the men in the Scottish Court of Sessions refuse to take the inherited lands of a Scottish peer, especially when that peer is someone they know. One of Alex's Keith cousins is on the court and many of the others hold Alex in high esteem. The lesson from the earlier rebellions was not lost on those men, Mary. We may be under England's yoke, but we will fight in any way we can. That's why the court appointed a new factor."

"Who is the new factor?" I asked, afraid of the answer.

Kenneth grinned. "Thomas MacNeill."

"Thomas? But he's already the factor. How . . . ?"

Kenneth laughed. "He's now the court's factor as well. It's happening everywhere. Stirling of Keir's estates have been given to his own steward, his kinsman Walter Stirling, and both Stirling and Walter Stirling are openly Jacobites. My favorite thus far is the Earl of Carnwath. The court appointed his mother as factor."

"But this makes no sense. If they mean to punish Alex . . ."

"The English mean to punish him, Mary, but the court are Scottish and they mean to keep Scottish assets in Scottish hands."

"What does this all mean?"

Kenneth smiled widely. "It means you can go home, Mary, with your children. You can go to Kilgannon and when the time is right you can discharge the debt to Alex's creditor. You can repay Will, but not yet. Perhaps not for several years, assuming he will not demand payment before then, which I will not," my brother said emphatically.

Kenneth nodded, and continued. "Someday it will be safe to pay the debt and clear the charges. In the meantime you can live openly at Kilgannon and raise your children there. I have been assured by the court that no one will evict you."

I closed my eyes. Home, I thought. We can go home. I opened my eyes and looked up at Kenneth. "I owe you an apology, sir," I said. "I thought you did not understand our situation. But it was I who did not understand."

"I know that, Mary," he said, his tone kind. "I just did not know how to tell you. I've known about the court's action for some time. That's why Gilbey and I were in Edinburgh. We were waiting for their decision and their assurances."

"Why did Harry not tell me this sooner?"

"He was afraid you could not stand the strain if his plan failed. What if the court did not recognize Harry's claim? What if they had decided otherwise? Harry had little faith in the Scots. He didn't want your hopes to be raised only to be dashed. He wasn't sure you could manage another disappointment."

Oh, Harry, I thought, *perhaps you were right.* I could not have stood another disappointment. I looked at the ring on my finger. *Alex,* I said silently, *we can go home.* How bittersweet it was now.

"And now," Kenneth was saying, "we apply for a release for Alex, based on the indictment being incorrect. Have you heard that General Gordon has been freed?"

Randolph's head snapped up. "General Gordon? The man who commanded the Jacobites' right flank at Sherrifmuir? He is free?"

"He was indicted and attainted. He was in prison," Will said.

Kenneth nodded at them. "He was, but he's free now. And Farquharson of Inveraray. The same thing. Both men freed."

"Why?" Will asked. "What happened?"

"They were attainted under the wrong Christian names. As Alex was." Kenneth's eyes met mine. "Absurd, but there it is. A fine point of the law and one we will attempt to use. Now that Gordon and Farquharson have been freed, the courts will have grown accustomed to such mistakes. We have nothing to lose if we try the same thing." I slumped against the back of the chair as Will squeezed my shoulder and Kenneth smiled at all of us.

"Start applying for Alex's release, Kenneth," Will said. "Name your fee, sir; I will gladly pay whatever you desire."

Kenneth smiled. "I will get my pay, Your Grace. First let me be successful."

"You will be," I said. "You must be."

"God willing, Mary," Kenneth said quietly.

"God willing," I echoed. I looked up into his kind eyes and then at Will and Louisa and Randolph. "I have to tell the boys. And we must find Matthew." Gilbey, who had listened quietly with the others, said he'd leave at once to try to catch Matthew and *Gannon's Lady* in Bristol, and Kenneth insisted upon accompanying him. They left within moments.

* * *

The next few days were quiet. Randolph and Will were wearing themselves out riding back and forth to London, but no one was looking for us, nor asking about us, and no soldiers had returned to Louisa's to search. There was no news of DeBroun. Nor of Alex. I suggested that we return to London, but my family would not hear of it. For once I did as I was told and stayed at Mountgarden while Randolph and Louisa returned to London without me, promising to send word of any announcement at once. The boys and I stood on the drive and waved until they were out of sight.

I tried to be calm as we waited for news and for Matthew and Gilbey to return, but I could not settle my thoughts. Where was DeBroun? He would have no reason to stay hidden. It made no sense. He must, though we'd not heard a breath of it, have returned to his home. Or was he in hiding, thinking that the Mac-Gannons would pursue him if he could be found at his home in London? I wondered just where in Cornwall his property was. The days passed slowly but they passed, each one shorter and colder as the year drew to a close.

Henrietta, the Mountgarden girl who had become the baby's nurse, was incessantly cheerful. She'd had vast experience helping to attend to her brothers and sisters and to her own small daughter, and taught me well how to care for my son. Henrietta called the baby Master Alex. The boys and I called him the baby. If I had considered it, I would have known that I would have to decide what to call him soon, but, like so many things, I chose not to think about it. Will was with me one morning when I rocked my son and he commented on what a good child Alex was. I looked at him, startled.

"It is what you named him, Mary," Will said.

"I'm not sure I will ever call him that," I said. "For me there is only one Alex."

My brother nodded at me. "And for most of us," he said. "Then call him Robbie. It's plain who you're talking about. If someone asks you, tell them he's named after his grandfather. Or his favorite uncle. Or Randolph."

"But they won't ask me, Will. They'll just talk about me behind my back and they'll say that he's named after Robert."

"Mary," said Will, "since when do you care what they say about you? Or if you do care, since when do you let it change your behavior? If it bothers you, call him Harry. Or Lowell. Or Keith. Or Boy. Or whatever 'boy' translates into in Gaelic. You're making too much of it. Decide and you'll grow accustomed to it in time."

I met his eyes and smiled at him. "Dear Will," I said, but could say no more. He gently took my hand in his.

"It's lovely to have you home, Mary. I hope you'll stay after Alex . . . I hope you'll stay. Betty and I must see to Grafton, so you and the boys could live here. I've told you, this will be your home forever. Despite the circumstances, despite everything, it's lovely to have you here." I nodded and ignored my tears and his moist eyes.

"Thank you," I said. "Thank you, Will."

I was walking down the terraces at Kilgannon, going slowly toward the dock. My skirts were rustling, the crisp swish of my taffeta petticoats sounding with every step, but I could hear nothing else. That was strange, I knew, for Kilgannon was seldom quiet, but I was unconcerned about that. Or anything. I was detached. There was no one about and I walked toward the loch as if drawn there. The mist hung low over the water, obscuring the surface and the end of the dock. The sun glinted above it and gleamed off the wet grass in the meadow to my right but could not penetrate into the white cloud. At the dock I stopped while the hush roared in my ears and the mist rose higher in front of me. I waited serenely. Faintly at first and then slowly, slowly more distinctly, came the figure of a man walking toward me from the end of the dock. He was tall and broad-shouldered and wore a kilt, and as he grew closer I realized without surprise that it was Alex. He wore the same clothes he'd worn when he'd left Kilgannon, although his legs and feet were bare and his bonnet was missing. His hair was loose and flowed around his shoulders, but something was different. A dark shape was caught in it. As I watched him walk slowly toward me I tried to determine what it was, but I could not. Behind him the dock disappeared into the fog. I could see him clearly now, his expression calm, and as he closed the gap between us I opened my arms for him and smiled.

And then he was in my embrace. Before I closed my eyes I saw that it was seaweed in his hair, and I reached up to touch it. His hair was dry, as were his clothes, but the seaweed was cold and wet, and I withdrew my hand, repulsed, and wrapped my arm around him. He was solid in my arms, his lips next to my ear, and he whispered, "Mary," as he held me to him. I could feel the wool of his plaid next to my cheek, and I tightened my grip. *Alex,* I thought. *At last.* But when I opened my eyes he was gone and I saw my arms holding only air. I lowered them slowly, looking at my hands. There was water on the fingers that had touched the seaweed, and I stared at it while the mist enclosed me.

I must have made some sound, for when I woke to find myself sitting in bed, my hands outstretched in front of me, the echo of my voice still hung in the air. Of my room. In Mountgarden. I looked wildly around, expecting at any second to be transported back to Scotland. I touched my face and the bedcovers to be sure, but this was all too real. Alex was dead. I was certain of it. I moaned and jumped from the bed, rushing to and fro in a frenzy, as if by moving things from one surface to another I could erase the images I'd seen. Alex was dead. The memory of my visit to the Tower washed over me, and I could hear my voice demanding, "Come to me after death. If it is possible, come to me. Promise me!" and his answering, "If it is possible, I will come to you." *Oh, dear God,* I prayed as I sank to my knees beside the bed. *Dear God, do not let this be true.* But I could not still the voice in my head that said it was. Alex had come to me as I had asked, and on this icy morning, as I stood on the brink of hysteria, I knew he was gone. He was with Angus now. And Harry. And Duncan.

How I got through that day and the next and the next I do not know. It must have been the children that kept me getting up each morning and functioning. I remember little of it, only Will worriedly asking me what was wrong and me muttering a reply about seaweed. I knew I was in serious trouble on the third day when Jamie came upon me talking to myself in the hallway.

"Mama," he said, taking my hand in his own and looking into my face with a frightened expression. "Mama, the baby needs you."

I stared down at him, noting the untidy hair falling around his face, the blue eyes dark with fear. Alex must have looked like this at his age. *Mary, you cannot do this,* I told myself. *You will not do this.* Taking a deep breath, I knelt before him, holding both his hands in mine. He looked into my eyes, waiting. I smiled at Alex's son. "And so do you, Jamie, my love. You need me too. And I need you," I said, gathering him to me. The embrace was no substitute for the one I had dreamed, but it would have to do. He hugged me tightly, his arms around my neck.

I waited. What exactly I was waiting for I never defined. News. Confirmation. A brisk letter from a stranger that would open, "Dear Madam, I regret to inform you . . ." Nothing came. I did not tell Will nor Louisa of my dream; I told no one. I had no doubt they would think me mad, so I kept my fears to myself. *They are only fears,* I told myself, *only fears. I know nothing for certain.* But every time I closed my eyes I saw my fingers touching seaweed caught in golden hair and heard his voice whisper my name.

The days passed. Our only visitors were the neighbors and the only letters from Louisa, who wrote daily. And then, on a cold and dark Thursday when Will and Betty were out, I got two letters, one from Gilbey, the other from the high judge, Lord Webster. It was addressed to Mistress MacGannon and I held it in my hand, terrified of what it would say. "Alex," I whispered, but there was no answer.

Lord Webster's letter was brief. He had written to ask me if I wanted to visit my husband. Immediately. I folded Gilbey's letter and put it in my pocket. "Alex," I said. It was a prayer. So my dream had been wrong. Alex was alive.

TWENTY-TWO

"WE BURIED ANGUS IN A SNOWSTORM, BUT I don't think Matthew noticed," wrote Gilbey. "He stood over his father's cairn until we led him away, and then he sat in the hall before the fire, staring into the flames. He fell asleep in front of a bowl of soup and he slept for two days." Angus had been buried on the steep slope that ran up to the mountains on the far side of the loch, next to his Mairi, and his two daughters, near the ruin of the house where Angus and Mairi and Matthew had lived, the house that Angus and Alex had pulled down after Mairi and the baby had died. When the short ceremony was finished, Matthew built the cairn over his father while Gilbey and Dougall and Thomas handed him rocks, their fingers frozen and shaking, then they stood as Seamus played "MacGannon's Return" into the storm.

"We will make sure all is well here, Mary," Gilbey wrote, "and then we'll return to be with you. I'm sending this with a MacDonald who's going to London for his own reasons. We won't be long."

I reread the letter and folded it neatly, putting it in my pocket again, and sighed as I looked out the window. It seemed we were no closer to London than we had been an hour ago. Beside me, Henrietta dozed, her head against the side of the coach, and on the seat opposite, my sleeping baby was strapped into a carrying cradle.

Lord Webster had sent more than a letter. He'd also sent men and a coach, saying that they would accompany me to London. He asked me to come at once, so that, he'd written, "you may see your husband before his sentence is delivered and performed." Performed. I had little doubt what he meant. One would not say performed of a pardon. Executions were performed, not amnesties.

Despite the staff's and the boys' strenuous objections, I had gone with the judge's men. It was only a trip to London, I told them. Once at Louisa and Randolph's, I would write and let them know I was safe. They had not been pleased but the thought of seeing Alex swept me past their protests and into the coach. We left an hour after I received the letter, for the judge's men were openly impatient to leave and so was I. *Alex*, I thought. Of all of our visits, this would be the hardest. And the last. Of that, I had no doubt. My eyes filled with tears again and I chided myself. I would have to find some courage before I saw him again.

As we entered London, I peeked out the window trying to see landmarks, but nothing was familiar. When we passed St. Paul's heading east I knew we were not going to Louisa's and knocked on the roof. When that was ignored, I called to the driver. Neither he nor the footmen would answer my questions, and I began to be alarmed. Still, I told myself, it was possible that I was being brought to see Alex before going to Louisa's. We were heading toward the Tower and I comforted myself with that idea until we turned north, away from the river. Then I demanded to know where we were going and threatened to scream unless they told me. That, at least, got a reaction, but not the one I wanted. The coach jolted to a stop and two footmen leapt into the coach with us, waking the baby as they pushed his cradle aside and sat opposite me, their expressions hostile. The coach lurched forward.

"Madam," said a footman through clenched teeth, "you are going to Lord Webster's house. If you scream or attract any further attention to yourself we will make you very quiet. Is that understood?" I lifted my chin but one look at the man, who put a hand on my son and looked at me with obvious meaning, silenced me. I nodded and reached for my child. We rode the rest of the way in uncomfortable stillness, Henrietta looking with huge eyes at me and then at the men. I looked at the baby or out the window, my anger growing. I would have something to say to Lord Webster about this.

When at last we arrived, I stepped onto the gravel driveway of a small manor house on the outskirts of London, isolated and fenced, the foliage dense between the house and the road. I looked up at the shuttered house with a sinking heart, telling myself that Lord Webster intended for me to meet Alex in this secluded spot for the simple reason that it was so hidden. With that thought in mind I went inside. We were led by a silent sullen woman to an upstairs room that faced the driveway. As she closed the door behind her I crossed the room and opened the shutters. And heard the bolt being shot on the door behind me. Turning, I looked across the room in surprise, certain I was mistaken, but Henrietta, who met my eyes with a startled look, had heard the same thing and said so. I tried the door. It was bolted from the outside and I knocked at first, then banged on it, shouting. There was no answer. Crossing the room again to the window, I looked at the men who had lingered on the gravel below and realized that they were not footmen. They were guards. "Oh, my dear God," I said aloud, "what have I done?"

What I had done was deliver myself, my baby, and the innocent Henrietta into the hands of our enemies. But I did not recognize that at first. No one came near us for two days except to bring us food or water or to empty the chamber pot. My luggage, scanty as it was, had been searched before it was delivered to us, and the speechless woman who served us also took the baby's linen away. She never looked at us. Two men stood guard at our door at all times.

On the evening of the second day, a carriage rolled onto the drive. Henrietta and I watched anxiously as Lord Webster stepped out and walked into the house. Twenty minutes later the guard summoned me. I followed him downstairs, my thoughts in a storm, and was shown into a small parlor where I waited. Within moments the judge swept into the room as though it were Westminster. I studied him, trying to determine his purpose. I did not want to anger him if he truly intended to let me see Alex, but I was less than pleased by this treatment. He bowed before sitting ceremoniously in one of the chairs opposite me and watched me with hooded eyes.

"Madam. You will, no doubt, have some questions as to why you have been sequestered here."

"I do," I said, trying to keep my tone equivocal.

"I grew very weary of you disrupting my court."

I bent my head. "For that I am truly sorry. It was not intended, sir. I was overcome by the announcement of the verdict."

"That was once, Mistress MacGannon. I meant every time you came to court. No one was paying attention to the issues. They were watching you and your husband."

"I am not responsible for that."

"Exactly what your husband said."

I waited, still unsure of this man or his mood. He leaned forward, his elbows resting on his bony knees.

"Mistress MacGannon, your husband is dead." I stared at him, unable to think, let alone speak as he watched me with that predatory gaze. "He drowned."

Drowned, I thought, remembering my dream.

"Do you understand?" Webster demanded. I shook my head. "Stupid woman. Your husband drowned whilst attempting to escape."

"From the Tower," I croaked. "He was escaping from the Tower?"

"No. Pay attention. Your husband was sentenced ten days ago."

"Sentenced? How? When?"

"Madam, we have the Crown's blessing to proceed as we deem proper. Your husband was sentenced in secret." His eyes narrowed. "We have not found Lord DeBroun and do not know if he's in hiding or if your husband's relations are holding him as they claim. I could not risk the two of you disrupting my court again and turning it into a shambles. I sentenced him in my chambers rather than in the court." He leaned back in his chair and folded his hands together. "We were very lenient, considering the crime."

"But how did he drown?" My voice was a whisper.

Lord Webster frowned at me. "Stop interrupting. Your husband was sentenced to fourteen years indentured service in the colonies. In Virginia." He straightened his back and watched me. *Fourteen years,* I thought. "He was put on board a ship bound for the colonies. It sailed eight days ago. Your husband threw himself over the rail and into the water. We have no doubt that he drowned." With a brusque gesture he took something from his pocket and held it out to me. It was a gold pocket watch and I took it from him with a pounding heart, remembering the day that I'd first seen it, the day Alex had bought it. I knew before I opened it that I'd find *June 5, 1712* engraved inside, and *Trenchant and Sons* on the face.

"Did this watch belong to your husband?" Webster demanded, bringing me back to the present.

I nodded. "Yes," I said hoarsely. *Alex,* I thought. I held the watch in my hand and felt Lord Webster's words begin to penetrate. "This does not prove Alex is dead," I said, "only that he was unable to prevent you from taking this from him."

"Mistress MacGannon, do not be witless. He was seen going over the rail. How long do you think he lived in that water?"

We sat in silence while I struggled not to let despair overcome me. Alex with seaweed in his hair. I had been right. He had come to me. Eight days ago, Webster had said. I tried to remember which night I'd had the dream. "You don't have his body."

He scowled. "Your husband is dead."

"He can swim," I said softly. "He can swim. It's not true."

Lord Webster's eyes narrowed. He sighed as though

he'd come to a conclusion. "And that is why you are being held."

"Why?"

"If, and there is always a remote possibility, if your
husband is alive, he will come to you. And if his barbaric
relations do have DeBroun, I would have had nothing
to trade them. Now I do."

"They are not holding DeBroun. I will swear to that."

"Then your husband will trade himself for you."

"Never."

"We both know he will. For you. Or your son. We
are searching both land and sea for him. I have told
them to bring me his head, and I will hold you until
they do."

I stared at him, wanting to doubt. But I watched his
eyes and believed all he had said. "You are the barbarian," I said.

Webster was not insulted. "I consider only my duty,
which is to crush rebellion. Make no mistake. I will
crush this rebellion, and when I'm finished, no set of es-
says aimed at the lower masses will sway London; no
dramatics by a handsome man in the courtroom will
move them, nor pleas for sympathy by his beautiful
wife. London will understand that the Crown has been
threatened and will be grateful that it has been protected. Whatever the cost, madam, I will succeed. The
Crown will be protected."

"You are repulsive."

"I am prepared to be such, madam. I am not Edgar
DeBroun. Marriage is not what I want from you."

"What do you want from me?"

"Your husband." He rose to stand over me. "Pref-
erably dead. It would be much simpler that way. But if I

have to ship him off to Virginia, I will do so. It makes little difference to me."

"My family will find me. It was clumsy of you to send your own coach with your own men. My brother will discover that it was you who wrote to me, and he will come looking for me."

The judge gave a short bark of a laugh. "He already has, with your uncle Randolph. I made our position extremely clear, that I will hold you until DeBroun is returned or your husband surrenders. Or . . ." He paused. "Until your husband's body is given to me."

"Will would never agree to that, nor my uncle."

Lord Webster was unmoved. "They did agree to it, madam. Readily. In exchange for your stepsons' continued freedom. I would have taken them next and I told them so. They are no relation of his and may be brought under my jurisdiction as wards of the court. Sons of a traitor, madam. Your brother has gone home and your aunt and uncle have withdrawn with him. And it was not clumsy of me to send my own coach. It was planned. It led them to me and then I knew who would come after you." He paused. "It was not the MacGannons, madam. Your husband's family has deserted you and I have dealt with yours. You are quite alone here unless you count your son and his nurse. If you do not cooperate, we will separate you from them." He met my gaze implacably.

I tried to control my fear. *He is lying,* I told myself. Will and Randolph and Louisa would not be so easily managed, and Matthew and Gilbey and Thomas would never abandon me. He must be lying.

"You will not touch my son," I said.

"I will do as I deem proper to solve this little problem. And make no mistake, this is a very little problem. In two years no one in London will remember your husband's name. Nor yours. And now, madam, tell me what you know about Edgar DeBroun's captivity. Tell me what you can quickly, madam. I may not always be so gracious."

"The MacGannons do not hold Edgar DeBroun," I said quietly. "To my knowledge, no one does. I believe he is free."

Webster was silent as he watched me. I could hear the clock ticking on the mantel and someone walking slowly across the hallway upstairs. Lord Webster rose abruptly and moved to the door, turning as he opened it. "Madam, the next time I come I expect the truth from you. And I hope to bring your husband's head. Will that be proof enough of his death?" I did not answer and the judge left me.

Upstairs in my room I shivered and pulled Alex's old plaid around me. Henrietta tried to comfort me but I had not told her everything Webster had said, only that he'd told me Alex was dead. It was bad enough that she had to be here with me, I thought. She did not need to know just how precarious our position was. But I did not lie to myself. I stood at the window and rested my head against the cold glass. Alex was alive. He had to be. But how could he be? Even if he were fit enough to swim to shore, what then? There would be no one to aid him. The MacGannons had all gone north, the Macleans with them, to bury Angus and Duncan. And I, idiot that I was, had delivered myself and our son into the hands of our enemies, leaving the boys at the mercy of others. But I could not believe that Will and Louisa and Randolph had abandoned me, and I did not want to believe that their hands were tied. I prayed for the boys' safety. And Alex's. And ours. And where was DeBroun?

Later I sat before the fire, staring into the flames, rocking my sleeping baby while Henrietta dozed on the bed. Alex was alive, I told myself, refusing to remember seaweed in his hair, and he would go to Louisa and Randolph in London. Or Will at Mountgarden. Or Grafton. Or strike out for the north and eventually get to Kilgannon. He was not without his resources. Perhaps William Burton, his shipping agent, would help him or, failing that, some of the men he'd known in London. Surely there would be someone. But I kept remembering the day he'd been attacked by the mob, just before Queen Anne's death, when the city had been terrified that a Jacobite invasion was imminent. London could be very fickle.

Louisa and Randolph and Will certainly knew Webster held us, and I didn't believe for a moment that they would simply stop searching for me. But who, I wondered, would ever suspect I'd be in this secluded house, surrounded by guards? They would have gone to the judge's town house or to his estate in Derby, not here. And what, I thought with a new pang of fear, what if the judge was not lying? I contemplated the window again. Three stories to the ground, a sheer drop, no porch roof or accommodating gable to block my fall. Impossible to consider with a baby or without. And the roof, another story above, was no escape. I looked around the room, with its thick plaster walls, coming back as always to the door. But the door was at least three inches thick, ancient oak that bore the marks of many blows. And I had no weapon save my mind. *Think, Mary,* I commanded myself yet again, *think. You will not sit here and rot like some character out of one of Thomas Mac-Neill's stories. Think.* But my thoughts ran in circles. At last I climbed into bed with the baby and Henrietta. And dreamed.

I was walking down the terraces at Kilgannon. The mist hung low over the water, obscuring the surface. At the end of the dock, I waited serenely as he walked toward me. In his hair was something dark and wet. . . . Alex was dead. I woke in the dark, my heart pounding and my breath coming in ragged gulps. *Oh, dear God,* I prayed, *do not let this be true.* But I could not still the voice in my head that said it was. He had come to me as I had asked. I climbed from the bed and paced the room. *Alex, my love, where are you tonight?* I asked silently. I held his watch to my breast and prayed.

The morning dawned gray and cloudy, the air heavy with moisture, and I huddled in the covers, still dressed in my clothes. I heard something but fought against waking until Henrietta sprang from the bed and went to the window.

"Lady Mary," she whispered, "it's a coach arriving." Her pretty face was pale, and I thought yet again how very unfair it was for them to imprison her with me. "There's more than one man," she said without looking away from the window. "One is the judge. He's very stiff this morning. I hope he has pain in every joint of his body."

I lifted my head with a horrible thought. "Is he holding anything? A box?" *A box big enough for a man's head?* I thought.

"No," she said with a puzzled glance at me, "he is

holding nothing. Here's the second man. Blond. A tall man. Dressed all in black, in English clothing. He's very big."

"Alex," I said, sitting up. "Or Matthew." I rose and moved to join her.

"They've gone in the house," she said.

I was waiting when the guard came to our room to summon me, and I went down the stairs with a lighter heart than I'd had in days. It was unlikely that Alex was here. He'd never have gone tamely into the house without some attempt to get my attention. So it must be Matthew, and he could at least tell me what was happening. Nothing could be worse than my imaginings. I'd find out what news there was and I'd ask the judge to release Henrietta, if not both of us. I was led to the parlor and offered a cup of tea by the same woman who served us upstairs. She still would not look at me. Men were quietly talking in the next room and I sipped the tea, trying to hear what they said. Negotiating, I thought. They kept me waiting a long time. I stood when the door opened, ready to greet Matthew. But it was not Matthew who entered with the judge. It was Malcolm.

TWENTY-THREE

I DROPPED THE CUP. AND I MUST HAVE LOOKED AS though I was about to faint, for Malcolm took my arm. I cringed away from his touch, backed into the chair I'd been sitting in, and sat down with a thump as I stared at him. Alex's brother smiled. The cup rolled on the floor, all of us ignoring it.

"Mistress MacGannon, your brother-in-law has come to give you his condolences," Lord Webster said as he sat slowly on the chair opposite me. "I assume you two will wish to comfort each other."

I hardly noticed the judge's words, nor did I look at him. I was watching Malcolm. The year had not been kind to him. He was heavier and his face, although still handsome, was more florid now, his eyes piggish in the folds around them. He reached a hand to me and I turned my head aside.

"Mary," Malcolm said in a wheedling tone as he sat in the chair beside me. "I am sorry about Alex. We must heal the wounds now. It's time to reunite."

I did not trust myself to answer.

"MacGannon has applied to be your stepsons' guardian," said the judge, shifting in his chair to look at us both.

"No," I said, my voice wavering. "No. I am their mother."

Malcolm shook his head and spoke as one would to a child. "Yer no' their mother. Their mother is dead."

"I am the only mother they have. And I am their guardian."

"They are my blood, Mary, not yers." Malcolm's tone was patronizing. I leapt up, ready to leave the room, but Malcolm beat me to the door, blocking my passage. I met his eyes. "They are my blood, Mary," he said again in a much different tone. "And now that Kilgannon has passed to Ian, he will need a man to guide him." I stepped back from him. Malcolm slowly smiled and my rage exploded.

"No!" I cried. "No." I drew myself as tall as I could. "Ian has not inherited Kilgannon. Alex is not dead, despite your best efforts. Over and over, Malcolm, you tried to kill him, and when you could not manage it yourself you got the English to do your dirty work. Well, you swine, you failed again. Alex is not dead."

Malcolm's smile widened. "Oh, but he is."

Lord Webster spoke from his chair, his brittle voice carrying easily. "Your husband is dead, madam."

"Dead, Mary." Malcolm smiled into my eyes. "Alex is dead. Dead. Yer a widow. And Ian has inherited."

I shook my head. "Bring me proof." I whirled to face the judge. "You don't have proof, do you? I knew it. Alex is not dead." I turned back to Malcolm. "Even if it were true, Ian would inherit nothing. Kilgannon is forfeited with all of the rest of Alex's property, or have you forgotten that?" Malcolm watched through narrowed eyes. If he did not know of the Scottish court's ruling, I thought, I would not be the one to tell him. "Even if you cleared all the obstacles, it would be Ian who inherited, not you."

"I will be his guardian, Mary," Malcolm said.

"Not while I live."

"As ye wish," he said coldly. "That can be arranged."

"No doubt," I said, my voice low with hatred. "And how long would you let Ian live? How long would it be until you removed him and then Jamie?" I glanced over my shoulder at the judge. "He will kill them both just to get the land. And you will be responsible."

Malcolm moved away from me with distaste. "What a horrible thing to say. I would never harm them, Mary."

"Oh?" I glared at him. "Just as you would never harm their father? No, Malcolm, you will have to kill me before I allow you to be their guardian, and if I'm dead, Matthew will kill you. And if he's dead, Gilbey will do it. Or Thomas. Or Dougall. Or wee Donald. A lot of people hate you for what you did."

"Ye dinna understand . . ."

"Oh, but you're wrong, Malcolm. I understand only too well. We all understand." He raised a hand as though to strike me and I glared at him, aware that the judge had moved to stand behind me. "Go ahead, Malcolm," I said. "It has never been difficult in the past for you to hit women. Or is it different with an audience?"

Malcolm lowered his hand. "Yer distraught, Mary. I'll return when ye can talk sensibly."

"No," I said, meeting the anger I saw in his eyes with my own. "Don't come back. You are dead to me, Malcolm. Dead."

"As is Alex," he sneered.

"No." I turned to the judge, who watched both of us

without expression. "Either you know he's not dead or you fear he's not."

"We believe that he is dead, madam," said Judge Webster.

"Until I see his body he is alive to me. If he were not, you would release me."

"You seem to forget that your husband's kinsmen hold DeBroun."

"They do not."

"Ah, at last, the subject I came to discuss. Pray be seated again, madam. You will not be leaving this room until we address this." I did not move, nor speak. Lord Webster glanced at Malcolm before turning back to me. "I have brought your brother-in-law here because you are a very stubborn woman and I am trying to have you tell me what you know. I am considering appointing MacGannon as guardian of your stepsons since their father is presumed dead." I was silent. The judge nodded. "Very well. That is exactly what I will do. I will transfer you to the Tower and I will appoint Malcolm MacGannon guardian of your stepsons and your baby since they will have become wards of the court. Then we will all wait for Edgar DeBroun to return." I met his eyes. I believed him.

"If you tell me what you know," Webster said, "I will reconsider the guardianship." I nodded and when he led me back to the chair I went willingly. He sat next to me. Malcolm stayed at the door. "Madam," said the judge, demanding my attention, "tell me what you know about DeBroun's captivity."

"DeBroun is not being held captive," I said. "He has gone."

"Gone?"

"Gone."

Lord Webster studied me. "How do you know this?"

"I saw him before I left London." That much at least was true.

"And where is he now?"

"I don't know. Truly, I don't. I hope he's in hell."

"Are the MacGannons holding him?"

"No. The MacGannons have gone back to Scotland. DeBroun is being held by no one."

The judge considered me with pursed lips. "Why have the MacGannons gone to Scotland, madam?"

"It is their home. They could do nothing here."

"Are they coming back?"

I shook my head. "I don't know. I have heard nothing."

"If I release you, what will you do?"

"Go to Mountgarden. Raise my children. My brother will help."

Malcolm spoke from the door. "As they are helping ye the now, Mary? Perhaps Robert will help as well?"

"Malcolm," I said, "unlike you, I will never betray Alex."

Malcolm laughed unkindly. "Who does yer child look like?"

Lord Webster rose and walked stiffly to the door, then turned to me. "Madam, remember that you are alive only because I choose to keep you so. I will return with the proof of your husband's death." He went through the door without a backward glance.

When the door closed Malcolm came to stand over me. "And what about Angus, Mary?" Malcolm asked quietly. "If Matthew and Gilbey will avenge ye, what about Angus? Where is Angus?"

I looked up at him. "We do not speak these days," I said and watched Malcolm's pleasure in my answer. How I hated him.

"Don't fight me, Mary. I am the one with the power here."

"You are dead to me, Malcolm," I said and turned my back. Eventually he left me alone and after a while I heard the coach drive away and the house become quiet again.

Locked in my room, I wrapped my arms around myself and went over it again and again. Webster was still not convinced that the MacGannons did not hold De-Broun. And Alex had to be alive. He had to be. I prayed for his safety. And the boys'. Until today I had thought we were in danger, not them, and I had never imagined I could be put in the Tower. I had no doubt that Webster would do just that if it suited him, but I had no way to warn Will of Webster's plan. The judge's men would arrive at Mountgarden without warning and tear Ian and Jamie away from my brother. I looked at my baby and his nurse with something close to panic and tried not to think about Malcolm as guardian of my sons.

We were left alone for the rest of that day, and when the woman brought our breakfast the next morning I did not even look at her. The door closed behind her and Henrietta attacked the food with energy while I listlessly watched her eat. And then I saw it. Under the plate was a small square of paper. Leaning forward without a word, I drew the paper out from under the plate while Henrietta sat and watched, her fork midway to her mouth. It was no more than four inches across, a scrap of dirty paper, and it had fit neatly under the plate. There were no words written on it but it lifted my heart and I smiled as I looked at it and showed Henrietta. The pattern of my wedding ring was drawn in intricate detail, each twist of the design clearly delineated. And in the center of the paper was the rose, the twin of the one on my ring.

"Alex drew this," I said and then stopped. I turned the paper over. There was no signature, no sign of the artist. I pressed it to my heart. *Alex, my love,* I prayed, *tell me you are alive. Tell me this is from you.* The drawing was silent but my answer could wait. Someone knew where I was. We were not alone.

I spent that day and the next at the window in a frenzy of emotions, thinking to see someone, or be seen by someone. But there were no visitors, no drawings. Each time the woman brought us something I searched her face for a message, but she would not meet my glances. The man at the door prevented any conversation, and the trays she brought held nothing but food and crockery. I hung the plaid out the window, which caused conversation among the guards, but no one came to tell me to remove it.

The baby was fretful, as though he'd caught my mood, and Henrietta sang to him as she walked him. I watched her and thought about what a comfort she'd been for me, a sweet and agreeable girl who never complained. I must keep her safe. And the baby. But how? I looked out the window at the drop again. Impossible. I sighed and watched the guards as they roamed the gravel drive. Four of them there. Two who were always at our door. And six more I'd seen when I'd been taken downstairs. At least twelve, then, without counting the woman. As I watched, four more men came from the house and joined the ones on the drive. Twelve? Or sixteen altogether? I paced the room and went over our situation again. Alex was alive. Since receiving the sketch I was sure of it. Or almost. But what did Webster plan? I could not be held here forever. Surely that would not be in the judge's best interests. If Alex were found, dead or alive, my usefulness would be over. And if he was not found in a reasonable amount of time, there would be no reason to keep me alive to tell the tale of this adventure. Or Henrietta and the baby. But then there was the drawing. Who had sent it and what did it mean? Was I to do something obvious that I had not thought of? I started to think again.

It rained that night and most of the next day. In the late afternoon the sky cleared and weak sunlight filtered through the clouds. I stood at the window and watched the guards below. Just as I was about to turn away, something flickered in the trees at the far side of the drive. Something red. "Henrietta," I whispered, "come here. Tell me if you see anything." I pointed out the clump of trees. As she watched, I saw the movement again and she gasped.

"Yes, Lady Mary! I saw it. There is someone there." She gripped my arm and we watched with growing excitement, but no one came out of the trees and none of the guards noticed the movement. Instead, a lone rider came to the door, encased in a long cloak. As he approached the house he threw back the hood and looked up at us, his blond hair bright against the wool. I caught my breath. I needn't have. It was Malcolm. I stepped back from the window, my disappointment hard to bear. It must have been one of Malcolm's men that we'd seen. No wonder the guards had not reacted. He had been expected. A few moments later I was summoned and went down the stairs with a heavy heart.

Malcolm, standing by the hearth, smiled as I entered the room.

"Mary." His voice was warm as he moved to me, extending his hands. "We were both so wrong the other day. Let us try again."

I ignored his hands as I sat down. "Why are you here?"

"We must unite the family."

"Why?"

"Because we are all we have left. Alex is gone and the boys and ye are all I have of my family. Mary," he said, his tone coaxing, "come to yer senses. I am in favor with the Whigs and allied with the Frasers. I am yer only hope of survival. Let bygones be bygones." I looked at my wedding ring. "Dinna be obstinate. Webster is coming to question ye about DeBroun again. He has allowed me to come here first and try to persuade ye to be cooperative. Tell me what ye ken and perhaps he will be generous."

Generous, I thought. Edgar DeBroun had also promised to be generous. "What do you want, Malcolm?" I asked.

"I only want what is best for all of us. Come home, Mary, and raise yer children in Scotland. If not at Kilgannon, then Clonmor."

"I cannot."

"Ye mean ye will not."

"I mean I cannot," I said crisply. "I mean I am being held captive, Malcolm. I can go nowhere."

"I will speak to the judge. I'm sure that once ye tell him what ye ken about DeBroun, he will release ye."

"I don't know where DeBroun is."

"I don't believe you."

"It is the truth, Malcolm, but then you always did

have difficulty with the truth," I said and watched his eyes harden.

"What happened between ye and Angus, Mary?"

"We did not agree on the best way to help Alex." That much was true and I met his eyes without a flinch.

"Where are my mother's jewels?"

The question, so unexpected, caught me off guard. "What?"

His eyes were icy. "My mother's jewels. They're not at Kilgannon. Where are they?"

"Why?" I asked, stalling for time.

"They are all I have left of her."

I laughed unkindly. "They're gone, Malcolm. I sold everything to try to free Alex. Everything's gone," I lied. It was true that everything else salable was gone from Kilgannon, but Margaret's jewels were in the bottom of a trunk at Mountgarden.

"We could sell them, Mary. We could get Kilgannon back."

"They are gone, Malcolm. Perhaps I should speak more slowly?"

He considered me for a moment, then shook his head. "Mary, ye have disliked me from the first. Why?"

I paused and looked at him thoughtfully, then decided to answer with the truth. I certainly did not have to worry about sparing his feelings. "It is true that I have always disliked you, Malcolm, and at first I did not even know why," I said. "But I soon discovered that I not only disliked you, I despised you. For many reasons, the first of which is that you were disloyal to Alex. You were always contemptuous of him and you sneered at everything he did and ridiculed him when he was kind and fair to others. And I learned to hate you when you tried to kill him and were silent when he lived. I despise you because you prey on women and those who are weaker than you, because you beat Sibeal when you were the one at fault, and I hate you because you betrayed Alex to Robert. Your own brother, and you showed the enemy where to find him. I despise you because you are intelligent and you use your mind for harm instead of good, because you cannot be Alex and so you would destroy him instead of becoming like him. Because, even now, when we all fear Alex is dead, you only think of yourself. You are incapable of thinking about anyone else's needs. I hate you because you are everything I've said, and a coward as well."

He took a step back as though I'd struck him. After a moment he took a deep breath and opened his mouth, then closed it and turned and left the room without a word. When I heard the front door close I climbed the stairs and returned to my room.

Henrietta turned from the window with shining eyes. "Lady Mary," she whispered, "I've been watching. There is someone in the trees. Several people, I think. Some are wearing red and some green. We can see them because we can see over the underbrush. Look." She pointed to the trees as I came to stand beside her. "There. See? The brush prevents the guards from seeing them."

She was right. I could see the small movements in the trees, but couldn't tell who was there. There was no movement from the underbrush. The sun moved lower on the horizon and the shadows lengthened. It was almost dark when we heard a thump and then another from downstairs and then silence. And another series of thuds. We ran to the door and pressed our ears to the wood but there was nothing else to hear. On the other side of the door the guard moved his feet and let us know he was still there. He must have heard the noise as well, I thought. I ran to the window, but the six guards who patrolled the front were behaving normally.

And then a horseman thundered into the yard. Alex vaulted from his mount, grabbing one of the guards by his collar and shouting at the others. They started toward him but stopped when Alex put his sword to the guard's throat.

"Back off or he dies," he growled at them. "Back off!"

The guards stepped backward, then circled him slowly. I watched in horror. He was one against six. It was only a matter of moments before at least one of them could reach him.

"Mary Rose!" Alex shouted, turning his captive so they faced the house. "Get yer things together, lass. I've come to take ye home." And then, seeming to come from all directions at once, I heard the roar of a battle cry. The MacGannon battle cry. And men poured from the trees to come to Alex's aid.

TWENTY-FOUR

The house rocked with noise. The battle cry had been legitimate, for I saw Dougall and other MacGannons, Macleans with them, but there were Mountgarden men mixed in as well, fighting alongside the Scots. I watched some of the guards on the drive lay down their weapons as the yard filled with kilted men. Those who did not surrender did not live long, and soon the rest were raising their hands in submission. But I did not see Alex again. I raised the window and leaned out, calling Dougall, but the noise below drowned out my voice.

From inside the house we could hear shouts and thumps and an occasional shot, and then both Henrietta and I turned from the window as the door behind us opened. The guard entered, closing the door behind him, his eyes wild. The man stood with his back to the door and stared at us. We stared back.

At the sound of running feet in the hallway, we all turned to face the door. The guard raised his weapon, a pistol, and took a knife from his belt to hold in his other hand. The footsteps stopped and there was the sound of the bolt being shot on the door. The guard ran to the door then, shouting and pounding on the wood, and when there was no answer he turned to look at Henrietta and me.

"We're locked in," he said unnecessarily.

I turned to the window again, but dusk had fallen and I could see little. I leaned out and saw torches were being lit on the far side of the drive. As they were held high, I could see Dougall standing over men who were being bound. The fighting was finished at the front of the house. "Dougall!" I screamed. "Dougall!"

He looked up at me and grinned as he crossed the yard. "We'll be with ye shortly, Mary. Thanks for the plaid. We ken where ye are and we'll be there, but first we have some mopping up to do."

"Alex?" I called, but Dougall had gone into the house and I got no answer. I turned to find the guard looking over my shoulder. "Did you come in here to protect us?" I asked.

He snorted. "I came in here to escape. I can hear what's going on downstairs. They'll butcher me. They're Scots."

Before I could argue with him we heard a man shouting my name. I ran to the door while the guard moved to stand behind me. The voice was muffled and I closed my eyes as I listened and prayed. His voice came closer and then he was in the hallway. "Mary!"

I opened my eyes and smiled. "Alex!" I called and pounded on the door. "Alex!"

"Mary?" Alex was on the other side of the door. The bolt was pulled and the latch tried but it must have been locked as well. "Mary, are ye aright, lass?"

"Yes! Yes! Yes!"

He tried the door again and cursed in Gaelic. "Get yerself back, Mary Rose," he said and waited a moment. "Are ye away?"

"Yes," I said. The door slammed inward with a splintering crash, Alex's left foot still on the lock, his sword in his right hand. He hopped as he regained his balance and then stood in the doorway looking at me and then behind me. I had already started moving toward him, but he held up a hand to stop me. I watched as his expression hardened and followed his gaze to see the guard pointing his pistol at Alex. I screamed.

"Dinna scream, Mary Rose," Alex said, his voice very calm while he kept his eyes on the guard. "The man's nervous enough." He gestured to his right. "Move aside, lass, get out of the way."

"He thinks you'll kill him," I said breathlessly as I moved back. The baby wailed in Henrietta's arms, but none of us paid attention. Alex's eyes never left the guard.

"I just might do that. It depends on what he does," he said.

"I have the gun, Scot," said the guard, his tone deep.

"Aye, and the advantage," said Alex, taking a half step into the room. Behind him I could hear footsteps stopping abruptly at the doorway. "Ye could kill me before I got to ye. I'm well aware of that, Englishman."

Alex took another half step forward and the guard backed away. Alex moved forward again. Will came through the doorway and stood behind Alex, his eyes on the guard and a pistol in his hand. The guard sighted down the barrel, his pistol aimed at Alex's heart. I stepped forward to stop him as his finger moved to the trigger, but I need not have. Will, with one swift movement, lifted his gun beside Alex's shoulder. And fired. The guard fell at once, his pistol clattering to the floor. I screamed. Henrietta screamed. And the baby wailed.

"He's all right, Mary," Will said. "Alex is all right."

Suddenly the room was crowded with men who got between Alex and me, MacGannons, weapons drawn, calling my name and his and asking what had happened. But all I could see was Alex and his face as he reached for me.

"Mary," he said hoarsely and opened his arms. I was in them before the sound of my name died in the room. "Mary Rose. Thank God." He spoke in Gaelic then, without regard to our audience, saying words of love that I had waited so long to hear. I laughed and cried, touching his face and his chest and his shoulders, trying to convince myself he was real and not just another vision.

"Alex," I sobbed, clutching him to me. "Alex."

He leaned over me, his face against my hair. "Are ye aright, lass? Are ye aright?" I nodded.

"Are you all right, my love? I thought he would shoot you."

Alex laughed and nodded at my brother. "Not while yer brother's at my elbow, lass." He looked at Will. "Ye were braw, Lowell. Remind me to take ye with me when I go into battle. Yer a grand champion." Will laughed, pleased.

"Oh, Will," I said, throwing myself at him. "You saved Alex's life. You might have been killed!"

My brother shook his head, but welcomed my embrace. "He was aiming at Alex, Mary. All I did was stop him."

"Thank you, thank you, thank you," I said, clasping him to me. "You are wonderful. You were so quick, so calm."

"So accurate," Alex laughed.

Will beamed and released me, gesturing to Alex. "It was him in danger. As always. Damned Scot," he laughed. "And do ye not admire my knees, lass?" Will's accent was, as always, terrible. I blinked at him and then realized what he meant. He was dressed in Highland clothing, complete with kilt and plaid and bonnet and a sword in his belt. He laughed at my expression. "It was Alex's idea. The Duke of Grafton does not burst into people's houses, but a Scot can and no one is surprised."

"Told ye," Alex laughed, then reached for me again. "Did Webster harm ye, Mary Rose?" he asked as his arms enfolded me.

"No, my love," I said, leaning to look into his face. "But he told me you had drowned." I stroked his cheek. "You're not dead. Oh, Alex. You're not dead."

He laughed. "Not the last time I looked, lass, although there have been days lately when I couldna tell ye for sure. I came close enough to drowning for the report to be true." He pulled me to him again and I tightened my grip on him. "Mary," he said, his lips against my ear. "Oh, lass, I thought to never see ye again. 'Tis a miracle to have found ye."

"Are the boys safe?" I asked, looking from Alex to my beaming brother. "Are they all right? Where are they?"

"Safe and sound aboard the *Mary Rose*, lass," said Alex. "With a guard of thirty clansmen and wee Donald in charge. No one will get his hands on my sons," he said grimly, "unless it's me."

Dougall appeared in the doorway then and nodded at me before turning to Alex. "Hello, Mary. I see yer well." I smiled. "All is quiet downstairs, Alex. They're waiting for ye."

The baby whimpered, and Henrietta, still cradling him, peeked out from behind the clansmen. "I'll be down soon, Dougall," Alex said. "I've more important things to do now," he said, clasping me to his chest again and giving me a hearty kiss.

Dougall grinned as he left. "When yer ready, chief, we'll be waiting." He gestured to the men and the room emptied.

Alex released me with a smile and we turned together to Henrietta. At my nod she handed the baby into Alex's arms as Alex smiled with joy. "Your son, my love," I said.

"Aye," Alex said softly as he held the baby's cheek to his own. The baby whimpered again and Alex rocked him. "Whist, laddie, dinna fret. Hush now. It's yer da, come to find ye. All is well." He kissed the baby's head. "Hello, my son," he said in Gaelic. "Welcome to the world." Alex looked up at me, his eyes shining. "What's his name, Mary Rose?"

"Alexander Robert Harold Lowell Keith MacGannon. I've been calling him Little Alex."

Will laughed. "She has not. She's been calling him 'the baby.' I told her to call him Robbie." Alex looked from Will to me. "After his grandfather," Will said softly. "As your Ian is named after his. My father will be remembered in your son."

"Robbie," Alex said quietly and exchanged a long look with Will while I held my breath. "Yer father. Aye," Alex said at last and nodded, his decision made. "We'll call him Robbie, lass, if ye will. One Alex is quite enough in this family." He shifted the baby and smiled at him. "Welcome, Robbie MacGannon," he said in Gaelic, and then looked up at me, his eyes very blue. "Mary Rose, we have a bonnie son."

I nodded, unable to speak. Alex laughed and leaned to kiss me. "Speechless, aye? Well, I'm glad to know I can still render ye such." He looked around the room, then grinned. "Let's get out of here, aye?" And Will laughed.

Downstairs we found what was left of the judge's men, some of whom I discovered were no more than workers on his nearby farm, neatly bound and sitting against the walls of the kitchen with MacGannons standing over them. They gave us hostile looks as we entered. The woman who had served us was sobbing at the table, but stopped when Alex gave her money and thanked her for delivering the sketch. She refused both and pled for the lives of her husband and sons and friends.

"What?" asked Alex scornfully as he gestured to the men. "Mistress, do ye really think I'd kill them now? Get ye gone from here and return with help in an hour. It may be raining again by then and they'll be sitting on the drive getting wet." He pressed the money in her hand again. "Give the judge, when he returns from wherever he's hiding, a message from me," he said. "Tell him Alexander MacGannon will return to thank him for the hospitality he showed my wife and son. Tell him to be expecting a visit from me. And tell him I'm no' pleased."

She nodded, gulping, as she crossed the room to the door and flew through it. Alex looked at Dougall, Thomas, and the others who waited for his orders, and then turned to the prisoners.

"Get yerselves outside now. I'm burning the house."

A short time later we stood on the drive with the clansmen and my brother and watched the flames reach toward the sky. Dougall said that the rain might start again and put out the fire.

Alex shrugged. "It doesna matter. It's only a symbol," he said quietly. "The judge will no' mistake it. I dinna care if it burns to the ground or if the rain stops it. No one will ever live in this house again." He turned to me. "We have to go, lass," he said and I nodded, but he lingered, watching the flames. I glanced at the bound men at our feet. I had not asked where Matthew and Gilbey were, afraid to know the answer, but Alex kept looking at the entrance of the drive as though expecting someone. At last Alex shrugged and turned his back on the house.

"Here they come, Alex!" a man shouted from the foot of the drive. "All four of them!"

"Aye," Alex said softly and muttered something to himself. Will moved to one side of Alex and I to the other. I could feel how rigid his body was and wondered as I looked from his tense face to the dark entrance who he was preparing to meet. MacGannons were moving forward with torches, their greetings loud in the night air.

Matthew was the first into the light and I breathed a prayer of thanks. Matthew's expression lightened as he nodded at me, and he turned to the man behind him. My uncle Randolph. I was astonished that Randolph would be part of this, but I smiled at him as he drew closer. Randolph grinned at me and waved.

The third man was Malcolm, his hands tied together and his face bruised. I watched him approach, remembering his brother coming home to me in Kilgannon in much the same condition. I glanced at Alex, but he looked at his brother without expression. And then Gilbey came into the light and I took a deep breath. *All accounted for,* I thought. But what now? Everyone

watched Alex. He stood silently, the flames lighting his
hair into a glow around his head, his arms at his sides.
Matthew and Gilbey helped Malcolm to dismount and
then the three of them faced Alex.

"Malcolm," said Alex tonelessly.

"Alex," Malcolm said. No one else spoke as the
brothers looked at each other. Around me the men
moved nervously.

Randolph broke the silence when he dismounted in
front of me. "You're all safe and sound, Mary? And the
babe?" I embraced him and he kissed my cheek and
shook Will's hand. "Thank God. We've been terribly
worried. Your aunt hasn't slept in days."

"I'm sorry . . ." I began, but Randolph waved my
words away.

"Not your fault," he said. "And never fear, we'll take
care of Webster. Duke John has already started. And so,
I see, has Alex."

"We have to go, Alex," Dougall said. Alex nodded,
at last shifting his gaze from his brother to his cousin.

"Aye," he said, his voice flat. "Put him with the
others."

We were ready to leave in just a few minutes. Alex sat
atop his horse next to me, watching the first of the
clansmen file out the drive. He looked back at the men
still tied up on the gravel, then climbed down from his
horse. I watched in horror as he walked toward them,
drawing his sword. Behind me Matthew and Gilbey
were suddenly still and Dougall exclaimed but did not
move. Malcolm watched Alex approach without expression. Will and Randolph exchanged a look. Alex
stopped in front of Malcolm, the sword glinting in the
light from the flames. Malcolm looked up at his brother

and Alex raised his arm. I closed my eyes, but there was no sound and I opened them to see Alex stick the sword into the gravel between Malcolm's legs.

"I should kill ye, Malcolm," Alex said. "If our positions were reversed, ye would kill me. But I willna. No' because ye dinna deserve it, or because I'm afraid of retribution from the English. I willna kill ye, Malcolm, because ye would dirty my hand and my name. And my soul, but that's something ye'll never understand." He kicked gravel onto Malcolm's lap with a toe. "I am taking Clonmor back. Dinna try to go there. And never . . ." He leaned over his brother. "Never come to Kilgannon. Never come near my family. Or I will kill ye with my own hand. Do you understand?"

Malcolm nodded and Alex turned, grabbing his sword as he strode away. He climbed into the saddle and nodded at us. "Let's go," he said.

The crackle of the flames was the only sound behind us.

TWENTY-FIVE

WE GALLOPED AWAY FROM WEBSTER'S HOUSE SO rapidly that there was no time to speak. At last we paused at a crossroads to make plans, our conversation hurried while clansmen stood guard for us. Will and Randolph would return to Mountgarden, taking Henrietta and the men who had aided us with them. And then they'd return to London. They were confident that this night's escapade could not be traced to them.

And we, I was told, were off to the *Mary Rose*, and then to Scotland. I did not argue, knowing it would be foolish to stay in England. But I did remind Alex that our luggage, and all the Kilgannon papers, and Margaret's jewels, were still at Mountgarden. If my brother's home was searched and they were found, it would not go well with him. Alex nodded and frowned and at last it was determined that Matthew and Gilbey would take a few men with them to retrieve our possessions.

I wrote a hasty note to Louisa, and then it was time to bid my brother and uncle goodbye. I embraced them both fiercely. "Thank you," I said to each, and each waved my words away as though this sort of adventure were commonplace to them. I was overcome then, realizing that I might not see them for years.

Randolph embraced me, his eyes full of unshed tears. "Hush, Mary," he said. "We love you. What else would we have done? Thank God you are all safe." He glanced at Matthew and I knew we both were thinking of Angus. "Well, almost all." He squeezed me to him again. "Go with your husband, my girl, and be safe. Write to us when you can."

I turned to Will. "No sad goodbyes," my brother said with a smile. "This is the time to applaud, not cry. We'll come to see you if you send one of your ships to get us. I'm the best first-footer Kilgannon's ever had and you won't want anyone else. In fact, you can't have anyone else. I claim it as my right and I'm a duke now, so you can't say no. What's the use of being a duke if one cannot have one's way?"

I laughed and embraced him. "Dear Will," I said.

He squeezed me. "Go, Mary," he whispered. "Go and be safe in your home with your family. Just keep him out of England, for God's sake!" I nodded and turned to Alex.

"My love," I said. "Take me home."

"Aye, Mary Rose," Alex said. "I will."

We arrived at the *Mary Rose* without incident and the boys fell on us with delight, grumbling that they had not been allowed to rescue me and the baby. They'd wanted to accompany their father on what they considered to be an adventure and complained that wee Donald had not even let them go on deck. Alex ruffled their hair and picked them up, turning them upside down until they giggled, then left them with me and the baby to settle into the big cabin. The *Margaret* was already sailing offshore, waiting for us and *Gannon's Lady* to join her. We'd wait for Matthew and Gilbey, then all meet at sea and head for Kilgannon.

When Alex returned to me he talked with his sons, holding the sleeping baby while they sat with him. And then he sent them off to wee Donald's care again, and turned to me with a smile.

"I'm thinking this one should be abed as well," he said and I reached for Robbie, thinking Alex was right. He put a hand on my arm. "Lass, I dinna mean that bairn. I meant ye."

I met his eyes over our son and felt the stirrings again. This man never failed to rouse me and now was no exception. We laid our sleeping child safely on another berth, then fell into each other's embrace. I tore his clothing from him and he mine from me in our frantic haste to be together. Our union was swift and joyous and I submerged into a sea of sensations. His whiskers were rough on my skin, but his lips soft and his hands gentle, and when he paused above me I pulled him to me with a throaty laugh.

"Alex," I said. "Come to me."

"And two shall become one," he said, then glanced at the baby. "Or three," he laughed, then concentrated on his task.

I heard some of Alex's story later that night as we lay entwined in our berth, and more in greater detail when we talked together before dawn. Alex made light of his fear and anger during his trial and how after being beaten unconscious at the verdict, he'd been kept isolated in the Tower, but the timbre of his voice had changed when he told his story, and I studied him, noting cheekbones that were much too prominent and lines now permanently etched around his mouth. He'd noticed that DeBroun was missing during the last of the trial, of course, and suspected Angus had made a move, but since he saw Angus in the courtroom every day, he did not know what it was.

And he'd brushed over his escape from the transportation ship, explaining that Webster had lied. The ship, a former East India Company merchant ship, now used as a prison transport, had not set sail. *The Hammer of Scotland* was still moored in the Thames, just off the Tower, and Alex had escaped late one afternoon while being rowed out to it, throwing himself and several of his companions into the water with those guarding them. The other men had grabbed for the boat, but Alex had struck out for the south shore. They had pursued him, searching for him with a flotilla of small boats, shooting at everything that broke the surface of the water. Blocked from land by their pursuit, he'd headed east down the river and had been rewarded at last by the approach of a merchant ship that had hindered his pursuers just long enough for him to reach the shore, half drowned and exhausted. I closed my eyes but the vision his words had brought was too evocative of my dream, and I opened my eyes again. He'd huddled under a dock until nightfall, then he'd started walking westward in the dark.

It took him a very long time to get to Louisa's, where Bronson, as only Bronson could have, had greeted him with the news that Louisa and Randolph had gone to Mountgarden, that Angus was dead, that I was being held by Lord Webster, and that London was buzzing with the news of his escape. But Bronson had sheltered and protected him, and he'd spent a safe night in Bronson's own bed, safely hidden even when the house was

searched in the wee hours by soldiers. I made a mental
note to apologize to Bronson the next time I saw him.
If, I thought, I ever did.

In the morning Alex had gone to Mountgarden to
find his sons. And my family, about whom Webster had
lied to me as well. Will, Louisa, and Randolph had been
busy and, through bribery and forceful questioning of
the judge's staff, had discovered my location. They'd
been waiting for Matthew to return to put their plan
in motion. When Alex had arrived at Mountgarden,
Louisa, Randolph, and Will had told him all that had
happened, and again of Angus's death. And Duncan's,
which Bronson had not known.

Matthew had arrived that night and within hours
Alex had assured himself of his sons' safety on board the
Mary Rose, then had left for Webster's house where he
had waited for the others to join him. It had been a
simple matter, he said, to bribe the serving woman to
get the sketch to me. It had been much more difficult
to wait for the others, especially when Malcolm arrived,
but Alex said he watched me through the window. And
when Matthew and Dougall had arrived with the clansmen and the Macleans, and my family and the Mountgarden men, they had attacked immediately.

The Duchess, meanwhile, had arranged for Webster's
treachery to be made public. The scandal sheets and
gossips had loved it. Webster, it was rumored, had left
for the Continent. But no one had heard any news of
DeBroun.

And Murdoch, Alex said, was aboard *The Hammer
of Scotland.*

I had not known Alex had been gone until he slipped
back into the berth with me, his limbs cold from being

out in the early morning air. I murmured as I turned and drew him against me, warming his skin with my touch. I snuggled against him, feeling his hand stroke my hip and thigh. When he did not speak again I raised my head and tried to sit up, but he pulled me tightly to his chest.

"My love," I said, "what's wrong? Where were you?"

He didn't speak for a moment and I listened to the rhythm of his heart, thinking that whatever it was could not be so dreadful if he was so calm. But when he took a deep breath his breathing was ragged and I tightened my arm around him, waiting. I was in our berth on the *Mary Rose* and my love was in my arms. What could possibly be wrong with the world?

"Nothing, lass," he said at last, his voice husky. "I just wanted to touch ye so I'd ken ye were real and no' my imagination working again."

"I'm real," I said, threading my fingers through the hair on his chest and feeling his heartbeat quicken as I moved my other hand down his side.

"Aye," he said with a throaty laugh. "That ye are, lass. That ye are." He buried his face in my hair. "Mary Rose, I love ye so. There were times I feared never to see ye more. Mary," he said, brushing my hair back and kissing my cheek, "there has never been a woman like you. God only made one."

He turned on his back and stared at the ceiling with a heavy sigh and I closed my eyes, remembering his earlier grief, at last expressed, at Angus's death. And Duncan's. He had been inconsolable and I knew the loss of Angus would affect us always. He felt responsible, which I told him was not reasonable, and then told him of my own guilt. He had shaken his head.

"Guilt? I see no guilt on your head for Angus's death, lass."

"I do," I'd answered. "He was protecting me, Alex, and our son. And he kept his response to DeBroun in check partly because of me, because I had argued so much against violence, and partly to prove that he was not the barbarian the world believed him to be. Angus wasn't the savage that DeBroun was, and that's why he died. Because of me." Alex had mulled this over and I had studied him as he considered. Thin and scarred now, he seemed older by much more than the weeks he'd spent away from me, and I wondered if my laughing Alex would ever return. At last he'd kissed my forehead.

"Mary Rose," he'd said, "Angus was the finest man I've ever known and the finest friend I'll ever have. We'll remember him that way, lass, and no' guess what could have been. Yer no' to blame for his death. DeBroun is. No' ye. And if ye think Angus worried a minute about appearing barbaric or that ye changed his actions, ye dinna ken him as I did." He'd patted my cheek. "Put it out of yer mind, lass, and come here to me."

The baby brought me back to the present with a whimper, and I watched Alex get up and lean over his son with a smile, the first rays of morning lighting his hair in the dim cabin. "Mary," he said as he bundled the baby up and brought him to me, "tell me again what ye named him. Seems like a lot of names for a wee one."

"Alexander Robert Harold Lowell Keith MacGannon." I smiled and sat up to take my son. "And your name is just as long. MacGannon because it's your

family name. And his. And just before that is his grandmother's family name, and just before that his mother's
family name. I named him after you and my father and
Uncle Harry. And," I sighed, "if I had known we'd lose
Angus . . ."

Alex nodded, his mood growing somber. "Aye," he
said and took a deep breath. "Mary," he began and my
heart froze. I knew that tone of voice. There was something he hadn't told me.

"What? What is it, Alex?"

He frowned to himself, then met my eyes. "I'm
sending ye home with the *Mary Rose,* lass. And the boys
as well."

"And where will you be?" When he did not answer
immediately, I stiffened. "Alex, where will you be?"

"Going back for DeBroun."

I stared at him openmouthed, then closed my mouth
and raised my chin, furious. "Alex, we have just moved
heaven and earth to get us all safely out of London.
What in God's name do you think you can accomplish?"

"Mary, Matthew willna leave London without finding DeBroun. And Dougall's with him. Apparently Angus asked them to kill DeBroun. And I'll be damned if
I'm no' part of it."

"How will you find him?"

"Duke John's men have found him." He looked
down as his son stirred, his expression softening as he
gazed at the baby.

"What are you going to do?"

He rubbed his neck, drawing my eyes to the scars he
still bore from DeBroun's "questioning." His voice was
quiet. "Do ye see these, lass?" I nodded. "I owe De-
Broun, Mary. For this. I owe him for having Murdoch
and me beaten and then going off to parties and telling

the stories, and for coming back the next day and telling us how the people laughed when they heard his tales. I owe him for asking ye to be his mistress while he battered me for his amusement; for frightening ye into thinking he'd treat me with kindness in exchange for yer body. Yer my wife, carrying my child, a defenseless woman, and the bastard is making arrangements to have ye when I'm dead. He's a bully, lass. And a murderer. He's the reason Harry's dead. And he killed Angus in cold blood, and Duncan as well. In front of ye. I'm not forgetting any of it. I owe him. Even if Angus hadna asked Matthew and Dougall to kill him, I would ha' done it. But with Angus asking . . . well, let's just say I'm no' running for home until it's done."

I sank back against the cushions and studied him. I knew this mood. And this man. "What if I asked you not to do this?"

"It would make no difference."

"Alex," I said, feeling my temper rise, "what will this do? Will this bring Angus back to life? Or Duncan? Will it erase the scars on your neck, or all the other scars he's responsible for? Will it erase the memories of what you've been through?"

He shook his head. "No. And Mary, it willna erase the memories ye have either. Nothing will change any of that."

"I see. So you think this is the answer."

"Aye."

"When are you going?"

"Now. I'm meeting Matthew and Dougall." I put Robbie down carefully and climbed out of the berth, standing in front of Alex.

"Tell me you're not that foolish. Alex, this is madness. We're on our way home. What can this accomplish but risking your life again? And this time Matthew's and Dougall's as well?"

"It's justice."

"Justice? It's foolhardy! I forbid you to do this!" As soon as the words had been uttered, I knew they were a mistake. He smiled slowly, then reached for his clothes and began to dress. "Alex?" When he ignored me, I put a hand on his arm, stopping him in the act of putting his shirt on. "Alex, talk to me." When he did not answer again, I stepped back and watched him dress.

"Alex," I said at last, "how can you succeed? De-Broun will have half the English army protecting him. How can three men get through his defenses?"

"It willna be a battle, lass." He met my eyes and raised his chin. "I've aready sent word to him. It's a duel."

I stared at him, horrified. "Have you gone mad?" I whispered.

"Perhaps," he said and moved past me.

I beat him to the door and threw my arms wide to prevent him from leaving. "No! Alex, don't do this. It is madness! It is lunacy!"

He shook his head. "No, Mary Rose, it's the fairest thing I could have done with the man. I could have killed him in his bed or attacked him on the street. Instead I'd doing what Harry would have done. Harry canna do it, so it's my turn. I willna kill the man in a cowardly way, lass, but he'll be as dead. And die with the knowledge of who it was put the sword in his heart." He kissed my forehead and moved me out of the way. "I'll see ye in Scotland, Mary," he said and was gone.

TWENTY-SIX

I STARED AFTER HIM, THEN TURNED TO LOOK AROUND the cabin. One baby, sound asleep on a berth, a pile of my clothes on the floor next to the bed, and charts and maps on the table in the center of the cabin. No weapons. No sense to this. I moved slowly, as though in a dream, and dressed for traveling. Outside there were the noises of men moving on the dock and then silence. *Alex must be gone,* I thought, and looked out the window. *Gannon's Lady* was berthed beside us. *Somewhere east of London,* I thought, looking across the river, *but still west of Greenwich. Damn fool,* I thought, with a lurch of my heart. *I was right. This is madness.*

I opened the cabin door to find wee Donald blocking my way. "I thought you were with the boys," I said.

"They're fine, Mary," he answered. "They're still asleep. Alex told me to make sure ye dinna leave the ship."

"I see," I said and closed the door. Pacing the cabin, I thought furiously. There were three children to be cared for and I was the only woman. But I would not stay here and wait to discover if my husband was alive or dead. I'd had enough of that in my life. I put a bag of money in one pocket and sat at the table, waiting for time to pass. Then I opened the door again.

"Donald," I said when he turned to me. "Have my trunks been brought over from *Gannon's Lady* yet?"

Donald shrugged. "I dinna think so, Mary."

I frowned. "I need clean clothes." I glanced back at the cabin as though trying to decide what to do, then back at Donald. "Will you watch the baby while I go and get something else to wear? We can bring the trunks over later, but I won't spend another day in these clothes."

"I dinna think that's a good idea, Mary," Donald said. "Alex said no' to let ye leave."

I frowned. "To *Gannon's Lady*? Donald, either you can go and get what you think I need, or I can go and get exactly what I need. It makes no sense for you to go digging through my trunks. *Gannon's Lady* is next to us. It won't take me long."

It took me another few minutes to convince him, but I soon was on deck, talking with the men, and in another minute, on the dock, walking away from the *Mary Rose* with a pounding heart. I turned the corner before any of the men realized what I'd done. And kept walking, ignoring the curious looks I received. Wapping. I was in Wapping. Not the best part of town, but at least I knew where I was and how to get where I needed to be.

DeBroun's house was empty and his staff wide-eyed with terror. They answered my questions with stiff nods and excited gestures. Yes, the Scots had been here. But Lord DeBroun was not here. He was at Lord Webster's house. I climbed back into my hired carriage with a feeling of destiny. I should have known.

And it was with that same feeling of having already known what would happen that I stood beside the coach a few minutes later, watching men battle the fire that raged in Judge Webster's mansion. All the people had been roused from their beds, an excited neighbor told me, at swordpoint, and told to get outside. And then an army of Highlanders had set the house ablaze and had carried off Lord DeBroun. At first no one seemed to know where they'd gone, but a coin to a sly young man had gotten me the information I needed.

I went on foot, passing the streams of people going the opposite way. London never took fire lightly, not even fifty years after the Great Fire. Webster's house would be attracting the attention of people for miles around, for fire was everyone's enemy. No one spoke to me as I passed, and I was grateful for that. I was just one more hurrying woman in a cloak this cold morning, and no one knew that my heart was pounding with fear.

The churchyard was where I'd remembered, the walls still shrouding the quiet spot. It was a surprisingly large plot of land, surrounded on one side by the ruins of a church burned down in the Fire and never rebuilt, and on the other three by tall walls that hid it from the city. I had shown it to Alex on one of our visits, commenting that this was one of my favorite secret spots in London, for no one seemed to have remembered it, and it amazed me to find such a peaceful corner in the middle of all the bustle of London. He'd smiled but had not commented, and I had thought he'd forgotten it until that sly boy told me where to find him.

They were here, but they didn't see me enter through the side gate. Alex stood in the center of the garden, mostly dirt now, and faced Edgar DeBroun with a grim smile, his sword in his hand. Matthew stood at his side and Dougall behind Matthew. And behind Dougall ten other Kilgannon men, Thomas among them. I should have realized they'd all be here. If Dougall or Thomas had seen me this morning, I'd still be on the *Mary Rose.*

DeBroun was not alone either. Behind him was an assorted band of men, looking hastily dressed and terrified. DeBroun, his expression haughty, had a sword in his hand as well. He reached behind his back, under his coat, to adjust something, then bowed mockingly and saluted Alex with the tip of his sword. And across the garden Matthew met my eyes, but said nothing.

Alex, hatless and wearing only a white shirt and his kilt, grinned and tossed his head. "DeBroun," he said cheerfully, "prepare to die."

"I'll see you in hell," DeBroun said and lunged forward.

"Sir," Alex said, "I insist you go first." He parried the thrust and the two battled, Alex going forward, then back.

Alex laughed when he drew the first blood, a stripe down DeBroun's cheek, and smiled when DeBroun backed him into a bush. He lunged forward, forcing DeBroun backward in rapid little steps, while Alex grinned and said something that made DeBroun curse. Alex sidestepped, then spun around as DeBroun's swipes grew more ragged and desperate. Alex was concentrating now, his expression hardening as he backed DeBroun against the wall. And leaned into DeBroun's face, talking quietly. Alex pushed himself backward and let DeBroun regain his feet, then began the process anew. The only sound now was their ragged breathing and the horrible slither and clanging of steel on steel. Alex was getting tired.

I looked across the garden, silently pleading with

Matthew to intervene, but Matthew watched the battle with a grim expression and crossed his arms over his chest. DeBroun backed Alex onto a pathway and Alex missed his footing, spinning aside just as DeBroun's blade lowered. As he turned, Alex saw me and exclaimed, losing his concentration, and DeBroun's sword grazed his arm. I cried out, bringing the attention of the watchers to me, while Alex threw himself out of De-Broun's reach. They battled anew, Alex's arm bleeding now and both men visibly weary.

Alex backed DeBroun across the garden and De-Broun tried a savage kick, which Alex blocked. With a snap of his arm Alex broke DeBroun's grip on his sword and the blade clattered to the ground beside them. Alex brought his blade to DeBroun's throat.

"Say a prayer, Edgar," Alex snarled. "Is that no' what ye said to me in the Tower? 'Say a prayer'? I was un-armed then. How does it feel, Edgar? No' as much fun to hear it as to say it, eh?"

DeBroun took a step backward, then reached be-neath his coat. And brought a pistol out. Matthew lunged forward, Dougall at his side. DeBroun raised the gun to Alex's chest, struggling to reach the trigger. But Alex batted the gun aside and it fired into the air. And Alex plunged his sword into DeBroun. I closed my eyes.

DeBroun died quickly, but not before Matthew said several things to him and Alex stood over him watch-ing. "Ye swine," Alex said with contempt, leaning over the fallen man. "Ye canna even fight a duel fairly. Ye filthy swine. Get yerself to hell where ye belong."

The other men fled and the Kilgannon men moved to my side with uneasy glances at me. Except for Dougall, who glared at me, then came to my side. "Mary,"

Dougall hissed, "what are ye doing here? Why can ye never stay where yer safely put?"

"I have as much right to be here as you," I said softly.

Dougall frowned. "The two of ye will be the death of me yet."

I ignored him and watched Alex. Dougall went to his side and declared DeBroun dead. Alex wiped his sword clean on DeBroun's clothes, then turned and met my eyes across the garden. He came to me without a word, taking my hand and leading me from the garden.

We returned to the *Mary Rose* silently and I to our cabin. No one had spoken to me, and Alex did not come to me for hours. I sat shivering in the warm cabin with the boys pestering me with questions. I held my baby while I tried to erase the memories of what I'd seen. It was Matthew who came and sat with me, silently at first, then slowly talking, telling me what they'd done before I'd arrived. He smiled just once, when he said he and Alex had flipped a coin to determine who would fight DeBroun.

"I lost," he said, and I met his eyes over the boys' heads, both of us knowing DeBroun would have killed him.

Alex came to me in the dusk, smiling with the boys, and taking the baby from me without a word. He sat on our berth and rocked his third son while the first and second plied him with questions.

"Where did ye go, Da?" Ian demanded again.

Alex met my eyes briefly, then looked at Ian. "To settle a score, lad," he said quietly, while I stared at the wall. "To settle a score that only I could settle."

"It was unnecessary," I said quietly.

Alex shook his head. "No, lass," he said softly. "It was necessary. And it's done."

"What about Webster? Will you go after him as well?"

Alex met my look evenly. "Perhaps. Perhaps when he returns, I'll pay him a visit, lass. Not a duel, but a visit."

"I see. And burning the house? Houses?"

"My calling card, Mary. Something to remember me by." Alex rocked Robbie, who had become fretful. "Mary Rose," Alex said, and I looked at him again. "I love ye, lass. Dinna forget that. No man harms my wife or my family and escapes my wrath. I love ye, lass."

"And I you, Alex. But this could have ended much differently."

"Aye." He kissed the baby's forehead. "But it dinna."

I shook my head, unwilling to argue in front of the boys.

It was a quiet night. We were both awake for large parts of it, silently turning in our berth. Alex reached for me just before dawn, and I cried in his arms while he whispered words of love.

"Take me home, Alex," I sobbed. "Take me home."

"I will, Mary Rose," he said, and wiped the tears from my cheek. "I will, lass. But, Mary, ye ken I canna stay there. They'll come after me now for sure."

"I know, my love. But we can go home for a while anyway."

"Aye, for a while. We'll go soon."

"Why not now?"

"Soon."

The dawn brought rain. And unwelcome tidings. Gilbey brought us steaming cups of tea at first light, and with it the news that *The Hammer of Scotland* was preparing to set sail. Alex took the cup from Gilbey with a blank expression, and I looked from my husband to the younger man.

"So?" I said. "So?"

"So," Gilbey said, clearly unhappy to be putting his thoughts into words. He gave Alex a questioning glance and at Alex's nod, continued. "So *The Hammer of Scotland* is carrying two hundred Jacobite prisoners, Mary. Bound for the colonies, where they'll be sold into indentured service for fourteen years."

"Poor souls," I said, then turned to Alex with narrowed eyes. "But what has this to do with us?"

Gilbey cleared his throat and looked at Alex for help. Alex straightened his back and met my eyes. "Murdoch's on board, Mary," Alex said. "And we're going to go get him."

I started to laugh, which startled both men, and I rose to my feet, carefully putting my cup down on the table. "Alex MacGannon," I said, "one of us has gone mad. I'm not quite sure which it is, but one of us has gone mad." And I left the cabin.

He found me on deck, wrapping my arms around myself and staring at *Gannon's Lady*. When he put a hand on my shoulder I did not turn, and when he leaned to kiss my neck I batted him away.

"It won't work, Alex. It won't work." I turned to meet his eyes. "Why can't we just go home? I'm sorry that Murdoch is going to the colonies, but why must we risk life and limb yet again? Was yesterday not enough? Do you now crave danger?"

"I willna endanger ye, lass, nor our sons. Ye'll be safe aboard the *Mary Rose* and well away from the action." He stroked a hand across my hair. "And remember,

Mary. The Macleans aided us in freeing ye from Webster. Is it no' right to aid them in freeing Murdoch?"

"So you'll take two small ships, two brigs, against *The Hammer of Scotland*? An East Indiaman twice the size. You'll be outgunned and outmanned. What are you thinking, Alex?"

"We're faster."

"You're smaller."

"We can outmaneuver her."

"She has twenty-four guns, Alex. Twenty-four. The *Margaret* has four and *Gannon's Lady* eight. That's half the gunpower."

"We canna use the cannon, lass."

I felt my eyes widen, then realized why he said that. "If you use the guns you'll destroy the ship."

Alex nodded. "And perhaps the men she holds."

"You're going to capture her."

"Aye."

"How?"

"We'll fire into her sails and then we'll board her. Murdoch kens we'll try. I told him if I got freed I'd try."

I stared at him, then shook my head. "You're going to become a pirate off the coast of England?"

He nodded again. "Just outside the mouth of the Thames, lass."

"You've gone mad."

He laughed and nodded. "I may have. But I'm enjoying it."

"Why?" I breathed. "Why, Alex?"

He pressed his lips together and stared into the distance, at last returning his gaze to mine. "When I was in the Tower, lass, I realized how much I hated to be powerless."

"Everyone does."

He nodded again. "And I determined that if I was ever free again, I'd do my best to free every Scot under lock and key."

"At the risk of your own life?"

He looked at his boots, then raised his eyes to mine. "They'll hunt me for the rest of my life, Mary. They have no choice. I'm too well known now, too dangerous, to be left alone. Even if we go to Kilgannon, lass, I canna stay. At best I'll visit ye sometimes, but I canna stay. And if I'm no' there, who will guard ye and the boys? And the clan?"

"And this is better?"

"This, Mary Rose, is two things. A ship big enough to transport many of our people across the sea in safety, should we decide to go. And a means to thumb my nose at England while freeing my countrymen and a good friend and paying my debt to the Macleans."

"I see."

"I thought ye might."

"And you cannot resist."

He shook his head. "I canna. I willna."

I turned from him then, thinking of what he'd said. He was right, I'd known that, and had thought enough about it myself. We could go to Kilgannon, but we would never be left to live our lives there in peace. And by returning we endangered not only ourselves and our sons, but the entire clan. The reasons that Alex had given himself into Robert's custody were still valid. Alex had been pleased to discover that Harry's schemes had proved successful, but even if Kenneth cleared the obstacles to the legal ownership of Kilgannon, Alex was still an escaped convict, a condemned traitor, and a notorious one at that. They would never leave him at Kilgannon. The soldiers would come, or the ships. One day, they'd come after him. Was the saving of one life worth the loss of five hundred? I sighed.

"But where can we go now, my love?" I asked quietly.

He wrapped his arms around me. "I've been thinking, lass. We have few choices. We canna stay in Scotland or in England."

"A ship big enough to transport people across the sea in safety," I said, remembering his words. "You're thinking of going to visit Becca." He nodded. "The Carolinas . . . Where you would have been sent as an indentured servant."

"No, that was Virginia. That's a thought too." He kissed my neck and I bent my head to allow him more access. "And there's always the Caribbean, but that's full of English ships and pirates."

"How would we live? Would you trade?"

"I've no' thought it all out, Mary Rose. I thought ye could help with the details." He turned me and held me against him.

"The details. Like where we'd go and how we'd support ourselves. Those sorts of details."

"Aye." And then he kissed me and for a moment or two I forgot we were in full sight of all the men on deck. I wrapped my arms around his neck, closed my eyes and concentrated on his lips. "I dinna ken what's coming, Mary," he whispered into my ear. "But I can tell ye I'll love ye forever."

"And I you, Alex," I said, my breaths coming faster now. "We'll sort the future out together later. All that matters is that you come back to me in one piece."

"I intend to do just that."

"You always intend to. Make sure you do."

"Aye." He smiled wickedly. "But, lass, I'm thinking

ye should send me off with a special reminder of what I'm leaving."

I leaned back from him, suddenly aware of the clansmen trying to pretend we were not embracing in full view of them all. It was hopeless, I thought for the thousandth time, to have any shred of privacy on board a ship this size. They'd seen me come on deck angry and Alex follow me, and now they saw us with our arms wrapped around each other. Alex followed my gaze and then laughed as he met my eyes. And swung me up into his arms.

"Calum," he said to the captain standing not far from us. "I'll be busy for a bit and then we'll leave."

Calum nodded and fought his smile. "Aye, sir," he said without inflection.

"Alex!" I cried, half scandalized, half entertained, as he carried me to the stairs. "I'll go down these by myself," I said crisply. He released me and I straightened my clothing, then went belowdecks with as much dignity as I could muster. Alex turned to say something as he followed me, and the sound of the clansmen's laughter drifted behind us.

Once in our cabin, our mood changed and we turned to each other with quiet smiles. I shook my head as I reached for him. "What will I do with you, Alexander MacGannon?" I asked softly.

He kissed me with a lingering touch and ran his finger along my jaw. "Ye'll think of something, Mary Rose. Are ye angry with me, lass?"

I met his eyes while my thoughts tumbled. Images of Alex flew through my mind: Alex, chin raised, making his way toward me in Louisa's ballroom; quoting a poem of seduction to me in Westminster Abbey; climbing Robert's garden wall to tell me he loved me; introducing me to the cheering clan while we stood atop a table in the hall at Kilgannon; and swinging me up into his arms as he carried me off to spend our first night together there. And the sadder, wrenching memories as well: Alex rowing me out onto Loch Gannon and trying to explain why he was going to leave me to go to war; raising his arm in farewell as he led our men away from home; the horrible image of him returning, battered and defeated; and standing, defiant, in a hall full of his enemies while he was tried for defending his homeland.

"No, my love," I said gently. "I'm not angry. And I don't know what to do with you except love you. And I do love you, Alex. Beyond life. Beyond death. Until the end of time."

He bent to kiss me with a tender touch. "And I ye, Mary Rose. Until the end of time."

"Of which we have not much," I whispered, untying the lace at his throat.

"We'll have enough, lass," he said. "And then I'll go and get us a new ship."

"I want only that you come back to me safe and sound," I said, then gasped as he shrugged out of his shirt and pulled me to him. "Alex," I said to his naked chest, closing my eyes as he bent and ran a hand along my ankle and then up my leg under my skirt.

"Alex," I said again a few moments later as we lay entwined on our bunk.

"Hush, lass," he murmured, and threw the last of my clothing over the edge of the berth. "Hush. Dinna talk. Dinna think. Just feel." I closed my eyes again and followed his instructions.

"Alex," I said sometime later, "you have to take the *Mary Rose* against *The Hammer of Scotland*."

He looked at me evenly. "And why is that?"

"She's the fastest. And holds the most men."

"And my wife and sons are on her."

"We'll have to go to *Gannon's Lady*. We should be on the *Margaret,* but that's too difficult to do now." He was silent for a moment, then nodded. "Alex," I said and his eyes met mine. "Everyone in London knows the name *Mary Rose.* You'll have to cover it or paint it out. Or they'll know it's you immediately." He nodded again. "And you'll have to change the name of that ship."

He grinned then. "Aye, I'm thinking the same thing. How about *The Pride of Scotland?*"

I shook my head. "I have a better idea, my love. *The Rose of Scotland.*"

He laughed. "Aye. *The Wild Rose of Scotland.* After ye, Mary Rose."

Later I decided that it had been I who had gone mad.

The Hammer of Scotland passed us at nine in the morning, and a few moments later the *Mary Rose* glided silently out of her slip, *Gannon's Lady* just behind her. The boys and I were safely tucked into the big cabin on *Gannon's Lady* and had promised to stay safely out of sight. Most of her crew had gone on the *Mary Rose.* And Dennis, her captain, had agreed to flee if the action went badly. I rocked Robbie and sat on the berth with Ian and Jamie. But my thoughts were with Alex.

It was a daring and dangerous plan. The *Mary Rose* would cross the bigger ship's bow and fire once into her staysails, then the *Margaret* would come behind her and do the same. And then the two brigs would come up on each of her sides and the men would board her. A simple plan, laid out like that, but not so simple in execution. The *Mary Rose* and *Margaret* were each less than half the size of *The Hammer of Scotland*, 140 tons to her over 350, and she had twice the cannon of them combined. And would not hesitate to use them. And the size made other things difficult. The brigs' sails would be vulnerable to attack when they came alongside, but the East Indiaman's would be out of reach until the clansmen got on board her. Once the prisoners were freed they could help, but until then the Kilgannon men would face well-armed and trained soldiers and sailors alone. I rocked my child and prayed.

All went well at first.

TWENTY-SEVEN

THE HAMMER OF SCOTLAND SAILED INTO THE OPEN ocean with the poise of a ship well accustomed to the sea. Her sails were all unfurled now, and five miles from the shore her escort began to slip behind her. We met the *Margaret* as planned, and three brigs kept well behind and close together, as though they were merchant ships off on a trading trip. Designed to be fleet, they slid through the water with ease, their crews alert to every slight change in their prey's course.

The *Mary Rose* was the first to pass the escort ships, two small men-of-war. But she caused no alarm, for she flew British colors and signaled as though she were a private merchant ship, not a privateer. The *Margaret* passed the escorts in the same fashion, then *Gannon's Lady.* The boys and I stood on deck as we passed them, safe for the moment. And then Dennis ordered us below again.

We sailed all afternoon, quietly pursuing *The Hammer of Scotland,* but careful not to attract attention or to get too close. And then, as the dusk gathered, Alex made his move.

The *Mary Rose* and the *Margaret* slid forward into their places, catching the East Indiaman by surprise. We

heard the first gun and the splintering crash of the top-
sail and knew the gunners had been successful. The
cries of the crew on the huge ship carried over the water, angry and fearful, and I paused for just a moment to
remember all those who would lose their lives today so
that others might go free. A moment later the second
gun sounded and the crack of a mast was heard, and
then I could not distinguish noises, for *The Hammer of
Scotland* had found her cannon. I opened the cabin
door and stood at the foot of the stairs to the deck, trying to tell what had happened, but the sounds were
deafening. I crept up a step or two, then three, while
waving Ian and Jamie back down. And then I lifted my
head above the hatch and stared in shock.

Smoke was everywhere. The forward sails dripped
down over the bow of the merchant ship, and the dam-
aged mizzenmast at the stern hampered her crew's
attempts at steering, for the wreckage of the mast
lay across her wheel. There were men everywhere,
scurrying up the rigging and running across the decks.
The *Mary Rose,* closest to us, was circling and, as
we watched, pulled tight alongside the bigger ship. I
could not tell if the *Margaret* was on the other side.
I could see Alex directing men up the ropes they'd
thrown to the East Indiaman's decks, and the English
soldiers, their red coats visible even through the haze,
leaning over with drawn swords and pistols to repel
them. Men fell from the ropes on their companions below and from where I stood it looked as though the
clansmen were making little progress.

Two men climbed high into the rigging of the *Mary
Rose* and aimed pistols at the English soldiers, who shot
at them. Matthew, I realized with a shock as his head
flew back and his bonnet fell to the deck far below. But

he did not seem hurt and reached calmly down for the pistol that Gilbey handed to him. And shot one of the soldiers repulsing the invaders. The smoke was too thick for me to see then, and Dennis fell away from the action, circling between the three ships and where the escorts would soon be. I looked back at the scene, but could see no signs of victory for either side.

When we came closer again I could see that some of the Kilgannon men were now fighting on the deck of the East Indiaman, battling with swords and knives. There was no sign of the Jacobites, who must still be below. And then I could see no more as we pulled away, far from the action. I stood with clenched hands and waited while we made our turn.

We circled closer again and this time we could see both the *Mary Rose* and the *Margaret*, still intact, tied to the sides of *The Hammer of Scotland*, and red coats littering the deck of the merchant ship. There were too many men on deck to be just the soldiers and Kilgannon men, and I realized that the prisoners must have been freed. I breathed a prayer of thanks. It was almost over.

We fell away again and this time our circle was wider and led us far from the action. And revealed one of the escort ships approaching. I came on deck then and went to stand with Dennis, who gave me a glance but did not order me below. He narrowed his eyes as he gauged the escort ship's speed, then looked behind us to where the smoke still cloaked the three ships. Anyone would know at once that a battle was under way, I realized, and *Gannon's Lady*'s position, neither in the battle nor running from it, would be suspect. We had little time before the escort ship realized that all was not as it seemed.

Dennis gave me another glance, then gestured to the escort ship behind us. "We're leaving, Lady Mary," he said.

"Captain," I began, but Dennis cut across my words.

"I ha' my orders, madam. And I'll no' be the one to have to explain to Laird Alex how I delivered his wife to the English. Get ye below, please, madam, and mind the wee ones. We're off."

"But, Captain, the battle is almost over. They've taken the ship. We can join them."

He gestured to the escort ship. "Lady Mary, we'll head for them, but it's almost dark and the wind is rising. The escort ship is closer to us than we are to them. I must mind yer safety. Please, madam, get ye below and out of the way."

I scrambled to obey, confident that we'd be with the *Mary Rose* and Alex before long. I was wrong. Darkness fell and with it came a squall that drove us south. And with us, its sails white against the dark sky, one of the escort ships. A man-of-war, with twenty-eight guns, Dennis said, and a contingent of soldiers to aid its sailors. We had only a skeleton crew with us, for most of Dennis's men were with Alex.

With the dawn came the empty sky. And an empty sea as well. I was pleased, thinking that we'd head for Kilgannon and meet the others there, but Dennis was not, for the air was still. We changed course and he cursed, for we had turned to meet the escort ship. She was well armed, but heavy, built for war, not speed, and Dennis was confident that *Gannon's Lady* could outrun her if he could find some wind. He cursed again a short time later, for the second escort ship had been blown south with us as well and now followed us.

I stood on the deck with the captain, watching the

two ships, one on either side of us. Dennis turned to look further out to sea and nodded to a crewman. "Fall off," he growled. "We'll have to head out further. Find some wind. Take us to France if ye have to." The man followed his order.

But the escorts followed and Dennis cursed again. "We're no' acting innocent, ye ken, Lady Mary, and now we've aroused their interest. No doubt they saw that *The Hammer of Scotland* was taken and they've an idea who it was." He frowned. "We'll have to hope the wind doesna rise offshore, for if it does they'll get it first and be here with the wind. We can outrun them if we get the wind." He frowned again. "But no' without it."

They got the wind first and bore down on us while we waited, all but becalmed. Dennis ordered his men to arm themselves and me to barricade myself in the cabin. I sat on the berth, the same berth, I realized, where I had seen Alex, all those years ago, lying ill, brought close to death by Malcolm's treachery. I thought of all that had happened since then. And I prayed. *Gannon's Lady* held much of my personal history, and I was not ready hand her, nor my sons, over to the English.

I felt the first breeze find us and heard the orders Dennis shouted. And a moment later clutched my baby as the ship lurched forward. The boys cheered as we turned more fully into the wind and caught a huge gust that propelled us ahead. As we veered north I saw our pursuers, close now, turn to match our course. And then, behind them, the sails of a much larger ship, *The Hammer of Scotland*, with the sails of two smaller ships just before her. The escort ships changed course, running for the south. And I laughed.

*　　*　　*

Kilgannon. Home. There were times I thought I'd never see it again. The air was cold this winter morning and the sun glinted off the water, turning it from sapphire to silver. Above us the mountains loomed deep blue against the pale sky; white clouds scudded overhead. And the bare branches of the trees reminded me that this was the season of death. So much death.

All those months, when I had thought of coming home, I'd assumed we would all be here. Matthew's face was shuttered. He had been silent for most of the journey, but when we had stopped at Duart, he'd stood at the edge of the cliff and cried with us, and Murdoch, as we piped his brother home. We bid Duncan welcome. And farewell. And farewell for us possibly as well. If we were wise, we would visit those still here and then we'd leave, away in the dark like the criminals we'd become.

I glanced at Alex, standing so quietly next to me, with our son in his arms, then gripped the rail of the *Mary Rose* and watched us turn into the inner loch. And a few moments later, as we sailed around the headland, there it was, the most beautiful home on earth. The dark stones rose into the sky, the roof of the keep pointing at the clouds. The gulls overhead called their welcome. Kilgannon. Home.

It was the same and I sighed with relief. There was our room, and there the parapet where I'd watched so many sunsets. And there, in the meadow beyond the castle itself, was the knoll where Alex had given the prizes, and where I had welcomed him home. And in front of us now, the dock where we had welcomed the MacDonald to change our lives. Next to me the boys bounced impatiently. I smiled at their eagerness and took a deep breath. Nowhere else on earth smelled like Kilgannon. The sea met the mountains and their scents mixed with an overnote of roses. Roses. Impossible, but there it was. Kilgannon smelled like heaven. I turned to look over the boys' heads, to the other side of the loch where Angus's grave was, and I sighed. It would be, I knew, the first place we'd visit.

"Home," I said.

"It seems so strange without my da," said Matthew quietly, following my gaze. "How can it be home if he's no' here?"

"He is here," I said softly, turning to him as he towered over me, his handsome face drawn. "He is here, Matthew," I said again.

Next to me, Ian nodded. "It is home," he said and looked up at me. I smiled and put my hand on his shoulder.

"And I'm glad to be here," said Jamie, his voice bright.

"So am I," said Alex, his voice full of emotion. When I turned to him, he gave me a weary smile and I patted his arm, knowing he felt the empty space next to us.

I had imagined that Kilgannon would be deserted, that all the people would be gone, but the hills were dotted with tartan-clad figures running toward the loch, and on the dock a small group waved. I could see Ellen, her babe in her arms, and Dougall's wife Moira, and Berta. And Thomas's Murreal. And Seamus Mac-Crimmon with his pipes. And despite my best efforts, I felt my tears fall as the first lonely strains of "MacGannon's Return" came over the water to us.

Home.

For a while.